P9-BYM-101

"I think if we gave it a try we could be great together."

Those words barely penetrated before his lips settled on hers.

His arms went around her back and pulled her close. She fisted her hands in his shirt and held on because she seriously thought her legs would give out from the tremble of need that shook through her.

His tongue swept across her bottom lip and she stopped thinking about anything but tasting him. She opened her mouth and he dove in, sweeping his tongue along hers. He did so with a skill that curled her toes but also carried a hint of hesitancy, like he wasn't sure, or maybe like her, it felt so new and wondrous he needed a second to settle into it.

"Damn, sweetheart, I should have kissed you forever ago."

By Jennifer Ryan

The McGraths Series
WAITING ON A COWBOY

Stand-Alone Novels
SISTERS AND SECRETS • THE ME I USED TO BE

Wild Rose Ranch Series
TOUGH TALKING COWBOY • RESTLESS RANCHER
DIRTY LITTLE SECRET

Montana Heat Series
TEMPTED BY LOVE • TRUE TO YOU
ESCAPE TO YOU • PROTECTED BY LOVE (novella)

Montana Men Series
HIS COWBOY HEART • HER RENEGADE RANCHER
STONE COLD COWBOY • HER LUCKY COWBOY
WHEN IT'S RIGHT • AT WOLF RANCH

The McBrides Series
DYLAN'S REDEMPTION • FALLING FOR OWEN
THE RETURN OF BRODY MCBRIDE

The Hunted Series
EVERYTHING SHE WANTED • CHASING MORGAN
THE RIGHT BRIDE • LUCKY LIKE US
SAVED BY THE RANCHER

Short Stories
CLOSE TO PERFECT
(appears in SNOWBOUND AT CHRISTMAS)
CAN'T WAIT
(appears in ALL I WANT FOR CHRISTMAS IS A COWBOY)
WAITING FOR YOU
(appears in CONFESSIONS OF A SECRET ADMIRER)

WAITING ON A COWBOY

A McGRATHS NOVEL

JENNIFER RYAN

AVONBOOKS

An Imprint of HarperCollinsPublishers

This is a work of fiction. Names, characters, places, and incidents are products of the author's imagination or are used fictitiously and are not to be construed as real. Any resemblance to actual events, locales, organizations, or persons, living or dead, is entirely coincidental.

Excerpt from *Love of a Cowboy* copyright © 2021 by Jennifer Ryan.

WAITING ON A COWBOY. Copyright © 2020 by Jennifer Ryan. All rights reserved. Printed in the United States of America. No part of this book may be used or reproduced in any manner whatsoever without written permission except in the case of brief quotations embodied in critical articles and reviews. For information, address HarperCollins Publishers, 195 Broadway, New York, NY 10007.

First Avon Books mass market printing: September 2020
First Avon Books hardcover printing: August 2020

Print Edition ISBN: 978-0-06-285193-2
Digital Edition ISBN: 978-0-06-285186-4

Cover design by Nadine Badalaty
Cover images by © SalvadorCelis/iStock/Getty Images Plus; © thierry-dehove.com/Getty Images; WLDavies/iStock /Getty Images Plus
Cover photography by Rob Lang Photography
Author photo by Steve Hopkins

Avon, Avon & logo, and Avon Books & logo are registered trademarks of HarperCollins Publishers in the United States of America and other countries.

HarperCollins is a registered trademark of HarperCollins Publishers in the United States of America and other countries.

FIRST EDITION

20 21 22 23 24   QGM   10 9 8 7 6 5 4 3 2 1

*For those waiting on love.
I hope you find it.
Perhaps it's been right in front of you
all along and all you need to do is open
your heart to the possibility.*

WAITING ON A COWBOY

Prologue

Back in the day
Kindergarten Playground

Hey, Lizard, I'll trade you my grapes for one of your chocolate chip cookies."

"Stop calling me that."

Tate sat next to Liz, rolled his eyes, and stuck his tongue out at her because she told him that *all* the time. And he ignored her *all* the time.

Liz handed over the cookie and popped one of the grapes into her mouth. She'd rather have the cookie but didn't mind sharing with Tate—even if he did call her names. He didn't mean it.

He's weird.

But she liked him. He always picked her first to play a game, let her ride the pony at his birthday party before anyone else, and always sat with her to paint during free time and at lunch. She liked that. Daddy picked Mama to do everything with him, too.

Tate stuffed the whole cookie in his mouth, and Liz announced, "I'm going to marry you."

Tate stopped chewing and stared at her. "Na-uh."

"Yes I am."

He shook his head. "Na-uh."

She smiled, confident she knew better. "You'll see."

Chapter One

Today
All Grown Up
Mostly

TATE WALKED into the Backroads bar ahead of his brother Declan and spotted the woman who'd been dodging him for weeks. A you-done-me-wrong country song blasted through the overhead speakers as he closed the distance, his eyes locked on the girl he'd known since preschool but who couldn't be bothered to call him lately. It used to be all he had to do was think about her and the phone rang. But ever since her parting "you just don't get it" shot weeks ago, he'd heard nothing from her. And he wanted to know why.

He wanted things to go back to the way they used to be.

"What the hell, Lizard?"

She turned on the stool, her head tilting to look up at him, fiery dark red hair falling over one shoulder, down her arm, and brushing the tabletop. "What do you want?" Not an ounce of welcome tinged those words or filled her annoyed green eyes.

"I want to know why I haven't heard from you."

Her head fell back with her exasperation and those green eyes that always saw everything about him narrowed. "Have you missed me?"

The question set off an alarm in his head, but he didn't know why. Answering her question seemed like stepping on a land mine, so he evaded it. "Why are you avoiding me?"

"After our last conversation, I thought that'd be clear."

He tried to remember what they'd talked about. But the last few weeks he'd been distracted—his ex-military brother, Drake, had fallen into a dark place, but Adria helped him claw his way out, then her twin sister, Juliana, had died of an overdose. The man responsible for Juliana's death faced off with Drake and Adria, though it didn't end well for him, and they took Juliana's death hard. It was a lot to deal with, and the whole thing had been traumatizing. He'd been so happy for his brother when Drake and Adria worked things out and ended up engaged. At the time, everything else in Tate's life had faded to the background—until recently, when he woke up and realized he hadn't seen Liz in weeks.

"Lizard, you know I've been helping Trinity and Adria get their business up and running. And the situation with Juliana turned tragic. I lost track of everything and had to focus on my family."

Sadness and regret filled her eyes. "That's just it, Tate, you unloaded all that on me at the time, yet you can't remember what I said to you."

He thought back and recalled the thing that stuck with him. "You told me that if things were meant to work out, Drake and Adria would make it happen. They did. They're married and expecting and Drake's happier than I've ever seen him."

For the first time since he walked in a soft smile tilted her lips. "I'm happy for him."

Of course she was. Their lives had been intertwined forever. She knew everything that happened in his life and with his family.

"So what's the problem?"

"You," she snapped. She never raised her voice to him. "And me for hoping for something that is never going to happen because you're *you*."

He held his hands out wide, then let them fall and slap the sides of his thighs. "What the hell does that even mean?"

Before he got an answer, some dude with dark hair and a fuck-off look in his eyes walked up and inserted himself between him and Liz.

Tate immediately hated the guy.

"She's with me."

That's what you think.

Liz was *his* best friend and no one got in between them.

Tate glared at the guy in the odd-for-a-honkytonk-bar tie, button-down shirt, and slacks and took a step closer. But the guy stood his ground and didn't move out of Tate's way.

Liz slipped off the stool, linked her fingers with the guy's, and leaned into him. "Clint, it's okay. Tate's an old friend."

One of Uptight Dude's eyebrows shot up at that. Liz looked a little sheepish.

Tate refocused on *Clint*. "I'm her best friend."

Clint's stance relaxed even if he didn't back down. "Ah. She told me about you." Whatever Liz told him obviously didn't impress the guy.

Tate couldn't care less. "Then you'll excuse us while I have a word with her."

Liz spoke before Clint said anything. "I said what I wanted to say the last time we talked."

"And you haven't said anything since," he pointed out, his gut tight. Obviously, he'd missed something big. From the sound of things, it just might cost him the person who knew him better than anyone and who had always been there for him.

"It's not like you called or came to see me in the last six weeks."

"It hasn't been that long." They never went more than a few days without talking or seeing each other. Maybe it had been a couple weeks this time, but not six. Right?

"You're busy doing your thing. It's time I did mine. If you'll excuse us, we'd like to get back to our date."

What the fuck?

Liz dismissed him and turned to take her seat again.

Tate couldn't let things go on this way. They definitely didn't end this way. "Wait."

Clint put his hand on Tate's chest to stop him from touching Liz's shoulder.

Tate went still and pointedly looked at that hand on him. "You want to keep it, you'll take it back. Now."

They locked eyes and the energy around them became charged with animosity.

Clint dropped his hand but still didn't get the hell

out of Tate's way. "You didn't want a shot with her, so I took it. Back off. She wants to be with me."

Like she didn't want to be Tate's friend anymore. *What the fuck was going on?*

Tate felt Declan come up behind him before Declan's hand settled on his shoulder. "Come on, bro, let's get a beer and leave Liz and her date alone to enjoy their evening."

Tate glared at the back of Liz's head. She sat there not saying a word. She wouldn't even look at him.

"We'll talk later, Lizard."

Clint shook his head. "She hates that silly nickname."

No she didn't. Though she'd never admit it. It had become a thing between *them*. It didn't have anything to do with Clint. "What the hell do you know?"

"From what I've heard, I know a hell of a lot more about her than you do."

Declan grabbed Tate's arm and pulled him back a step before he decked the guy. "Let's go."

Tate had known Liz practically his whole damn life. "You don't know anything about me and Liz."

"I know she wants a man who appreciates her and doesn't take her for granted."

Tate took a step closer, not liking Clint's smug smile or the way he puffed up his chest.

Liz jumped in between them and planted both hands on Tate's shoulders and shoved him back into Declan. "Don't you dare ruin this for me!"

He had no idea what she meant.

She held up her hand. "Just go." The plea in her eyes killed him.

His gut constricted and his heart had trouble beating against the tightness around his chest. "Liz?"

Her lips tilted in a half frown. "Go get a beer with Declan. Flirt with the waitresses, pick up one of the dozen women staring at you right now. Do what you do and let me be."

That almost sounded like goodbye.

It couldn't be.

But Liz turned her back on him again.

Clint took her hand, pulled her close, then walked her to the dance floor where he took Liz in his arms and swayed to the slow song with her head resting on his shoulder.

Declan smacked his hand on Tate's shoulder. "It was only a matter of time."

Tate couldn't take his eyes off Liz in that asshole's arms. "What the hell are you talking about?"

"She's a beautiful woman. You had to know that at some point she'd want a serious relationship with someone who wants to make her his wife and have a family. He seems decent enough."

Tate turned on Declan. "You don't know anything about him."

"He'd have to be a good guy for Liz to like him so much."

"How do you know she likes him?"

"She let him step in to get you away from her."

She picked *Clint* over him.

She never chose anyone over him.

What the hell is going on?

The crack about flirting with waitresses and picking

up a woman hinted that she didn't like him choosing others over her either.

He knew that. He wasn't blind or an idiot.

But she was Liz. Hands off had always been his rule.

"It's unusual for women and men to be friends." Declan headed for the bar.

Tate followed. "We've been friends since we were finger painting and eating Play-Doh."

Declan took one of the open stools and held up two fingers to Tami behind the bar, who nodded she'd get them their usual. "Liz has been in love with you since then, but you can't expect her to love you, and only you, for the rest of her life when you dismiss her feelings the way you do."

"What are you talking about?" Tate didn't want to go there.

Declan glanced over and laughed. "Oh come on, you can't tell me that you don't revel in the fact that she loves you and puts up with all your shit while you treat her like your favorite pet."

That pissed him off. "I do not." Did he? That sinking feeling in his gut intensified.

Declan shoved his shoulder so he'd turn in his stool. "Look at her. Do you want to strip her bare and get your hands on her?"

"That's Liz." He didn't dare think such things about her. They were friends.

Or they used to be.

"Exactly. How long did you expect her to wait for you to stop seeing her as pigtailed Lizzy Lizard? She's a grown woman now, Tate, with hopes and dreams of love and marriage and a relationship that isn't all about you."

"Our relationship isn't all about me."

Declan laughed in his face. "Keep telling yourself that, bro, but you're the one who has no idea what happened six weeks ago that made her take a huge step back until she fell right into Clint's arms."

Fucking Clint.

"*He* made her dump me."

Declan saluted Tami with his beer bottle in thanks for filling their order. "Dumped? Is that how it feels?"

Kinda. But he denied, denied, denied.

"It's not like that. We've only ever been friends."

"And it's been clear for years she's wanted more." Declan frowned. "Don't shake your head at me. You know I'm right. Everyone can see it. She settled for friends because you mean that much to her, but you can't expect her to settle for that for the rest of her life. You can't expect her to watch you date other women, listen to you tell her all about how it's going and cry on her shoulder when it doesn't work out and think she doesn't feel jealous and left out."

"She dates."

"And nothing ever comes of it because you've got her heart." Declan took a sip of his beer. "Were you even a little happy when those relationships ended?"

His stomach clenched. "Of course not." As soon as the words left his mouth, he heard the lie. He'd never been jealous of her relationships. He was just happier when she was focused on him.

I'm an asshole.

And a terrible friend.

He should be happy for her. He should want her to find someone special. He wanted to see her as happy as Drake and Adria looked when they were together.

He glanced at Liz on the dance floor smiling and clapping her hands as she spun and swayed her hips in the line dance, Clint trying to keep up with her.

He just didn't want her happy with Clint. "Something about that guy bugs me."

"Mom always told us we have to share our toys."

Tate smacked Declan upside the head. "She's my best friend, not a Hot Wheels."

"Maybe she'll make you her maid of honor at her wedding."

Tate fumed and downed half his beer. "Fuck you."

"Nice comeback." Declan turned and leaned back against the bar, sitting like Tate, watching Liz on the dance floor. "You ate up all her attention. Are you upset that she's giving it to someone else or pissed that she might be falling in love with him and you want to be that guy for the rest of her life?" Declan held up his hand to stop Tate from spitting out another expletive. "Don't answer. Think about it. Because she deserves to find someone who treats her the way she's treated you all these years. Don't take this chance away from her just because you want her to love you and no one else when you don't really want her."

Tate slammed his beer down on the counter, stood, and walked out of the bar without looking at Declan or Liz because he didn't know what to do with Declan's question or how Declan's words made him feel.

This was *Liz*. Liz! The girl who played in the rain with him and raced him on horseback and never won but always took it in stride. They double-dated to all the school dances. She warned him when one of his girlfriends did something behind his back and always consoled him after a breakup. She had no problem pointing out all his faults and where he'd gone wrong but in a humorous way that made him smile and laugh and somehow feel better despite the fact that she was probably right.

Honest. Dependable. Smart. Kind. Generous. The list went on of all the good things he liked about her. Her sweetness drew him to her when they were kids.

She was a part of his life. A piece of him.

And with that thought, he went back to what Declan asked.

Did he want to keep her from falling for some other guy just because he didn't want to lose her as a friend?

He wanted her to be happy. She deserved to have everything she wanted.

What really got to him was that it wasn't that he hadn't ever looked at her as a woman he wanted, but that he always stopped himself from crossing that line because he didn't want to lose what they already had together.

But if he lost her to some other guy, would he forever wonder what might have been if he took a chance on them?

What if he'd waited too long?

What if she really was done with him?

Chapter Two

LIZ CAUGHT Declan's eye after Tate stormed out of the bar. Declan shrugged and gave her a half smile. She hated to upset Tate, but she needed some space. She couldn't keep holding on to him. It left no room for anyone else to come into her life because she was always looking at Tate. What if she missed a good guy who wanted what she wanted because she was pining for Tate and hoping he'd miraculously love her?

He didn't.

He wouldn't.

And it hurt to admit that and feel like no matter how hard she loved him it would never change.

After all this time, she'd finally accepted that he'd put her in the friend zone and had no intention of moving her out of it.

Clint hooked his hand around her middle from behind, planted it on her stomach, and leaned down close to her ear. "You came here with me. Forget him." He nuzzled her neck and gave her a soft kiss. "You're kind and sweet, beautiful, and sexy as hell."

They swayed to the music and she leaned back into him, loving the feel of his arms around her.

He took her hand and spun her out, then pulled her

back in to his chest as they made their way from the edge of the dance floor back into the flow of couples circling the center and keeping time to the music.

"Was everything okay with your car?"

She focused on him. "Yes. And thank you again for going out of your way to help me out." She'd put off the oil change and tire rotation longer than she should and took the first available weekday appointment. Clint drove her to work, then to pick up her car during his lunch hour. He did so many nice things for her. He didn't mind picking up a bottle of wine and the mushrooms she forgot for dinner at her place. He repaired a broken hinge on one of her kitchen cabinet doors. He didn't get upset when they had to rearrange their plans because she got called in to work on her usual day off. Anything to accommodate her.

"Happy to help. All you have to do is ask."

These past two months had been really great. Too bad Tate had to remind her that she hadn't put her whole heart into being with Clint. And he deserved her full attention.

Out of the blue, Clint grabbed her wrist, pulled her off the dance floor, and leaned down close to her face. "I told you to let it go. Stop thinking about him. He doesn't want you. I do."

Taken aback, she tried to explain. "I'm sorry, Clint. I just didn't expect to see him here, or that he'd be so upset."

His eyes narrowed. "Is that what you wanted? Are you just using me to make him jealous? Because you're wasting your time. If he wanted to be with you, he'd have dragged you out of here with him."

Harsh!

She didn't much like the "dragged" implication but let it go because Clint was right. Tate didn't fight to be with her. He'd walked out like she'd been the unreasonable one.

"I'm sorry," she apologized again. "I didn't mean to upset you." She liked Clint. Maybe she didn't have the same kind of connection with him she did with Tate, but things were moving in the right direction as they spent more time together. She needed to focus on him and the future, not Tate and what would never be.

She tugged on her hand to get him to let her go. His grip didn't hurt, but she didn't like the possessive way he held on to her. In fact, it gave her pause, because he'd never shown any kind of animosity toward her over anything.

She chalked it up to jealousy and hoped he'd get over it if she dropped the whole Tate thing and they settled back into their evening together.

But Clint didn't let go. "Don't make a fool out of me, Liz. I thought we had something." The sharp tone startled her.

"We do," she hurried to assure him. "I'm sorry." She wasn't used to apologizing this much, but he deserved it, because the last thing she wanted to do was make him feel like a runner-up to Tate. "There's nothing between me and Tate. Now he knows that."

He raised her hand and kissed the inside of her wrist where his fingers had left red marks. "Good. Then let's enjoy the rest of our evening." He tugged her toward their table. "Come on, let's get a drink."

She went along with a smile she didn't really feel.

Clint touched her back when she settled onto her stool. "Don't move. I'll be right back." He walked up to the bar.

She sat staring at his back, a nagging feeling prickling the back of her mind about the way he spoke and acted tonight.

Seeing her with Tate sure did set Clint off. But the show of jealousy didn't make her giddy with excitement. Instead of being happy he didn't want another man near her, it made her uneasy. The way he spoke to her, bluntly stating that Tate didn't want her, made her feel like she didn't measure up and she should be grateful Clint wanted her.

It didn't sit well.

Of course Tate didn't think she wasn't good enough for him. He just didn't feel the same way about her that she felt for him.

She looked down and realized she was gently rubbing her wrist. Her gaze snapped back up to Declan's. She read the disapproval over Clint's rough treatment of her and the question in his eyes. She nodded and smiled to let him know she appreciated his concern but she was fine.

She didn't blame Clint for being upset about Tate. She'd talked about Tate a little too much on their first few dates. She'd made it clear they were just friends, but Clint picked up on the fact there was something more. On her part anyway. She'd forced herself to be open to someone new in her life. She'd made a point to try to get to know Clint better. And up until tonight, she'd managed to keep her thoughts and feelings for Tate out of her head and heart and be in the moment with Clint.

But seeing Tate tonight made it harder to forget him.

How could she? They'd been friends practically their whole lives.

You don't meet the man you're going to marry in preschool. It just didn't happen.

And if Clint didn't measure up to Tate in looks or charm, well, that didn't mean he wasn't a good guy. When she was with him, he made it clear that he enjoyed her company. He wanted to spend time with her. He made her feel wanted and sexy. She'd be out of her mind to turn down a guy like him.

For what?

Tate didn't want to be with her. Not like that.

And every time she came face-to-face with that and reminded herself of it one more time it made her heart break all over again.

And being alone was far worse than being with a cute guy who really liked her.

She needed to stop this vicious cycle of thinking something Tate said or did hinted that maybe he wanted more and accept that was never going to happen.

Clint set a glass of white wine in front of her, took the seat next to hers, and took a sip of his beer.

She stared at the wineglass. "What's this?"

He narrowed his eyes. "Your drink."

"I'd prefer a beer."

He dismissed that and checked out the dancers getting rowdy to Dierks Bentley's "5-1-5-0." "Women drink wine. It's classy." He shook his head as everyone called out the numbers in the song, leaned over, and kissed her. "And sexy. Try it. You'll like it."

She picked up the wineglass and took a sip of the lukewarm chardonnay. "It's a little dry."

His lips pressed into a tight line and his eyes went flat. "You're trying to ruin this date."

The accusation stunned her. "No, I'm not."

He looked away. His annoyance grew with every second she didn't say anything.

Feeling like it was up to her to salvage this evening, she put her hand on his arm and squeezed. "Clint, I'm sorry. Thank you for the wine." *Even though I'd rather have an ice-cold beer.*

It took him a second to stop watching the dancers pumping their fists in the air, yelling out the chorus to the song, and focus on her again. "You should appreciate that I'm trying to make you better."

Excuse me. "Better than what?" She leaned away from him, completely stunned by that offensive statement.

He hooked his hand at the back of her neck and drew her close. "You're just trying to pick a fight. I thought we came here tonight to have some fun."

She wasn't having any fun. And the men in her life made it feel like she was the one making their lives miserable.

She picked up her glass and took a deep swallow and still didn't like the wine.

"That's my girl." Clint clinked his glass with hers and took a long pull on the beer she wished were hers. "You shouldn't let things get to you so much."

Prickly much? You're the one with the passive-aggressive attitude tonight.

She didn't want to prove him right by pushing the argument that she didn't need him to make her better. *Whatever!* She was fine the way she was. Except for the Tate thing. But she was working on it.

You don't just forget your first love.

She was trying to put Tate in the past.

One date at a time, even if this one had gone off the rails.

"Let's dance." She loved to dance. She'd lose herself in the music and movement and closeness with Clint.

He took her hand and led her to the dance floor and right into his arms. She lost herself in the rhythm of the two-step and by the third song she was having fun as Clint twirled her around and right back into his chest where he held her close and pressed a soft kiss to her temple.

This was more like it.

Out of breath, she made her way back to their table and downed the last of her wine before she even took her seat. Clint slid onto his stool and tipped back his beer. He ordered another and wine for her from the passing waitress, but she held up her hand. "Forget the wine, I'll take a water."

Clint nuzzled her neck again. "Here I was hoping to get you tipsy so I could persuade you to let me stay the night with you."

She planted her chin in her hand and stared at him with a flirty smile. "Is that your plan?"

"Oh, I have plans for you."

This was the fun, easy guy who showed up to all their other dates.

The waitress set their drinks in front of them. She wanted a taste of his cold beer to wash away the dry wine still on her tongue. She snagged his mug, took a big gulp, and handed it back. "Yum. That's good."

His brows drew together, but he was still smiling,

even if it didn't reach his eyes. While they caught their breath and finished their drinks, she asked, "How was work?"

"My boss is on my case about a proposal that was missing one key component in the bid amount. My assistant screwed up, but I got blamed because we lost the job."

"I guess you missed it when you checked her work."

"My assistant should do her job right if she wants to keep it."

Sounds like she did your job.

She kept her mouth shut because she really didn't know exactly what he did at work, and changed the subject. "What are your plans for the weekend?"

"I'm having the guys over to watch the game. Do you want to come over?"

"Football isn't really my thing. Besides, your friends don't want me hanging out while you're all shouting at the TV, cheering on your team."

"Someone needs to make the snacks and serve the beer."

She expected that line to come with a smirk. It did not.

When did I become the domestic assistant?

Lucky for her, she had better plans. "I actually promised a friend I'd help her this weekend."

"Doing what?"

"Selling food at the farmers market."

His gaze sharpened. "With who?"

"Trinity."

He tilted his head. "Who is that?"

"Tate's sister." The minute she said it, she wanted to take the words back.

Clint leaned in and put his hand on her thigh in another grip that got her attention. "I thought you were done with him."

She put her hand over his to soothe him. "Trinity has been my friend since we were kids. She opened a shop in town a while back. Her business partner married her brother Drake. Adria needs to stay behind and run the shop, so Trinity asked if I wanted to help at the market. Tate won't even be there."

Clint jerked his hand away and shifted his focus back to the dancers. "I thought you were moving on with me."

"I am," she assured him.

He turned back to her. "It doesn't feel that way when you continue to associate with Tate and his family."

She'd seen Tate once in all the time they'd been dating and this was the first weekend she didn't spend doing chores and seeing Clint. "Just because Tate and I are taking a break, doesn't mean I have to give up my friend, even if she is his sister."

Clint clamped his hand over her arm on the table and leaned in. "You're on a break?"

She sighed and tried to make him understand. "Tate and I *are* friends. That's all."

"Then why the break? He should be happy for you that you're with someone who wants to make you happy."

Her mind hesitated to agree with that.

"I'm sure he will be, once he gets over the fact I needed some space, and that doesn't mean I'm not his friend."

Clint pressed his lips tight and shook his head. "Women and men can't be friends."

"I think the best married couples are best friends." Her parents and Tate's were the perfect examples of that.

"That's different. Your wife should back you no matter what."

She agreed with that to a point. "A relationship should be based on friendship."

"I agree. But between men and women, there's gotta be heat." He leaned in and brushed a soft kiss just under her jaw, then whispered in her ear, "That's more important than anything. All I want to do is get my hands on you, not talk about my day, why you won't spend your weekend with me, or that your friend is an asshole and you're better off without him."

So getting laid is all that matters? What happened to the guy who ran errands and went out of his way to please her? "So you do all those nice things just to sleep with me?"

"Said every guy, ever."

She pressed the heel of her hand to her forehead, mostly because it pounded to the beat of the loud music, but also because she couldn't believe he said that. "I'm ready to go. That wine gave me a headache."

His fingers contracted on her arm. She tried to pull free, but it took him a second to let go.

"Let me guess, you don't want me to go home with you."

"My head is throbbing." She pointed up. "The music is really loud. I just want to go home, down an ibuprofen, maybe have a cup of tea. If you want to relax and watch a movie, I'd like that." But sex was off the table because her head was spinning after everything that had happened tonight.

He stood and tossed some money on the table to cover their drinks. "You take care of yourself. I guess I'll go home and take care of myself." If he meant it as a joke, the bitterness in his voice didn't help it sound like it.

She tilted her head and raised an eyebrow at the innuendo and outright jab at her for denying him what he wanted.

He shook his head and relaxed his shoulders. "Chalk it up to a bad day. I hoped seeing you tonight would make everything right, but you and I seem to be off."

No. *He* seemed off. The charming guy who held doors open for her, sent her sweet texts just to say hi and ask about her day, and complimented her nonstop those first few weeks seemed to think he didn't need to try anymore.

"I blame your friend Tate for ruining tonight." Clint held his hand out toward the door.

Tate started it, but Clint made it worse.

She slid off her stool. "I'm sorry tonight didn't go as planned." What else could she say?

"Let's hope you're back to your old self when I see you next."

Right. Totally my fault. Not! "Maybe I should book you a massage at the spa."

"Aren't you my personal masseuse?"

"Not tonight." How much did Clint actually pay attention? That's not what she did at the spa. She managed it and ran the front desk. She loved helping customers plan a relaxing, exceptional experience.

Clint should sign up to be a member. Little things seemed to agitate him. Especially when he didn't get his way. He needed a relaxation regimen.

After the way tonight unfolded, she just wanted to go home and sleep and hope tomorrow would be a better day.

They walked out of the bar. The second the door closed on the raucous music, her head stopped pounding. She breathed in the cool night air and relaxed even more.

Clint took her hand and tugged her toward her car. She didn't mind rushing to keep up. Home and her bed called to her. But still, he didn't need to make it seem like he couldn't wait to be rid of her.

She hit the unlock button on her key fob. Clint opened the door and stood back. His impatient vibe made her slip in without even attempting a kiss goodbye to end the night right. Or at least what should have been the right way to end a night with her boyfriend.

That description felt as off as their relationship.

The deeper glimpses she got into his moods and the way he thought about himself, her, and others triggered too many doubts. Tonight, they made her second-guess whether or not they were right for each other.

She didn't expect Tate to act the way he did tonight, and she certainly didn't expect Clint to react to Tate the way he did.

"I'll see you soon." Clint closed the door and stood back while she started the car and backed out of her parking spot.

She waved goodbye, but he didn't even crack a smile or wave back.

He had no reason to be so pushed out of shape.

She drove through the lot and turned onto the main road. Curious—and a little suspicious—she glanced out the side window just in time to see Clint walking right back into the bar.

Was he going back for another drink to take the edge off this night? Or was he looking for someone to take home because she'd turned him down tonight?

She didn't know the answer. Surprisingly, she didn't care one way or the other.

If you don't care, what are you doing with him?

Every girl Tate had ever dated had made Liz out-of-her-mind jealous.

Not that she should feel that way if she and Clint had a solid relationship, but they didn't. Something about him just didn't feel right anymore.

Tonight he'd shown her a whole new side to him. Jealous. Aggressive. Judgmental. Even possessive.

She didn't like the way he talked to her or manhandled her.

She stood up for herself. But she could almost feel him testing her to see how far he could go.

Or was she just riding this train of thought, nitpicking things Clint said and did because of Tate showing up and acting like she'd betrayed him, and she wanted to believe it meant something when it didn't?

She needed to stop wishing for impossible things.

Tate wasn't thinking about her. He liked her fine as a friend, but he did not want her.

Two men in her life. One she liked but couldn't see herself falling in love with forever, because the other still held her heart.

Chapter Three

TATE DROVE the truck in silence along the ruts in the grass to the south pasture. He couldn't stop thinking about seeing Liz at the bar last night with *that* guy. He couldn't believe the way she spoke to him. They'd been friends forever, yet she could barely look at him last night. She let her new guy get in his face and say things that just weren't true.

He didn't know what happened to make Liz take a huge step back. If he could get her alone, maybe she'd talk to him the way she used to, all open and honest, tell-it-like-it-is even if he didn't want to hear it.

He sighed and slammed his hand against the steering wheel, letting out some of the pent-up frustration that had kept him up most of the night tossing and turning thinking about Liz, their relationship, and everything Declan said to him last night.

"Her boyfriend walked her out to her car last night, then came back into the bar alone." Declan leaned back in the passenger seat, head back, eyes closed, calm as could be as he dropped that bomb.

Tate had been so lost in thought, he'd forgotten his brother was with him. "Why'd he go back in alone?"

"To dance and flirt with a few of the women."

Declan didn't bat an eye. "One took a shine to him. They had a couple drinks." Declan fell silent after that.

"And?"

Declan opened his eyes and rolled his head to look at Tate. "After a lot of flirting, he left alone."

"Are you sure she didn't go with him? Maybe in her own car?"

"She stayed another ten minutes or so, then left with friends."

Tate didn't know if he wished Clint left with another woman or was relieved that the shithead hadn't cheated on Liz. She didn't deserve that. And she deserved a hell of a lot better than her boyfriend hanging out and chatting up other women in a bar behind her back.

Wait, something seemed off. "Why didn't he go home with Liz?"

"Is it really any of your business?"

Yes! Why was there even a question about it? "I'm looking out for my best friend."

"I thought I was your best friend." Declan's mocking pouty tone nearly got him decked.

"Do you want a friendship bracelet to prove it?" Tate teased back. But he wanted Declan to start talking, because his brother held something back.

Declan stared out the windshield for one long second, then spilled. "After you left, they danced and seemed to be having a good time. Then . . ."

"Then what?"

"He grabbed her arm on the dance floor and again at the table while they were talking. Looked intense."

"Did he hurt her?"

Declan's mouth dipped into a frown. "Not sure. But it didn't seem friendly."

"I don't like this." You do not grab a woman that way. Ever. End of story.

"You mean you don't like him."

"I don't like anyone who thinks they can put their hands on her."

Declan's head rolled toward him again. Mirth shone in his eyes. "Is that right?"

Tate swore and huffed out a frustrated sigh. "That's not what I mean."

"Are you sure?" The teasing tone said Declan already knew the answer.

Yes.

No.

He wished he knew.

He spent half the night thinking about that and still hadn't untangled his jumbled thoughts and didn't even want to consider his feelings one way or the other because . . . *Liz.* Enough said. She was his friend. He liked it that way. Simple. Uncomplicated. Easy.

They'd never mucked things up by getting personal. Yet their relationship went deeper than any other he'd had with another woman. Maybe because those had been heavy on the physical side of things and light on deep emotion. Liz knew him better than anyone. If he mixed in a physical relationship with her—

He couldn't go there.

The friendship meant too much to him. And yet, it was because of her that they'd remained so close. She drove the relationship.

He counted on her to keep them connected.

Not that he didn't call her or drop by to see her now and again. He did. But he reluctantly admitted that normally that was because he wanted something.

"I can practically feel you thinking." Declan interrupted his thoughts. "You keep grinding away on this, smoke is going to come out your ears."

"Shut up."

"Very mature." Declan settled back, eyes closed. "If you want things to be different, if you want to keep her, *you* need to be different."

He'd taken her for granted. He owned that. He owed her an apology for it, but it didn't mean they shouldn't be friends anymore. He could do better. He would.

If she'd give him a shot.

That *if* scared him.

He didn't want to lose her.

Liz was special.

Clint saw that. Maybe whatever they had wouldn't last. He hoped it didn't because Clint seemed like an asshat. The arm-grabbing thing definitely sent up a red flag. And he'd talk to Liz about it if she didn't do something. Like leave the guy.

But someone else would surely come along and see what a wonderful person she was and he'd be right back here faced with losing her as a friend. Because no way some guy would allow her to be best friends with him when she was with them.

He wouldn't want to share her.

I don't want to share her.

Fuck.

Did that mean he wanted her for himself?

He wasn't ready to go there. Not with so much at stake.

Declan opened the passenger door the minute he stopped in the pasture. "You think on it too long, it might be too late." Declan climbed out and slammed the door on the ominous declaration.

The cows made their way across the pasture, the sound of the truck bringing them for the feed Declan started tossing out the bed of the truck.

Tate slammed his hand against the steering wheel. "Shit."

He needed to talk to Liz. Clear the air. Get their friendship back on track. Figure out where her head was at, and why the hell she'd give that guy the time of day.

Could they still be friends if she was with someone else?

If she left Clint, did Tate want something more with her?

Could he risk what they had for something more?

If he lost her either way, could he live with that?

He didn't want to think about it.

Either way, he was tired of not knowing what she thought and what she wanted.

He'd always known she'd liked him more than as a friend. He never acknowledged it or threw it in her face. Maybe his avoiding it had grown tiresome for her.

He'd been careful not to hurt her feelings.

Maybe his silence hurt more than if they'd talked about it and put it out there in the open.

They'd had their share of spats in the past—mostly because he'd pissed her off about something—but they'd always worked things out.

Most of this was probably his fault. He accepted that, no problem.

If she had something to say, if she was angry with him for something he'd done, she should have come to him, not shut him out for six long weeks.

And okay, it shouldn't have taken him that long to figure out they had a problem.

Having a lot going on in his life didn't excuse him from being blind and deaf when it came to his best friend.

He'd fix this.

He had to, because he didn't want to think about his life without Liz in it.

Chapter Four

Liz looked up to greet the next customer coming in the door at *Zen Out*, the day spa she managed, but the only thing she could see of the guy behind the huge bouquet of flowers he carried were his black pants and shoes.

"Hello there," she called.

"Delivery for Liz Scott." The delivery guy set the basket on the counter and stepped to the side to see her.

"That's me."

He handed over a tablet. "Sign here please."

She squiggled what would have to pass as her signature with her fingertip and smiled. "I can't believe they're for me."

"Enjoy. Have a good day." He walked out without her even attempting to give him a tip.

She couldn't take her eyes off the pretty flowers. Red roses, white carnations, pink lilies, purple asters were mixed in the greenery.

She pulled the card out and read it.

> *Even these aren't as pretty as you.*
> *See you tonight. Clint*

She woke up this morning with a sense of relief that she'd decided to pump the brakes on her relationship with Clint. If it didn't feel right, she didn't want to waste time waiting for it to give her the feelings she thought she should have with someone.

And then Clint went and did this and her heart soared. The unexpected gift made her second-guess how she felt about him. Maybe she'd been too rash to think that one bad night meant they were doomed to a bad relationship.

The bell dinged again. She tore her gaze from the flowers and took in the long, tall cowboy walking toward her without his signature good-natured smile.

Tate stuffed his hands in his jeans pockets. "I'd have gotten you those pony flowers you like."

"Peony," she corrected, but had to smile at his folly, though she suspected he knew the name of the flowers she liked and purposefully used *pony* to make her laugh. It worked. With Tate, it all worked. Except for the one thing she wanted with him: their friendship *with* sex.

"And these are lovely."

Tate's gaze took in the huge bouquet. "That's a pretty big apology for him acting like a jackass last night."

"Imagine if we were dating and you had to make up for being a jackass for the last six weeks," she shot back.

Tate sighed and hung his head.

Damnit, she hated when he looked all adorably apologetic. She usually let him off the hook without a second thought. But not this time. Not when he'd ignored her for weeks and didn't even notice her absence.

It hurt. Deeply. He owed her an explanation and a real apology.

Tate's gaze came up and met hers. "Lizard—" He shut up the second she glared at that stupid nickname. "Liz. Please. Give me a chance to . . ."

She waited ten seconds for him to finish that statement.

In the end, nothing came out of his mouth. He just stared at her.

One of their best customers and her friend Emmy came out of the back room. "Mrs. Bendle is finished with her facial and mani-pedi." Emmy touched Mrs. Bendle's shoulder in goodbye, then focused on Tate. "Sweet of you to bring Liz flowers."

Tate's lips tilted in a lopsided frown. "They're not from me."

"Too bad." Emmy gave her an I'm-not-a-Clint-fan look, a tilt of her head in Tate's direction, silently telling her to stick with him, then headed back to her work area. They'd had a couple conversations over the last few weeks about her budding relationship with Clint. Emmy thought her lack of enthusiasm meant she should stick with the man who made her heart race.

What good was having all the feelings when she was the only one feeling them?

Mrs. Bendle handed over her credit card. "I didn't think men sent flowers anymore unless it's one of those silly picture things they text. That's not real. It lacks emotion. Flowers say something. He took the time."

Liz handed over the receipt for Mrs. Bendle's signature. "That was my thought, too."

Tate glared at her.

Mrs. Bendle took her copy of the receipt and turned to Tate. "Looks like you've got some competition." She walked out, leaving those words hanging between her and Tate.

She didn't like the intense look in his eyes that she couldn't read when usually she could practically speak every thought in Tate's head. "You were saying?"

He checked his watch. "It's time for your break. Can I buy you lunch? I'd like to talk."

"Do you actually have something to say to me?"

"Yes. Starting with, I don't want to lose you."

Shocked, she gasped and braced her hands on the counter. "Tate—" The rest of what she wanted to say evaporated and her mouth snapped shut as Clint walked in the door, surprising her even more than Tate's blunt words.

"Hey baby." Clint walked right past Tate without a word or look and came around the counter, took her face in his hands, and kissed her softly. "I missed you today. Thought we could have lunch together."

She stared up at him completely at a loss.

"Did you like the flowers?"

"Uh . . . They're beautiful."

"Like you." He brushed his nose against hers and his smile lit up his face and eyes.

She had to admit, underneath her stunned surprise, her heart actually melted a little at his unexpected arrival, the sweet kiss, and his desire to see her.

He didn't stop with the flowers, he showed up.

And it kind of made up for last night.

Clint released her and turned to Tate. "Did I interrupt something?"

Tate looked at her and cocked an eyebrow, expecting her to say something.

"He came by to ask me to lunch, too."

Clint smiled down at her, then looked back at Tate. "I guess we both behaved badly last night." Clint slipped his arm around her back. "I thought about it and you've been her *friend* long before I came along. It's natural you'd look out for her and want only her happiness. I plan to keep making her happy, so I don't see why we'd have a problem with each other."

Tate's gaze bored into Clint's. "I hope your night ended better than it started."

Clint shrugged with a mock frown. "Dancing with Liz made my night." He looked down at her. "I only wish we'd stayed together last night. Instead, I let my jealousy get the better of me. I upset you. I'm sorry."

She pressed her hand to his chest. "I wasn't at my best last night either. Let's just forget it." All that fretting over what happened last night seemed silly given Clint's apology and change in attitude toward Tate.

"Great. Let me take you for a burger at that place you love down the street. You can have one of those thick chocolate shakes."

"She likes vanilla shakes," Tate pointed out.

Clint kept the smile on his face and didn't even blink. "Vanilla, it is."

She'd rather go over to *Almost Homemade* and get one of Trinity's yummy Cobb salads, but how could she refuse Clint after the flowers and coming to her workplace in person to invite her to lunch.

She glanced at Tate, who immediately read her mind. "We'll hook up later."

That got an eyebrow raise from Clint, but he held his tongue, taking Tate's veiled taunt in stride.

"Come by the cabin tonight," Tate implored. He'd never spoken to her with such a need in his voice. "Please, Liz. We can't leave things like this."

"We're seeing that rom-com movie tonight at seven thirty."

She didn't know anything about a date tonight. Clint had rolled his eyes when she mentioned she wanted to see that movie rather than whatever robot, blow-up-the-world thing he wanted to see. Again, he was trying to be nice and do what she wanted to do. Even if he hadn't exactly asked her.

The frustration in Tate's eyes and voice made her sympathy spike. Tate's unusually serious gaze held hers. "We will talk about this. I'm not giving up twenty-five years of friendship or you."

Startled he'd specifically say that last part, she cautioned herself against reading too much into it. Again.

Tate shot Clint a deadly glare and walked out the door.

Her stomach knotted watching him leave and not knowing if they'd ever get back to being what they used to be. Or to at least a more balanced friendship.

"Ready to go to lunch?"

Emmy walked out of the back to take over the front desk for her right on time. She stopped short at seeing

Clint instead of Tate, gave Liz a confused look, then took a seat behind the counter and pretended not to pay attention to her and Clint.

"Let me just grab my purse from the office."

He leaned over and kissed her on the head. "Take your time, babe."

She headed for the office door, but turned back. For a split second she saw the anger on Clint's face before he gave her another smile. She didn't blame him for being upset when he found her with Tate. She wondered how to manage seeing one man and wanting another.

Not that she didn't like Clint and think their relationship could turn into something more. For much of the past six weeks, that's what she'd thought. Relationships had their ups and downs. Some more than others.

So they'd hit their first bump in the road. With Clint's apology, she could get over it and move on.

She pulled her purse out of her desk drawer and headed back out to the lobby area. Emmy helped check in a new customer.

Clint scrolled on his phone but looked up when he heard her approach. "Ready to go?"

"Can't wait." She walked out of *Zen Out* ahead of him.

Steps away from the front door, he hooked his hand around the top of her arm and halted her beside him. He leaned into her. "What was *he* really doing here?" He pushed the words out through clenched teeth.

"He wanted to talk about what happened last night and why I've distanced myself from him."

"I hope you made it clear it's because you're with me." Clint made it clear he wanted to keep her all to himself.

She looked down at the grip he had on her arm. "You're hurting me."

His touch gentled but he didn't let go. "Are you going to meet him later?"

"I . . ."

"It's yes or no," he snapped.

She put her hand over his on her arm. "Clint," she implored. "I've explained many times that Tate is a friend."

"I know you want him to be more."

"I did once, but I know that's never going to happen. He doesn't see me as a desirable woman." Her chest ached admitting that. "You and I are something different than what I have with Tate. Before, Tate's and my relationship was very close. We knew everything about each other."

"Yeah, he just loved pointing out that you like vanilla, not chocolate shakes."

"That's because he came to all my birthday parties where we celebrated with shakes instead of cake."

His head snapped back. "You don't like cake?"

"I do. I just like vanilla shakes more." She turned to face him. "I've known Tate forever. You and I have only been dating for a couple months. We're just getting to know each other. I learn something new about you every time we're together and vice versa. It takes time to get to know all the little things about a person."

He cupped his hand at her neck, his thumb skimming her jaw. "I want to know everything about you." The sincerity and urgency in his eyes made her smile.

"We'll work on that."

"You're not ending this?"

"Why would you think that?"

"Because of the way you look at him."

She didn't know what to say about that because she couldn't help how she felt or how she looked at Tate. "And yet I agreed to lunch with you and not him because I want to move on with my life with *you*." She backed away from Tate because she needed to make room in her life for someone new.

Clint showed up just when she decided to put herself and her wants and desires first.

While she liked Clint, and they'd had some fun up until last night's odd and questionable encounter, she didn't know if they'd go the distance.

If he kept reacting with anger and resentment about Tate, their new relationship might never have a chance.

Why did relationships with the men in her life have to be so complicated?

Clint brushed his thumb back and forth against her skin. "If that's what you really want, then make sure your *friend* knows it."

"I will."

"Call him. Tell him. There's no reason for you to go see him." His gaze hardened when she raised a brow at that order.

He gave her whiplash. He didn't mind that Tate was her friend, but oh yes, he did. Talk to him. Don't talk to him. She couldn't keep up, but she would make her own decisions about her life and who was in it. Or not.

"I will talk to Tate later." She tried to distract him. "Right now, I'm going to put Tate out of my mind and go to lunch with you."

Clint didn't look quite convinced to drop it.

"I loved my flowers and your showing up to ask me to lunch. Why spend our time together talking about Tate instead of talking about each other?"

Clint yielded with a nod. He peppered her with questions about her childhood and high school years during the drive to the restaurant and all through lunch. After the second story she told that included Tate, and Clint's hands fisted on the table, she avoided stories that included him and focused on herself.

When they arrived back at the spa, she turned to him in the front seat of his car. "Thank you again for the flowers and lunch."

"Are you sure I can't convince you to ditch working for your friend this weekend and spend it with me?"

"Sorry. I promised I'd help Trinity." She didn't want to leave her friend in the lurch.

Clint brushed his hand over her hair. "Promise me we'll have more dates like today."

"I don't know. You took a little too much enjoyment in that story I told you about James putting that toad in my locker when I broke up with him."

Clint laughed again. "Come on, it jumped out and landed on your chest and made you scream. I would have paid money to see that." Clint's laughter started anew.

She could laugh about it now, but back then, she'd been scared and humiliated in front of everyone. She hated frogs and toads and lizards. James got her back for breaking up with him in front of everyone at lunch in the quad, but he'd deserved it for trying to cop a feel under the football field bleachers the day before and not taking no for an answer. The exchange ended in an awkward struggle. She ran away before anything terrible happened, but he'd scared her a little bit then, too. The next day, someone vandalized James's car. She always wondered if Tate flattened James's tire in the student parking lot. Her heart wanted to believe it. But Tate refused to fess up about it.

"I'll see you soon." She kissed his cheek and rushed out of the car, hurrying to get back to work before she was late.

Emmy was still working the reception counter. Even though four customers waited to be checked in or out, Liz headed back to the office. The memories of Tate prompted her to send him a text before she went over the reservations for the afternoon and started on the accounts.

LIZ: Sorry about lunch.

She tucked her purse in the desk drawer, sat in her chair, and booted up the computer.

TATE: We still need to talk
LIZ: I know. Okay if I come by tonight at 6

It was out of her way to drive out to see him, then back into town to meet Clint for their seven thirty movie date, but she didn't want to let this thing with Tate simmer any longer.

TATE: Yep

The man of few words wanted to talk. She'd go and let him talk, because if he expected her to fix this, he had another think coming. She went out of her way to be there for him. If he just wanted them to go back to the way things used to be, he'd find that for the first time, she didn't want to be his everything—excluding what she really wanted to be to him.

She liked being his friend, but if that's all he wanted, then he needed to let her take the time and space she needed to find someone who wanted to make her happy.

Clint had made a real effort today and she appreciated it. For a while there, they'd talked and laughed and enjoyed their time together.

Her phone dinged with another text. She picked it up.

CLINT: Never leave me wanting again with just a peck on the cheek

She laughed under her breath and realized that after all he'd done she owed him a sexier goodbye than a friendly peck.

CLINT: Miss you already

She smiled at the simple words that meant so much.

CLINT: I'll pick you up at your place for the movie
CLINT: I expect a kiss good-morning to make up for the one you gave me at lunch

Which meant he wanted to spend the night.

The thing about the kiss niggled at the back of her mind.

Why hadn't she planted a kiss on him filled with heat?

Because she'd been thinking about Tate rescuing her from James and making him pay for tormenting her and how sweet that was for Tate to do just for her.

She needed to stop thinking about Tate and impossible things and focus on the here and now and the man who missed and wanted her.

Maybe she couldn't unlove Tate, but she could make room in her heart to love someone else.

She sat back in her seat and stared up at the ceiling hoping Tate hadn't doomed her to never falling in love with someone else and a life of loneliness pining away for a man who didn't want her.

People settled all the time. If that's what she was doing with Clint, well, he wasn't such a bad guy. She could do worse.

At least she wouldn't be alone.

That's what had changed between her and Tate.

All those calls they shared, all the time they spent together, it hit her all at once weeks ago when they hung up after a long call where he'd talked about how much he wanted to meet someone like the woman Drake fell hard and fast for. Tate wanted a real relationship with someone. He wanted to be in love. And after pouring out his heart, he'd hung up with her and she'd felt dismissed.

Even though they'd never talked about how she felt about him, he'd never acknowledged it or even thought about accepting her love for him. He'd never considered her for the person to be the one who filled that longing in him.

She couldn't make him love her.

She couldn't flip a switch in him and make him see her in a different way.

To him, she'd forever be his best friend, Lizzy Lizard, and nothing more.

Tonight she'd let him know she accepted that now, even if it left a crack in her heart.

In time, that persistent ache would heal. She'd find happiness with someone else.

So would he.

And when he did, her heart would break again, but she'd wish him all the happiness in the world because she loved him that much.

Chapter Five

TATE PUT the last plate and fork in the dishwasher and shut it. He and Declan shared a roof over their heads and split the chores, while the meals were prepared courtesy of their little sister, Trinity, with prepared food from *Almost Homemade*. Trinity and Adria put together a week's worth of meals for them, and Trinity delivered them every Sunday. He and Declan knew she just wanted to come out there to make sure they hadn't burned the place down, or left their underwear strewn all over the house.

The thought made him chuckle under his breath.

What did she expect, that they'd turned into heathens when she moved out and into the apartment over the shop?

"What are you smiling about? I thought you were worried about this talk with Liz."

"I am. I was just thinking about Trinity and how she brings food out to us every week."

Declan rolled his eyes. "She thinks we can't do anything domestic on our own."

"I have to admit I liked it better when she did the dishes."

Declan frowned. "There's so few to do now, it's not that bad."

Tate understood all too well how Declan felt. "The ranch is quieter nowadays." Mom and Dad bought an RV and spent their time driving cross-country, making the house feel empty without them and Drake and Trinity living at home anymore. Tate wiped down the counter. "I'm looking forward to moving out to the cabin when Drake and Adria move their stuff out." Their new house was being renovated, but they'd recently moved in anyway. They just hadn't taken all their stuff yet, what with the rushed wedding and their honeymoon.

"I need a change." Not just of where he lived but in his life.

"I do, too. This place feels too much like the family house instead of mine." Declan ran the ranch now. He deserved the big house.

Tate could make do with the cabin. He didn't need much room. "Well, Mom and Dad took care of the kitchen renovation before they left on their cross-country excursion. But the whole place still needs a new coat of paint. You should buy some new furniture, I don't know . . . redecorate."

"Yeah, because I have time to do that."

"If you want me to hire on the new guys we need, I'll do it and free up some of your time."

"I'm talking to a few people. I just haven't made up my mind yet."

Tate didn't push. The whole family simply accepted that Declan ran the business after Drake ditched this place and joined the army. Declan liked to do things his way. Tate didn't resent Declan for taking the lead and not giving up any of the management responsibilities. Back in the day, Tate ran a little wild. But he'd grown up and tried to step up as much as Declan would allow him because he loved working the ranch. When Declan asked him to do something, he did it. He offered to take on more all the time. Declan took him up on it when he absolutely needed to. Otherwise, Declan did the work himself.

One of these days, Declan would resign himself to the fact that he couldn't do everything—and no one asked him to. When that day came, Tate would be there to partner with Declan in a more even way. Until then, to keep from stressing Declan out, he took his cues from Declan and did his job. Declan counted on him to do it well.

Tate didn't ever want to disappoint Declan.

But he'd disappointed Liz. And it ate away at him. He needed to make it right.

He checked his watch. "Liz should be here any minute."

"Are you going to finally admit you have feelings for her?"

He hoped getting her alone so they could talk would help him figure out exactly how he felt. "Do I? Or am I just holding on to her because I don't want anyone else to have her?"

"That's what I asked you."

Tate held his hands out and let them fall and slap his thighs. "Fuck if I know."

"Kiss her."

Tate's brain slammed to a halt. "What?"

"Have you *ever* kissed her?"

"No." He'd never crossed that line, because they were friends.

"Maybe you should. It might tell you everything you need to know." With that, Declan walked out of the kitchen into the living room where a football game Declan recorded on the DVR blasted out of the TV.

Tate tossed the dishcloth into the sink and headed for the front door. Just as he hit the bottom step, Liz drove toward him and parked.

His heart sped up at the sight of her. He'd barely slept last night or gotten anything done today thinking about this conversation, what he'd say, what she'd say. How this would go. How it might end.

He didn't exactly blame her for choosing lunch with her boyfriend instead of him, but he didn't like it either.

"Hey," she said without looking at him when she got out of the car and closed the door. Instead, she put her hand up to her forehead and stared out at the pasture and hills. "Look at that gorgeous sunset."

He had eyes only for her. The sweep of her cheek, the set of her jaw, freckles sprinkled over her nose, the copper in her hair shining in the waning light. He looked at her as a man looks at a desirable woman. Every line and plane from her beautiful face, down her softly rounded body, tight ass, and trim legs. Something stirred. She drew him in, and for the first time he fantasized about kissing her.

Or was that just Declan getting into his head?

She finally turned and smiled at him, her green eyes bright, then turning wary. "Are you okay?"

"Yeah." She did that all the time, asked about him, made sure he was okay and happy. How often did he neglect to ask about her?

She always looked good. Happy. Content with herself, her life, and everything going on. So he accepted what he saw and didn't ask.

But then she stopped calling and it took him weeks to notice.

What else had he missed by not paying attention to her?

"How are you, Liz?" He made sure not to call her Lizard. She said she hated it. He always thought she secretly loved it. But maybe he'd been wrong.

Maybe he'd been wrong about a lot of things.

Her head tilted to the side. "Are you sure nothing is wrong?"

Irritated, he frowned. "Why? Because I remembered to ask about you?"

The smile faded from her pink lips as those resentful words left his mouth.

When did her lips ever look that tempting?

She walked toward him. "Tate, are you mad at me?"

"I think I'm mad at myself."

She chuckled under her breath. "You think you are?"

He waved his arm toward the house. She walked ahead of him, but instead of going inside, she sat on the top porch step and stared out at the pasture and the horses he knew she loved to ride. His dad taught her along with him when they were still little tykes.

She still didn't look at him. Or maybe she just didn't want to look at him.

He took a seat next to her, stared at the sky turning from a deep orange to a soft pink, and asked what he really wanted to know. "Why did you stop talking to me?"

"Why did it take you so long to notice?"

Frustrated, he ran his hand over his head. "We're never going to get anywhere if you answer my questions with questions of your own."

"Your answer to my question will help you answer the question you asked me."

"Because I was busy and got caught up with Trinity's shop and Drake and his issues, and then Juliana died and everyone, including me, was stunned by her death. Once everything settled down, Drake and Adria got married. Declan and I had a lot to do here. We're shorthanded and fell behind with everything else going on."

"You called all the time to talk about Drake, the problems at the ranch, how Juliana's death hit all of you hard. Then, nothing. Not even an invite to Drake's wedding."

He'd wanted to ask her to be his plus-one, but then he'd been in a strange headspace seeing Drake all happy and moving on to a better life. It messed with him in a way he couldn't really explain. He'd wanted to be alone.

"You didn't need me"—she went on, even though that wasn't true—"because there was nothing going on in your life that you needed to offload on me."

He turned to her, but she still faced the pasture. "Is that what you think?"

"It's mostly true, Tate. You can't deny that you rely on me to call and check on you, to be there anytime you need me."

"I do. And I'm here for you." He touched her shoulder. She jerked but settled quickly.

"Look at me, Lizard." He used the nickname hoping it took her back to better times.

Instead, she sighed and turned to face him. "What?"

"I care about you, you have to know that."

"That's the problem, Tate. You don't see how much *I* care about *you*."

His stomach went tight and he looked away because he wasn't sure he wanted to go down this road. If they did, there was no turning back.

"Right. You do see it." She stood, walked down the steps, and turned back to face him. "Do you remember what you said to me on our last call?" He hesitated to talk about that weird mental space he'd been in, so she prompted him. "About Drake and Adria and their relationship."

"Drake is nuts for her. He married her in like a split second after meeting her."

"Because he loves her. He can't live without her. *You* said you wanted something like that. For a second, put yourself in my place hearing that from you." Her voice softened and filled with emotion with that last part.

She loved him.

It still went unspoken, but he knew it. He'd always known it.

He felt it in his chest, warm and comforting with a zing of excitement in his gut in contrast to the apprehension that went with it. He liked knowing someone felt that deeply for him. But it scared him. Because look what happened. Without ever trying he'd hurt the one person he'd do anything for.

And when he said that he wanted what Drake found with Adria, he'd thrown it in her face that she offered it to him on a daily basis and he never accepted it because he didn't—

Wait. He did have feelings for her. The depths of which he was just starting to allow himself to explore because, well, he was afraid of losing her.

"I want you to have that kind of love in your life, Tate. I want it for myself. And I'm afraid that if I focus too much on our friendship and not on what I want, I'll never have it."

Being friends with him wasn't enough to make her happy. If he understood what she was saying, it actually made her sad and lonely.

He never intended that. Yes, he loved having her in his life, there for him whenever and however he needed her. That's the kind of friend everyone should have. But he hadn't been that to her. Not in a way that made her feel that way. It kicked her in the gut. Somehow, someway he'd fallen short.

And that's what he feared would happen if they took this thing to another level and he'd lose her.

He didn't like feeling inadequate.

Unsettled by her words, his chest ached.

This didn't feel like a conversation that brought them back together. It felt like goodbye.

He couldn't let things end this way. "Liz, I can't say that what you want can't be what we have."

Everything about her went still. "What are you saying?"

He gave her the absolute truth. "I don't want to lose you."

She deflated with a sigh. "We will always be friends, Tate." That gave him some relief. "But I want more in my life than just a friend." She bit her lip, then admitted, "I want someone in my bed. I want to be with someone who wants me to be the last thing they see at night and the first thing they see in the morning, and they're happy for that small but huge thing. I want to be something special to someone."

"You are special to me." He didn't think he had to say it.

"It's not the same, Tate, and you know it. You saw it with Drake and Adria. That extraordinary bond they share got to you. You wanted it with someone. You wanted to feel what you saw in Drake."

Damn her for making him feel like he wasn't enough for her.

His lungs seized and his brain halted all other thoughts.

Is that what always held him back from thinking they could be more than friends?

How many times did some guy he knew comment on Liz, and he confirmed she was great. Fantastic. She'd be a great girlfriend, wife, mother, all-around best person you could have in your life.

They'd ask why he never got together with her. He'd say the same thing every time. She wasn't for him.

They'd always look at him like he'd lost his mind.

Why wasn't she for him?

Because he cared so much about her, he thought she deserved better than him?

He didn't know if he could answer that question without being confronted by other deeper thoughts and feelings.

Better to never go down that road.

But faced with losing her . . . he didn't know if he

could let these thoughts go and not do everything in his power to hold on to her.

"Tate, are you all right?" She always read him so well. He liked that most about her. He didn't have to say a word and she heard everything he didn't say.

"I'm confused," he admitted. "I don't like that you feel like our friendship isn't equal." He held up his hand. "It's my fault. I took for granted that things would always be the way they were up until a few weeks ago. Before that I'm sure, which is why it upset you that I wasn't putting into the friendship all I got out of it."

Her green eyes went soft. "Thank you for understanding."

"Why didn't you just say something to me?"

She held her hands up, then let them fall to her sides again. "Things change, Tate. We're adults now. What we want now has changed. We both want to move into the next phase of our lives. We can't do everything together."

"So you found someone else to do things with." And for whatever reason, this time it irritated the shit out of him.

"Clint and I were moving in the new direction I'm hoping to take until he met you in the bar."

"He's not a fan of mine."

"Understatement."

"Because he sees how much you care about me?" He wasn't throwing it in her face, he was trying to let the reality of it settle in his mind in a new way.

Her eyes narrowed and she crossed her arms at her chest.

Nope. Not looking at her breasts.

That road led to doom. Right?

Yes.

No?

"He wants me all to himself. Which at first sounds like a good thing, but in reality, it's made things a bit difficult."

"Are you sleeping with him?" His hands fisted with the thought of that ass putting his hands on her. Tate never liked thinking of anyone with her. It used to be easy to ignore. Usually because he went off with someone of his own. But now . . . the urge to slam his fist into something—preferably Clint's face—overwhelmed him.

"That's none of your business. I don't ask about the women you're sleeping with, do I?"

No. She never asked. She listened when he talked about other women, gave him advice, and occasionally weighed in with her opinion on someone, but they never talked about sex.

I'm a dick.

He winced with the gut punch that came with that thought.

He didn't want to hear about her love life. Why the hell did he discuss his with her?

Because getting her, a woman's, opinion helped a lot in most situations. Because he was a dude who accepted he'd never figure women out.

But he wanted to understand Liz better. Especially if it kept her in his life.

But he'd been the ass who'd known how much she cared about him and never considered how she felt discussing one of his girlfriends.

"If he's that threatened by our friendship, maybe he's not the guy for you."

"That's for me to decide, not you," she snapped.

Tate offered his opinion anyway because he couldn't seem to hold his tongue about Clint. "I don't like him."

"Why? You've never cared about anyone else I dated."

"None of them ever prompted Declan to ask me if I just wanted to keep you all to myself."

She did that thing where she went statue still again.

"He thinks I have deeper feelings for you than I want to admit." Why not lay it out there and see what she thought?

"How did you answer him?"

"I couldn't." He went with the truth and didn't even hint that his thoughts lately had slid on the scale from No Way to Maybe to sliding ever closer to a Yes when it came to dating her.

Liz's green eyes shone bright with unshed tears and a lump formed in his throat because the last thing he ever wanted to do was make her cry. "Then it's as it's always been."

"What the hell does that mean?"

"If you felt that way about me, Tate, you'd know it. You don't. You never have. And that's okay."

His stomach dropped, because he didn't think she was right, and he might actually have some real, deep feelings for her. "It's complicated."

She shook her head. "No, it's not. It's yes you do, or no you don't. You love me in a different way."

He'd loved her as his friend forever. He'd never stop.

"That's why we've always been friends. I hope that

never changes. But I need a little space to explore other options."

"Clint's another option?" That didn't sound like the right thing for Liz.

Her lips scrunched into a pout. "Not all of us get the one we want."

"It sounds like you're settling, and you deserve a hell of a lot better than that."

She shrugged. "I don't know where things are going with Clint—"

"Don't you think if he was the one, you'd know that by now?"

Anger flashed in her eyes. "See, you did answer Declan's question."

This time, he went stock-still.

The tears in Liz's eyes spilled over and rolled down her cheeks, tearing his heart in half.

He didn't know what to say, but something deep inside him called out for him to say something to stop her from leaving.

Not one word left his clogged throat.

All he had to do was shout, "Stay!"

But fear stopped him.

She walked to her car, climbed in, and drove away, leaving him sitting on the porch step reeling from the loss and his own cowardice to make a decision or allow himself to want something he always felt like he shouldn't.

She's not for me?

Well, why the hell not?

His heart pounded in his chest and something shifted inside him as that thing that had been nudging and expanding inside him burst free.

He didn't want a life without her in it.

Intense urgency to find and tell her that, and a hope for a wonderful life with her, filled him up.

Tate jumped up, ran into the house, grabbed his keys, and rushed back out to his truck. No way things ended like this. No way he would let her get away without them exploring if this thing that had always simmered between them—admittedly ignored by him until now—was everything and more than he'd ever hoped he could have with her.

Chapter Six

LIZ DROVE a mile from the McGrath ranch before she pulled her phone out and looked at the string of texts she'd ignored during her talk with Tate. She hated that she hoped the last few came from him.

She stopped at the intersection to the main road back to town. With no traffic coming from any direction, she took a second to read the messages.

CLINT: U there

Five minutes later . . .

CLINT: What r u doing

Three minutes later . . .

CLINT: Why are you ignoring me

One minute later . . .

CLINT: Call me
CLINT: Now

Two minutes later . . .

CLINT: Ur with Tate aren't you

It took him eight minutes to follow that one up.

CLINT: I just want to hear from you
CLINT: Where r u
CLINT: I need to see you
CLINT: I thought we left things good

She thought so, too. Why all the texts when they had already made plans for a movie tonight? Why did he need to know where she was when they were supposed to meet in an hour?

She wiped the last of the tears from her eyes and texted him back.

LIZ: We r good. Ran an errand. Heading home now.

She dropped her phone in the cup holder and turned right onto the main road. It didn't take more than five seconds for her phone to start chiming. She never texted and drove, so left the phone pinging with new incoming messages where it was, turned up the radio to blot out the sound and ease her heart with one of her favorite Sugarland songs, and tried not to think or feel anything for a few minutes.

She wished she could just go home, curl up in bed, and not think about what just happened for a little while, but she wasn't going to cancel a date because of Tate.

She wasn't going to put her life on hold for him anymore.

She never expected her talk with Tate to take such a turn.

Why would Declan ask Tate such a thing? Did Declan think Tate really did have feelings for her?

Didn't matter.

If Tate wanted to be with her, he'd have said so long before now or done something to show it.

Her absence from his life these last few weeks prompted him to say those things because he thought she didn't want to be his friend anymore. She didn't want him to do something he didn't feel just to keep her as a friend.

And that's what confused Tate. He thought maybe he was feeling something now that he hadn't ever felt for her because she took a step back.

That wasn't real.

So much for not thinking for a while. She couldn't not think about Tate.

That's why she'd needed the distance these past weeks.

She pulled into her spot under the covered parking area for her condo, shut off the car, grabbed her phone and purse, and climbed out. Her phone dinged with yet another text. She held it up and read the long string.

CLINT: What errand
CLINT: When will u be home
CLINT: Why didn't you tell me you were going out

CLINT: What's taking so long
CLINT: Where are you
CLINT: I expect you to answer me

Fuck you. I don't owe you a play-by-play of my day. What I do is my business.

Rage burned through her.

She sighed and reined in her temper. Clint didn't deserve for her to take out her frustration on him. He wanted to see her. He wanted to talk to her.

He didn't want to share her with another man. Seemed reasonable.

She wouldn't like it if he was always talking about and seeing another woman, even if they were just friends.

It created problems just like this.

Before she got a chance to text him back, Tate pulled in behind her car, stopped, turned off the truck, and jumped out.

"We're not done talking," he announced and closed the distance between them.

A car squealed its tires on the road drawing Tate's and her attention for a moment.

She recognized Clint's car heading in their direction and talked fast. "Tate, I don't like the way we left things either, but maybe we need to take a minute—"

"No. We've had since junior high hormones kicked in and you got breasts and things got a little uncomfortable between us to figure this out."

She couldn't help the smile that tugged at her lips. "We're not kids anymore. We're not talking about puppy love and crushes. We're talking about wanting marriage and family." She thought that would put things into perspective for him.

Guys usually balked at commitments like that.

"Damnit, Liz, you feel like family."

She didn't expect that answer.

Tate stuffed his hands in his front pockets, vulnerability in his blue gaze.

"I know that, Tate. I feel the same way about you. But you've ignored my feelings for you all through the stages of our lives. I can't help the way I feel. I can't shut my feelings off. I can't make you feel something you don't."

Frustration lit his eyes. "You don't know how I feel."

"And you admitted you're confused about how you feel now when you've always maintained our friendship status and I've been clear about how I feel."

Clint came to a jarring stop inches from Tate's truck bumper, got out, and slammed his car door. "What the hell is going on?"

Liz caught her breath at the fury in his words.

Tate stepped in front of her. "We're having a private conversation."

Clint closed in, standing nearly chest to chest with Tate, who had a couple inches on Clint. "She's my girlfriend. You don't like it, fine, but that's how things are now."

"Did you tell your *girlfriend* about the woman you were dancing and drinking with at the bar after she went home?"

Clint's eyes narrowed. "So she can have you as a friend, but I can't have any women friends." Liz didn't like the satisfied grin Clint shot Tate for turning the tables on him.

When she left the bar and saw him go back inside, she suspected he might be doing something she wouldn't like, but she hadn't cared enough to stop him.

Blinded by flowers and pretty words. Damn. She'd been so pleased by them, she'd completely dismissed his behavior.

Tate glanced back at her. "Are you buying this?"

Not really, but Clint had a point. They were seeing each other, but that didn't mean he couldn't talk to other women. But she got how irritated it made him when she did so with Tate.

She tugged on Tate's shoulder to get him to move aside. "Stop. Both of you." She raked her fingers through her hair and focused on Clint. "What are you doing here? Our date isn't for another half hour."

Tate put his arm across her middle and pushed her back a step in a protective move she didn't think necessary. "He was waiting down the street for you to come home."

Clint reached for her hand and held it in his. "I couldn't wait to see you, so I came by early, but you weren't here. Then you wouldn't answer my texts and I got worried, so I stayed and waited for you to get home."

It sounded good, but the string of texts touched a nerve. The impatience and insistence in his texts showed a possessiveness that didn't sit well with her.

"I told you I was running an errand and on my way home. I couldn't text you back while I was driving."

Clint dropped her hand. "You mean you went to see"—he pointed his thumb at Tate—"*him.*"

"Yes. I did. Because we've been friends since we were kids and I wanted to clear the air between us so that we can both move on with our lives." She didn't feel like she needed to justify her actions but she did owe him an explanation.

"So you told him you want to be with me and to leave you alone."

"Tate isn't trying to take me away from you. He never was."

Tate jumped in again. "We're not done talking. I've still got things to say to you."

She turned to Tate. "We can go round and round on this, but it still comes back to the way we left it."

He stepped closer, making it so easy to see the sincerity in his eyes. "No, it doesn't."

"Look, man, she doesn't want you."

Tate's gaze never left hers. "You don't know what she wants. I do. I've always known. And it's her choice."

Clint didn't back down. "She chose me. You turned your back on her all this time. She's done with you. She wants someone who really wants her, not some pity date."

Rage filled Tate's eyes as he turned to Clint with his hand already closing into a fist.

She jumped in between them with her back to Clint and her hands planted on Tate's chest. "Tate, please don't do this."

Tate talked right over her head. "The last thing I feel for Liz is pity. Nothing, not even you, can ever break the bond between us."

"I'm the one in her bed, not you."

She spun around and faced Clint. "Oh. My. God. What the hell is wrong with you?" She'd had enough. What she and Clint did in private was none of anyone's business. She didn't want it broadcast like this, where any one of her neighbors could hear them.

The last thing she wanted was Tate knowing about her sleeping with another man. Stupid as it was. He had to know she'd been with a couple other guys. She couldn't wait for him forever. But still. Clint went too far throwing it in Tate's face.

"Me? He won't leave us alone so we can be together without his interference. He's got you all turned around. He tugs on the leash and you run back to him."

She sucked in a breath and stepped back as those insulting words hit her.

"Do not talk to her that way." The restrained anger in Tate's voice didn't even touch the rage she felt, but under it she felt the pain.

Liz turned to Tate but embarrassment kept her gaze from going any higher than his throat. "Please go home, Tate. I know you mean well, but your interference is making things worse. We'll talk later. Right now, I need to talk to Clint."

Tate put his hands on her shoulders and drew her back with him several paces. He leaned in and whispered in her ear. "Will you be okay?"

She nodded but didn't look up at him.

He hesitated a good ten seconds, then kissed her forehead like he often did before all this got complicated. "I don't like leaving you like this, but I'll do what you ask. Call me later so I know you're all right."

He walked toward his truck. "You talk to her like that again, I'll fuck you up."

Liz leaned against the side of her car. Clint glared at Tate until he drove away, then he finally turned back to her. "How can you possibly be friends with him?"

"Why should I be with you when you talk about me like I'm a dog on Tate's leash?" Humiliation heated her cheeks because it did feel a little true.

"Babe, come on, you know I meant that's how he treats you." Clint walked to her and put his hands on her shoulders. "Can't you see? He's not jealous. He just wants to keep you to himself because you feed his overinflated ego."

She pushed past him, grabbed her purse off the trunk where she left it to talk to Tate, and headed for the stairs to her place. "Thanks. I feel so much better."

He followed her. "You don't need someone like him in your life. You've got me. I care about you."

Halfway up the stairs, she turned to face him. "Really? Then what is with all those texts insisting I answer you immediately."

"I figured you were with him and things would end badly again. And I was right." He looked her directly in the eyes to make sure his point hit home. "I thought you might want to be with me, someone who doesn't want to push you away but pull you closer." He put his hands on her hips, turned her around, and nudged her to finish walking up the steps to her door. "When you didn't answer, it bothered me."

She pulled the keys from her purse, unlocked the door, and stepped inside.

Clint slammed the door before she took more than

three steps into the entry, grabbed her arm, and pulled her back so hard she stumbled and slammed her head into the door before her back hit with a thump.

His fingers dug into the outside of her shoulder. "I am so tired of doing this with you. The bar, your work, at your condo. Every time I want to see you, there *he* is. You're with me. You will not see him again."

She put her hand on his wrist and tried to push his hand away, but his punishing grip never ceased. "Let go. You're hurting me."

"Say you understand. You will not see him anymore."

"Clint, you're hurting me," she shrieked, unable to focus on anything but the pain in her arm.

Someone frantically pounded on the door. "Liz, it's Ava. Open the door right now or I'm calling the cops."

"Who the hell is interfering now?"

"Let me go. It's my neighbor."

Clint looked at his hand like he didn't even realize he was holding her at all and released her.

"Liz, I'm not kidding," Ava called.

She waited for Clint to step back before she dared to move. She could barely breathe, but managed to suck in a breath as she stepped to the side of the door and stood so she could keep Clint in her peripheral view.

"Oh for God's sake, open the door." Impatience and frustration infused his words.

Her hand shook on the knob, but she turned it and pushed the door open and away from her.

Ava locked eyes with her. "Are you okay?"

"Fine," she automatically replied.

"See, she's fine. You can go," Clint ordered.

Ava held Liz's gaze for another moment, then glanced at Clint. "Maybe you two need time to cool off."

"This is none of your business," Clint bit out through his clenched jaw.

Ava stared at her, silently prompting her to speak up.

She found her voice, shaky as it was with anger and embarrassment burning through her. "I think she's right. You should go. We'll talk about this later."

Everything changed about Clint in that moment. His eyes filled with apology and he came forward and cupped her cheek.

She jumped, but he ignored it. "Babe, come on, let's talk. I'll take you out to a nice dinner. You'll have a glass of wine. Everything will be better."

She brushed his hand away. She hated wine. And right now, she hated that he didn't know that and kept pushing what he wanted on her. "It's been a long day. I'm tired."

"We'll order in, watch a movie. Whatever you want, baby."

This time she made her wishes clear. "I want you to leave."

Clint stared her down, but Liz didn't give in. "Fine. But if I find out you called him . . ."

"Leave now, or I will call the cops." Ava held up her phone, 911 showed on the display. All she had to do was hit the call button.

"We'll talk about this tomorrow." That sounded like a threat.

Liz stepped back, indicating he should go. She needed time to calm down and gather her wits. Think. After all that happened with Tate and Clint over the last few hours, she simply couldn't deal with anything more.

Some things were better dealt with at a distance. Clint's volatile temper was one of them. She wanted him out of her condo and away from her.

Clint let out a frustrated sigh and brushed past Ava on his way down the stairs.

Ava stepped into Liz's condo, closed the door, and locked it. "Are you okay?"

Liz crossed her arms and brushed her hands up and down them. "I am now. Thanks."

"I had a boyfriend like him once. Started out great. He was sweet, loving, everything I always wanted in a man. Then one day a guy made a pass at me in front of him. A switch flipped. He became jealous. Obsessed with knowing where I was, what I was doing every minute of the day. At first, you think it's cute he's so interested. The first time he hurt me, it came out of the blue. We'd had dinner together at this cute little bistro. We got to the car to drive home, and wham! Out of nowhere he backhands me across the face. He said if I ever looked at another man the way I did to our waiter, he'd do more than slap me. I didn't know what to say. I should have jumped out of the car and run for it. I stayed longer than I should have because he always had a heartfelt apology and spoiled me with flowers and gifts. It took me too long to see that they didn't mean anything and didn't make up for the bruises. It took a friend making me take stock of the relationship to see that I spent more days afraid of him than happy."

"I don't know what happened to the guy I thought I knew. It's like you said, everything seemed fine until he saw me with a guy friend and he changed. I thought he was just afraid of losing me."

"If he's like my ex, losing you is not an option even if he needs to force you to stay."

Liz didn't think Clint had become that extreme. "I think he just let his anger get the better of him."

Ava shook her head. "I used to make up excuses for my ex, too. Don't let him get away with treating you that way."

"Oh I won't." Liz raked her fingers through her hair. "I just wanted someone to date. Someone to have fun with. Someone who set off fireworks inside me when he kissed me."

"We all want that, Liz. But it doesn't have to be with that guy. Dating sucks. You've got to kiss a lot of frogs to find a prince. Toss that fish back. Something inside him is rotten."

"You're mixing your metaphors."

"You get my point."

Liz nodded. "Thanks again for stepping in. I've had one too many arguments today and I just didn't have it in me for one more with him."

"People use words to argue, not their hands."

Ava stepped in to hug her, hit Liz's sore shoulder and winced for Liz. "Sorry. Arguments don't leave marks. Arguments should turn into compromises." She smiled. "And makeup sex."

Liz nodded. "Thanks for the rescue and the advice."

"Want me to stay awhile? Just in case."

"I appreciate it, but I really just want some peace and quiet and time to think."

Ava put her hand on the doorknob. "I'm just across the

landing if you need me." Their doors faced each other. No doubt, if Clint came back, Ava would hear him.

"Thank you. I'll be okay."

Ava unlocked the door, opened it, and turned back. "Keep this locked all the time." With that, she stepped out and closed the door.

Liz locked up right away, went into the kitchen, opened the fridge, pulled out a beer, unscrewed the cap, and took a deep swallow just as her phone beeped with a text.

Her hands shook as she went to grab her purse where she'd dropped it on the floor just inside the door. She checked her phone, dreading a text from Clint, but it was Tate, and her relief eased away the trembling in her body.

TATE: You ok
TATE: I'm sorry things didn't end well again
TATE: I still need to talk to you
TATE: Call me PLEASE

Tears cascaded down her cheeks. Overwhelmed from her talk earlier with Tate, and from Clint's . . . she didn't know what to make of Clint right now. It seemed like nothing went right with the men in her life today. Neither of them were acting like she expected.

Uneasy, feeling a little lost, she called Tate, needing to simply hear his voice.

"Hey, Lizard. How's my girl?" His deep voice washed through her easing her heart. He'd never called her his girl before, but the nickname brought a slight smile to her lips even as she wiped the tears away.

"I'm a little out of it right now. My best friend and I aren't syncing anymore. The guy I've been seeing is . . ."

"What?"

She shook her head, unwilling to get into it. Tate would overreact. Maybe she was blowing this out of proportion, too. "Never mind."

"Liz, if something's wrong, you can talk to me. Even if it's about him."

"He has every right to be angry that—"

"You love me, not him."

She sighed and hung her head. "That's not fair."

"It's true. Right?" He sounded unsure.

"We had this talk at your place. Nothing has changed."

"Maybe it has for me." His voice softened with those words.

All too familiar hope sprang up inside her, but she squashed it down because she couldn't be disappointed again or feel the fool for thinking he might actually—finally—return her feelings.

"After how we left our talk and what happened tonight—"

"What happened?" Urgency filled his voice.

She hesitated too long to answer because she didn't want him to know that Clint scared her.

"What. Happened?" The force he put into that question hit her in the chest and made her heart beat faster.

"Never mind."

"Liz, seriously, you've never had a problem speaking your mind with me. Just tell me."

"Let's stick to us."

"That's what I'm trying to tell you, I think we should try *us*."

"Don't you get it, Tate, I've hoped so many times that you would look at me differently. That you'd feel the way I do. And now you give me *maybe* something has changed for you and you want to *try.* Do you have any idea how crushingly disappointing it is to hope you mean it but know it's probably not true. It's not real."

"How do you know when I don't?"

She pressed the back of her hand to her forehead where a headache started to pound. "I can't do this right now. Not after . . . everything that's happened today. I need time to think. I'm going to take my beer into the shower and wash this day away."

"Take the bag of OREOs you keep in the cupboard over the oven instead of the pantry so you don't see them when you go in there and eat them all instead of real food."

Of course he knew that about her. He knew everything. "OREOs are real food."

He chuckled. "I know you think that." He paused. "I don't want to hurt you, Liz. I don't want to lose you either."

"You won't. We'll always be friends." She barely got those words out her choked-up throat before she hung up on whatever he might have said. Wrung out, she left the phone on the charger on the counter, grabbed the bag of cookies, and headed down the hall to her room.

Texts started dinging on her phone. One after the other as she set the cookies on the bathroom counter, stripped off her clothes, winced at the red marks marring her left shoulder, gulped a significant portion of her beer to ease the wave of anger and fear that washed through her, then popped a cookie in her mouth before she turned on the taps and stepped under the steaming spray.

She let the tears fall again, remembering Clint's dark and angry eyes and the fear that overtook her when he didn't let her go. If Ava hadn't stepped in to help . . . she didn't want to think about what Clint might have done next.

She tried to focus on Tate and the sweet, hesitant way he tried to repair their relationship. Not that it was broken. She just wanted more. And if she couldn't have that, she wanted to find what she wanted with him with someone else who loved her like she loved Tate.

He put it out there, kind of tested the water, by telling her he wanted to try. She appreciated that he'd do that for her, but she'd come to terms with him not loving her. That's why she'd forced herself to start dating and how she ended up with Clint.

He started out a good guy. But tonight it became clear that he wasn't the right guy for her.

And Tate, she'd rattled him by making him think she didn't want to be friends anymore.

Any minute, he'd come to his senses and tell her that their friendship meant everything to him and that's all he wanted.

Her heart ached with the echo of all the other times he'd made that clear to her in so many words.

She stepped out of the shower, dried off, ate another cookie, turned off the light, listened as two more texts came in, closed her bedroom door, and crawled into bed despite not having dinner or it even being close to her bedtime.

She let the quiet punctuated by text dings surround her. She felt the aching loneliness of her home and especially her bed. She wished Tate was here to wrap his arms around her and hold her safe and loved in his arms.

Dreams.

She wished they were real and not the reality she'd lived today.

She closed her eyes and remembered the way Tate had called her his girl. After all the bad, that one thing chased away the nightmare of today and gave her some peace.

Chapter Seven

TATE HEFTED the last hay bale off the trailer and handed it to Declan to stack in the barn. He wasn't sure who got the better end of the deal when he stood tall and groaned at the ache in his lower back. He jumped down. The thud of his boots hitting dirt reverberated through his knees to his back, setting off a new round of spasms.

"You're getting old, man." Declan smacked him on the shoulder.

"I'm two and a half years younger than you."

"Then you're seriously out of shape."

Tate held up both arms and flexed his biceps. "Who's out of shape?"

"What did Liz think of those guns?"

Tate dropped his arms. "I'm still trying to pin her down."

"And do what to her?" The mirth in Declan's eyes made Tate grin, but the last couple days hadn't been at all funny.

"Shut up. You know that stuff you asked me?"

Declan raised a brow. "Yeah."

"I thought about it. Maybe there is something there if her seeing this guy makes me want to punch him every time I see him."

"You not liking this guy means you want to *pin Liz down*?"

More hard questions.

"There have been times," he admitted. "But I always put the brakes on it because it's Liz. Our friendship meant too much to me to mess it up. And . . ."

"And?"

"I thought she deserved better."

Declan's hand clamped down on his shoulder. "Tate, man, that's not true."

"True or not, she was always the girl who wanted a commitment."

Declan held his hands out wide. "Doesn't everyone?"

"I guess. When the time is right." It had never been right for him. At least, not for long. Sure, he'd had girl-friends for months at a time, but he never lasted much past a year.

Declan pushed again. "The time hasn't been right for you. But things change. Do you want to make a commitment to her now?"

"I see how happy Drake is with Adria."

Declan nodded. "It's such a huge change from how he was before he met her."

"Exactly. I can't remember ever seeing him that happy. And settled. Like no matter what happens, he's good, because he's got her."

"You've always had Liz. Good times and bad, she's always been by your side."

"Exactly. And I don't want to mess that up. But it's not the same as what Drake and Adria share."

"They have sex." Mischief and teasing filled Declan's eyes.

Tate rolled his. "Yes. And there's also a closeness that bonds them." He didn't know how else to explain it and knew he fell short, because he didn't know how to put his finger on that intangible but so evident thing Drake and Adria shared.

"You don't think you have that with Liz?"

"The question is should I risk our friendship to find out? I was ready to tell her yes yesterday, but her boyfriend showed up and threw a wrench in the whole damn thing. I think something happened between them when I left." He should have stayed to be sure nothing happened to her. It nagged at him.

"Like what? A fight?"

"He definitely wasn't happy when I left." Understatement of the century.

"Do you think he hurt her?"

If he did, he's dead. "I hope she'd tell me if he did."

"You think she would, knowing you'd hunt the guy down and beat him into the ground?"

Tate had to concede the point. "She held something back last night. She never does that. She puts it all out there. Every conversation we have is real. It's not like that with other women. I don't like this sudden distance between us."

"I keep telling you to get closer to her. There's something there, Tate, whether you want to admit it or not."

"What if she's built *us* up in her mind so much, there's no way I can live up to it?"

"What if reality is better than anything she or you could ever dream up?"

Tate's belly tightened with . . . anticipation. And

maybe hope. He'd never feared losing a woman in his life.

He'd never hoped things would work out with one this bad.

Declan read his mind. "If you go into it worried that you'll mess it up instead of intending to make it work, you'll doom yourself to failure. From all I've heard"—Declan feigned ignorance though he'd had his fair share of women in his life, though not lately—"relationships take work and require compromise. You're friends already. You've got an easy rapport. I have no doubt any challenges that come up, you guys will work them out. If you want her."

The more he thought about it, imagined them together, yes, the more he wanted it.

Now he couldn't stop thinking about it.

Tate checked his watch. "She should be home soon."

Declan waved him away. "Go see her. Figure this out before your mind spins out of control and you talk yourself out of what you've always wanted again."

One side of Tate's mouth drew back. "I'm not talking myself out of it."

"You're spending far too much time talking yourself into it rather than just doing it."

Tate gave him a dirty look.

"Go. *Pin her down,*" Declan mocked.

Tate went to the truck door. Before he climbed in, he overheard Declan say under his breath, "I'll hold down the fort alone." Tate wasn't the only one who wanted a partnership—and love—like Drake had found.

On the way into town, Tate thought about how things

had been for him and Declan the last few years, running the ranch, working hard, and hardly living. Tate found a few hours here and there to get out and have some fun. Declan mostly stayed back, finishing paperwork, placing orders, paying the bills. He'd shouldered the burden without complaint, oftentimes pushing Tate to hang with his friends.

Tate went because he'd rather have fun than do more work after a ten- or twelve-hour day. But now he wondered how Declan did it. How much of a toll had all that work and no play worn on Declan?

The drive into town didn't give him enough time to figure out what he was going to say to Liz. Maybe he should just take Declan's advice, not say anything, and just kiss her already.

One thing for sure, she needed to dump Clint if she hadn't already.

That guy was no good for her.

Tate wouldn't stand by and let some asshole disrespect her.

He pulled into her complex and parked the truck in a visitor slot. Since her carport was on the other side of the building, he didn't know if she was home yet and headed up to her condo to find out.

He took the stairs up, stared at her door for a second, and sucked in a deep breath, gathering himself to finally get this done. He wasn't leaving until they settled things between them.

He knocked on the door and waited but didn't hear her moving around inside.

The door behind him opened. "Oh, it's you. Good. That other guy is a dick."

He didn't have to ask who she was talking about. "What happened?"

"She didn't want to talk about it, but I overheard them fighting. Sounded like things got physical."

A wave of rage made his blood boil.

"I pounded on her door, told them I'd call the cops if I didn't see her. She looked rattled but okay. She asked him to leave, but he didn't, so I made it clear I'd call the cops if he didn't."

"Jeez. Did he go?"

"He wasn't happy about it, but yeah. I think she crashed after that. I didn't hear anything more last night."

She'd talked to him and not said one damn word about any of this. "Good. Okay." He didn't know what else to say or do. He needed to see her.

"She usually gets home about now. If you want to wait in my place, I might have a beer. It's probably some crap IPA my ex liked."

Tate laughed under his breath. "Thanks." He hoped Liz got home soon. He wanted to know exactly what happened last night.

What he really wanted to do was hunt down Clint and kill the fuck for making one second of Liz's life unhappy. If Clint hurt her, he'd wish he was never born.

That voice in his head yelled, *And what does that tell you about how you feel about Liz?*

Chapter Eight

LIZ WALKED out of work and headed for the parking area, but stopped short when she passed the first row of cars in the lot and spotted Clint leaning against the hood of her car. He smiled like nothing happened last night. Like she hadn't woken up with a gasp in the middle of the night and a nightmare image of him trying to strangle her.

Things hadn't gone that far, but who's to say he wouldn't do something worse next time. She wasn't about to give him a chance.

"I texted you last night and today. You didn't respond. You didn't answer my calls."

Twenty-seven texts. Fourteen phone calls. One very sweet voice mail. Three that became increasingly angry and bitter. "I was working. Besides, I have nothing to say to you."

"I'm sorry, Liz. I would never hurt you. Things got out of hand . . . I just wanted you to listen and understand that I care about you. I want us to go back to the way things were before Tate got in the way."

"Tate wasn't in your way."

"No? You're in love with him."

She couldn't deny it. "I do love Tate. He's been my

very best friend since we were children. He knows me better than anyone."

"I want to have that with you."

"I thought we might have a chance at that, but you are so obsessed with keeping me away from Tate you've ruined the last few times we were together."

"I just don't understand how you two can be friends."

"We are, and that's not going to change. But you've changed. Or you're just not the man I thought you were."

Clint stood and took a step away from her car.

She held up her hand to keep him from coming any closer. "Don't."

"Don't what? Apologize? Touch you? Kiss you? You're my girlfriend. Of course I want to make this right. Of course I want us to be everything, and more than we were before he showed up during our date."

She shook her head. "No. I'm not your girlfriend. Not anymore."

"Come on. Don't say that. You don't mean it."

She hated that he told her what she meant. "You put your hands on me last night. You scared me. I don't want to see you anymore."

He put his hand out again to touch her, but she stepped out of his reach. "Babe, come on. I didn't mean any harm. You wouldn't listen."

Anger flashed. "Are you saying it's *my* fault you left bruises on me?"

"Let me take you to dinner. We'll talk about it."

"Now who isn't listening?"

His eyes narrowed and darkened. "Don't do this, Liz. You'll regret it."

"That sounds like a threat." She regretted that she hadn't listened to her intuition about those little things that niggled at her in the back of her mind before what happened last night. She wasn't sticking around to see if even more of his real personality came out and she regretted that. Or worse.

"I'm done, Clint. No more dinners out. No more texts. No more phone calls. I don't want to see or speak to you again." She couldn't make it clearer.

"Do you really think he's changed his mind about you? He hasn't. He just doesn't want to share. Like I don't want to share you with him."

"What's between Tate and me has nothing to do with you."

"The hell it doesn't. Because of him, you're acting like this." He waved his hand at her. Deep displeasure and annoyance filled his eyes and added lines around his frown. "Before, you and I had fun. We'd laugh and smile at each other and you'd kiss me like you meant it. We made love like we couldn't get enough of each other." He laid it on thick and painted a picture of a happy couple and a fulfilling relationship.

Yes, she'd been enamored by his charm and attention. She didn't mind the make-out sessions. She could have done without the pouting and simmering anger when she denied him a sleepover. Eventually, she'd given in to her desires and slept with him. It had been a long time. She'd craved that closeness. And hoped it would make her feel closer to him. She thought it would strengthen their relationship. But he'd proven a selfish lover, leaving her unfulfilled and wanting more often than not. The other times, she'd had to make it happen for herself before he finished and promptly fell asleep.

Some guys just didn't get it. Clint deluded himself into thinking he was the perfect boyfriend and lover. Well, she wanted someone who put her first and wasn't satisfied until she was satisfied.

She didn't delude herself into thinking that was Tate. She'd accepted he didn't care for her in that way. Fine. But that didn't mean she had to settle for Clint.

She didn't like being alone. Who did? But having no boyfriend was far better than being scared and intimidated by Clint's aggressive messages and threatening anger.

"Clint, I'm sorry, but I just don't feel like you and I want the same things. Yes, we started off great, but—"

"Tate! He ruined it. He made you turn on me. Well, he can't have you." Clint rushed her, took her by the shoulders, hurting her sore one, leaned down, and smashed his lips to hers.

She dropped her bag, fought to get her hands between them, and pushed him away. The second she was free, she swiped the back of her hand across her mouth. "What the hell?"

He tried to pull her close again, but she struggled out of his hold and took several steps back. "Stop!"

He took a step closer.

She pointed a finger at him. "No! Another step and I scream bloody murder."

"You're being ridiculous."

She spread her fingers and held her hand up to him. "I do not want you to touch me ever again."

"Oh come on. You don't mean that."

"Yes. I do. Do not call me. Do not come to see me. We're done." She ran forward, grabbed her purse, rummaged for her keys, unlocked the car door, opened it, and rushed inside, slamming the door and locking it again. Her hands shook so badly, she scraped the key against the ignition several times before she pushed it into the slot.

She glanced over her shoulder to back out and found Clint standing dead center of her bumper glaring at her. "Move!"

"We aren't over."

"Move, or I'll call the cops!" She didn't have it in her to go another round about how this was over and done. For good. She didn't care what he thought or said about it.

Clint's mouth drew tight and his eyes narrowed. "I'll see you soon." He hesitated another second, then slowly stepped out of the way.

The second he was clear, she stomped on the gas pedal and backed out, braking only long enough to put the car in Drive and push the gas again. She sped out of the lot way faster than she should have, but her heart pounded in her chest so hard she couldn't help but respond to the fear and get out of there as fast as possible.

She checked her rearview mirror and spotted Clint's car about five cars behind her. She sped up and barely made it through a yellow light that turned red before she fully crossed the intersection.

Tears clogged her throat, but she choked them back. No way she shed another tear over that asshole.

She didn't deserve to be treated this way. No one did.

She sucked in several deep breaths and let them out. Her heart slowed and she could breathe and think straight again. She let off the gas before a cop pulled her over. She didn't see Clint on her tail but kept checking every couple minutes to be sure he hadn't caught up to her again.

When she pulled into her carport she wished she had a garage with a door for added protection. Her hands shook when she shut off the engine and sat in the quiet for a minute with her forehead on the wheel.

"You're okay, Liz. You're home." The pep talk didn't really ease her mind, but she sat up, gathered her purse, keys, and phone, and got out of the car. She walked out of the parking area and around the corner of the building to the walkway. Still hyperaware of her surroundings, the sound of a car pulling up drew her attention. She peeked over her shoulder and spotted the back end of what looked like Clint's car. She didn't wait to see if it was him. She dashed down the path and up the stairs to her condo door.

She fumbled with her keys and stopped when she heard a deep voice coming from Ava's condo followed by Ava's laughter, then the man's. The sound was so familiar, she turned and knocked on Ava's door.

"Hey there," Ava said by way of a greeting.

"I thought I heard—"

Ava stepped back and there was Tate sitting on the sofa with a beer in hand. Another sat on the table.

She backed up a step. "Sorry to interrupt." She shoved the key in her lock, turned it, and went through the door, and pushed it to close the second she stepped in. But it didn't slam like she wanted.

No. Tate shoved it open and walked right in. "Liz, what's wrong?"

She kept her back to him and tossed her purse on the dining table. "Sorry I walked in on . . . whatever that was." It was only a matter of time before Tate met Ava and got his flirt on like he did with every pretty girl he met.

She shouldn't be surprised.

She shouldn't feel hurt and rejected again.

"Ava asked if I wanted to wait at her place instead of sitting on the steps for you to come home. That's all. I was waiting for you. I came to see *you*."

Ava was a good friend and a kind person, which made Liz feel worse for thinking something was going on between them. Ava gave Tate a warm, but not flirty smile from her condo door across the short hall. "Nice to meet you, Tate."

"Thanks for the update and the beer."

Ava nodded. "I'll leave the two of you to your evening." She gave Liz a reassuring nod and closed her door.

Liz felt like a complete and utter fool. Humiliation burned her cheeks and made this day even worse.

Pity washed over Tate's face, and she couldn't stand it. "Just go. Leave me alone." It was all too much. Hot tears fell down her cheeks.

Tate didn't leave. He shut the door, walked right up to her, wrapped his arms around her, and held her close, his cheek pressed to her hair. "Sweetheart, I have no idea what is going on, but everything is going to be all right."

She let the tears come in a torrent and shuddered in his arms.

He held her tighter. "I've got you, Liz. I won't let you go."

How come that sounded so good when Clint's denial that they were over felt like a threat?

She pushed against Tate's rock-solid chest and stepped back, but his hands came up to cup her face.

His thumbs swept over her wet cheeks. "What's got you all unraveled?" When she didn't answer, he took her shoulders in his hands and pressed on the swollen bruise on her left arm.

She winced and tried to move out of his grasp.

His eyes narrowed with concern and he hooked his finger in the collar of her shirt and pulled it down her arm as much as he could, revealing the purple splotches on the outside of her shoulder.

"Liz! Oh my God! What the hell!" He lightly brushed his fingers over the marks.

Even that small touch hurt and she hissed and stepped away, pulling her shirt up again. "Stop touching it."

Tate pointed his finger at her. "Did *he* do that to you?"

She didn't know what to say or do. She felt stupid and embarrassed that it happened. "It's over." That's all he needed to know.

"Fucking right it is. I'll kill him." Tate turned for the door, but she grabbed his arm and managed to wiggle her way between him and the door before he opened it.

"Stop. Don't go. He . . ." She tried to catch her breath, but her heart pounded so hard she could barely breathe.

"He what?"

She didn't know when she planted her hands on his chest, but she gripped his shirt and held on. "Please don't go."

Tate went perfectly still. "You're afraid to be here alone."

Her head fell forward. "I already spoke to him."

"When? Before you got home? Is that why you're so out of it and yelling at me?"

"I didn't yell at you."

"Yeah, you did when you thought I was hot for your neighbor." He put his hands over her fisted ones on his chest. "I'm not into her, Liz. Ava is nice and all, but she's not you."

Her head snapped up and she met his steady gaze. "What?"

"You heard me." A soft smile notched up his lips. "It's kind of cute when you're all pissed and jealous. You usually hide it better than this."

"Did you come here to humiliate me even more?"

"No. I'd never do that to you, Liz, and you know it. I came here to tell you that you're wrong about me not having feelings for you."

She released him and pushed past him. "I know you care about me. I get it. I don't need another we're-better-as-friends speech."

Tate took her arm and pulled to get her to turn around and face him.

She expected him to say what he always said about not wanting to lose what they had, but instead he took her face in his hands and stared down into her eyes and just like that she fell deep into the blue depths and all the sincerity and honesty staring back at her.

"I think if we gave it a try we could be great together." Those words barely penetrated her ears before his lips settled on hers and he scrambled her brain.

His arms went around her back and pulled her close. Her breasts pressed to his chest. She fisted her hands in his shirt at his back and held on because she seriously thought her legs would give out from the tremble of need that shook through her.

His tongue swept across her bottom lip and she stopped thinking about anything but tasting him. She opened her mouth and he dove in, sweeping his tongue along hers. He did so with a skill that curled her toes but also carried a hint of hesitancy, like he wasn't sure, or maybe like her, it felt so new and wondrous he needed a second to settle into it.

"Damn, sweetheart, I should have kissed you forever ago." Those sweet words were followed by another searing kiss.

They got lost in each other for another long moment until Tate broke the kiss, drew in a ragged breath, pressed his forehead to hers, and stared deep into her eyes.

She rubbed her hands down his back along his taut muscles and held his waist. "I don't know what to do now." She waited to see if she woke up from this dream.

Tate brushed her hair behind her ear. "Let's go out to dinner. On a real date." He took her hand and pulled her forward as he stepped back toward the door.

"Wait. No." She shook her head and tugged him to stop.

He tipped his head to the side and studied her. "Why not? I thought this is what you wanted, too."

If the kiss hadn't been enough to tell her Tate had

changed his mind about dating her, that *too* he added at the end confirmed it.

"I . . . um . . . a date would be so nice."

"But," he prompted, then caught the fear she couldn't hide from him. "This is about *him*. What else did he do?" She tried to pull her hand free, but Tate held on. "Na-uh. You start talking. I mean it, Liz. What happened?"

Her heart shot up to her throat. She tried to get the words out, but fear shot through her again.

"Shit." Tate drew her to the dining table and pulled out a chair. "Sit before you pass out. You're white as a sheet." He loomed over her.

"I'm okay."

"You don't look it. Start talking or I'll go find that fuck and make him talk."

She leaned back, stuck her foot on the edge of the chair across from her, and pushed it out. "You sit and calm down."

Tate took the chair, pulled it out and close to hers, then sat down. He took both her hands and held them in his. "Talk to me, Liz. You're tough. Nothing really gets to you. So what did he do to rattle you so much?"

"He wouldn't stop."

Tate's eyes went wide with shock. "What does that mean?"

She knew his mind had gone to a dark place. "No. Not that. He didn't force me or anything." She took a breath and tried to explain. "He showed up at the spa as I got off work. He was waiting at my car. I told him it was over."

"Good. Then there's nothing stopping us from seeing each other."

She dipped her head, then looked up at him. "You're really serious about this."

"If you need me to prove it, I can kiss you again." He squeezed her hands.

"I really can't believe this is happening."

"It's strange. But that will wear off. And I really do want to kiss you again." The sweet smile warmed her heart and made her giddy with anticipation even if she was having trouble switching gears from he-just-wants-to-be-my-friend mode.

Someone honked a horn outside and she jumped.

Tate frowned. "Okay, sweetheart, you need to tell me what he did when you broke up with him."

She sighed. "He didn't believe me."

"Well, that's too damn bad. You said you didn't want to see him again, that's the end of it."

"He tried to convince me otherwise."

"How?"

She pressed her lips together and fought the urge to wipe her mouth again because she really liked holding hands with Tate. "He forced a kiss on me."

Rage filled his eyes.

"I pushed him away and told him I was done. He thinks I didn't mean it, that I'm delusional to think you'd ever want me unless it's out of pity, and that he and I can find our way back to when things were good."

"Of course you didn't believe any of that bullshit."

She didn't know what to say because there was a ring of truth in what Clint said. The last thing she wanted to do was discover that all the times she'd foolishly hoped Tate would love her back only made her a fool.

Tate cupped her cheek in one hand. "The best couples I know—Drake and Adria, my mom and dad—have one thing that helps keep them together. At the heart of their relationships, yes, they have a deep love, but it's more than that. They're best friends. They trust each other. They know how to talk to each other with respect and consideration. We have that already."

"That's not the same," she couldn't help pointing out. Their friendship didn't mean they'd have a long and lasting romantic relationship.

"I admit that up until now, I purposefully didn't allow myself to think that you and I could be more. I didn't want to lose what we had. Truthfully, I thought you deserved better."

She squeezed his hand, stunned by that admission. "Tate. No. The truth for me is that no one else ever measured up to you. I tried to do the same as you, protect our friendship and find someone else so I didn't screw *us* up."

"I'd see you happy with someone and think that proved my point."

"You'd go from one woman to another and I'd think, 'Why can't he see that I'd make him happy?'"

"I never meant to hurt you or make you think that—"

She touched her fingers to his lips to stop him from explaining. "I know, Tate."

"I wasn't ready to make some big commitment. I never thought about being someone's long-term anything. Boyfriend. Husband. That just wasn't in my head. I don't know if this will work. I'm scared as hell I'll fuck it up and lose you. But I'd rather let the feelings I've buried all these years out and see if we could be more than lose you to some other guy and wonder why the hell I never even tried to make you mine." He leaned in closer. "It's not that I never felt something for you, it's just that with you it felt too . . . important. I knew it would change everything between us, and I didn't know what that really meant. Now I do."

He knew it meant a life together. Marriage. Children. Forever. Everything she wanted only with him.

Tate squeezed her hand. "I'm ready to try because it's what *I* want. You're what I want." He tugged her out of her chair and right into his lap. They shared another searing kiss that left her breathless. Just like Tate intended, it knocked out all her worries and made her focus on him and the way he made her feel.

She forgot all about Clint.

Her fears dissipated.

And she stopped second-guessing Tate's feelings and motives.

After the day she'd had, she just wanted to wallow in this amazing moment.

Tate kissed her one last time and hugged her. She pressed her cheek to his head and held him close with her arms around his neck. She breathed in the shampoo and sunshine scent in his hair and the solid feel of his body pressed to hers.

"Get used to it, Liz. We've always been close." He squeezed her to him. "We're going to get closer."

She sat back so she could look him in the eye. "It's just so much all at once." She broke up with the wrong man and got the one she wanted all in one day.

"Then let's take a little time and settle into it. If you don't want to go out, we'll stay in. I'll order pizza. You find a movie." Tate stood with her, which made their bodies brush together. Every nerve ending attuned to him.

She caught her breath and looked up at him.

He slipped his hand underneath her hair at the back of her neck and stared down at her. "I love it when you look at me that way, but I'm trying to take this slow because it's important and there's a lot at stake. I don't want to rush. Well . . . I do, but I think it's important to not skip the getting to know you stuff."

She understood all too well. "We've been friends a long time, but that's not the same as dating and being together."

"Trust me, now that I've opened the door to us being together, I can't stop thinking about it and wanting you. I just feel like if we jump too soon, we'll miss something important and it'll get messed up." He raked his fingers through his hair.

She placed her hand on his chest, liking that she could reach out and touch him without it being weird or seeming to cross a line. "I understand, Tate. The last thing I want to do is force this or think that because we're such good friends that the rest will be easy."

"I know you in one way better than I know most people, but as a girlfriend . . . that's different."

To lighten the mood, she teased, "Are you my supercute boyfriend now?"

He hooked his arm around her waist and drew her close. "You think I'm supercute?"

"You're gorgeous, and you know it."

"I didn't know *you* thought that."

"Oh come on, everyone knows it."

"You want to hear a confession?"

"I'm pretty sure I know all your deep dark secrets."

"Did you know that I hate it when guys look at you like they want to f—kiss you."

She knew that's not what he meant, but the ego boost made her smile, even if it wasn't wholly true. "They do not."

"Ah, yeah, they do."

"But I don't notice because I'm always looking at you." She traced her finger along his rough jaw, flirting and enjoying this new closeness with him.

"I tried not to notice it. Or at least not let you know I noticed."

"But you liked it."

"Deep down, yeah. It made me wonder, *What if?*"

She could think of lots of those, but the one that worried him most also stood out for her, too. "What if this doesn't work out?"

"What if it does?" Optimism filled his deep voice.

She buried her face in his neck and hugged him. He really had opened himself up to the possibility of them being more than friends. It boggled the mind, but also made her heart soar.

He squeezed her closer. "Feel that, Liz?"

Her whole body was aware of him. Mind, body, soul—everything inside her wanted, craved, needed him. "I feel it."

She'd never felt this way about anyone but him. Those early ripples of awareness, anticipation, and attraction she felt with other men, with Clint, fizzled out because none of them were Tate. None of them ever turned her attention away from him. Not for long. Because her heart had always belonged to him.

It probably always would.

Tate's hands came up to cup her face. He stared down at her, his eyes intent. "This is serious, Liz. It's real. Believe in that and let the rest happen."

This time, she initiated the kiss. Soft. Sweet. She lingered with the press of her lips to his. She took in the way his mouth fit hers and how her body nestled against his like it was made to fit.

She pulled back and stared into his eyes, the blue depths serene and welcoming. "A movie."

"Pizza."

"You and me."

"Sounds good," he agreed.

She slipped out of his arms as he pulled his phone from his back pocket. She went into the living room, taking in a breath and all that happened this evening. She picked up the remote, turned on the TV, and pushed buttons until she got to the On Demand feature. As she scrolled through movies looking for something she and Tate would both like, a movement outside the window drew her gaze. At first she thought it was one of her neighbors walking a dog but her gaze rose to the glimpse of the parking lot between two neighboring buildings and Clint standing there staring at her while he leaned against the back of his car. Too far away to really see his expression, she knew he saw her. Watched her.

A cold chill raced up her spine.

He raised his hand and typed something into his phone.

Her phone buzzed a few seconds later with a text. Afraid to stand there letting him watch her like some creep, she walked to the dining table, retrieved her phone, and stared at the message.

CLINT: We're not over!!!!!!!!!!!!!

Tate's hands gripped the tops of her shoulders. She jumped under his soft touch.

He read the text over her shoulder. "Bullshit." Tate snagged her phone. "I'll make him believe."

LIZ: This is Tate Liz is with me now
LIZ: Leave her alone
LIZ: Or you deal with me
CLINT: She's mine!!!!!!!!!!!

Tate's head snapped up and his gaze locked with hers. "He's delusional."

"I told you, he wouldn't listen to me."

"You need to stay away from him."

"I intend to, but . . ." She glanced at the window.

"What?"

"I saw him out in the parking lot watching me."

Tate ran to the window and stared out, his head turning one way then the other. "Where?"

She came up behind him and peeked around his shoulder, not wanting to see Clint or feel that creepy shiver up her spine again. But . . . "He's gone."

Tate glanced down at her with a question in his eyes.

"I swear. He was there." She pointed to the empty parking spot between the two buildings across from hers.

"I believe you, Liz. I'm just wondering, what's his

game? You broke up with him, but he still thinks you're his."

"Ever since that night at the bar, nothing between us has been the same. He's been . . . possessive, demanding, and a little mean. It was all good the first two months but . . . something about him always bothered me. I could just never put my finger on it. Until now."

Tate stared down at her. "I didn't know you were seeing this guy for that long."

"I don't tell you everything."

"You used to."

She pressed her lips tight, then confessed, "This time I wanted to really make a go of it with someone. He was nice and flirted and made me feel like he really wanted me."

Tate let out a frustrated sigh. "Okay. But then it changed."

"It was subtle. But when you came into that bar demanding to talk to me, I don't know, he took it as a threat to our relationship."

"Maybe it was." Tate handed her back the phone. "You stopped talking to me, and I saw you with him, and I thought . . ."

"You thought I left you for him?" It sounded so implausible he'd think that.

"Yeah. And for the first time, I really thought about what we have and how much it means to me."

"Declan prodding you had something to do with that."

He nodded, but added, "Kinda. But it's more that what he asked wouldn't let me shove the thoughts and feelings away again." He took her hand. "And before you start thinking that I wanted to do just that, you're wrong. I've been trying to tell you since that night at the bar. It's why I came to your work for lunch. I tried to tell you when you came to the ranch. It's what I came here tonight to tell you."

"The kisses told me a lot, but what exactly are you saying?"

"It's simple, Liz. Be mine."

She went up on tiptoe and kissed him softly, eyes locked. "If I'm dreaming, don't wake me up."

"You're in mine." His dazzling smile made her belly flutter. "And they're really hot."

He never failed to make her laugh, even at the end of a very difficult day. His words and what they shared today held a truth she couldn't deny.

He pressed his forehead to hers. "Is that a yes?"

"Yes."

He gave her a quick kiss because the doorbell rang. "Good. And if that's Clint and not the pizza, I'm going to deck him."

Liz held her breath while Tate opened the door. He looked completely at ease and ready to take on any threat at the same time. He just had that kind of confidence. Luckily, the only thing he needed to do was pay the pizza guy.

Tate handed her the box and went into the kitchen to get napkins, plates, and drinks while she set the pizza on the coffee table and pulled up the haunted house series everyone had been talking about at work.

Tate took the seat beside her.

"Since you're my new boyfriend, I thought we could start a new series together."

He chuckled and shrugged one shoulder. "Why not." He read the series description. "I heard Trinity talking about this show. Sounds good, but I thought you hated scary movies."

"Well, I have you here to chase away the ghosts."

And so they sat eating pizza like they'd done a hundred times or more. After they ate, she snuggled against his side with his arm around her and laughed when he poked her in the side during a particularly tension-filled scene where she anticipated a scare, but he jumped the gun and spooked her instead.

She didn't think about Clint at all because all she could think about was the buzz of electricity between her and Tate and the anticipation that he'd kiss her again.

She wanted him to stay the night. The desire in Tate's eyes said he did, too. But after three episodes, he stood, helped her clean up, then kissed her like he wanted to do a hell of a lot more, said, "Sweet dreams, Liz," and went home, leaving her giddy with anticipation to see him again.

As soon as possible.

And she did in her dreams that night, though they didn't do justice to one real-life kiss from Tate.

For the first time in a long time, and with Clint in her rearview, she woke up smiling and happy and eager to start her day because she'd get to see Tate later that day.

Chapter Nine

Liz jumped when Trinity came up behind her and put her hand on Liz's shoulder.

"What is with you today?" Trinity reached past her for another postcard advertising *Almost Homemade* to add to the bag that held her customer's order.

People crowded the farmers market. They'd had an endless line at the *Almost Homemade* booth, which Tate helped them set up this morning before he rushed back to work on the ranch.

Ever since he left, she got this creepy feeling. Like someone kept staring at her. But no matter where she looked in the crowd, she couldn't pinpoint anyone paying her special attention.

She didn't see Clint, but she felt his presence. Whether real or imagined, the sense of danger loomed.

And she didn't like it.

After the events of the last few days, she anticipated seeing him here. Lurking. She hoped he'd given up, let her go, and it was over. She wasn't so sure.

It creeped her out.

She hated feeling paranoid.

The growing anxiety, tightened her gut and notched up the dread building inside her.

When Tate got ready to go home last night, she'd desperately wanted to ask him to stay. Yes, because she wanted to finally get her hands on him, though she appreciated that he wanted them to take their time. But also because for the first time she'd been afraid to be alone at home.

Thanks Clint.

The last thing she wanted to do was ask Tate to stay because she was scared of Clint—instead of simply wanting Tate.

"Earth to Liz!"

"Huh? What?"

Trinity handed over change to a customer and turned to her. "Are you okay?"

"Yeah, I'm fine." She pulled out a chicken pot pie for her customer and accepted the twenty-dollar bill. It took her a second too long to calculate the four dollars in change.

Trinity touched her shoulder again. "Is this about Tate kissing you on the forehead before he left? I know how much you like him. He doesn't think sometimes when he does things like give you a friendly peck goodbye."

She actually appreciated that Tate hadn't picked this morning to announce their new status by kissing her silly in front of his sister. "Tate and I are good." She sucked in a breath and tested the water with Trinity about how she'd feel about her and Tate getting together. "We're dating now."

Trinity's eyes went as wide as the pumpkin streusel muffin in her hand. "Excuse me?"

"I'll take two meatloaves and a spaghetti with meatballs," the next customer requested.

Liz went to the cooler and pulled out the prepackaged meals customers loved to take home, heat, and eat. She turned around and practically ran right into Trinity.

"You and Tate are dating." Underneath the initial shock rose enthusiasm.

"Yes."

"When did this happen?" Intense interest filled those rapid-fire words.

"Last night. After I broke up with Clint."

Trinity's mouth drew back in a half frown. "I heard about the scene Tate made in the bar."

"Declan pushed Tate to confront his feelings. I expected Tate to be upset that I took a step back to find what I really wanted, but I never thought he'd come to me and confess that over the years he's thought about us."

Trinity put her hand on her chest. "Oh. My. God. He did?"

Uncertainty rippled in her belly. "Is that so hard to believe?"

"That Tate would talk about his feelings and not brush them aside with a clever remark? Yeah."

Relief swept through her. "Oh. No. I thought you meant . . ."

"What? That he didn't have feelings for you. Of course he does." Trinity said that with absolute certainty. "He's just been too stupid to see that you're perfect for each other."

Stunned, Liz stood there unable to come up with anything to say to that.

She leaned in and dropped her voice. "Did he kiss you yet?"

"He short-circuited my brain. Now it seems every time he looks at me, he can't help but kiss me. It's weird. And exciting all at the same time."

Trinity laughed. "I knew you'd turn him inside out one of these days."

"It's new." And for all she hoped it would be everything she wanted, she still harbored fears it wasn't real at all.

Trinity touched her shoulder. "It's been coming for a long time."

They couldn't ignore the customers any longer and got back to filling orders, but Liz still felt a heavy presence watching her. It took all her energy to focus on the task at hand, but eventually, she ignored the warning tingling inside her and fell into the routine of helping one customer after the next.

Just when the crowd thinned as the market wound down for the day, she spotted Clint standing next to a building across the street. His intense stare made her anxious. Her heart pounded so loud she thought Trinity could hear it.

He held up his hand and crooked his finger for her to come to him.

Fear made her want to run. But a wave of anger and indignation that he'd followed her here—watched her—made her scared and paranoid, and incited her to move before she thought better of it.

"Liz, where are you going?" Trinity called.

She didn't answer or stop, but rushed across the street and ran right up to Clint. "What the hell are you doing here?"

Surprise filled his eyes, though he shouldn't have

expected anything less than her boiling hostility. "I wanted to see you. I miss you." He reached out to touch her but she slapped his hand away.

"Don't touch me. I told you yesterday. We're over. I do not want to see you anymore."

Clint dismissed that with a shake of his head. "I saw you with him this morning. He doesn't really want you. Not the way I do. He kissed you on the forehead like you're his sister."

She'd thought the gesture sweet. And appropriate given they were in public with Trinity watching them.

"Don't let him make a fool of you again, Liz. You deserve better. Come back to me. We're so good together."

"You got one thing right. I do deserve better than a man who leaves bruises and forces himself on me. You hurt me. Nothing you say or do would make me want to take you back."

"How about this?" He grabbed her by the arms and pulled her in for a kiss that punished more than it soothed or coaxed her to see his side.

Because he held her arms pinned to her sides, she struggled to back away. Panic swept through her and made it hard to think and act appropriately.

Fear gave her the strength to fight. She turned her face away and kicked him in the shin.

He shoved her away. "What the hell, Liz?"

She should have known better than to confront him. It only gave him the attention he craved. She should have made her intention to stay away from him clear, by not giving him the time of day.

Lesson learned.

She swiped the back of her hand across her mouth. "Don't ever touch me again." She didn't wait around to hear any more of his declarations that they belonged together. She didn't give him a chance to hurt her again. She ran back across the street, straight to the *Almost Homemade* booth.

Trinity stood staring at her, concern and a hint of suspicion lighting her eyes. "What was that?" Anger filled her words.

"He just showed up. He's been watching me." She raked her shaking fingers through her hair. "Why won't he just leave me alone?"

Trinity responded to Liz's distress and hugged her. "I don't like this."

Liz didn't either. Clint gave up his plans to watch a game at his place with his friends to come all the way downtown to the farmers market just to spy on her.

"Hey, did you guys sell out again?" Tate startled her.

She hadn't seen him walk up behind her, but just hearing his voice, knowing he was here, eased her thrashing heart. She turned away from Trinity to him and threw her arms around his neck and held on.

Tate's arms wrapped around her. "Hey now, I'm happy to see you, too."

"Clint is stalking her," Trinity announced.

Liz tried to pull away from Tate, but he held her close and rubbed his hand up and down her back to soothe her. "What happened?"

She pressed her face into his neck, then raised her head and looked him in the eyes. "He just showed up. All day I've felt like someone's been watching me. I thought I was just being paranoid because of what happened, but then I saw him across the street. He motioned for me to come over."

Tate's eyes narrowed. "And you went?"

This time she stepped away from him, needing a chance to stand on her own again. "Yes. To tell him to stay the hell away from me. To let him know that I don't want him anywhere near me ever again."

Tate took her hand. "Okay. I take it he didn't want to hear that."

"He thinks he can convince me that we belong together and you're just . . . pretending. Or something. I don't know."

Tate pulled her into his chest and kissed her softly. His hand came up to the side of her face, warm and protective. His lips brushed against hers, then settled for a moment. Her heart melted and settled into a rhythm that seemed to match his pressed against her chest.

Tate kissed her again, then leaned back just enough to look her in the eye. "Does that feel like I'm pretending?"

"No." She dropped her forehead to his chin.

He kissed her head and buried his fingers in her hair. "Don't let his lies get into your head. He wants you to question me, us. If you do, this is never going to work. If all I'm doing is trying to convince you I mean what I say and I want to be with you, how long before you start really thinking I'm trying to convince you because it's not real?"

He had a point. When he left last night, she thought they'd taken that fork in the road that led them down a path where they ended up together, happy and in love.

Eventually. She didn't delude herself it would happen all at once, but she believed there was something there on Tate's part. He'd finally opened the door on his feelings and the possibility of what they could share.

And here she was not even a full day later and all the ground they'd made toward turning their friendship into something more got derailed because Clint made her think Tate's intentions weren't real or based on his true feelings for her.

Tate didn't lie. He didn't do anything he didn't want to do. He wouldn't manipulate her. He'd give it to her straight.

He cupped her face and tilted her head back so they were looking at each other again. "I'm not playing. This isn't some hookup or pity thing. This is me and you and what we make it. I'm all in, Liz." He brushed his thumb across her cheek. "Now that I know we're doing this, I can't tell you how hard it was to leave you last night."

"You guys should get a room." Declan smacked Tate on the back, pushing him into Liz.

Trinity punched Declan in the gut, making him bend forward and expel his breath in a whoosh. "Leave them alone." Trinity turned to Liz and Tate. "I'm glad you two are so happy, but what are you going to do about Clint?"

Tate held her hips and gave her a little tug closer. "Let's hope he finally got the message and stays away."

Liz wished she shared Tate's optimism.

While they cleaned up the booth and loaded the trucks, she had a hard time convincing herself that Clint had left. She felt him lurking. The creepy feeling tingling at the back of her neck kept her internal alarm blaring and her anxiety jacked up to high. Whether her imagination or reality, it didn't matter because he'd gotten to her.

Infected her.

He'd become a thing between her and Tate.

She vowed to herself that she'd stop questioning Tate's motives for wanting a relationship with her and just go with it and explore the new feelings they were both just starting to accept.

She'd wanted to be with Tate forever. She wouldn't let anything stand in the way or destroy it now that she had a real shot at happiness with the only man she'd ever truly loved.

Chapter Ten

LIZ DIDN'T know it, but Clint watched her all day. He sat at a café a block away, a view of her every move. Unaware of him, she'd served customers and chatted with Tate's sister. They smiled and laughed with each other through the morning and afternoon. Tate hadn't made an appearance after they set up and Clint thought maybe Liz had come to her senses and realized that was a lost cause. He'd only hurt her again.

He'd tried to remind her of that, but she refused to listen.

Then Tate returned.

She'd pined away for a man who didn't really want her. A man who didn't deserve her.

Didn't she see that if Tate loved her at all, he'd never have let her be with someone else?

Clint loved her like that.

She was just too blind to see it because Tate kept stringing her along.

Well, he'd make her see that she belonged to him.

They'd only scratched the surface of what they could have together. It had been going so well. He'd taken things at her pace. Slow and steady. In the past he'd pushed too hard, too fast for what he wanted.

Those women didn't see how hard he'd tried to love them.

Liz made him lose his temper. He never meant to grab her that hard, but he'd wanted her to listen. Was that so much to ask after all the time and effort he'd put into showing her how much he cared?

It hit him the first time he saw her. Something about her shone. She'd smiled at him and he'd known instantly that she was the one.

If Tate were out of the picture, she'd see him as the one and only man who could love her the way she deserved.

And she did want him.

When they made love, it had rocked him.

She had to have felt it, too.

Every kiss they shared set him on fire. The taste of her, her sweet seductive scent, the way she smiled and looked at him, everything made him want her even more.

Tate thought he could distract her with empty promises and lies.

Clint offered her everything. She'd be happier with him, not that dumbass cowboy who had the perfect woman standing right in front of him and had been too stupid to take her.

No other woman compared to Liz.

No one else would ever have her.

She belonged to him.

Tate might think he could move in and try to take her away from him, but Clint would show him that no one got in his way.

And he'd show Liz who she really loved.

His subtle reprimand hadn't worked to bring her around.

She needed a heavier hand and a push to see past Tate's disingenuous interest and that they could be happy together again.

Chapter Eleven

A FEW DAYS later, Tate raced after Liz on horseback across the pasture toward the stables. It had been a while since they took a ride around the ranch. Being with her here, with the way things were between them now, made him look at the ranch in a whole new way.

What would it be like to live here with her?

It seemed even more important than ever to close up the gaps in some of the areas he and Declan simply put off. They had to prioritize projects and let other things slide until they could get to them later. But perhaps "later" was "now."

They raced past the cabin where Drake and Adria were living now until the renovations were done on their new house.

Soon, it would be Tate's place.

He didn't mind taking Liz back to the big house where he lived with Declan, but it would be nice to have his own place. He and Liz could enjoy their own quiet evenings in, making dinner together, watching a show, and spending some time alone. Preferably in bed.

God, how he wanted her.

It amazed him how quickly his mind took *You can*

have her to imagining all the ways he wanted to be with her.

Liz reined in by the stables, turned the horse toward him, and pointed right at him. "I won!"

He couldn't help the laugh that bubbled up inside him and burst out. "You wish. I just liked the view from behind you."

She giggled and it made him smile even more. "I knew you let me win." She shook her head. "That's a first."

"Purely selfish on my part. I'm hoping you'll console the loser with a kiss."

She walked her horse right next to his, leaned over, and met him in the middle. He desperately wanted to taste her again. She kissed him with a passion that made him feel like he'd won everything ever in life.

The deeper they got into this relationship, the more he asked himself why the hell had he waited so long to have something like this?

He was just beginning to see and feel how having someone in his life who loved him made all the difference. Yes, she'd always been in his life. But opening himself up to her and all she offered—it opened his eyes to what he'd been missing in all his other relationships.

He could talk to her about anything. She didn't let him get away with being an ass. She laughed at his jokes. And when she kissed him . . . damn. He felt it.

They were taking things slow. He didn't mind. In fact, he liked this part a lot. The touching and kissing. The revving things up and letting them simmer. He could have her anytime he wanted. She wanted him just as bad. But they needed this time to transition from best friends to lovers.

But that didn't mean he couldn't turn up the heat. So he dismounted, hooked his hands under her arms, plucked her off her horse, and held her close. She let out a surprised gasp, and Tate dove in for a deep kiss. He slid his tongue along hers, getting that sweet moan he loved, and brushed his hand up her side and swept his thumb along the outside of her breast. He wanted to palm the whole thing, but they were in the middle of the yard where anyone could see them.

Liz leaned back and stared at him, a touch of shyness in her eyes. "Are you going to let me win now because I'm your girlfriend?"

"Maybe." In the past, labels like that came with expectations that seemed daunting and overwhelming. They made him twitchy. Not with Liz. She was so much more than just another girlfriend.

"Why would you do that?"

"Because I love it when you smile at me full of excitement."

She touched her fingertips to his jaw. "I'm not used to you being so sweet."

She was used to him teasing and trying to outdo her. Remnants of them growing up together and being a boy who wanted to show up and show off for the girls. But he didn't want to best Liz just because he could. He liked that they could be playful with each other, knowing it wasn't done out of spite or just to rile the other person.

Sure, sometimes he annoyed her, but she got over it quick. If he ever felt like he'd gone too far, he'd always apologize.

He'd been careful never to flirt or be too nice and give her false hope. He'd ridden that line a long time. Being with her now, like this, freed something inside him. Something he hadn't realized he'd kept locked down along with his real feelings. "Get used to it."

The horses shifted restlessly beside them. He reluctantly released Liz and followed her lead, taking his horse's reins and walking behind Liz and her horse to the stables. Her ass looked good in a saddle and swaying as she walked.

God, he had it bad.

"Declan should have dinner ready soon. Hungry?"

She glanced over her shoulder, a sweet, sexy smile on her lips as her eyes dipped and traveled down him and back up, leaving a blazing trail of heat. "Yep."

He'd always liked her. He thought he knew everything about her, but he'd never seen her like this. "This side of you fascinates me."

She stopped her horse by its stall and glanced at him. "What side?"

"You seem so . . . open."

"I don't have to hide the way I feel about you."

And he didn't have to stop himself from noticing things about her. Like the long column of her neck where he wanted to kiss her. The way she cocked her hip when she stared at him. The temptation of her pink bowed lips. "It's sexy as hell."

"It's just me, Tate. You just never noticed."

"I can't stop noticing now."

Her sweet smile widened. "I like you flirting and all sweet on me. It's nice." She'd waited a long time for him to see what was right in front of his face.

They unsaddled the horses and brushed them down in companionable silence, working hard to get the job done. With the horses settled in their stalls, fed and watered, he held his hand out to her. She took it, sliding her fingers through his. They walked up to the house, exchanging silly smiles and shoulder bumps along the way. This all still felt new and a little weird at times but fun and exciting and like an adventure to someplace you couldn't wait to see and experience.

They walked in the front door and caught Declan pulling a casserole out of the oven.

Tate reluctantly let go of Liz at the breakfast bar and headed for the fridge. "Hey, man, what can I do?" He pulled two beers from the fridge, set his on the counter, unscrewed the cap from Liz's, and handed it to her. He uncapped his, clinked the neck of his bottle to hers, then took a deep sip. After the dusty ride, he needed the cold wash of liquid down his throat.

Liz took a deep sip and sighed. "That's good."

Declan set the casserole on a hot pad on the counter. "Can you set the table?"

"I'll do it," Liz offered.

Tate put his hand on her shoulder to get her to sit on the stool at the counter. "Drink your beer. We got this."

Liz sat, but didn't let it go. "You know I've eaten dinner here with you all many times and always helped with the meal."

"Not tonight." Tate wanted to do something nice for her. Let her relax and just enjoy the time they had together.

Declan winked at her. "He's trying to impress you."

Tate rolled his eyes. "Yeah, with my mad place setting skills."

Liz laughed and it hit him in the gut and tied it in knots.

Tate walked past her with the plates, utensils, and napkins stacked in his hands.

Liz did that sexy once-over of him again. "He is impressive."

God, how that inflated his ego and made him want to strip her bare and make love to her all night.

Declan shook his head. "Gross." He slid the garlic bread into the oven, then turned back to Liz. "You guys are going to be just as annoyingly happy as Drake and Adria, aren't you?"

Tate really hoped so. "Get used to it." It seemed they all had to take a little time to settle into the changes between him and Liz.

"I love lasagna." Liz changed the subject.

"Tate brought it home after you guys took everything back to *Almost Homemade* after the farmers market. Since it's my night to cook, he asked me to pop this in the oven and make some garlic bread and a salad."

Liz turned on the stool to face him. "You did?"

"It's your favorite meal. Simple enough to make what you like when I could grab most of it from the shop."

Appreciation shone in her eyes as she picked up her beer and looked at it then saluted him with it. "Thank you for being so considerate."

He tilted his head, not getting what was so special about getting her a beer and making her favorite meal. But if it made her happy, he was glad for it. "You're welcome. No big deal."

"It is to me." The sincerity in her voice drew him to her.

He kissed her softly. "I just wanted to have dinner with you tonight."

She looked up at him, joy and gratitude in her eyes. "I know. It's really nice."

He brushed his fingers over her cheek. "Okay."

"Let's eat," Declan announced, taking the bread from the oven, filling the kitchen with the smell of melted butter and garlic.

Tate took Liz's hand and helped her stand. "Take a seat at the table. I'll grab the lasagna while Declan grabs the salad."

With dinner on the table, they passed plates so Tate could dish up the lasagna. Declan doled out salad, and Liz plopped bread on each plate. Family style. Everyone chipping in and around the table. Liz had eaten at the house too many times to count. She'd always fit in with the family, just like he'd always felt at home at her parents' place.

Declan had no trouble starting the conversation with Liz. "How was the ride?"

"Beautiful. I love it out here. The ranch is so pretty this time of year."

Tate agreed. The grass was as green as her eyes, blue skies, and miles of open country for them to explore. "Lots of hawks up today. We saw a few deer down by the cedars in the south pasture."

"They've been moving around the property for a few weeks now," Declan confirmed. "I saw them in the orchard the other morning."

"That orchard needs some work. Especially if

Trinity and Adria want to start harvesting fruit from it next year for the shop."

Declan chewed and gave him a thoughtful look. "Those two are creating a lot of work for us."

Tate nodded his agreement. "It's business and we're making money right along with them." Though they did give their sisters a deep discount on the beef and he was sure the fruit, too. The ladies liked to advertise their products were produced with locally grown and sourced ingredients.

"What they've accomplished in such a short time with the shop is amazing," Liz praised. "The line at the farmers market never let up. I was afraid we'd run out of products before the end of the day."

Declan took a sip of his beer and set it down. "We've learned to expect a crowd. They're talking about opening a few more stores in other locations. Adria's already scouting for properties."

"Wow."

Declan stared at Liz. "How's the spa gig?"

"Good." She rolled her shoulders and squirmed in her chair. "I think I'm going to need a massage after that ride. It's been a while since I've been in the saddle."

"You know you're welcome here anytime." Declan's words touched Tate and lit up Liz's eyes.

He appreciated that Declan made it clear, though Liz knew she was always welcome here.

"I think you'll be seeing a lot more of me now." Liz's careful tone didn't match the smile she gave him, but he got that she was treading carefully because this was Declan's house, too.

"Happy to hear it. I always thought the two of you

would be good together." Declan turned his gaze to Tate and pointed at him with his fork. "This one needed a huge wake-up call."

Liz laughed. "He's a tough one to crack."

"Yeah, and now he's oozing all kinds of happy because of you."

Tate could take the teasing, but under Declan's words he heard a deeper ring of . . . not jealousy, but something akin to it.

He draped his arm over Liz's shoulders. "Timing is everything." What else could he say about him and Liz? Also, maybe Declan needed to know that his time would come, too. Maybe when he least expected it, the way it hit Tate.

Declan eyed him, then finished off his dinner without comment.

Liz glanced at Tate, getting that Declan was in a mood. He'd been in that mood for a while now. Maybe like Tate, he'd seen Drake fall hard and fast for Adria and wanted something like it, too.

More than likely, it was their age. They were getting older and nights out at the bar didn't seem quite so fulfilling and fun anymore. Not when they worked so hard and wanted to have someone to go home to instead of spinning the wheel on the dating scene and hoping your number came up and you won the prize. Declan, like Tate, had busted many times with relationships that started out fun but washed out quickly.

He played with Liz's copper red hair, knowing their relationship was different. This would last. How he knew that, he didn't know, but it was the first time he felt all in and ready to do anything to make Liz happy and want to be with him. He wanted to hold on to this feeling inside him that glowed whenever he thought about or saw her. It had always been there in the background. Another thing he'd ignored. But now that he knew it was there, he felt it all the more.

Declan slapped the back of his hand across Tate's shoulder. "You took your sweet time with Liz. It's a wonder she waited for *you*."

"She knows a good thing when she sees it."

Declan leaned forward and pinned Liz in his gaze. "Really? You couldn't do better than him?"

Liz laughed. "Well, he always shared his lunch with me in school and he held my hair back once in high school when I got really drunk on Jägermeister."

Declan fell back in his chair, chuckling and shaking his head. "No. Never drink that stuff."

Liz laughed with him. "My date was as drunk as me when he tried to pick me up off the bathroom floor to take me home. Tate wouldn't let him."

Tate remembered this. "I got to the party late because Dad asked me to stay in case one of the mares had trouble birthing a foal. I'd had like half a beer when I found Liz."

"Confession?" Liz asked.

"Oh please," Declan said leaning forward again.

"I only drank so much because I was upset Tate didn't show for the party and I thought maybe I'd make Tate jealous and I'd finally get him to kiss me that night. Instead, I puked and looked ridiculous drunk."

"You were kind of cute. As far as rag dolls go. I had to carry you out to my truck."

Liz put her elbow on the table, her chin in her hand,

and gave him a mischievous look. "I may have exaggerated how uncoordinated I was that night."

Tate laughed. "Seriously?"

"She got her big strong man to carry her to his car." Declan saluted Liz with his beer.

"Yeah, but I didn't dare kiss him after I'd puked. He'd never kiss me again if I did that."

Tate hooked his arm around her neck and pulled her close. "You probably wouldn't have remembered it anyway."

She gave him a sideways glance. "You were pissed when you got me into the truck."

"All I could think about was what could have happened to you. The guy you were with was so drunk he probably would have killed you both driving you home. I knew he'd sleep it off there, so I took you home to your folks to be sure you were safe."

"He found me after school that Monday and said it was better that we didn't see each other anymore. I'm pretty sure it's because you said something to him."

Tate shrugged that away, neither confirming nor denying.

Liz stared at him for a long moment, then leaned in and kissed him. "Thank you."

"For what?"

"Looking out for me. Taking care of me."

"I always did." He hugged her close to his side and kissed her on the temple. "I always will."

Declan grabbed his plate and beer and stood, looking down at them. "I'm glad you two finally got together." He headed into the kitchen.

"You cooked," Liz called. "We'll do the dishes."

"We will?" Tate teased.

She elbowed him in the gut. "Yes. We will."

"Fine."

She didn't buy the long-suffering sigh he put into that acquiescence.

They gathered the dishes and took them into the kitchen. Declan had already retreated to the family room to watch TV or back down to the office to work. Either way, he made himself scarce, but Tate enjoyed having dinner, the three of them.

Liz made quick work of the dishes while he put away the leftovers in the fridge. He turned to her and found her watching him with her back to the counter, hands clasped in front of her. She shifted from one foot to the other, fatigue and discomfort in her eyes.

"You okay? Sore after our ride?"

"A little. And being on my feet all day at the farmers market made my feet and knees ache. I'm getting old."

He chuckled at that. "My back agrees with you. I used to be able to do all the ranch work and then some and feel fine. Now I groan when I get out of bed." He took her by the hips and pulled her close. "Come on. I'll walk you out. You've had a long day. I'm sure you'd like a hot shower and some sleep."

She walked with him to the front door. "Thank you for inviting me out for a ride and dinner."

"I like having you out here. You know that."

She smiled at him as they took the steps down the porch and headed for her car.

He took her hand before she got in and turned her to him. "Listen, there's something I want to talk to you about."

Her eyes turned wary. "What?"

"Clint." The guy worried Tate.

Her head tilted. "What about him?"

"I don't like that he showed up at the farmers market today. I want you to be careful. Alert. And let me know if he's still giving you trouble."

"I think he got the message today."

"He should have gotten it the first time you said you didn't want to see him anymore."

Her hand brushed up his chest. "I'm done with him. I've stopped reading his texts and listening to his voicemails."

"He's still calling you?" Tate couldn't believe the guy's audacity.

"He's persistent, but that doesn't matter. I'm with you."

"You should block his number." Tate didn't know why she put up with this.

"I thought about it, but if he's stupid enough to leave all that evidence, let him." She had a very good point.

Tate didn't know what to make of Clint's behavior. It didn't follow reason.

Liz wanted to be with him and that's all that mattered to Tate. "Text me when you get home, so I know you're okay."

"I will." She started to turn to the car, but he hooked his hand at her hip, spun her toward him, and kissed her, long and deep, letting her know how much he wanted her. How important it was that she stay safe and sound.

He tried to keep things tame for the sake of his own sanity since she was headed home and not up to his bed. But damn, it was hard to stop kissing her and let her go.

Liz broke the kiss, stepped back, but still had a fistful

of his shirt. "You know, I'm not sure I would have been ready for all that when we were younger." She held her free hand up in front of him and circled it in the air to mean all of him and the heat between them.

He chuckled. "Think you're up for it now?"

"Looking forward to it. Immensely." She exaggerated that word and it only made him smile more.

"Go home. I'll see you soon."

She slipped into the front seat of her car. He leaned in and gave her another quick kiss because he couldn't help himself, then closed the door for her. She backed out of the drive and gave him a wave before she headed to the main road.

He went back to the house, missing her being there with him already. It made him stop on the porch and turn to the vast ranch and confront his memories of his time here and what it felt like now. He loved working here, but he wanted more in his life.

He and Liz had been a part of each other's lives forever. They had shared many experiences and a gazillion conversations. It seemed like enough. He enjoyed what they had and felt lucky to have a friend like her. But he wanted them to join their lives in a more meaningful and permanent way.

They were moving in that direction, but the desire to hurry it all up and get to what he really wanted surprised him. The more he thought about the concept of *him and Liz*, the more he wanted it. Her. *Them* to be an *us*.

He never expected things to go like this, this fast. But there it was. And he was ready for more.

Chapter Twelve

TATE JUMPED when someone put their hands over his eyes, but he immediately recognized the smaller hands as a woman's and smiled, hoping it was the woman he hadn't expected to see today.

"Surprise," Liz said, moving her hands to his shoulders as she leaned over him and kissed his cheek.

He grabbed the file he'd been using to fix the mare's hoof, stood, turned to Liz, and got himself a real kiss. "I thought you were having dinner with your folks today."

She shrugged. "I turned Sunday dinner into Sunday lunch so I could come out here and see you for a couple hours."

"Did you get your laundry and other stuff done?"

"For the most part. I might have gone down the rabbit hole on a couple of design shows."

He touched her back to get her to walk out of the horse's stall ahead of him. "You're obsessed with decorating."

"No, I just like looking at all those pretty places. They're all clean and neat when real life isn't. My place is small, it's just me, and I still can't keep it as picture-perfect as those places look on TV."

"I'm so glad you changed your plans and came out to the ranch to surprise me."

"You don't mind?"

To show her how much he appreciated her making the drive and taking the time, he kissed her softly, hoping to convince her to stay for dinner—and maybe the night.

He didn't know if they were there yet.

With any other woman, he'd simply seduce her into inviting him back to her place.

But this was Liz.

And he didn't want to go to her place, he wanted her right here with him, sharing *his* bed.

Big difference.

While he'd never brought anyone home to the ranch—because he shared the house with his siblings—he wanted Liz to stay.

He'd thought about it a lot yesterday and all day today.

She fit.

She belonged here.

It scared him. In a good way. Because it felt real and important and like he was on the cusp of changing his life and getting what he really wanted.

He didn't expect them to go from friend to forever without taking the time to explore and experience this new phase of their relationship.

He didn't want to rush.

He wanted to show her that this was important to him. She meant something to him. More than he'd ever let himself feel or acknowledge.

So he poured that into the kiss, hoping she understood and felt everything he didn't know how to say to her.

His phone rang in his pocket.

He broke the kiss and stared into her dazed eyes, happy to see he'd made an impression. "Sorry. Trinity said she might need some help tonight at *Almost Homemade*."

Liz swept her hands over his chest. "Take it."

He wanted to take her up to the house and have his way with her. But he pulled the phone from his pocket and smiled at the caller ID. "Hey, Ma. How are you? What are you and Dad up to today?"

"Not much. I'm checking in on my kids." She did that at least once a week no matter where they were on their cross-country tour.

"Where are you?"

"Yosemite. It's beautiful here. Dad says hi. How are you?"

"I'm good. Great actually. A beautiful woman swung by for a surprise visit." Tate winked at Liz.

She smiled, leaned in, and said, "Hi, Mrs. McGrath."

"Is that Liz?"

"Yeah, Ma." He brushed his hand over Liz's hair and filled in his mom on the biggest change in his life. "She and I, well, we're seeing each other now."

"About time."

He rolled his eyes. "What does that mean?"

Liz cocked up an eyebrow, wondering what his mom said to him.

"I knew eventually you'd want to settle down with her." Absolute certainty filled her voice.

"You did?"

"You've loved her forever." She said it as matter-of-factly as saying he liked beer.

Did everyone see what he'd missed all these years? "How did you know when I didn't?"

"Tate, you picked her to be yours when you were still talking in one-word sentences. You looked at her, said, 'Mine,' and that was it. I saw it in you when you two played together. She's been your friend and confidant your whole life. Most people drift apart as they get older and especially when they aren't in school together anymore. Not you and Liz. You made a point to stick close to her. She did the same with you. I always thought you were meant to be. I bet her parents feel the same, though I bet her mother wants to know what's taken you so long. Me, I know you needed time to live a little and decide what you wanted your life to be." She sighed, and he imagined her raising her shoulders and holding up her hands, the way she did. "Boys take longer to figure things out."

He rolled his eyes at that.

"Liz always knew," his mom announced, like he didn't already know that. "I'm glad you see it now."

So was he. He'd never felt this hopeful about any of his other relationships.

"I hope you two will be happy together." The warmth in her voice assured him she was happy for him and Liz.

"Thanks, Ma." He weaved his fingers through Liz's. "We're figuring it out, but it feels right."

Liz locked eyes with him. Her green eyes brightened with happiness and surprise that he'd say something so open and blunt to his mom and her. He hoped it eased her mind about just how serious he took their relationship and he really did want them to work out.

"It took you a long time to get here. Enjoy it. There's no rush."

Maybe not, but it felt like he needed to prove something to Liz, thanks to Clint and how he'd made her doubt Tate's feelings and intentions.

He hoped the more time they spent together as a couple, the more she'd settle in and see the truth.

Clint better stay the hell away or Tate was going to have to take matters into his own hands and make sure Clint understood Tate wouldn't tolerate him harassing Liz anymore.

"I'm hoping we can have a nice dinner tonight, maybe go for a walk on the property and look at the stars."

"Sounds like a nice evening. It makes me happy to know you're happy and looking to the future. Now, what's going on with Declan? I got the 'everything is fine' line from him, but it sounded like something is bothering him."

Tate got that same feeling, especially last night at dinner with Liz, but Declan hadn't confided in him. "It's business as usual around here for him."

"I sometimes wonder if he spends too much time working instead of living. Reminds me of your father. That's why I pushed for Dad to buy the RV and get away from that place for a while."

"You guys getting tired of wandering, yet?"

"When we do, we settle into one spot. The Sierras are nice. We'll probably stay awhile. We plan to come back and get a little place, especially since we'll have a grandbaby soon. Or two," she hinted with a teasing tone.

"And that's my cue to say I'll talk to you later." Kids were not in his near future, but someday. A little girl with Liz's dark red hair and her smile. A boy with her heart and his love for riding and the ranch. Though he bet any little girl of theirs would be wild for the horses, too, and just as bold as he and Liz.

"I'll fuss over Drake and Adria's little one. I really can't wait to be a grandma. Those two went from meeting each other to getting married with lightning speed. You and Liz could take a little more time than they did."

"Drake didn't want to let her get away."

"And you tethered yourself to Liz all these years. Reel her in, Tate."

That made him chuckle. His mom didn't usually weigh in on his relationships. But he appreciated how much she liked Liz for him. "I'm working on it."

"Who knows, maybe your dad and I will be home for another wedding soon." *Take his time. A wedding soon.* His mom needed to make up her mind.

"You're getting ahead of yourself." But he could see it. Liz walking down the aisle to him dressed in a gorgeous white gown, her hair piled on top of her head, fiery tendrils dangling around her face and that smile she gave him every time she saw him.

"I thought you finally figured out you can't fight fate."

Yeah, he felt it now. They were meant to be. But that didn't mean it would just happen. They were almost there, but they needed some time to settle in and figure out how to be a couple.

He'd never done that with another woman. He had

relationships, but none that made him want to stick it out when things got tough. He and Liz knew how to be friends. They needed to learn how to be partners.

"I'm not fighting anything anymore." He walked to where Liz stood a few feet away petting the mare and listening to his side of the conversation. He kissed her softly. "Gotta go, Ma. I want to spend more time with my girl."

"Enjoy each other, Tate. Be happy."

"We are." Yesterday had been great. No pressure. No expectations. Just the two of them out for a ride, talking about nothing and everything, enjoying a few hours together.

They needed more time to explore the new closeness between them and allow themselves to explore their desire for each other.

"I'll talk to you soon, Ma." He hung up after their goodbyes and his promise that he'd keep in touch.

Liz reached out and tugged on his T-shirt. "It's sweet that you told your mom about us."

"I'm surprised she didn't know already. I figured Declan, or especially Trinity, would have told her."

"Maybe they weren't sure you wanted anyone to know."

He cupped her face. "I want everyone to know you're my girlfriend." He kissed her softly, his tongue sliding against hers in a long, slow sweep. If that didn't convince her he wanted her, nothing would. "Besides, it seems like everyone but me knew we'd eventually end up together. I'm kind of kicking myself for taking so long to figure it out."

The hesitant sweep of her hand over his chest felt

more like her testing the waters of how much freedom she had to touch him. "It kind of still feels like a dream."

He pressed her hand against his heart. "I've had a few fantasies of my own these last few days."

A sexy smile spread across her lips. "Oh yeah?"

"They're never as good as this." He kissed her again, letting loose the reins on his desire and pulling her into his arms so her body fit against his. Every time he held her close, a ripple of awareness shot through him.

She felt it, too, and moved in closer, her thighs brushing his, her breasts pressed to his chest as she settled against him.

He swept one hand up her side and over the mound that fit his palm to perfection. He brushed his thumb over her hard nipple. She sighed and rubbed her belly against his hard shaft. It sent a bolt of lust through his system so hot he wanted to lay her out in the soft grass, strip her bare, kiss every inch of her creamy skin, and bury himself deep inside her.

His phone rang in his pocket. He ignored it and kept kissing Liz and making her moan every time he brushed his thumb over her nipple. He wanted to dip his head and suck the peaked bud into his mouth.

His phone dinged with a text. And then another.

Like a prize fighter at the bell, Liz broke the sexy kiss. "Aren't you going to answer that?"

He palmed her ass and pulled her snug against his throbbing erection. "I'm trying to answer another call."

She smiled and laughed under her breath and hugged him closer. Just as her lips were about to touch his again, his phone dinged with another text. A breath away from his lips, she stared into his eyes with hers narrowed with concern. "Maybe it's an emergency."

"It's definitely an urgent need." He rocked his hard dick into her belly and groaned. Damn but she felt so good in his arms and they hadn't even gotten their clothes off yet.

"Tate."

"Fine." He reluctantly let go of her very fine ass to pull his phone from his pocket. He swiped the screen with his thumb and stared at the notifications. "Shit."

"What?"

"Trinity needs me at the store." He let his head fall back and sighed.

Liz's fingers slid into his hair. She pulled his head back up so she could look at him. "Another time."

He touched his forehead to hers. "Count on it." The mare nudged him in the back. He pushed her big head away, then looked down at Liz. "I don't want to let you go, but I've got to get down to the store."

"Go. Trinity needs you." She slid her hand over the mare's face. "I'll head home and catch up on *Outlander*."

He didn't know what that was, and before thinking, words poured out of his mouth. "Or you could wait here for me. It'll only be a couple of hours."

She took a few seconds to think about it. "Um, that sounds good." The tone didn't back that up.

"But?"

"It's a little odd to just go up to the house and hang with Declan while I wait for you to come home."

He understood. It felt like everyone was watching them. Waiting.

Once he moved in to the cabin when Drake and Adria came home from their honeymoon and officially moved out, she probably wouldn't mind. He couldn't wait to have his own place and eliminate issues like this.

"How about dinner tomorrow after you get off work?"

Her shoulders relaxed as relief washed over her face. "That sounds great." She gave him a shy smile. "Maybe we'll end up back at my place."

Usually going to the woman's place sounded good, but not with Liz. He wanted her here. It seemed important to include her in his life here at the ranch. At home.

He didn't say anything about that and kissed her softly. "I'm really glad you came by. I wish we could spend more time together."

"I worried that showing up might make you feel like I'm crowding you."

"Not at all." He shook his head. "No. Don't think that. I was bummed when you said you had Sunday dinner with your parents and I had a bunch of stuff to do here today. You can come and see me anytime you want. I really hope you'll take me up on it as often as possible."

She nodded, relief replacing the apprehension in her eyes. "I'd like that."

He hugged her close. "Me too, Liz." He brushed his fingers down the side of her beautiful face. "If I didn't have to help Trinity, I'd stay here and show you how much I mean it."

Liz placed her hand on his jaw and stared up at him. "I know you mean it, Tate. I'll see you soon."

He lingered over the see-you-later kiss they shared. Letting her go was harder than he thought. Driving away and not following her to her place turned out to be a test of his will, because all he wanted to do was be with her and take her to bed and love on her for the rest of the night. Maybe longer.

It might take him a while to get his fill now that he discovered his need for her ran so deep.

He never expected it to happen so fast, but she lived in his mind and heart now. Maybe she always had and he'd been too stubborn to acknowledge it. Now that he had, he didn't want to wait for them to have . . . everything. Days doing things together. Nights making love. Mornings that started with her smile.

Friends. Lovers. Partners.

A life together.

That sounded pretty damn good.

All he had to do was figure out how to make it happen.

Where would they live? How could he give her everything she needed and wanted? How could he hold on to her?

What happened if he screwed it all up?

He didn't have the answer to some of those questions and others he didn't want to think about. But he needed to because his future not only included Liz— his future was Liz.

Chapter Thirteen

LIZ PULLED into the lot at the spa, but didn't get out of her car right away. Instead, she took a second to search her surroundings, to be sure Clint wasn't there waiting for her before she rushed inside for her shift.

He'd become the specter in her relationship with Tate. There, but not there.

When she left the ranch on Sunday, she'd made herself so anxious about whether or not Clint would confront her again that she'd been sick to her stomach. When she arrived home, she rushed in her front door and locked it.

She hated being too afraid to go out and do what she wanted.

And she had reason to be scared and hyperaware of her surroundings.

Tate picked her up after work on Monday as promised. They enjoyed a lovely dinner out at the local steakhouse. She loved sitting with him in the intimate booth. They shared their day over drinks and turned dessert into a sport when they each tried to keep the other from eating the triple chocolate cake with a fork sword fight that left them both laughing.

All the fun and joy faded when they walked out of the restaurant and she spotted Clint across the street watching them. He didn't do anything but make sure she saw him before he turned and walked away.

She found that creepier than him confronting them.

Tate noticed her distraction, but she didn't tell him about seeing Clint. She didn't want to spoil her evening with Tate with another talk about Clint's odd behavior and unwillingness to let their breakup go.

She spent Tuesday and Wednesday evenings out to dinner with Tate trying to focus on him but on constant guard for Clint. She didn't see him, but she felt him. Whether it was real or not it made it hard for her to simply be in the moment with Tate and enjoy herself.

Tate picked up on her strange vibe and asked her if everything was okay several times. She always said yes, but Tate didn't quite believe her, and she couldn't blame him.

Clint was coming between them.

After the smokin' hot moments they shared at the ranch over the weekend, things had cooled down. Her fault. She didn't blame Tate for thinking that her distraction meant she wanted to slow things down.

She spent the last three days eating lunch in her office, afraid to go out and give Clint a chance to confront her again.

Not today. At lunch time, she pulled her purse out of her desk drawer, stood, put the strap up on her shoulder, and walked out of her office and the building, all false confidence and bravado.

Today she vowed to start living like Clint wasn't

part of her life. No more being scared of seeing him. No more hiding. No more letting him ruin her dates with Tate.

Her favorite sandwich shop was only two blocks away. Maybe her gut tightened with anxiety during the walk. Maybe she glanced around more than usual to be sure she didn't have a shadow following her. But she didn't turn back and return to the relative safety of her office.

She wouldn't let *him* win.

Win what, she didn't know. She didn't understand the point of him lurking in the background of her life. It didn't endear him to her. She didn't find it sweet or romantic.

But Tate had been both those things the last few days. He tried so hard to please her. And it wasn't that hard because all she really wanted was more time with him. And to kiss him. And more.

More of everything.

On one hand, she didn't know why he waited to take her to bed. On the other hand, she found it sweet that he wanted to date her. She enjoyed their nights out. She didn't mind working their way up to being more intimate with each other. If she could stop thinking and worrying about Clint, she might actually settle in with Tate and their newfound closeness.

They were so close to having the kind of relationship she'd always wanted. The last thing she wanted to do was ruin it because she wasn't focused on them and distracted by Clint.

The bell over the sandwich shop door dinged, announcing her entry. She barely spared a glance for the lunch crowd filling the tables and headed for the line in front of the counter.

Liz shuffled along behind the person in front of her lost in her Instagram feed where it seemed like every one of her friends had happy photos of engagements, weddings, and family snapshots with babies and toddlers. She envied them their happiness and milestones she still hadn't hit but wanted more each day.

"Hey, Liz," Pat called from the counter, stealing her attention away from the phone. "Want the usual?"

It hit Liz all at once that maybe her life had become too predictable. Her internal warning system went off again. It had gotten a workout lately. "Yes, please. And thanks, Pat." She handed over the cash to cover her roast beef and cheddar on a crusty roll. Yum. Her favorite. Especially with a bag of barbecue potato chips and an iced tea, no lemon. "Keep the change."

"Here's your number." Pat handed her a numbered plastic placard to place on her table. "We'll bring it right out."

Liz took the stand and her drink and snagged a seat after a couple of guys got up to leave. She dropped her purse on the table and fished out her cell again.

She texted Tate, excited to check in with him and make plans.

LIZ: What do you want to do tonight?

About to set her phone down, she turned it over when it dinged immediately. Surprised Tate got back to her so fast when he said he'd be out of cell range most of the afternoon checking on the herds at the farthest part of their property, she read his response.

TATE: Staying home tonight
TATE: Maybe we jumped the gun on this thing
TATE: It's just not there for me
TATE: I can't give you what you want

Tears pricked her eyes and clogged her throat. She blinked them away when Pat set a tray with her food in front of her.

"Can I get you anything else?"

"No, thank you. I'm good." Far from it. Her heart ached. Her stomach pitched but she swallowed back the cry of agony and the tears clogging her throat.

How could Tate do this to her?

Why?

Over text message!

Why would he break things off like this when everything seemed fine last night? It didn't make sense.

TATE: I think we should stay away from each other for a while

He kissed her last night like he couldn't get enough of her. Yes, he pulled back before things went too far, but that's because they had silently agreed to . . . what? What were they waiting for? The right time? So they could get to know each other better? They knew each other better than anyone else knew them.

They were made for each other.

They were meant for each other.

But Tate didn't think so.

He wanted out.

He didn't want to see her.

A tear slipped down her cheek just as someone brushed their finger through her hair and pushed it behind her ear. Her head shot up and she gasped.

"I hate to see you so sad." Clint stared down at her with concern in his eyes. "Are you okay?"

She drew herself up and away from him. "I'm fine." She glanced around the crowded deli. "What are you doing here?"

"Lunch." The obvious answer didn't sound like a lie, but it made her hesitate and question his motives after catching him lurking and stalking her at the farmers market and outside the restaurant where she and Tate ate Monday night.

"Thank you for the concern, but I'm fine."

"Listen, things between us got screwed up." What sounded like genuine remorse filled those words. "I'm sorry about that. I'd like to help if I can, even if it's just to listen." He didn't wait for her agreement and sat across from her. "Eat, babe. You'll feel better."

She didn't want the food, she wanted to go back to ten minutes ago when she thought she and Tate had a future filled with Instagram posts of their engagement, wedding, and babies.

She wanted Clint to leave so she could think and try to understand why Tate did this now.

"Come on, it can't be that bad."

It devastated her. "Tate broke up with me."

Clint leaned in, his arms crossed on the table. "He's an idiot for letting you go."

She slumped in her chair and fought the tears again. "Thanks." She appreciated the sentiment even if it came from him.

"It's how I felt after screwing things up with you. I don't know what got into me. Seeing you with him . . . I should have handled things better." The sincerity in his voice sounded real, but she had a hard time believing him. "I should have trusted you more." In her mind, you either trusted someone or not. "I should have believed you wanted to be with me and that your friendship with him didn't mean you weren't committed to our relationship."

This was the Clint she remembered. Open. Easygoing. The guy she liked and fell for before it all went bad.

She couldn't put the blame all on him. She'd had one foot out the door the whole time wishing for Tate. Her heart had always belonged to him and doomed all her other relationships.

Well, she and Tate had tried and her fears came true. He didn't really want her. He'd warned her that her questioning his true intentions might drive a wedge between them. In the end, he realized his feelings didn't run that deep.

Fooling around, spending time together, it didn't amount to more than a good time. Not enough to make him want to build a life with her.

Clint's hand settled over hers. "Listen, babe, let me brighten your day. I'll take you out for drinks, maybe some dancing. We'll laugh and have fun and you'll forget all about what's-his-name." Clint gave her a coaxing smile.

The last thing she wanted to do was repeat past mistakes. And right now, a quiet night at home with a book or movie, her favorite blanket, and a gallon of rocky road sounded like a plan she could get behind.

"Thank you for your concern and the offer, but I think I'll head home after work and take some time to myself."

Clint patted her hand. "Another time then. I really would like to make things up to you. I'm not that guy, Liz. I hope you know that."

To keep the peace and put it in the past, she said, "Let's just forget it."

His smile spread into genuine glee. "I knew you wouldn't hold it against me. You're kind, Liz. You see the good in people." Clint glanced around the room, then focused on her again. "If you're sure you're okay, I'll leave you to eat your lunch, but I hope we can get together soon."

She didn't want to ruin the mood by ending yet another encounter with Clint by shooting him down and making him . . . upset. She preferred him reasonable and nice.

She'd never forget that he turned on her.

"I'll be okay." She couldn't help but look down at her phone, think about Tate and how he ended things, and wonder what might have been.

"Haven't you spent enough time waiting for him?"

Did she read a hint of bitterness in that question? Or was that her own sour heartbreak?

She'd waited forever for Tate. To come so close and have him end it like this felt so inconsiderate and callous. He had to know she'd be devastated.

After all they shared, the breakup seemed so impersonal.

Clint leaned down and kissed her on the head. "When you're ready, call me. I'll be waiting for *you*." His hand slid across her shoulder as he walked away.

For a split second, knowing someone was waiting for her felt damn good, but that fleeting moment didn't last because it wasn't the right person waiting for her.

She pushed her phone away, picked up her sandwich, and took a bite. She'd lost her appetite, but the first bite tasted good and helped ease the tension.

A woman walked toward her, planted her hand on the table, and leaned down. "Whatever he said to you, he's lying. Don't trust him. Don't let him into your life. He'll destroy it."

The certainty and force in those words made the hairs on the back of Liz's neck stand up.

Liz set her sandwich back in the basket and stared up at the pretty brunette. "Who are you?"

"Someone who's been where you are now. Clint and I used to work together. He made me think he loved me. Soon, I didn't have any friends. I didn't see my family. I did everything he wanted just to make him happy. My whole life became about keeping the peace. Arguments turned into fights. A rough grab here and there turned into . . ." Choked up, the woman couldn't speak, but Liz got the picture. "When I tried to leave, he talked me back. When that didn't work, he tried to force me by making sure I had nowhere to go. He sent everyone at work a video he took of me naked and doing something I thought was only for him. It was supposed to be p-private." Tears filled her fear-filled eyes, the devastation she suffered so clear to see. "Whatever you think he is, he's not. He's a m-monster." The woman ran past her and out the shop door.

Liz fell back in her seat and raked her shaking fingers through her hair.

That poor woman. Clint put her through hell. Liz had gotten a glimpse of Clint's temper and didn't want another up close look. She appreciated his attempt to be nice to her today, but that didn't excuse how he'd treated her in the past. It didn't erase the memory or panic she'd felt when he grabbed her and she feared he'd do a lot worse.

Taking a private moment between a couple, recording it, and sending it to others . . . how downright mean and vindictive. Did Clint really think embarrassing and humiliating her would make her want to be with him?

That's not how you love someone.

That's how you terrorize them, and make them fear and hate you.

She didn't want to live like that. She didn't want anything to do with someone like Clint.

She hoped she never saw him again.

That led her right back to thoughts that she'd never see Tate again either and it hurt too much to bear.

Just when love seemed so close she could touch it, it barely brushed her fingertips before it slipped away.

She didn't get a man like Clint who tried to force love, or Tate who had it handed to him free and easy and turned it away.

Well, she couldn't make Tate love her and she wouldn't keep offering him something he didn't want.

She didn't know how she'd get over losing her best

friend and the man she loved all at the same time, but she'd find a way. Because she couldn't endure a lifetime of feeling this heartbroken and alone.

But that didn't mean she wouldn't grieve with a good long cry under the covers and a gallon of ice cream. And brownies.

This kind of sad required copious amounts of chocolate.

Chapter Fourteen

CLINT WAITED for Aubrey to rush out of the deli and head for her car. Lucky for him, she was distracted and had parked behind the nearby dry cleaners because of the lunch crowd that flooded this area. She walked right into his trap.

The second she hit the unlock button on her key fob and reached for the driver's door handle, he came up behind her, covered her mouth and the scream with his hand, snatched her keys from her hand, and dragged her to the back of the car.

"You should have kept your mouth shut."

She mumbled some dramatic plea against his palm and struggled to turn and face him, but he kept her subdued. He didn't care what she had to say. He didn't accept excuses.

She knew better.

He'd taught her better.

He expected her to keep up the fight, but she was a timid creature who bent to his intimidation and strength far too easily. That's why she hadn't been the one. He broke her too easily.

Boring.

She hadn't challenged him.

Not the way Liz did.

He unlocked the trunk and lifted the lid. Aubrey found some guts and used her feet to push him back a step before he locked his arm around her waist, held her head back against his shoulder with his hand over her mouth, and said into her ear, "I love it when you fight."

All the struggle went out of her as tears dripped down her cheeks and wet his hand.

Too bad. When she fought, he got to play.

Her submission took away his fun. She knew he hated that. He wanted her to struggle and fight. She wouldn't win, but he'd have a damn good time watching her try. He got off seeing how much pain she could endure.

But poor Aubrey had lost her fight and her will long ago.

Weak. Timid. Useless. She disgusted him now.

Clint's father had tried to make him weak and control his outbursts when he was a kid with the same heavy hand he used on Clint's mother. She'd been willful and defiant, sometimes crazy, pushing his father's temper. Dad took control. He made Clint's mother behave. And when he got tired of disciplining her, he'd moved out, leaving Clint to console his wild mother and keep her in line.

As a weekend father, his dad tried to maintain their relationship, but Clint didn't much care what his father thought anymore. He didn't submit to his father's new tempered discipline, his stupid reasons for why Clint should act and be better, or how he'd tried to tell Clint how to live his life.

Clint did what he wanted, when he wanted.

When he got in trouble in high school because a

girl said yes, then she regretted it the next day and reported him to the principal, his father laid into him good. By then, Dad didn't tower over him anymore. He may have outweighed him, but he didn't have Clint's strength and speed. When his father threw that right cross, Clint didn't cower with his hands up, he blocked that punch and threw one of his own. And then a dozen more, until his father lay on the floor a bloody fucking mess, his nose busted, eyes cut and swollen, whimpering and moaning in pain.

Dad didn't hit him anymore.

The girl took back her accusation because he'd made it clear she'd regret it if she didn't. She'd wanted it. And he wouldn't let her get away with saying otherwise.

From there, his relationship with his father deteriorated until they no longer spoke.

Good riddance. Family sucked.

He didn't need someone criticizing him and telling him what to do.

Clint wanted a woman equal to him.

Aubrey wasn't that woman.

But Liz . . . "If you fucked things up for me and Liz . . ." He shoved Aubrey into the trunk, yanked her purse away from her, and slammed the lid.

She kicked and pounded against it, screaming and begging, "Please! Let me out! I didn't do anything! Let me go!"

Her cries and pleas had no effect on him.

He'd already checked the back of the building. No cameras and only small high windows. He pushed the seat back and slid behind the wheel of her car, confident no one saw or heard anything.

He drove out of the lot and headed for the one place he could get rid of her and make it look like she'd finally lost it.

He went over his conversation with Liz in his head. It went well. He'd consoled her over that fuck, Tate. She realized now that Clint was the right man for her. After he got rid of Aubrey and finished work for the day, he'd give her a call, ask her again if she wanted to go out. Women wanted to be pursued. He'd give her that. For now. Then, they'd get back to the way they were before everyone tried to interfere.

Of course, he'd have to tell her that Aubrey was nothing more than a jealous ex who wanted to make Liz hate him so Aubrey could have him all to herself. Easy enough.

Liz wouldn't want anyone else to have him, because she wanted him all to herself.

Luck was on his side as he pulled into the park that backed up to a small lake. A lot of people liked to hike the trail that circled the water, but hunting season just opened and the north trail was closed, the small lot empty. He parked the car in a haphazard angle to the locked gate, turned off the car, and found Aubrey's cell phone in her purse. He pulled up her text messages, found *Mom*, and sent a text.

AUBREY: I'm sorry. I love you.

He made sure to punctuate just like she'd done in her other texts, then wiped the phone with his shirt and tossed it on the passenger seat.

He climbed out of the car, found a sweatshirt in the

back seat, and used it to wipe down the steering wheel and car handle. He draped it over his shoulder, left the driver's door open, popped the trunk, and warded off the attack he expected from Aubrey. She swung her hands wildly trying to hit and scratch him, but his long-sleeve dress shirt kept her from doing any real damage. He grabbed her by the shoulders and hauled her out. Her feet hit the dirt and she nearly fell, but caught herself and swung her hand again. The slap stung his cheek and left a tiny cut from her nail scraping his jaw.

He shook her hard enough to make her head bobble back and forth on her shoulders. "Knock it off."

She kicked his shin and pushed against his chest to get free.

He slapped her across the face, splitting her lip.

For a second she stood stunned, then her eyes turned to fury. "I hate you!" She spit on him.

He grabbed her hair at the side of her head into his fist and held her still. "You bitch." He wanted to slam his fist into her face, but that would fuck up his plan. She'd ruined enough things for him today. "Let's go."

He hooked his arm around her throat, used his free hand to wipe down the trunk lid, slammed it, and walked her to the open car door. He tossed the sweatshirt onto the passenger floorboard, then sidestepped the door and headed for the gate and the path that pedestrians used to bypass it. He forced her to keep in step with him, making sure she walked more than dragged her feet. He needed it to look like she'd willingly walked down the path, even if it looked like she was unsteady from the distress and anguish that she couldn't live with anymore.

Or so everyone would think.

He stopped on the footbridge by the raging water-fall, which cascaded over boulders the size of cars, tumbling down thirty feet or more before flowing into the lake. Teens came up here to drink, fuck, and party.

They called it Lover's Leap because several teens had committed suicide here.

And now one jealous, distraught ex-girlfriend who thought she lost him to another woman.

"Please, Clint, I'll go away. You'll never see me again." She struggled to back away from the railing, using her feet to push him back. "I'll tell her I lied. I'll swear that I made it all up."

"It's too late, Aubrey." He spun her around, cupped her face between his hands, and held her so tight her cheeks pressed in and squeezed her little nose. He stared down into her eyes, so filled with fear and a plea that didn't even make him think twice. "You did this to yourself."

She tried to shake her head, but couldn't even budge his hold on her. "Please. I'll be good. I'll do whatever you say. Please!"

He wiped away the tears with his thumbs and frowned at her. "You make promises, but you don't keep them. You act out. You make me punish you."

He didn't give her a chance to respond and hooked his hands under her arms. Short and thinner than he remembered—probably because of her fucked-up head and not taking care of herself—he easily lifted her skinny ass onto the railing. Before she could grab hold of him, he hooked his hand under her legs, spun her around, and pushed her right off the wide top board.

Just like that, she flew, arms out wide, legs spread. Her scream ended the second she hit the rocks. The raging water swept her down several more boulders until she disappeared under the force of the water and raging whitecaps flowing into the lake.

He stepped back and stared down at her black shoe. He used the toe of his to turn the flat toward the railing so it looked like she stepped right out of it, up onto the railing, and jumped right off.

So easy.

He stuffed his hands in his pockets and followed the bridge to the path that led around the lake to the other side away from where he'd left Aubrey's car. When the trail wound close to the water, he tossed Tate's cell phone in, then enjoyed the rest of the two-mile hike back that ended not more than a mile or so from his office.

The energetic hike invigorated him. He liked to keep in shape, so a couple miles barely made him break a sweat.

His assistant, Kelly, stood the second she saw him, ready to do his bidding just like he'd taught her once upon a time. "You're back early."

Yep. It didn't take him even an hour to fix things with Liz and take care of Aubrey's meddling.

Her gaze narrowed and fixed on his chest. "Did you spill lunch on your shirt?"

He glanced down at the small red stain. "Ketchup."

She raised an eyebrow. She knew better than to question him. He'd taught her that, too.

"Something you want to say?"

She rigorously shook her head.

"I didn't think so." He went into his office, took off the shirt, grabbed a clean one from the credenza, stuffed the dirty shirt in the plastic bag from the clean one, and went out to his assistant. "Kelly, take this to the dry cleaners when you pick up my suits."

She put her hand on the bag and stared up at him. "Sure." She may not like running his errands but she'd never say no.

Not to him.

She knew better.

Unlike Aubrey, Kelly took their breakup in stride, but continued to pine for him. Not that he cared. She hadn't been the one either. But she did what she was told, so he strung her along, giving her just enough attention to keep her in line. And every now and then, he took pity on her and gave her a night to slake her need for him.

She was a good, obedient girl.

He went back into his office and sat at his desk, smiling, free and clear.

Chapter Fifteen

TATE TOSSED the post hole digger into the back of his truck, rolled his sore shoulders, and went to the driver's side door. He leaned in the window and tugged on the sleeve of the jacket he'd left there earlier. He felt all the pockets but didn't find his phone. He must have left it at the ranch in the stables, or up at the house in the kitchen where he'd grabbed several bottles of water before heading out here to check fences and the herd.

The cows were fat and happy, but he passed grumpy and went right to pissed that he'd left his phone and couldn't call Liz once he got back in cell range. He had a nagging urge to hear her voice and know she was okay.

Funny how things had changed so quickly. There'd been an appropriate distance between them as friends. They shared things, but not everything. Now he wanted to know all he didn't know about her. What she wanted and needed. What she dreamed about for the future.

And he wanted to get his hands on her.

He didn't know what happened after the weekend and the hot kisses they'd shared. But he felt something off in her the last few nights.

He didn't think she was pulling away, but maybe

settling in to take things slow and let them build again. He could do that. For now. But he had plans. Dirty, sexy, sensual plans that would leave no doubt in her mind he wanted her desperately.

And he had other plans for their future.

Drake bought a house with Adria and hired contractors to fix it up, including the dream kitchen Adria always wanted.

Tate wanted to turn the cabin into a place for him and Liz to call home.

His finances needed help. He'd been wise enough to save a little here and there, but he could have done better. The ranch made good money, especially now that they increased the herd and supplied *Almost Homemade*.

He made a decent income. He could provide for him and Liz. Modestly.

He'd like to fix up the cabin, maybe add on to it. It would save them money. But he had no idea if Liz wanted to live way out here on the ranch and away from town. She loved her place because it was so close to shopping and restaurants and anything else she wanted to do.

It would be more expensive to live in town.

He'd have one hell of a drive every day, back and forth, but he'd do it if that's what she wanted.

And there it was, his thoughts and plans turning to make her happy. Sure, he'd been accommodating and generous with other women. Now he thought, "What would Liz want?" before he made decisions.

He didn't want to fast-track their relationship just because they'd been friends forever, but he was getting impatient to move things to a more permanent status.

Which led his thoughts to rings and vows and a

life of making decisions together. And that led him to thoughts of how he didn't want to screw this thing up because it felt too important.

He didn't know what his life looked like without Liz in it, and he didn't want to find out.

Tate jumped in the truck, searched the floorboard and seat but came up empty on his phone. He drove back to the stables anxious to find it so he could call Liz, check in, and make plans for tonight. Maybe he could convince her to come out to the ranch for dinner and a sunset ride. He'd kiss her under the stars. And beg her to stay the night.

At this point, he was desperate to be with her.

He pulled into the yard and sighed with relief to see Declan. He parked the truck and met his brother in front of the stable doors.

"I can't catch a break."

Tate stopped in his tracks and stared at Declan. "What's wrong?"

"The guy I hired to help out got a better offer."

Tate shrugged that off. "You'll find someone else."

Declan glared. "It took me three weeks to find this guy. We need help now."

Tate understood Declan's worry. They had fallen behind and spent every day trying to catch up and keep the operation running smoothly, but taking care of a herd the size that they ran on the ranch required more hands than they had right now.

"I'm happy to help any way I can. Let me call a few guys I know and put out some feelers. Maybe something will come of it. Right now though, I need to borrow your phone."

"Did you forget to charge yours again?"

"No. I can't find it." He accepted Declan's phone and hit the speed dial to call his as he walked into the stables. He didn't hear it ringing before voice mail picked up. "Maybe it's up at the house." Until he went up there, he used Declan's phone to call Liz.

Strange, it went right to voicemail. "Hey sweetheart, it's me. I lost my phone. Call me back at the ranch number or Declan's. I can't wait to see you tonight. Missed you today."

Tate handed the phone back to Declan. "If she calls back, find me. I'm going to check up at the house for my phone, shower, then head over to see her."

"Tate, we need to talk about the ranch and prioritize what needs to be done."

"I hear you, man, but I need to see Liz."

"First Drake, and now you."

Tate cocked his head and stared at Declan. "What does that mean?"

"A woman walks into your lives and you ditch work for them and leave me to handle everything."

"I just spent all fucking day working my ass off to check things off your list. If you've got something that needs to be done right this minute, I'll do it, but I'm worried about Liz. That damn ex of hers hasn't gone away quietly and without my phone, I don't know if she called today."

Declan threw up his hands and let them fall. "Fine. Go check on her. I've got this." He turned and walked down the stable alley to the back office.

Tate nearly went after him. Declan was under a lot of pressure, mostly because he shouldered the responsibility for the ranch and had a hard time letting loose the reins to someone else. But the need to talk to Liz outweighed Declan's concerns about the ranch. They'd been dealing with those for months now. Declan could wait. His need to see Liz couldn't.

He searched the house for his phone and came up empty, even when he called it from the house phone to see if it ringed in one of the rooms. He really couldn't believe he'd lost it. He could have sworn he tucked it in the front pocket of his jacket when he headed into town this morning to pick up their order at the feed store. He remembered taking off his jacket before he headed inside to pay for the order and help load it into the back of his truck.

Maybe it fell out of his pocket while he stood outside the door and tossed his jacket onto the seat.

He used the house phone, called Liz again, and left another message. "I'm heading over to see you after I take a quick shower. See you soon."

Why didn't she pick up? She had to be off work and home by now. He hoped that she was driving out to see him and that's why she didn't answer her phone.

Whatever the reason, he'd see her soon. They had a lot to talk about. Their future. And the next steps, which included them taking this relationship to the next level because he couldn't stand another long and restless night dreaming about making love to her when she could be in the bed with him.

Chapter Sixteen

LIZ JUMPED at the knock on her door. She'd barely had time to put her purse down and crack a beer before someone intruded on what she hoped would be a quiet evening of drinking, sulking, and not talking to anyone.

She put her hand on the lock, but took it away before she just opened the door. She peeked through the peephole and studied the tall dark-haired man. "Who is it?" She had no idea.

"Detective Wayne Valdez. I need to speak to Liz Scott about Aubrey Pittman."

"Who?" She didn't recognize the man or that name.

"Pat at the sandwich shop said she saw you talking to Aubrey at lunch today. May I come in?"

"Hold your badge up." Paranoid? Maybe, but she lived alone and didn't take any chances.

Sure enough, the guy had a badge and credentials. She unlocked the door and stepped back to allow him to enter. He checked out her place in one long sweep from her living room into the bedroom down the hall and around the kitchen to her beer sitting on the dining table behind her.

"What is this about? I did speak to a woman today, but I don't know her name. I'd never met her."

Detective Valdez pulled a picture from his jacket inside pocket. "Do you recognize her?"

Liz had a bad feeling. "Yes. Is she okay?" The cops didn't show up just because of an innocent conversation between strangers.

The detective didn't answer. "If you didn't know her, why were you having lunch together?"

"I went to lunch alone," she clarified. "Aubrey stopped by my table before she left."

"Pat said you spoke to a man before you spoke with Aubrey."

"Yes, that's right. Clint, my ex, saw me sit down and came over to talk."

The detective's eyes narrowed. Everything about him went on alert. "Clint Mayhew?"

That sparked her suspicions. A ripple of dread went through her. "How did you know?"

He didn't answer that, but asked, "Was he already in the restaurant?"

She shrugged. "I guess so. But I'm not sure. I didn't see him when I walked in." She thought about the texts from Tate and added, "I was distracted and upset."

"About what?"

She didn't want to share. Or cry in front of him. "Does it matter?"

The detective's gaze sharpened again. "Maybe."

Someone else knocked on her door.

"Excuse me." She turned her back to the detective and looked through the peephole again and spotted Tate. "Go away," she yelled through the door.

Surprise shone in his eyes before they narrowed.

"What? Let me in."

She pressed her hand to the door and tried to tamp down the wave of sadness and rejection. "We have nothing left to say to each other. Leave."

She took a step back to finish her conversation with the detective, but Tate walked right in the door.

He looked from her to the detective and back. "Who the hell is that?"

"None of your damn business. Get out." She pointed to the door.

Tate genuinely looked shocked.

The detective faced off with Tate. "Maybe you should go. I have important business to discuss with Liz."

Tate turned back to her. "Who is he? And why is he here?"

Liz sucked in a breath, let her drama with Tate go for now, and introduced the two men. "Tate McGrath, this is Detective Valdez. He came to ask me about a woman, Aubrey, who spoke to me at lunch today after she saw me with Clint."

Tate stared down at her. "What the hell were you doing with him?"

At this point, Tate had no say in who she spent time with anymore, though she appreciated what sounded like concern.

"I wasn't with him. We ran into each other at lunch." Resigned to the fact that Tate wouldn't leave until he was good and ready, she met the detective's direct gaze and asked what she didn't really want to know. "What happened to Aubrey today?"

The detective delivered the devastating news. "Her body was found by a hiker at the bottom of Lover's Leap."

Shocked, her knees went weak.

Tate caught her before she fell to the floor. He helped her sit in one of the dining chairs. "Who is Aubrey? And what does this have to do with Liz?"

It couldn't be. Liz just saw Aubrey a few hours ago. It had to be a mistake.

But it wasn't. There was a cop in her condo questioning her.

"Aubrey was Clint's ex. She had a restraining order against him. He's been accused numerous times of harassment. Aubrey and concerned neighbors called in several domestic disturbances during their relationship. She and other past girlfriends never followed through, so he's gotten away without the charges sticking." The detective sighed out his resignation that he couldn't fix the past. "Tell me about your meeting with both of them today."

She sucked in a breath to settle her nerves and grief over what happened to Aubrey and spelled out the events as concisely as she could. "I left my office around twelve fifteen for lunch and walked the two blocks to the deli. I eat there often. Pat knows me. I placed my order and found a table."

She'd done the same many times. It never ended like today. "Clint approached my table. I don't know if he walked in after me or was already there." The thought of him following her creeped her out and amped her paranoid thoughts of what else he'd done without her knowing. His sitting in the restaurant waiting for her creeped her out more. "I've seen him watching me from a distance several times since we broke up."

Angry lines marred Tate's already perturbed face.

"That's why you seemed distant this week. Why didn't you say something?"

"Because I didn't want him coming between us again." But he had, and she hated it.

The detective wrote everything down. "Did he know you frequented that place?"

"We met there for lunch a couple times when we dated."

She focused on what happened and not Tate's presence and what he'd texted her at lunch. "Clint was nice. Comforting. The good guy act reminded me of the guy I liked." She couldn't believe she'd bought the conciliatory attempt to get back in her good graces.

Fool me once. Never again.

Tate frowned. "You think he played you."

She reminded herself that she'd had her suspicions. "I appreciated that he tried to make me feel better but it didn't make me forget how he'd hurt me."

"Was there a physical altercation in the past?" the detective asked.

She hated remembering how scared she'd been. Echoes of that fear rippled through her now. "Yes. Here at my condo. My neighbor stepped in. I made it clear to Clint we were over before that confrontation and again before he left that night."

"He's not the kind of guy who takes no for an answer." The detective scribbled more notes. "What else about the conversation today?"

"Nothing. He asked if he could see me tonight, I told him I wasn't up for it. I don't ever want to reconcile with him. He left thinking that maybe we'd see each other soon. I didn't want to upset him after we'd had a nice conversation. I thought to just leave it at that and move on."

So much for leaving it in the past. Clint had no intention of letting her go. She rubbed her hands up and down her arms to ward off the cold shiver of fear.

The detective wasn't done with his questions. "After Clint left, what happened with Aubrey?"

"She walked up to the table and told me that everything Clint says is a lie and I should stay away from him. She told me that he'd ruined her life and sent a recording of her in a . . . compromising sexual situation to her coworkers."

"Did he ever record you?" The deadpan look didn't ease the embarrassment of that question.

She pressed her hand to her sour stomach. "Oh God, I hope not." Though she didn't want to think about her limited time with Clint, she thought back to those intimate moments, searching her memory for anything that seemed odd, or like he'd been performing. But looking back only made her realize it all seemed like a performance now. "I suppose he could have recorded us without my knowledge." She swallowed back the bile rising in her throat and shook off the eerie chill that raced through her. "We only had sex a couple times." Not that it mattered, but she wanted Tate to know . . . Oh, who cared. That wasn't important right now.

She wanted to put it all behind her, but Clint wouldn't let her. He kept coming back into her life and mucking it up.

She shook off the past and tried to stick to the here and now. "Aubrey warned me away from Clint, then left. I appreciated that she said something even though

I'd already decided that Clint and I were never going to be a thing again." She sucked in a breath. "After she left, I tossed my lunch and went back to work and tried to put Clint out of my mind until I came home to . . . this."

The detective replaced his no-nonsense look with a sympathetic one. "Have you heard from Clint since then?"

"No." *I hope I never do again.* "Do you think Clint killed Aubrey?"

"Her mother received a text message around twelve forty. 'I'm sorry. I love you.' She left her car at a trailhead at the lake and it appears she walked up to Lover's Leap and . . ." The detective left it to her to fill in the blank.

"Do you seriously think she left the deli and killed herself?" Liz didn't buy it. No way.

"Did she seem distraught or upset?"

"It was obvious she feared Clint. Enough that she warned me. She seemed determined to make sure Clint didn't hurt anyone else. But distraught? No. Nothing about the way she acted makes me think she wanted to hurt herself or jump off a bridge." She shook her head. "No. I don't believe it."

The detective nodded like he felt the same way. "After things got really bad with Clint and the video went out to her coworkers and friends, her mother said she did attempt suicide. Pills. But she called her mom to say goodbye. The paramedics arrived in time to save her."

Liz felt so sorry for Aubrey and all she'd endured. "Sounds like a desperate cry for help after a traumatic event."

Tate pressed the detective. "You think Clint saw Aubrey talking to Liz, kidnapped her, and pushed her off a bridge?"

It sounded so farfetched. And yet, she didn't know how far Clint would go.

The detective closed his notebook. "I can't prove it, but yes, I do. Her mother said things were good in her life. Aubrey liked her new job and had made several new friends. Nothing about her recent history gives even the slightest sign she was depressed or contemplating suicide. I went through the events of Aubrey's day. Everything seemed routine. She showed up to work on time, did her job, then went to lunch. Her mother swore to me that Aubrey wouldn't kill herself that way. She was terrified of heights."

Liz thought out loud. "Clint probably found it poetic, tossing his lover off the bridge and convincing himself she deserved it for not loving him enough."

Anger and disgust drew lines across Tate's forehead. "Have you spoken to Clint?"

The detective shook his head. "I wanted to start with Aubrey's day, make sure there wasn't anything else going on in her life and make sure I didn't reach the wrong conclusions by getting caught up in her past." He fixed his gaze on her. "It appeared you were the last person to speak to her today. As soon as you mentioned Clint, I knew my suspicions were correct. I'll track him down and talk to him, but I don't anticipate it going anywhere. The guy is careful. I doubt we'll find any evidence of him in her car or at the bridge, but you never know. The car was wiped down, but they found a few prints. We'll see if anything comes back from the lab. Until then, I'd stay away from Clint from now on. If he's targeted you as his next obsession . . . well, I can only say it won't end well. If he does anything to you, call the police. Make sure there's a record of it. Don't let him get away with hurting you the way he got away with all the others." Detective Valdez fished a card out of his pocket and held it out to her.

"That's it. That's all you've got for her?" Tate snatched the card and held it up. "How is a warning and your number supposed to protect her from this psychopath?"

Frustration lit Detective Valdez's eyes, though he took Tate's anger in stride. "My hands are tied. I need more than accusations and assumptions. Without evidence, I can't arrest him."

"And he gets away with killing someone." The contempt and disgust in Tate's voice matched exactly how Liz felt. Tate was scared for her.

But he didn't want anything to do with her, so . . . "Tate, thanks for your concern, but I'll handle this. Just go."

"That's the second time you've tried to kick me out for no reason. What is wrong with you?"

She turned her pointed finger into her chest. "Me?" She let her collective emotions fly. "After what you did, you want to know what's wrong with *me*."

Tate's eyes went wide. "Whoa. What did I do?"

"After all these years, everything we've shared, you don't have the decency to say it to my face. You send me a text!"

He held his hands out wide. "Say *what*?"

She shook her head. "I'm not doing this with you again. You can't say what you said and expect that we'll still be friends."

His hands dropped and his eyes went soft. "We are more than friends. I don't know what happened between last night and you not picking up when I called you twice today, but whatever it is, just tell me. If I upset you, I'm sorry."

She stood to face off with him because she couldn't take this sitting down. "Upset me! You send me those texts, then you show up here like nothing happened!" Tears threatened and roughened her voice.

"Hey now, hold up. I lost my phone this morning. I tried to call you from Declan's phone to let you know."

Rational thoughts broke through the hurt and anger. "You lost your phone?"

"Yeah. I had it this morning when I drove into town to pick up an order, but after that, I can't remember where I put it. Or maybe I dropped it and didn't realize it."

She crossed her arms across her fluttering belly. "Did you text me around lunchtime?"

"I told you I had work way out on the property. No cell service. Not that I had my phone to call or text you. Why? What is going on?" The plea in his voice made her believe him.

She went to her purse, grabbed her phone, pulled up the texts, and turned the phone to show him.

Rage filled his eyes as he read. "No fucking way. I did not send that. No." He took her face in his hands and stared into her eyes. "I would never break up with you via text. That's . . ." He touched his forehead to hers. The anger in his eyes dissipated to a plea. "No, Liz. I swear to you that wasn't me."

"Could it have been Clint?" the detective asked, sparking a whole new round of suspicions.

She and Tate both turned to him. Liz spoke first. "Why would you think that?"

"If he wants you back and Tate is in his way . . ."

She filled in the rest of that with dreadful thoughts. *Who does something like that?*

She glanced up at Tate. "But how did he get your phone?"

Tate shrugged. "I hardly ever lock my truck door. He could have walked right up to the truck and taken it out of my jacket without me or anyone knowing. I didn't think to call you until I finished work and was headed back into the stables. That was late afternoon. I wanted to make plans with you for tonight. You knew I'd be out of reach, but something nagged at me when I couldn't find my phone. I tried you twice."

"I didn't answer because I didn't think we had anything left to say."

He brushed his thumb over her cheek. "You mean so much to me, Liz."

She leaned into his palm and took in the warmth and comfort of his skin against hers. Relief swept through her so heady it made her feel a little buzzed and giddy. He still wanted her.

"Are you sure you lost the phone?" the detective broke into their moment.

"I didn't send her those texts." Tate's vehemence left her with no doubt he didn't do it.

The detective held up his hand to ward off Tate's further denial. "I want to be sure he took your phone and didn't clone it or something."

"I can't find it anywhere. I'm usually careful about keeping it on me in case of emergency. I tried to track it, but nothing came up on my computer. Either the battery is dead, or someone shut it off."

Liz didn't think so. "More than likely, if Clint stole it and sent me those texts, he got rid of it."

The detective nodded his agreement.

Tate got a far-off look. "I never noticed his car or him."

Liz voiced her suspicions. "He had to have been following you, too, otherwise how did he know you were in town?"

Tate sighed. "Why make it look like I broke up with you? He had to know we'd eventually talk and figure out that I didn't do it."

"He might have hoped she'd believe it long enough for it to drive a wedge between you," the detective suggested.

"He's been doing that from the start, making her think my intentions were bullshit to begin with." Tate stared down at her and her heart broke.

"I'm sorry he's made me question you and us. These last few days have been wonderful." She went right into his arms. God, it felt so good to be wrapped up in his strength, protection, and love. Because she did believe he loved her. They'd been friends too long for him not to feel that deeply for her. She believed that love had grown. "I won't let him tear us apart."

Tate hugged her closer. "Not going to happen." He

wanted to protect her. Just like he said, she meant so much to him.

"Just like with Tate's stolen phone and you receiving the text messages, there is no evidence it was Clint even if we think he did it. And I don't think it was an accident he showed up at lunchtime, just after Liz got those messages." The detective had only bad news for them. "Whatever you do, don't confront him about the phone and texts. He'll just deny it anyway and use your anger and her refusal to see him as an excuse to come after one or both of you again. The best thing you can do is nothing. Engaging him will only set him off. Aubrey got away only by cutting off all communication, switching jobs, and not associating with anyone who knows him."

"And so he found a new target. Liz."

"Let's hope Liz dating you deters Clint from taking this further."

"He killed someone who warned Liz away from him."

"Exactly. So maybe *she's* not the one in immediate danger." The detective hinted toward another target.

Her heart stopped for a split second as that hit her. "You think he might go after Tate."

"Women have always been Clint's victims, but I wouldn't put anything past him now that he's crossed this line. He beat Aubrey several times while they were together, but never too severely. If he took her from the deli, drove her to the bridge, and pushed her off all without being seen or leaving any evidence, that's cold even for him."

Tate went rigid beside her. "You mean it's an escalation."

"He wanted Aubrey to pay for interfering with his relationship with Liz."

Tate swore. "Aubrey spoke to Liz. *I'm* Liz's best friend and the guy who took her away from him."

The detective's lips pressed into a tight line. "Let's hope he doesn't start thinking of you in that way."

"I think it's a little late for that," Tate snapped.

The detective headed for the door but turned back before he walked out. "I'll update you with any relevant information. Call if you need help. Report anything he does." He turned to Tate. "Report your missing phone. You never know, maybe he kept it and we'll get him for that."

"Possession of stolen property. Big fucking deal."

"It could be the thing that trips him up. You never know." The detective left them with little hope anything would touch Clint, let alone put him behind bars.

She went to the door, locked it, and leaned back against it and stared at Tate. "I'm sorry. You didn't sign up for any of this."

"Are you kidding me? You think I'll let him mess up what we have because he's a dick who can't accept it when a woman doesn't want him? He wants to control you. Possess you. And since he can't have you, he thinks he can manipulate you back to him. When that doesn't work, will he try to force you? Hurt you again?" Tate grabbed the back of his neck and squeezed. "I can't stand to think of anything happening to you."

"The worst thing that happened to me today was thinking I'd lost you."

Tate held his arms out. She walked right into them again and held on tight as his arms wrapped around her. "You're never going to lose me." He kissed her on the head. "That's twice we've broken up and I didn't even know about it until it was too late."

She leaned back and smiled up at him.

He stared down at her and traced his fingers down the side of her face, his eyes filled with a mix of deep emotions she couldn't name. "It could have been you he pushed off that bridge."

A cold chill ran up her spine. She couldn't deny it.

Clint had to be out of his mind. Unstable. Volatile. Unafraid to do whatever he thought needed to be done to get what he wanted.

The chilling realization only made her believe even more that life was short and she didn't want to miss anything.

"What are we waiting for, Tate?"

He leaned down and pressed a soft, tempting kiss on her lips that had her rising on tiptoe to get closer as he pulled back and stared deep into her eyes. "Pack a bag. Come home with me. It's not safe here for you right now. And I need you with me. I know I was too stupid to see how much you mean to me, but now that I know, I can't lose you. I won't let him hurt you."

"Not stupid, just a whole lot of stubborn." She smiled up at him, hoping teasing him took the edge off.

The rumble of his chuckle vibrated against her belly pressed to his. "Thank God you're just as stubborn and held out for me to come around and realize everything I ever wanted was right in front of me."

Tears filled her eyes.

Tate's hand pressed to her cheek. "Don't cry. I don't think I can take it."

"They're happy tears. I love you."

He swooped in for a passionate kiss that left her breathless and clinging to him. He didn't say the words back to her, but the kiss showed her the depth of feeling inside him.

His tongue swept over hers one last time before he held his lips pressed to hers for a long moment. He broke the kiss and stared right into her eyes. "It's like a switch flipped inside me when I realized I could have lost you forever today. It started at the bar when I saw you with *him* and I knew you'd shut me out because you wanted someone else. Declan asked the question, but I knew I loved you. Of course I loved you all these years. But I want you to know I *really* love you. The kind of love that includes rings and vows and a home we share and waking up with you by my side, just like you've been by my side practically my whole life."

This time, the tears spilled over and down her cheeks. "I told you when we were five I'd marry you."

He brushed away the tears with his thumbs. "I should have listened. You're always right. And you're right about that." He kissed her again, but this time it felt like a promise. "Go pack a bag. Stay with me until we know for sure you're safe. I want to wake up to you in my bed where you belong and I've wanted you far too long."

The look in his eyes told her he was all in. He loved her. Knowing that erased the sorrow in her heart and fear from this day and shined a bright light on their future.

She couldn't wait to make her kindergarten prophecy come true.

But first, she needed to stay out of Clint's reach because he was a real threat to the future she wanted with Tate. A few days out at the ranch with Tate while the detective built a case against Clint and hopefully arrested him sounded like heaven.

She'd planted the seed of their life together years ago. Tonight, they'd take the first real step into their shared future.

Chapter Seventeen

TATE CHECKED the rearview mirror for the hundredth time since leaving Liz's place. Her car turned into the ranch driveway behind his truck. He watched the road behind her to be sure no one followed them.

Paranoid? Hell yeah.

Clint killed someone.

Unlike the cops, Tate didn't need the evidence to pin that on Clint. Fear that he'd come after Liz next drove Tate to keep her close and protect her.

Liz could be stubborn and independent. She fought for what she believed in and worked hard to achieve the things she wanted. He admired her for her persistence and tenacity.

Look how long she'd stuck it out with him.

If something happened to her . . . he didn't even want to think about it. He couldn't fathom a life without her.

He didn't want a life without her.

She parked next to his truck in the driveway. He got out and snagged both her bags from the back seat of her car.

"Come on." He walked up the path to the steps and right up and through the front door. She closed it behind them. He stood in the opening to the living room and met Declan's surprised eyes. "Liz is staying with me for a while," he announced without any explanation. He'd like to turn that "for a while" into forever. Soon.

"What took you so long?" Declan turned to Liz. "Hey."

"Hey," she answered back with a shy smile.

They'd known each other a long time, but Tate got that Liz probably felt a bit out of sorts letting Declan know she planned to stay with Tate—in his room. It kind of made him feel like a teenager, sneaking and doing something that felt naughty, but damnit he was a grown man. He and Liz were adults. He had nothing to feel embarrassed about, and neither did she.

Tate glanced down at her and ignored Declan's unabashed smirk. "Are you hungry?"

Liz shook her head.

"Maybe later." He didn't have much of an appetite after he heard about all that happened today. He hoped to help Liz forget her worries and that Clint made her believe he broke up with her. He couldn't imagine how much that hurt her. "Come upstairs, we'll put your stuff away." And he'd find a way to make her smile again.

Declan wore a stupid grin and gave him a thumbs-up that made Tate roll his eyes.

The heavy bags weighed him down as he took the stairs to the second floor, but anticipation sent him up and into his room where he dropped the bags next to his dresser.

Liz closed the door and looked around the room. "It's not like I remember."

"I took the Def Leppard and AC/DC posters down a while back."

"And the centerfold calendar." Her smirk made him laugh.

"I grew up."

"Naked girls are better in person," she teased, reading his mind.

He still didn't want to touch that with a ten-foot pole. They'd spent far too much time on what had come before they got together.

All he wanted to do now was show her that she was the only woman who mattered.

"I'll need to make some room in the closet or something." The four-drawer dresser by the closet was filled with his stuff, but he could clear a drawer for her. The two nightstands next to the bed offered little space, but she could plug in her phone and charge it. His clothes and jackets hung in the closet, but it wasn't packed, so she had some space in there, no problem.

Liz watched him while he tried to get through this tension-filled moment.

"You sure you don't want something to eat?" He wanted to put her at ease and help her relax.

She tossed her purse and keys on the dresser next to them.

Neither of them had glanced at the bed since they entered the room.

She didn't seem nervous at all. "I don't need anything but you, Tate." She'd always known exactly what she wanted.

He wanted to grab her and hold on. But he hesitated

because everything would be different. As ready as he felt for it . . . there was no going back.

When he didn't make a move, she tilted her head and stared at him. "Do you want me to stay here?"

"Yes."

"Have you thought about us here together?"

"It's all I think about now."

"You know how I feel about you, right?"

"The same way I feel about you."

She didn't take her eyes off him when she pulled her work T-shirt off over her head and that dark red hair cascaded down her shoulders, the tips of it brushing her creamy breasts encased in a white lace bra.

His mouth watered.

"Show me." Her hands went to the button on her skin-tight jeans.

"Stop."

One of her eyebrows shot up in question, but she froze.

"I want to do that."

She held her hands out to her sides. "Have at it."

Need made him want to rush, but something deeper tempered that drive. He stepped forward, cupped her face, stared down into her jade green eyes and just took in her beautiful face. Light brown freckles sprinkled across the bridge of her nose and across her pink-tinted cheeks. One cute little freckle sat at the outer corner of her right eye. Her lashes were the same deep shade of red as her hair. They looked almost brown except where the light hit and turned them red.

"Tate."

"Yeah, sweetheart?"

"If you're having second thoughts . . ."

He smiled because she was adorable when she was nervous. "Third. Fourth. A thousand thoughts about what I want to do with you. Starting with this."

Her face followed his for the kiss, but he dipped his head and kissed the spot just under her ear. He slid his hands down her shoulders and arms to her waist. He kissed his way down her neck, across her chest, up her throat, and planted a soft kiss on her lips. He clamped his hands tight on her hips and pulled her snug against him. Her sweet little sigh whispered against his lips. He swallowed her moan when he dipped his hand over her ass, squeezed, and lifted her so her body fit to his. Her hands went up under his shirt the second his tongue slid against hers. He tasted her need at the same time her nails bit into his back.

He loved that she didn't hesitate or hold back.

It made this transition from friends to lovers easier and less awkward.

He unhooked her bra and slid it down her arms. She pulled his shirt off over his head. When he pulled her back in for another searing kiss and her skin met his, something primal went off inside him.

He backed her up to the bed and laid her out on it, trailing kisses down her neck to her chest, and finally taking one of those tempting pink nipples into his mouth. He smoothed his tongue over the tight bud. She moaned his name and slid her fingers into his hair and held him to her as he feasted with her thighs pressed to his sides. He left one perfect breast for the other and cupped the abandoned one in his palm, molding it to his hand.

God, she was . . . amazing.

Her hands dipped between them and attacked the button and zipper on his jeans. She slipped one hand around his hard shaft and squeezed, then ran her hand up and down his length. Lost in the buzz of lust running though him, he backed away from her and practically tore her jeans, panties, socks, and shoes off her. He pulled and tugged as she scooted up the bed and fell back, her hair in wild disarray around her beautiful face and shoulders.

He stared down at all that pale skin and swept his gaze up her legs, past her tempting sex, over her round pink-tipped breasts to the come-and-get-me grin.

"Damn, babe, you're beautiful." Now that he allowed himself to really look at her and see her, he couldn't deny or miss the obvious: she was the most beautiful woman he'd ever seen.

"Don't call me that." The snap in her words made it clear she didn't like that particular endearment.

He pulled off one boot and the other, never taking his eyes off her. "Shall I stick with *Lizard*?" He stripped off his jeans and boxer briefs, completely satisfied to see her eyes dilate and fill with desire as her gaze roamed down his chest, abs, and throbbing erection.

"Try again." The breathless reply made him grin.

It was still there when he leaned down and pressed a kiss to the inside of her thigh. "How about *sweetheart*?" He trailed kisses up her thigh.

"Better," she said on a sigh.

Her thighs spread as he pushed them up and planted his hands on the mattress beneath them. He kept his gaze locked on hers as he dipped his head and teased her soft folds with the tip of his tongue. "What about *honey*?" He planted his mouth over her and sank his tongue deep into her slick core. The taste of her on his tongue sent a bolt of heat through him that made his dick twitch and the need to bury himself deep inside her intensify to the point he could barely contain the need to do so right now. He wanted to take his time, but his body and heart wanted to claim her as his.

Her hips rocked against his mouth. Her hands fisted in the comforter.

He took her right up to the edge, slipped one finger into her tight center, licked that throbbing bud, and sent her right into oblivion. Her back arched and her body pulsed against his mouth. Head back in the pillow, she never looked more beautiful to him.

He kissed his way up her belly and chest, reached over to the bedside table, pulled open the drawer, and fumbled through miscellaneous stuff for a condom.

Her body lay soft and supple below him as he tore open the condom and slid it on.

He brushed the hair away from her face, stared down at her, and asked, "How about I just call you mine?" He kissed her hard and deep and buried his hard shaft to the hilt.

She took him in with a moan. Her hands slid down his sides, over his hips and grabbed his ass. She squeezed and pulled him in deeper and sighed out, "Yes."

Desire overrode any other sweet words he might have conjured to please her. He couldn't think of any words to express how that yes made him feel, so he showed her with the push and pull of his body over and inside hers. Every kiss, sweep of his hands, thrust of his body said far more than he could put into words. Her moans and sighs, the demand of her kiss and body for more, drove him to satisfy her every yearning. No matter how much he gave, she wanted more and gave so much back to him.

He didn't want this first time to end. Not when it felt so right and perfect and real. He could feel her in a way that connected them. She breathed with him. Her heartbeat became his. He moved and she matched him until they simply gave themselves over to the moment, got lost in the rhythm and need until they hit ecstasy.

He collapsed on top of her, but tried to hold some of his weight on his forearms. She wrapped her arms around his back and held him close, her fingers brushing back and forth in a hypnotic rhythm that nearly put him to sleep.

"You left the lights on."

"The better to see you, my dear." He hoped she got the wolf to her Red Riding Hood hint. He felt a little wolfish and wholly satisfied at the moment.

"You sure know how to huff and puff and blow my house down."

He chuckled, lifted himself up onto his hands, and stared down at her. "That was . . ."

"Crazy amazing," she finished for him with a soft smile and sweep of her hands up his chest.

"It's almost like we read each other so well, we knew just what to do."

"Some of us have had more practice than others." The tone to those words was teasing, but there was a hint of resentment that it had taken him this long to see how great they were together.

"Which is why I know how special and amazing and different being with you is, and that I don't want to lose it, or you. Ever." He sealed that declaration with a kiss.

He eased them apart and lay on his side next to her. He planted his hand on her hip and rolled her to face him.

She hooked her leg over his and placed her hand on his chest. Something darkened her green eyes.

"What is it, sweetheart?"

"I never thought I'd be here. With you. Like this."

"I'm kicking myself for not doing this sooner."

She smiled, but it didn't light her eyes. "It happened when we were both ready."

He traced his finger along the side of her face. "You waited a long time for me to figure out you're what I want."

She brushed her fingers over his lips and along his jaw. "This kind of feels unreal and at the same time like the best thing that's ever happened to me."

He hugged her close. "I feel the same way." He sighed and said what was probably on both their minds. "After what happened today, it feels even more important. Like we almost missed this." He put his finger under her chin and made her look up at him. "I will do whatever I have to do to keep you safe and with me, because I can't lose you, Liz. Not now. Not ever. I mean it."

She buried her face in his neck and held on to him like her life depended on it.

He cuddled her close and offered her his strength and protection. His thoughts went to that poor woman who died needlessly and senselessly. He wouldn't let that happen to Liz. He'd kill Clint before he ever put another hand on Liz.

"Are you sure you don't want something to eat?" They'd both missed dinner. He wanted her to settle in here and feel like she belonged.

She rose up, pushed him onto his back, grabbed another condom out of the drawer, and held it up. "All I want is you tonight." She straddled his lap and stared down at him.

He gripped her hips, ready and willing. "Whatever you want, honey. I'm yours."

Chapter Eighteen

CLINT DIDN'T expect the cops to show up at his place the night Aubrey tried to ruin his relationship with Liz. He expected someone, most likely Aubrey's mother, would miss her and file a missing person's report in the next couple days. Some hiker or hunter would discover Aubrey's bloated body floating in the lake sometime in the next week. Then he expected the cops to rule it a suicide.

Done. End of story.

So what the hell was Detective Valdez doing holding up his badge on the other side of Clint's door?

He opened it just enough for the cop to see him, but not enough for him to step inside, blocking entry to the last person he wanted to invite through his door. "What's going on?"

The cop eyed him. "I'm here to ask you about your relationship with Aubrey Pittman."

"We don't have one. Not anymore. She broke up with me a while back. Why?"

"You sound bitter about that."

He tried to calm his racing heart with a deep breath and went with the obvious answer. "Does anyone like being dumped?" The bitch deserved what she got.

"What happened to Aubrey?" He tried to sound concerned.

The cop eyed him. "What makes you think something happened to her?"

Shit. Stupid. He shouldn't have offered an assumption that made him look guilty. He thought of a quick cover. "Cops don't show up for no reason. So what is it? Is she claiming I harassed her again? Because I haven't seen her in months."

"Did you see her today at the deli where you met Liz Scott?"

He shook his head. "No. I left after a brief conversation with Liz and went back to work."

"Did you make any stops?"

"No. It takes a good twenty minutes, maybe more, to walk back to my office."

"You walked?"

"I sit in an office all day. I like to get out, walk to lunch, and get some fresh air when the weather is nice. Like today." He stuck to the truth as much as possible. Once he left the large park and entered the downtown area again, no telling how many people saw him.

"Do you ever walk to the park by the lake?"

Maybe someone had seen him. "Not often, but every once in a while." He didn't panic. A lot of people who worked downtown went to the park for lunch. "Why are you asking about Aubrey?"

The officer looked past him into the entry and living room beyond Clint's shoulder. "May I come in?"

Twice he'd asked what happened and not gotten an answer. He wouldn't fall into the cop's trap and talk just to fill in the blanks. "Unless you actually have something to say about Aubrey, I'm done talking."

"We discovered Aubrey's body in the lake a few hours ago."

He leaned into the door frame and dropped his head. "She finally did it."

"Did what?" the cop asked, staring hard at him.

He looked up, putting on a mask of sadness and resignation. "Aubrey was . . . troubled. She had a hard time coping with life. She suffered long periods of depression. Sometimes she acted out and blamed others for her problems."

"She filed a restraining order against you as well as harassment charges."

He nodded. The restraining order she got, but he persuaded her to drop the harassment. For her own good. "A very troubled girl. She craved attention. Sometimes that meant she threatened to kill herself." He dropped his head again. "I guess this time, she followed through."

"Did you have something to do with that?"

He expected the question and snapped his head up and feigned shock. "What? Me? No. Hell no."

"Aubrey died not even half an hour after meeting Liz and warning her away from *you*. That conversation happened seconds after *you* left the deli."

"Exactly. I wasn't there. I never saw Aubrey. I'm sorry she fell into another deep depression and took her life."

"I never said she took her life."

That caught him off guard. "I . . . I don't understand."

"We found her body, but I never said she took her own life. In fact, the investigation is ongoing."

Crap. He tried not to show his anger, but inside he raged that the cops didn't just take the easy answer and go with it. "Do you seriously think someone killed her?" He expected the case to be open and shut. Leave it to Aubrey to cause him trouble even in death.

"The circumstances of her death are suspicious. I assume your office will confirm the time you returned after lunch."

"Speak to my assistant. Kelly saw me when I arrived."

Kelly wouldn't contradict him. Not if she wanted a favorable response from him. She craved his attention. Maybe he'd even get her a latte and one of those scones she liked so much. It was so easy to keep her in line.

The cop had nothing. If he wanted to fish, let him. He wouldn't find anything in this pond. Or the lake. No one would find anything.

"Where were you this morning between eight thirty and nine?"

That question caught him off guard. Apparently it showed, because the cop's gaze intensified. It took Clint a second to put the conversation back on Aubrey. "I thought you said Aubrey was seen with Liz at lunch?"

"That's right. Where were you this morning during the time I specified?"

"I don't see how where I was this morning has anything to do with Aubrey."

"And Liz is your ex?" The detective's abrupt switch from Aubrey to Liz threw him.

"That's right."

"Based on the conversation you had with her at lunch, are you hoping the two of you get back together?"

"That's none of your business."

"I'd say it's a no, especially after I saw her with Tate." The cop gave him a look.

Clint fumed. "He broke up with her."

"That's what she thought, too, until he explained he lost his phone this morning."

Shit. They tied the phone to him. Or so they thought. "Let me guess, he had a change of heart, came up with some bullshit story about losing his phone to cover, then pleaded with her to understand and take him back." He rolled his eyes. "The guy has been stringing her along for years. If she can't see this is just another game he's playing to keep her tied to him, that's too bad for her. *He's* the reason we broke up. He doesn't want her to be with someone who really cares about her. He just wants to keep her all to himself."

"Aubrey's mother said that's how you treated Aubrey. Like something that belonged to you."

No one understood his relationship, his dedication, to first Aubrey, and now Liz. "I tried to be there for Aubrey, to protect her from herself. In the end, I realized I couldn't help someone who didn't want to be helped. Someone who didn't think she needed help." Someone who didn't dedicate herself to being better and everything he needed her to be the way he'd been everything to her.

"Do you think Liz needs your help?"

"I tried to tell her that if Tate really wanted her, he'd have done something about it long before now. She's a beautiful, kind, loving woman who deserves someone who loves her, not someone who just wants her sole attention but doesn't want to give her the things she needs."

"You want to be that guy."

"She knows that. Tate messed that up for us, but we talked today and she knows that I still care. I want her to be happy. From what you said, it appears Tate is still playing games."

"I saw them together. Looked to me like Tate was all in."

That pissed him off, but he tried not to show it. "That's what he wants *her* to think." His well-laid plans fell apart too quickly. He needed a better tactic to prove to Liz she'd made a mistake with Tate.

He needed to help her see that before Tate hurt her again.

"So where were you this morning?"

"Getting ready for work and driving to the office."

"Anyone see you during that time?"

He crossed his arms and leaned against the door frame. "I live alone."

"What time did you arrive at work?"

He shrugged. "About nine."

"Do you always start that late?"

"My boss doesn't care when I get there so long as I put in my eight hours. Now if you don't mind, my dinner is getting cold."

"I have just a few more questions."

"Look, I'm sorry Aubrey took her life, but it has nothing to do with me. I've been out of her life for a long time. I've moved on, even if she hadn't."

"With Liz?"

"Good night." He shut the door in the officer's face. Let him think what he wanted, but Clint had no reason to fear he was a suspect, other than the fact that he was connected to Aubrey and Liz. The cop had nothing but suspicion. If he had any evidence, their talk would have been down at the police station.

Clint had been careful and used Aubrey's past and crazy threats to hurt herself against her.

He smiled as he walked back into his kitchen.

The cop couldn't prove a damn thing. Not even stealing Tate's phone and the texts to Liz.

The grin faded to an angry frown. That bastard Tate talked his way out of it and got back together with Liz. He made Liz believe Clint had sent the texts.

Well, just like he had with the cop, he'd make Liz doubt Tate once again.

She'd see Tate as a fraud and come back to Clint where she belonged.

Chapter Nineteen

"Did you sleep well?"

Liz handed the plate of eggs and fried potatoes to Declan. A self-conscious blush burned her cheeks despite his innocuous question. Being a redhead made it hard to hide such things. "Yes."

She'd slept better the last four days than she had in a long time. Not that she and Tate got much sleep. They'd been messing up the sheets every night on some unspoken mission to make up for lost time.

And she couldn't help but revel in it.

And with thoughts of all they'd shared, her blush deepened.

Declan, ever the gentleman, ignored it.

She never thought it would be like this. Oh, she'd imagined they'd be close, in sync, and get along well, but nothing her mind conjured came close to the depth of feelings Tate made her feel for him and about them when they made love.

It gave her a newfound optimism for their future.

The initial awkwardness and apprehension faded into oblivion after their first night together.

It felt damn good to look at Tate and know—all the way to her soul—he wanted to be hers.

She didn't question it anymore. Tate didn't give her any reason to deny it, and every reason to believe it. She finally saw that he did everything he could each day to show her he loved her.

Declan took his seat at the table and dug in. Mouth full, he moaned, then stuffed another bite into his mouth even though he hadn't finished chewing the first one.

"You act like you haven't eaten in a month."

"You're a better cook than me and Tate." He held her gaze. "So, how long do you plan to stay?"

"For a while. Until it's safe for me to be at home. Is that okay?"

Tate didn't have the only say. This was Declan's home, too, and she didn't want to put him out or become an unwelcome guest who overstayed her welcome.

Declan shrugged and scooped up a pile of eggs on his fork. "Fine by me. Drake and Adria got home yesterday from their honeymoon. They're up at the cabin now, packing their stuff. Tate plans to move in to the cabin after that. You guys can be *alone* there." Declan's knowing grin made her cheeks heat with embarrassment.

She couldn't believe he assumed she and Tate would move in together permanently. She and Tate hadn't made any plans or talked about what came next.

"I thought we could fix up the cabin, add on to it. Make it ours." Tate came up behind her, put his hand on her shoulder, turned her to him, and kissed her like he hadn't seen her in weeks. And just like last night, she melted against his big body. She gave in to the need to be closer to him. Her mind scrambled and she completely lost track of what he said and the unbelievable joy those words evoked—at the same time she was surprised as hell he'd simply say that's what he planned to do for them.

Tate pulled back way too soon. "Morning, sweetheart." His eyes were bloodshot and shadowed from lack of sleep.

It made her smile. "Morning." She placed her hand on his jaw and brushed her thumb over the stubble he hadn't bothered to shave before or after his shower this morning.

He leaned into her touch and stole her coffee mug off the counter at the same time. The mischievous grin made the butterflies in her stomach take flight and fill her with anticipation in hopes that she and Tate repeated everything they did last night again soon.

Tate took a sip of her coffee and stared at her over the rim. "Where do you think you're going?" He didn't miss a thing, like the barest glimpse of her work shirt under her sweatshirt.

"You heard Detective Valdez." He'd called after his interview with Clint and filled them in. "They don't have anything to arrest Clint."

"That doesn't mean he didn't do it."

"I believe he did. Which is why I'm taking the detective's advice." She picked up the sack lunch she packed before making breakfast for her, Tate, and Declan. "I won't go anywhere alone. I'll eat at work. I'll vary my schedule. I've already spoken to my boss. It's all arranged."

"Quit. Stay here. You don't need to work. I'll take care of you."

She understood his desire to keep her close and protect her. She appreciated it. It reinforced how much he cared about her. But . . . "Tate, honey, I'm not quitting my job and hiding here for the rest of my life. If I do, he wins."

"I'm pretty sure I win if you're here with me all the time." He tried to tease, but he was also serious. "Go to work at *Almost Homemade*."

She shook her head. "You can't hand out jobs at Trinity and Adria's shop."

"They won't mind. You're family."

She placed her hand on her melting heart. "Thank you for that. It means a lot that you think that."

"It's true," Declan added. "You've been a part of this family forever, Liz."

Tears filled her eyes. She always knew her friendship with Tate made her close to him and his siblings and parents, but she never imagined Declan and the others thought of her as family.

Tate set down the coffee mug and cupped her face. "This is where you belong."

She hooked her hands on his wrists. "But I still need a life that's mine." She hoped he understood.

"You won't have a life if Clint gets his hands on you." Declan pointed out the horrible truth.

Tate gave her a see-my-point face.

She got it. She felt the same way they did. But she couldn't quit her life and hide forever. She couldn't let Clint take everything away from her and get away with it.

She'd taken Thursday, Friday, and Saturday off work and stayed at the ranch all that time, not going back to her condo and giving Clint a chance to . . . do whatever he planned to do next.

How long was she supposed to put her life on hold because Clint couldn't take no for an answer?

She wasn't stupid. She had a plan, even if it wasn't foolproof.

"I have a new phone."

Tate bought her one when he replaced his. With a new phone number. Clint couldn't call or text her now. She'd cut him off just like the detective said she should do. Hopefully, Clint would get bored and sever his obsession with her. She hated to think of him turning his sights on some other unsuspecting woman. Aubrey must have felt the same when she delivered the warning to her on that fateful day last week. Liz hoped she had the guts to help someone else if needed.

"The phone means nothing if he takes you and kills you like he did Aubrey."

Frustrated and angry, she pushed away from Tate. "I'm going to work. I'll be careful. I promise. But I won't sit here on my ass doing nothing anymore. If I see Clint, or even think he's following me, I'll call the police. I'll text you throughout the day to let you know I'm okay."

"Damnit, Liz, I want you more than okay. I want you safe. Here. With me."

"I know." She sucked in a breath and let it out to calm down. "But you can't babysit me the rest of our lives."

"Just until the cops arrest him."

"For what? They have no evidence he did anything. No prints on your truck that he stole your phone. None left in Aubrey's car. No sign that she struggled or tried to fight him off if he was in her car. Nothing at the lake puts him there. He's going to get away with killing her. I won't let him get away with ruining my life."

Tate stared at her for what seemed like a full minute. "Fine."

"Thank you."

"I'll drive you to work and pick you up."

"Tate, Declan needs you here. You're already shorthanded. Spending three hours every day driving me back and forth to work is not a good use of your time."

"I'm going to spend the entire day worried about you," Tate bit out, his frustration etched in the lines around his frown.

"Try it Tate's way for a little while." Declan stood from the table to take his plate to the sink. "Clint hasn't been able to get to you here on the ranch. Let Tate take you to and from work and see what happens. If he tries to contact you at your office, we'll know he hasn't given up on you. If not, then we can reevaluate."

Tate stared at her. "You should be relatively safe at work with your coworkers and people coming and going all day. But on the road, that long drive where houses and ranches are few and far between, lots of open space and few cars . . ." He left off what could happen out there.

But she didn't need the details to come to a compromise. "Okay. For now. Maybe I can adjust my schedule and ride in with Adria when she goes in to work at *Almost Homemade*."

"You think Tate is overprotective?" Declan shook his head. "No way Drake lets his pregnant wife get involved in anything that puts her at risk along with you."

She threw up her hands and let them fall. "Great.

When he hears about this, I'm sure he'll revoke my invitation to stay here."

"Never." Tate touched her shoulder. "But you will be stuck with me driving you to work."

"I don't mind being stuck with you anywhere." She tried to put some humor in her voice, but it didn't come through or ease the tension in Tate's determined eyes.

Declan kissed her on the side of the head. "Stay safe. Be smart." He left her with Tate in the kitchen.

Tate brushed his thumb across her cheek. "We are all worried about you, Liz."

"I'm not taking this lightly. I just can't sit here and let him turn my life upside down."

He pulled her in for a hug. "I know, sweetheart."

"I won't live scared. He can't do to me what he did to Aubrey, isolating her from everyone she cared about. And as sweet as it is that you want to keep me safe here on the ranch, it's kind of the same thing."

"That's not my intention." The definitive tone made that clear.

She rubbed her hand up and down his chest and settled it over his heart. "I know you only want to keep me safe. But I won't give up the life I've built, or let him ruin what we've found together. I won't let him separate me from my family and friends. Or you. Because then, he wins. And I refuse to cower and let him win."

Tate put his hand over hers. "He knows we're onto him. He knows you're with me. Let's hope it's enough to keep him away." Tate's words didn't hold the assurance she needed, because nothing short of Clint behind bars for life would make her feel better and safe.

Chapter Twenty

TATE STOOD in front of the fireplace in the cabin and stared at his brothers and sisters. He'd called this family meeting because things were changing in his life. Fast. And he wanted them in on his plans.

Drake and Adria had already taken a seat on the sofa. Trinity walked in last and slid onto one of the bar stools behind them.

Trinity sensed something big happening. "What's the big news you couldn't share with me on the phone?"

He stuffed his hand in his pocket and pulled out the black velvet box.

A collective gasp went up from all of them.

"I'm going to ask Liz to marry me."

No one said anything, they just smiled and nodded.

"I know it's only been a couple weeks since we got together."

"You've known her since you were three." Trinity held her hand out. "I want to see the ring."

"Me too," Adria said, getting up to meet him as he walked over to show them.

Trinity hooked her arm over his shoulder. "It's gorgeous, Tate. She's going to love it."

"You don't think it's too much? Not enough?" He wanted Liz to have the perfect ring.

"It's stunning," Adria assured him.

"When are you going to ask her?" Drake glanced at the ring and nodded from his spot on the couch.

"I'm not exactly sure. Soon. I'm still trying to come up with the perfect way to do it."

"Take her out to dinner. Or for a ride and picnic on the property." Declan rolled his shoulders. They'd been working hard the last few days. "She's going to say *YES* any way you do it."

He dropped his shoulders and sighed. "I hope so. We haven't talked about it." He stared at the ring. "Then again, now that we're together it just seems inevitable."

"Are you not sure?" Drake never minced words.

"Oh, I'm sure." He'd never been more certain of anything. Ever. "We don't want to miss a second with each other. When she's not here, all I do is think about her."

"I can vouch for that." Declan teased, but it was the truth.

Tate had a few concerns he and Liz would need to address. "I don't know if she wants to live here, or in town. I haven't saved a lot of money. I can't buy her a house like you did with Adria. Because I work the ranch, and it's most convenient to live here, I think I can swing a loan to fix up the cabin."

Adria stepped in front of him and put her hand on his arm. "It's not about money. It's about the life you want to build with her."

He appreciated that, but he still needed to provide for her and any children they might have together.

Just like discovering the depth of his feelings for her, the reality of making a life with her hit him all at once.

He and Liz hadn't done a whole lot of talking about the future. They'd stuck to the here and now, mostly because the situation with Clint was nowhere near settled. How could they plan for the future when the present was so uncertain?

But they needed to start the conversation. To do that, he needed to know a few things from his family. "So you guys are good with her living here?"

"You know we are," Declan said, leaning his head back on the sofa and closing his eyes. The guy worked too hard, carrying the bulk of the ranch business on his shoulders even though he didn't need to. But that was another conversation for another time.

He focused on Drake and Adria, who Drake had pulled down into his lap. They were cute together. Seeing his brother this happy made him even happier because there'd been a time he and Declan thought Drake wouldn't make it out of the dark place he'd been in. Adria changed his life.

Being with Liz changed Tate's.

Drake read Tate's mind. "You're anxious to get this thing moving. I get it. I didn't give Adria a lot of time before we were walking down the aisle."

"I needed something wonderful after tragedy." Adria gave Drake a quick kiss. "We needed something good after all we'd both been through."

Tate got that. "Liz deserves to be happy. I want to make her happy. I want her to feel like this is home."

Drake nodded. "I get it. Work is nearly done on our

house. Adria and I should be able to move the last of our stuff in a few days. Maybe sooner. If you need help moving your stuff here, we'll help."

"Okay." That gave him time to ask Liz to marry him, come up with a plan with her for what they wanted to do to the cabin to make it theirs, and think about work, family, and the future they'd share. All of it overwhelmed him, but if they took it a step at a time and worked together, it would all work out.

Declan stood and raked his hand over his head. "I hope you'll be very happy together. Don't forget to call and tell Mom and Dad."

"I talked to them this morning. They love Liz and can't wait to marry off another son."

Declan arched his back and shifted side to side to work out the kinks. "The ranch is doing well. I project profits to increase fifteen to thirty percent over the next couple years. I'll give you a raise starting with your next paycheck."

"Thank you. That means a lot. But are you sure we can afford it? We still need to hire a couple more people to fill out the crew."

Declan waved that off. "It's fine. No problem. You and Liz will need the extra money to fix this place up."

"You'll be all alone in the big house," Trinity pointed out to Declan.

"I'm used to being alone." Declan walked out the front door, leaving them all speechless by his abrupt exit.

"How long has it been since Declan went on a date?" Drake asked.

"How long has it been since he left the ranch for

some fun?" Trinity scrunched her mouth into a sad frown.

Tate raked his fingers through his hair. The last time he dragged Declan out was the night Tate found Liz with Clint and lost his shit. "Declan never stops working. I think it's time to make him hand over more of the work. I'll talk to him about that and the other reason I wanted to talk to you guys. Liz tries to be okay, and make me think she's okay, but this stuff with Clint is getting to her. I want you guys to be on alert. Watch out for her when you're here. This guy got his hands on Aubrey without anyone seeing him take her. No one saw him push her off that bridge."

"Still no evidence?" Drake asked.

"The cops have nothing concrete, just a bunch of circumstantial stuff that adds up to nothing." His frustration filled every word and kept the muscles in his shoulders and neck tense.

"We'll keep an eye on her," Drake promised. "Trinity and Adria aren't here much, but maybe they can check in on her at lunch once in a while."

"Of course we can." Trinity smiled at him.

"I'm in," Adria added.

"Great." It relieved Tate to know they'd all be watching over Liz. "If you see anything suspicious or she tells you something she doesn't want to share with me for whatever reason, please remember it could be important and possibly save her life."

Drake pinned him with an intense gaze. "You really think he might go after her."

"So far, he's refused to give up. He tried to break us up with those texts." Thank God, it didn't work.

Tate never wanted to see Liz that angry and sad again. "What's he going to do next to get her back?"

"She doesn't want to be with him. Why keep trying to force it?" Trinity shook her head. "It makes no sense."

"He's obsessed with her. He thinks she belongs to him. He wants to save her from me." Tate didn't get it at all. He'd never hurt Liz. He loved her. And the thought of being responsible for even a moment of upset for Liz made his heart ache. Never. That's why he'd gone a little crazy when she took that step back and he'd been hell bent on making things right.

Adria frowned. "Take it from me, bad things happen when a guy tries to force you to like him."

Tragic things happened.

All of their thoughts turned to Juliana and what happened to her.

Drake hugged Adria close.

Tate couldn't help Juliana, but he could do everything in his power to keep Liz safe. "Thanks for the support and looking out for Liz. I appreciate it. I'm not sure when I'll propose, but it will be soon. Until then, don't say anything to her." He stared at Trinity. "Don't give hints that it's coming just because you can't help yourself."

Trinity pressed a hand to her chest. "Who, me?"

"You." He smiled despite how hard he tried to look intimidating to keep her quiet. He wanted to surprise Liz. She deserved a happy surprise with all the trimmings. All he had to do was pick a time and place and put it all together to make her smile—and say, *YES!*

He wanted them to have a long and happy life together.

If their friendship of the last twenty-plus years was any indication, they had plenty in common. They'd have the partner they needed in each other and a love that would keep them together. That love would continue to grow. He looked forward to a life filled with joy and laughter, a family of their own, grandbabies on their knees as they rocked on the porch in their old age, a real lifetime of memories shared.

Chapter Twenty-One

Liz HAD no idea what had gotten into Tate since yesterday, but he seemed anxious and secretive and . . . antsy. Totally unlike her steady, get-it-done cowboy. She didn't know what had him out of sorts. He assured her it had nothing to do with Clint. Relieved to have another day free of Clint's drama, she tried to put Tate's odd behavior out of mind and get her work done. The last few days had been busy, which helped keep her thoughts off things and settle the overwhelming nerves she'd had coming back to work.

She felt exposed anytime she left the ranch.

She wanted to settle into her life with Tate and let everything else go.

Her phone chimed with a reminder about her Thursday lunch date with Trinity, which made her smile. For the first time since everything happened, she was going out to eat with Tate's sister.

"I hope that sappy grin is because of my brother." Trinity stood in Liz's office doorway, hands braced on each side of the frame, looking lovely in a chic boho gauzy white dress with electric blue embroidery. Super cute, compared to Liz's navy slacks and white spa polo.

Liz smiled. "I was just thinking about how long and fast our relationship has been."

"And it makes you smile to think how stupid he was for waiting so long to figure out what was so obvious to everyone else."

Liz laughed and realized she hadn't really done that over the last few days because of her worries about what *might* happen. She needed to stay grounded in the moment and enjoy work, Tate, family, and friends.

She'd spent all this time waiting for something to happen instead of simply living her life, present and focused on what was important to her. Except maybe when she and Tate were in bed together. Then she'd been solely focused on him and the way he made her feel.

"It all happened at the right time." When she and Tate were both ready for it. Though he'd kind of taken her off guard. But she liked that it had been a wonderful surprise and he'd made the effort to come after her after all the years she'd been waiting on him.

"It's the way it's supposed to be."

She appreciated and loved Trinity's sentiment. It felt just like that now.

"Ready to head to lunch?" Trinity stood back, waiting for Liz to walk out ahead of her.

"Did Tate send an armed guard?"

Trinity giggled. "No. But I'm under strict orders to stay by your side the whole time." Trinity rolled her eyes. "I told him not to worry, girls never pee alone when they're out together."

Liz couldn't help but laugh with Trinity. It felt good to let go of her worries for a little while and have some fun. Lunch with Trinity was just what she needed.

They headed out into the reception area. Several ladies waited with glasses of sparkling water with orange slices. She loved it when groups came in for a girls' spa day.

Liz waved goodbye to Emmy manning the front desk with the phone to her ear.

She welcomed the bright sun and soft breeze as they exited the building but stopped short when a man approached and called her name.

"Liz Scott? Can I ask you a few questions?"

Trinity stepped in front of her. "Who are you?"

The dark-haired man adjusted the messenger bag strap on his shoulder. "Sorry." He patted the pocket on his somewhat wrinkled plain white dress shirt, then dipped his hand into his bag.

Trinity held her hand up. "Hold it."

The guy slowly pulled out a business card and held it up. "Tim Cobb. Investigative reporter for the *Examiner*."

Trinity took his card and handed it back to Liz. "Why do you want to talk to Liz, Mr. Cobb?"

"Tim." He stepped to the side to address Liz. "I'm doing a story on Aubrey Pittman's suspicious death and Clint Mayhew's possible involvement."

Liz stepped up to Trinity's side. "He killed her."

"Do you have any evidence to support that?"

"No." Liz scanned the parking lot and surrounding area, paranoid about being out in the open and exposed. "Listen, we're headed to lunch. Maybe we could do this over the phone or in my office."

"I'm happy to do it later today. I'm on deadline, and I really want your take on Clint and everything he's suspected of doing to Aubrey and the other women in his office."

That got Liz's full attention. "What are you talking about?"

"I interviewed people who worked with Clint and Aubrey at the company Clint still works at. People won't say it, but they're afraid of him. It's in the way they're so careful about what they say about him. Two women confirmed Aubrey's mother's story that Clint not only harassed and stalked Aubrey, but that they were also Clint's targets at one time. They never filed charges, but the details of their stories are eerily similar to Aubrey's account of how he used potentially scandalous things about them to keep them quiet and compliant."

"Aubrey told me he released a video of her to everyone in the office."

"He did."

"Why the hell wasn't he fired?"

"The company investigated but couldn't prove the email sent came from him. He used a generic and anonymous email that he set up and deleted once it served the purpose. The company didn't want to face a lawsuit for firing him without proof. He wasn't in the video and said Aubrey just wanted to get him fired because he broke up with her. She accused him of retaliation. He accused her of the same. Aubrey immediately left the company disgraced, so they swept it under the rug and Clint got away with it."

"He gets away with everything." Her mind and heart didn't want to believe Clint could be so cold and callous, but it was obvious the man she'd thought him to be in the beginning was nothing but an illusion hiding a monster.

"I'd like to see him face charges. The two women who were willing to tell me their stories did so with my promise to keep their anonymity."

Liz didn't blame them for wanting to protect their privacy while still trying to get Clint to pay for his wrongdoings. Still . . . "More stories with 'unnamed sources,' lending credibility but not enough to really get people to believe they're absolutely true."

Tim nodded his agreement. "It gives Clint wiggle room to claim they lied and made it up to get back at him for some slight. But it puts Clint on notice that people are paying attention. The cops are looking at him and so am I."

"But he knows interest will fade and he'll be right back to doing what he does." Bitterness filled Trinity's words.

Someone needed to stand up to Clint. "Here's my side, Tim."

"We can take this inside if you'd like." Tim notched his chin toward the spa doors.

She wanted to give him her side, add her voice to the other women who spoke against Clint, and be done with it. "It's a short story that echoes the ones you've probably already heard."

Tim went along with her wishes, pulled out his phone, clicked Record on an app, and held it up for her to speak into. "I dated Clint for nine or ten weeks. The relationship started out good. Normal. Little things tripped my radar. He wanted to keep me all to himself. At first, that seemed nice. Until he made a big deal about me spending time with friends instead of him. He didn't like it when I mentioned my best friend, Tate."

"The man you're seeing now?" Tim asked, making sure he had the details right.

She assumed Detective Valdez told him about her. "Yes. Things changed dramatically when Clint met Tate. Clint staked a claim and made it clear I should not see Tate anymore. I wasn't even willing to entertain the idea of cutting my childhood friend out of my life. Clint got angry. It became a *thing* between us. I didn't like the way Clint handled the situation. He became possessive and aggressive."

"How so?"

"When I broke up with him, he tried to convince me that's not what I wanted at all. I know my own mind. I didn't like being told what I thought. I didn't like the way he tried to make it seem like Tate was playing games with me. I know Tate. That's not him."

"Clint tried to undermine Tate to try to get you back?"

"Yes. And he didn't like that I saw right through him. He confronted me in my condo and things got physical. He grabbed my arm and left bruises. It wasn't the first time he aggressively grabbed me. He frightened me that night. If not for my neighbor pounding on my door threatening to call the cops, I'm not sure what he might have done to me that night. I made it clear we were over and he left. I hoped to never see him again."

"But you did."

"I spotted him watching my place from the parking area of my complex. Another time while I was working at the farmers market, and a couple times when Tate and I were out to eat. I didn't tell Tate because I didn't want them to get into another fight over me."

Trinity pressed her lips together, not liking that Liz kept something from Tate. She'd done it to keep the peace and not let Clint taunt Tate into doing something that would ultimately get him in trouble.

"Clint sent texts and tried to call. I ignored all of them. One day I received texts from Tate saying he didn't want to see me anymore. The texts were hurtful and unlike him, but I believed them because Clint had planted the seed that Tate's interest wasn't genuine. What I didn't know was that Tate had lost his phone that morning."

"You think Clint stole the phone and sent the texts."

"I can't prove it, but it seems suspicious because immediately after I received those afternoon texts Clint surprised me at a place I frequent for lunch. He was kind and consoling. The guy I liked when I started seeing him. He seemed to think we could reconnect since Tate was out of the picture. He played me."

"Because you found out later Tate didn't send those texts."

"Exactly. Tate and I have been friends forever. It was inevitable he'd wonder why I wasn't speaking to him all of a sudden and we'd talk."

"But Clint got you to talk to him again and see him as a good guy?"

"Yes. But I wasn't quite fooled, especially when right after he left the deli Aubrey came up to my table and warned me to stay away from him. Not even half an hour later, she was dead." Tears filled her eyes thinking about that poor, sweet woman who tried to do the right thing and warn a stranger only to end up Clint's victim again.

"So you were the last person to see Aubrey alive."

She shook her head. "I believe Clint saw her talking to me and he killed her."

As if conjured, her real life nightmare walked across the parking lot toward them with an engaging smile that sent a chill racing over every nerve.

"Oh. My. God."

Tim and Trinity followed her gaze.

She couldn't seem to take her eyes off him. You don't when a predator is stalking you. Her gut tightened with that fight-or-flight adrenaline pumping through her veins.

But she stood stock-still—that deer in the headlights stillness coming over her as danger drew near.

She wanted to pull off that amazingly agile leap out of the way, but a stronger part of her wanted to stand her ground, not show any fear, and let him know he wouldn't get away with terrorizing her again.

Tim positioned himself just about in Clint's direct path to her, keeping him from getting too close.

"Liz, you're beautiful as ever." She didn't believe Clint's easy smile or the charm in his voice.

Tim glanced back at Liz. "Go inside. I'll handle this." He held his phone out toward Clint. "Mr. Mayhew, Tim Cobb from the *Examiner*. I was just interviewing Liz about an incident at her home in which you forcibly grabbed her during an argument. Care to comment?"

Liz froze. She wanted to hear Clint try to wiggle his way out of this.

Clint's eyes went wide, dipped to the phone in Tim's hand, then landed and narrowed on her. "Telling lies, Liz. You know I'd never hurt you."

Tim continued his questions. "How many times did you hurt Aubrey Pittman?"

Clint took a step back but caught himself and bolstered his bravado with a hard glare. "You don't know what you're talking about."

"Six domestic disturbance calls where the police notes include visible bruises and marks on Aubrey's person. She filed a restraining order against you. Her mother details several altercations you had with Aubrey."

"Aubrey was a troubled woman with mental health issues. She craved attention and sought it in destructive and hurtful ways. She lied to her mother often to gain sympathy." The lies rolled off his tongue so matter-of-factly, with absolute surety that he was right. He believed what he said. He blamed Aubrey.

Liz got a sinking feeling in her gut.

Tim continued. "Liz is believed to be the last person to see Aubrey alive after Aubrey warned Liz away from you."

"Aubrey had a difficult time letting go. Her death was tragic."

"Her suspicious death is being investigated. Some say she didn't commit suicide but was murdered."

Clint didn't say a word, but the sharp gaze he turned on her incited fear and promised retribution, though she hadn't put the reporter onto this story. And Liz believed Aubrey's story should be told, that Aubrey deserved justice, and Clint should pay.

Tim hit Clint with even more. "Several of your co-workers, past and present, have told me stories of incidents that are incredibly similar to Aubrey's experiences with you. They speak to a pattern of harassment, threats, and abuse that's gone unreported because victims claim you intimidated them. Would you like to comment on that?"

"Print those lies and I'll sue." Clint shook his head at Liz. "I hope you're not involved in this."

"I simply told Tim the truth about what happened between us."

"There's a version of the truth and then there's proof." He glanced back at Tim to make the point that without proof all the reporter had was unsubstantiated accounts and hearsay.

Which is how Clint got away with this for so long.

Tim's phone rang and Clint snagged his arm and held Tim in a tight grip as he read the caller ID alert. "Why is Gabby calling you?"

Liz exchanged confused glances with Trinity.

Tim tugged his arm free. "Let's find out." He swiped to accept the call and put the phone to his ear. "Hello, Gabby." Tim listened, nodding to whatever Gabby said to him. "Thank you for the update. I'd like to speak with you and the others again to get your collective reaction as soon as the company takes action." He listened again. "Great. I'll call you later today." Tim hung up and stared at Clint. "The women I spoke to were reluctant to go on record. After I interviewed them, they got together to talk and console each other about their experiences with you. They compared notes, shared stories, and decided they couldn't face you alone, but together they could stand strong and take their case to your company's HR department as soon as you left for lunch. It doesn't look good for you."

Clint took a menacing step forward, but came up short when Tim didn't back down and stood his ground, blocking Clint from her. "Why the hell are you coming after me?"

"Time's up for guys like you who prey on women and think they can get away with it."

Before Clint did something stupid and acted on the tension between the two men and it came to blows, Liz stepped in. "Just go. I can't prove you stole Tate's phone and sent me those texts, but I know you did it. You haven't listened to me up until now, but I want you to hear this . . . I never want to see you again."

Clint tore his heated gaze from Tim and focused on her, his eyes softening with a plea she didn't believe. "Liz, come on, you can't believe this crap. I only ever wanted to make you happy."

Trinity hooked an arm through hers and stood close. "You hurt her. Tate makes her happy."

"Trinity." Liz warned not to engage with a shake of her head.

Clint pinned Trinity in a hard glare.

Like her, Trinity wasn't one to back down.

Liz put a hand over Trinity's, silently asking her to not antagonize Clint. She took a step back, pulling Trinity with her, and tried to make things clear for Clint one more time. "I have nothing left to say to you. I do not want to see you ever again. You've got a lot to deal with and answer for. Stay away from me." With that, she left Tim standing guard between her and

Clint, turned and walked with Trinity back into her office. Her appetite disappeared with just the sight of Clint showing up here again.

Emmy raised an eyebrow when they walked past her in the reception area, but didn't comment.

Safe in her office, she planted her hands on her desk, hung her head, and sucked in a steadying breath.

Trinity rubbed her shoulder. "He's something else, showing up here, thinking he can just play the nice guy and—"

"I know. But it's done. I hope this time he stays away." She didn't think he would. Liz stood tall and brushed her hair behind her ear. "Sorry about lunch. I'm just not up to going out."

Trinity nodded. "We'll do it another day. Do you want me to call Tate and tell him what happened?"

"I'll tell him when he picks me up."

"Can you believe the women at his work went to HR? I wonder how many there are?"

Liz didn't want to think about how many other women he'd hurt, harassed, or made uncomfortable with his behavior.

"He's finally going to get what's coming." Certainty filled Trinity's voice, but Liz wasn't so sure.

He'd gotten away with it this long. It had to stop, but Clint was cunning. You can't destroy someone's life over accusation and innuendo, but sometimes the bar seemed too high to reach to meet the burden of proof. And that left the door open for offenders to keep hurting others. It emboldened them.

It sounded like Clint's company took the women's claims seriously. She hoped they did the right thing when for so long companies swept this kind of thing under the rug.

"That reporter took me off guard. I had no idea this extended so far and reached into Clint's background and work life."

Trinity touched her arm. "Things like this, it starts off with small things and gets worse. It's a pattern."

Just like the relationship Clint started with her. Sweet talk, enjoyable dates, attention to reel her in, then a backhanded insult she didn't really take seriously, domination of her time and attention until she was solely focused on him. Arguments over small things that didn't really matter but seemed huge to him. Orders to never see Tate again. Her best friend. Promises that things would get better. Vows that he cared so much about her and wanted to make her happy that didn't match the way he acted and treated her.

Never in her life had there been violence in her relationships. That's why Clint's behavior stunned her. She didn't get it. For a moment, she'd wanted to dismiss it. He didn't mean it, she rationalized.

Heat of the moment, and all that.

Worse, he'd made her question whether it was her fault. Had she instigated it? No. But he'd made her second-guess herself more than once.

Clint wanted to wear her down so she'd do whatever he wanted. That's how it felt when Aubrey told her story, that Clint had simply been relentless in his pursuit and holding on to her even when she wanted out.

Liz got out before she got in too deep. So deep she suffocated and went along just so she could breathe.

"Tim's article will make people see Clint for who

he really is. Aubrey's death won't go unnoticed. People will read her story and know what really happened to her even if the cops can't prove what Clint did. Tim will make the public understand that unfortunately this kind of thing happens all the time. Maybe someone will even see themselves in Aubrey and that they're in a destructive relationship and get out."

"I hope so." Trinity adjusted her purse strap on her shoulder. "Do you want me to stick around for a while?"

Liz hugged her. "Thank you for the offer, but I'll be okay." She released Trinity. "I'm not really feeling like cooking tonight. Mind packing up something yummy for Tate, Declan, and me? We'll pick it up on our way home tonight."

Trinity beamed. "Do you really think of the ranch as home now?"

"Tate feels like home." Her heart grew heavy in her chest just thinking about him and how much she loved him. "Without him these last weeks, I don't know what I would have done. This thing with Clint is so worrisome."

Trinity's mouth tilted in a half frown. "Do you think he'll do something to you?"

"I don't know." Another lie she told herself. She knew he wouldn't give up.

She crossed her arms over her middle. "I hope this thing at his work will take the focus off me."

They stared at each other for a long moment, neither of them believing that would happen but pretending to agree her goodbye to Clint today ended this episode in her life.

All she wanted to do was focus on the happiness she found with Tate.

She hoped this dark cloud over their lives had passed and they'd have nothing but sunshine from now on.

Sure, they'd face a few showers in their future, but she didn't mind because with Tate she knew any storm they faced would fade with the brightness of their love.

Chapter Twenty-Two

THE STORIES these women are telling are disturbing."
Dustin, the HR guy sent by the higher-ups in the company to pull Clint into this fishbowl conference room and talk to him about the charges, shook his head. Like he didn't really want to high-five him for fucking the four women huddled together in an office behind them.

"They're lying."

"They were interviewed separately. Their stories are eerily similar."

"Yeah? That's probably because they got together, formed a plan to fuck my life, and handed you a load of bullshit."

Those bitches told every damn little detail about their personal relationships. He broke up with three of them. The other preemptively broke up with him when he'd made it clear he couldn't stand her sniveling one more second.

And today they retaliated because they'd been dumped.

Dustin stared at him. "Never shit where you eat. Four women in the same office. They were bound to talk and compare notes. Women, they do that." He shrugged, and gave Clint a you're-a-dumbshit-for-getting-caught glare.

Clint couldn't decide if the guy was giving him advice for next time or reprimanding him for dating multiple women he worked with.

None of the women who came forward were his subordinates. It didn't matter to HR.

At least his assistant, Kelly, remained loyal and kept her mouth shut about them dating.

But what did it matter, really? He was already screwed.

And Kelly was still in love with him, so she'd probably stick up for him, if nothing else.

"You've put the company in a precarious position. Your contributions have been invaluable, but your behavior can't be excused."

"You're afraid of a lawsuit." Getting rid of him didn't cost them anything.

"They've got a good case. Emails. Voicemails. At best they're unflattering for you, but some of them are outright threatening."

Maybe he'd let his anger get the better of him and he'd gone overboard, but only to ensure they kept quiet about some of the things he'd done because they'd gotten out of line.

All of them knew he had something on them. Still, they came forward. Bitches.

Maybe he'd post some of his home videos for all their friends, neighbors, and families to see. A couple of them had new boyfriends. He bet they had no idea how freaky a couple of those women could be.

Women loved to be wild—so long as they didn't get caught.

A couple of drinks, a few suggestions to see what they liked, what they fantasized about, and with a little coaxing, they forgot their inhibitions and performed for him.

He'd been close with Liz. She hid her passionate side. He wanted to bring that out—just like he did with those other women. With Aubrey.

They all loved it in the moment. Then they got all shy and reserved, but all they really wanted was for him to bring out that wild side again.

All he wanted was a woman who belonged to him. Someone who understood him and wanted to explore and share that kind of limitless passion. Someone who didn't want the outside world intruding on their relationship and the way they wanted to do things.

Women pretended to hesitate because of his appetites and tendencies—Kelly being one of them—but they wanted a take-charge man. They couldn't complain when they got exactly what they wanted.

Damn those women. They should have kept their fucking mouths shut.

Now probably wasn't the best time to think about his revenge, but it was coming. They knew it. They'd been warned.

At least Kelly was smart enough to heed that warning.

"So I don't even get to defend myself? I'm just fired and that's it." He fisted his hands under the table, trying to contain the rage roiling inside him.

Dustin held his hands out over the printed emails. "They used your words against you. I don't see how you can defend this." Dustin shook his head. "You can't." He slid an envelope across the table. "Your final paycheck. Your assistant cleaned out your office. You can pick up the box and I'll show you out."

Clint wanted to deck the guy. How dare they do this to him in such a public way! The entire office staff relegated to their cubicles behind him could see everything happening inside the conference room. He felt their eyes on him. Their collective judgment settled like a heavy blanket over him as Dustin walked him to his office where Kelly, head downcast, handed him the box filled with the few personal items he kept in the office.

She glanced at the women in the office three doors down from his. "All of them?" she whispered. Hurt filled Kelly's eyes.

He gave Kelly a hard glare that warned she better remain loyal and keep her damn mouth shut.

Fuming, he held it together as Dustin walked him past the closed-door office with the glass windows and the women sitting like hens, thinking they were safe from the wolf lurking outside. They weren't.

He walked out of there with his head high, a sly smile, and retribution on his mind.

Those women thought they got the best of him. Well, they'd see.

So would Liz.

Because of her, all this happened.

Aubrey.

The cops coming to his house.

The reporter.

The exes getting back at him.

Losing his job.

Fuck.

Someone had to pay for ruining his life.

Chapter Twenty-Three

LIZ WOKE up draped over Tate's chest. The steady beat of his heart thumped against her ear. His big hands lay warm on her back. The second she tried to move, he hugged her closer and grumbled in his sleep. His fingers brushed up her bare skin and tangled in her hair. Satisfied she was staying put, he settled back into sleep.

She smiled and snuggled into him, content and happy until disturbing thoughts intruded, keeping her from falling back to sleep.

It sucked. She had everything she ever wanted, but this thing with Clint had cast a dark cloud over everything in her life. The article about him would come out today. She'd be tied to him in the story the whole town would probably be talking about for days, if not weeks, to come. She hoped something came of Detective Valdez's investigation into Aubrey's death, but it appeared Clint would get away with that even if he got fired for harassing the women at work.

Those poor women. They endured daily trauma having to see him, knowing he targeted others in the office. They'd been too fearful to come forward until now.

What a mess.

And Clint refused to admit what he'd done to her.

Deny. Deny. Deny. That was his MO.

It worked, so long as he backed off when things got too obvious. And public.

But he was smart and conniving. He went out of his way to get away with his torments even though it drove women, and her, away instead of drawing them in.

What was the point?

Control?

He got off on hurting women?

Both?

Something even more disturbing and twisted?

"You're thinking so loud, you woke me up." Tate grumbled but still ran his fingers through her hair to soothe her. "What's the matter, sweetheart?"

"He won't quit."

"If he knows what's good for him, he'll stay away from you before he does something he can't squirm out of." Tate wiped his hand over his face. "Sorry. I'm still half asleep. That wasn't very comforting."

"I think it's true. He was furious yesterday, though he tried to control it. But for a second, I thought he might do something to Tim. Or me. He killed Aubrey because she spoke to me about what he did to her. What if he goes after the women at his work? What if he comes after me for talking to the reporter?"

Tate kissed her on the head. "I will do everything I can to protect you, sweetheart. With all the trouble he's in right now, let's hope saving his own ass takes precedence over revenge."

"That's just it, I think revenge is his default for every little slight. We were dating, but it wasn't serious. I break things off and he takes it so personally. Yes, it's personal. I get that maybe he wishes things could have been different, that his feelings ran deeper than mine, but you don't order that person to be your girlfriend again. You don't tell her it's not over because you say so. I mean, he never said he loved me or anything. So why hold on so tight."

"You gave him something he doesn't want to lose."

"I don't know what that was because things started off fun but that faded when we didn't connect on a deeper level."

"Stop analyzing it. You didn't do anything wrong. Nothing you did warranted his retaliation, or this continued pursuit. Maybe it's as simple as he can't have you, so he wants you."

"That's childish."

"Yes. It is. And it pisses me off. I don't like the way he's upset you and turned your life upside down. You spend your whole day looking over your shoulder. You jump when your phone rings. We talk far too much about your ex instead of *our* future." Bitterness tinged those words along with his frustration.

She raised her head and set her chin on her hand on his chest so she could look at him in the gray light. "I'm sorry, Tate."

"Not your fault," he snapped, then took a breath to calm down. "I want this to be over as much as you do so we can get on with living our lives. I want you waking up in the morning—not this godawful early—thinking about me. Us. Not him."

"What about us?" She slipped her leg over his thigh and rubbed her foot up and down his calf.

His hand dipped down to her hip and covered her ass. "I like where your mind is going now."

She brushed her fingertips down his belly and over his thick erection.

"And where you're putting that hand." His slipped over her rump, and his fingers teased her soft folds before one long finger dipped inside her.

She rocked back into his hand at the same tempo she stroked his length up and down.

"Damn woman, I can't get enough of you."

They'd made love twice last night. One quickie against the closed bedroom door because they needed to take the edge off after she told him about her confrontation with Clint at lunch. Then he'd made slow, sweet love to her after they cuddled on the couch and watched another episode of *Ray Donovan*.

Fast or slow, didn't matter. Every time they came together, it was never enough.

Like right now.

He stroked her with those magic fingers to a fever pitch. She kissed him hard and deep, then nipped at his chin. "Condom. Now."

She didn't need to ask twice or wait. By the time she slipped her leg over his hips and rocked back, he had the condom rolled on and her taking him in deep. She rocked against him. His hands clamped tight on her hips. She sat up and stared down at him. Golden stubble darkened his jaw and glinted in the soft morning light just starting to filter through the blinds. His blue eyes stared back at her full of want and need and so much more.

"I love you." She needed him to know that, to feel it in her.

Tate rose up and wrapped his arms around her, pulling her down harder on his lap. "I love you. I don't ever want to lose you." He moved under her. She rocked over him, her arms locked around his neck, their lips pressed together. They lost themselves in each other, the dawn, and a memory of this moment they'd never forget.

Tate fell back on the bed taking her down with him. She took advantage of more room to move and spent ten minutes making him crazy to the point he finally stopped letting her lead and took control, thrusting deep and grinding against that sweet little spot. Her body responded with an explosion of rippling pleasure that made her gasp and smile all at once. Tate thrust deep several more times and found that same burst of passion as she sank her teeth into the ridge of his shoulder where it met his neck. She ran her tongue over the small hurt as he settled into the bed beneath her, his big hands covering her ass, his breath heaving in and out.

She smiled against his neck.

"Pretty proud of yourself, aren't you?" His deep voice vibrated against her lips nibbling at his neck.

"Yes I am. Why? Should I try again?"

His hands squeezed her ass to hold her still. "I'm good. So good."

She giggled, feeling wicked. "Just good?" She rolled her hips against his still-hard flesh.

He clamped down harder. "Great. Fantastic. Totally spent. I won't walk for a week." He adjusted his back.

He'd been working so hard to keep up with things on the ranch and take her to and from work.

She leaned up on her hands and stared at the dark smudges marring the underside of his eyes. She brushed her thumb over his cheek. "I'm sorry you're not getting much sleep."

"I'm not." He didn't look one bit unhappy about it. His gaze dipped down between the two of them. His hands came up and covered her breasts, then went up her neck to her face. "You're the best way to wake up in the morning." He pulled her down for a sweet kiss. "I want to wake up to you naked on top of me every morning."

She smiled down at him. "Well, I will be naked all the time if I don't go pick up some more clothes from my place. I need to do laundry and clean out my fridge." She'd been staying at Tate's so long some of the stuff had to be spoiled by now.

His smile vanished.

Anxious butterflies filled her stomach. "What?"

"What if you didn't go home?"

She tilted her head and teased him. "Am I supposed to just buy new clothes?"

He shook his head. "No. Um. I mean, what if you didn't move back into your condo? What if you moved in here? With me. Permanently."

Stunned, she stared at him, trying to make her brain function when her heart jumped up and down in her chest like a toddler who got a puppy.

"Um."

Tate held her face, the way he did when he wanted her to really hear him.

"Move in with me. I don't want to spend another night without you. I don't want to wake up without you."

"What about Declan?" Why the hell was she thinking when her heart wanted her to spit out the only acceptable answer? *YES!*

"He has to get his own woman."

She smacked his shoulder. "Not funny."

"Neither is making me squirm while you make up your mind."

"I can't believe this is happening."

"Haven't we waited long enough for what we both want? It's not ideal to be here with my brother two doors down the hall, I get that. But Drake and Adria will be out of the cabin soon. It'll be ours. Declan and I already talked about it."

"You did?"

"Yeah, when Drake and Adria got engaged and bought their place."

So not because Tate started seeing her.

"Wipe that look off your face. I want you to live with me. I've never wanted that with anyone else."

She pressed her finger to his lips. "You don't need to convince me, Tate. I've only ever wanted you." That was a truth she'd learned to live with.

"Say yes," he pleaded. "I have plans to fix it up. Add on a couple more rooms and stuff to make it ours."

She couldn't believe she'd ever doubted Tate's sudden change in feelings for her. Or his commitment to her. He loved her. All the way. All in. "I'll put my place up for sale. It shouldn't take long to find a buyer. We can use the money to redo the cabin."

He shook his head. "I can't let you do that."

"Why? It's going to be our house, right?"

"Yes, but . . ." He didn't finish that sentence.

"If it's ours, then the money I get from the sale of my place is ours, too, right?"

"I want to take care of you."

"You do, Tate. In so many ways. But a relationship is a partnership. Maybe it's not always even, but both people have to contribute so that it feels fair and balanced to both people. I want to do this. In fact, I've often thought of how we could turn that place into our place."

One eyebrow shot up. "You have?"

"Daydreamed about a life with you? Yes. All the time."

He sank his fingers deep into her hair. "This might be new to me, but I can't see my future without you in it anymore. All I think about is you and me and the life we'll have together."

She met him halfway for the kiss they both craved.

The shower down the hall went on.

Tate tore his lips from hers and swore. "I was supposed to have the horses fed and the stalls cleaned before Declan went down to make breakfast." He tried to set her aside and roll out from under her, but she put her hand to his chest.

"I'll go start on the horses. You grab a cup of coffee and take a shower."

Tate shook his head all through that. "I'll take care of it."

"You take care of too much. Let me do this. I'm more than capable of shoveling shit and feeding the horses."

Tate laughed. "I could use a hot shower." He squirmed beneath her.

She helped ease the pain in his back by sliding off him and out of bed to grab her clothes. "Take your time. Bring me some coffee when you're done." She wiggled on her panties and jeans and found her bra in the corner of the room where Tate tossed it last night.

"I just want to lie here and watch you get dressed." His mischievous grin made her smile with him. "Though I prefer it when you strip."

"Later, cowboy. I've got horses waiting on me." She hooked the bra in place and pulled on Tate's T-shirt from yesterday. It smelled like him. And so did she after she'd spent the night snuggled up to him and they'd made love.

She quickly put on a clean pair of socks and found her pair of worn boots next to the dresser. She turned to kiss Tate and found him still smiling at her, adorably rumpled along with their bed. "God, you're gorgeous." She took in every rippling muscle and the sheet barely covering his hips and legs. Centerfold worthy. "I can't believe I'm moving in with you."

"I can't believe it took me so damn long to ask you."

"It's only been a couple weeks."

"You know what I mean."

"We have the rest of our lives together now." She leaned down and kissed him. The same zing of lust ran through her along with that other thing that always made her heart glow so warm and bright in her chest she expected it to burst free. Instead, it filled her up with so much love she felt lucky to have found something so wondrous.

"Watch out for Mugsy. He likes to nip to get your attention."

"Maybe I should do that to you." She leaned down and softly bit his chest.

He hissed, but it was pure pleasure, not pain. "You have my full attention anytime you're near."

She pressed down on her hands, kissed the spot she'd nipped, then stood and headed for the door. "Don't keep me waiting on that coffee, cowboy."

"You waited on me long enough."

She stopped in the open doorway and turned back to him, her gaze taking in his toned, bronzed body and the smile that was just for her. "Totally worth the wait."

"I'm going to marry you, you know?" That cocky grin made her laugh, but the words took her back to kindergarten and lunch on the playground when she'd announced her intention to marry him.

"I told you, you would." With that, she left him with the biggest smile she'd ever seen on his face and headed down to do the chores and bask in the love brightening her whole life and future.

Chapter Twenty-Four

LIZ COULDN'T stop smiling and thought she wouldn't mind being this happy the rest of her life. Nothing could kill this buzz. Not even Mugsy and his incessant attempts to take a bite out of her. She caught his head with her hand on his long nose and shoved him out of the way again as she tried to fill his water bucket.

"Keep it up and I'll bite you."

He shook his big brown head up and down and neighed at her.

"Flirt," she teased him and locked the gate behind her as she exited his stall. Only three more to go.

She hoped Tate enjoyed his shower, but she could sure use a cup of coffee about now. She'd prepared the pot and turned on the machine before leaving the house. Declan usually made pancakes on his mornings to cook and after all the work she'd done, she'd need a triple stack to fill the hunger gnawing at her belly.

The physical labor loosened her tired muscles and worked some she didn't even know she had. No wonder Tate had all those ripped muscles.

She tossed the hose on the floor and went to the grain bucket to get a scoop for the next horse.

"This is what you wanted instead of being with me." That accusing voice stopped her cold.

She froze, bent over the grain pail, at the sound of Clint's resentful voice.

"Horse shit and dirt. Horses trying to bite you at the crack of dawn." His voice drew nearer as he spoke those bitter words.

She spun around to face him. "What the hell are you doing here?"

The smell of stale whiskey and vomit clung to his rumpled clothes. His hair was a mass of haphazard brown spikes and curls. Bloodshot eyes locked on her and filled with hate. "Do you seriously want this?" He held his hands out wide to take in the massive stable.

She remained calm and didn't bother to answer his question because she'd made what she wanted perfectly clear. "Have you been up all night?"

"Well, I have an empty apartment and no fucking job to go to today, so I went to the bar last night to drown my sorrows."

"Did you spend the night there?"

Swaying side to side on his widespread feet, he squinted at her. "Sleep?" He made a *pfting* noise that sent spittle flying and tried to stay upright and not face-plant on the cement floor. "Got me a bottle and drove way the hell out here to bum-fuck-nowhere and waited for a chance to see you *alone*." He shot his pointed finger out at her. "He never leaves you alone!"

For good reason. Look what happened when she was by herself for an hour.

Clint glanced around, his body swaying in the direction his head went. "Where is Loverboy?"

She didn't want to rile him with talk of Tate. "Clint, what are you doing here? We have nothing left to say to each other." So much for disengaging. She wanted him gone, but he shouldn't be driving anywhere in his condition. She wished she'd brought her cell phone down to the stables with her. She'd call the cops as soon as she could—or as soon as she could make a run for it to the office.

She chanced a glance down the alleyway and gauged whether she could run for the office and make it before Clint caught her.

"I have things to say!" He took a step toward her.

"Don't fucking move." Drake's booming voice echoed through the stables as his dog, Sunny, crouched low beside him and growled.

Clint's eyes went wide when Drake cocked the rifle, put the butt up to his shoulder, and aimed for Clint's head.

Clint stared at her. "This is all your fault."

Anger simmered in her gut. She wanted to unleash it on him. But she didn't say a word, just watched Declan and Tate walk in the stables at Clint's back and out of Drake's line of fire.

Tate made his way closer, never taking his eyes off Clint. "Step away from her. You're trespassing. Cops are on the way."

Clint notched back one side of his mouth. "He is constantly coming between us."

She held her hand up to signal that she didn't want him any closer. "I'm sorry things didn't work out for us, but you knew how close I was to Tate when we started seeing each other."

He fisted his hands at his sides. "So you get what you want and I get fucked."

"You did that to yourself," Tate snapped. "She never did anything to you."

"She was mine first!" Clint looked over his shoulder at Tate. "She was in my bed before yours. I know every inch of her," he taunted, making her stomach pitch.

Her skin crawled just thinking about him putting his hands on her. She hated that she'd ever slept with a monster like him. Liz regretted every second she'd spent with Clint, never more so than right now. "That's enough."

Throwing sleeping with her in Tate's face was lower than low. She would hate it if someone Tate once dated threw it in her face. Decent people didn't do stuff like that. Their pasts didn't matter. Only what they shared now.

She glanced at Tate. His lips pressed tight with anger that matched the fury in his eyes. He shook his head like nothing Clint said would get to him. She hoped not, but it made her worry and even angrier. And she focused that anger on Clint.

"I haven't gotten near enough of you." The lascivious look Clint gave her made her skin crawl. The thought of him ever touching her again disgusted her.

"Touch her and you're dead." The venomous tone conveyed how much Tate meant every word.

Clint used his liquor-fueled courage to take a step toward her. "I will make you pay for Aubrey, talking to that reporter, those women turning on me. Everything." Clint lunged for her, his hand brushing her face, a nail scratching her cheek as Tate grabbed a hatchet from the work bench next to her and clubbed him with the wood handle. Clint fell to his knees, then landed in a heap on his side. Blood poured out of a cut on his temple where a goose egg lump rose.

Tate caught her before her knees buckled and wrapped her in his arms, her head pressed to his chest.

She put her hand over her stinging cheek and stared at Clint's limp body.

Drake came up beside her. "You okay?"

"Yeah. Thanks for coming to the rescue."

Adria appeared at Drake's arm and put her hand on his shoulder. "I saw someone sneaking into the stables, sent Drake, and called Tate."

Tate brushed his hand over Liz's hair. "I grabbed Declan and hauled ass down here."

Declan didn't even have his boots on. "I called the cops." Declan notched his chin toward Drake. "Better put that away before the cops get here."

Drake handed the rifle to Adria and pushed Clint over onto his stomach with his booted foot, none too gently. He grabbed a rope off the wall and tied Clint's hands behind his back.

Tate walked her away from Clint. He pulled a paper towel from the holder on the wall above the sink across from them, wet it, and pressed it to the cut on her face.

She hissed in pain. For such a tiny thing, it stung like hell.

"It's not bad. Probably heal in a day or so."

She leaned into Tate's hand. "Why the hell would he come here? He had to know it would only get him in more trouble."

Tate pulled her into his chest and held her tight.

"Christ, Liz, I thought he might hurt you before I got here."

She pushed out of his arms letting her adrenaline-fueled anger reign. "I should be able to walk around my home without worrying about being jumped by a drunk ex, for God's sake."

Tate gave her a silly and completely out of place grin. "What?"

"Your home?"

"I live here. With you. So why the hell does he think anything he does will change the past or the future. I'm here. I don't want to even see him let alone be with him again, so what the fuck!"

"He's a serious threat." Drake stated the obvious, and the impact of it hit hard. "He's bold enough to come here knowing you've got the three of us to protect you. Even if he didn't count on me and Declan, he knew Tate hasn't left you alone outside of work where you're surrounded by people since Aubrey's death."

Liz waved her hand out toward Clint. "He's drunk. He wasn't thinking."

"This time. Next time . . ." Tate left the rest unsaid, because there was no telling what Clint might do.

Declan waved the sheriff's deputy inside and met him halfway, explaining what happened with an angry, disgusted look on his face and a pointed finger at Clint lying on the floor.

Tate held her hand as the officer approached.

"I'll need to take your statement and a picture of your injury." First, the officer and Drake helped Clint sit up. Drake muscled Clint up with his hand hooked under Clint's armpit and practically plopped him on his feet with a thud. Clint wobbled, spotted her again, and tried to come after her. Drake held him in place and frowned at the sad, drunken attempt Clint failed to pull off without looking stupid and weak.

And it made him even more dangerous.

"This is all your fault. You're going to pay for this." The slurred words didn't erase the veracity of the threat.

The officer tugged Clint away from her with a "Keep tacking on the charges, buddy."

It took ten minutes for all of them to give their statements separately. The officer laid out the charges—trespassing and assault the only ones that carried any weight—Clint would be in and out of jail in a day. If that. Especially if Clint did the smart thing and got a lawyer.

Drake and Declan offered to finish off the three horse stalls she hadn't done.

Lost in her swirling thoughts, she headed for the house.

Tate caught up to her in the driveway. "Hey, where are you going?"

"I'm going to shower and head over to my place to get some clothes and other things I need."

"I'll drive you."

She shook her head. "You don't need to do that."

"I want to."

Frustration got the better of her. "He's in jail. I can drive myself."

Tate's lips tilted in a dejected half frown that made her feel guilty for snapping at him. "I'm sorry." She raked her fingers through her messy hair and tucked it behind her ear. "I'm tired of not being able to do what I want, when I want. I can't even do chores on the ranch without him mucking that up. He ruined a perfectly great morning."

Tate reached out and put his hand on her shoulder. "I know, sweetheart, I'm sorry."

"Don't be sorry. He's the shithead who can't take no for an answer. And he blames me! I'm supposed to pay because *he's* a jerk. What the hell did I do?"

"Nothing." Tate's even tone only irritated her more because it proved she'd lost her mind and was yelling for no reason.

She sighed out a huge breath. "Sorry. I'm doing exactly what he does—taking out my anger on someone who doesn't deserve it."

"I'm pissed, too. I can't even protect you on my own property. He got close enough to hurt you." Tate brushed his thumb over the barely anything scratch. "What if he'd done worse? Or he took you. Hell, he had enough time to shoot you." Luckily, only Drake brought a gun, just in case.

She put both hands on his chest. "Tate, I'm fine."

"He took Aubrey without anyone seeing him. He got her up to that bridge and pushed her off."

The nightmare image that evoked sent a chill through her.

Her first instinct was to soothe Tate by telling him they didn't know that for sure, but in her heart, she knew. Clint was capable of much worse violence. She saw it in his flat eyes and heard it in his heartless words. He didn't express any sympathy or remorse for what happened to Aubrey or what he did to her and others.

He never apologized for accosting her in her condo. Everything was someone else's fault.

"It's not your sole responsibility to guard me. I know you want to—"

"I want to lock you in a room until he's behind bars for life or dead." Tate glanced down to the stables. "If Adria hadn't seen him coming . . ."

"I had a shovel at hand and a bunch of tools. Like the one you used," she pointed out. "I'd have screamed for you. I'd have run."

Tate's eyes filled with a plea and dread. "And what if none of that was enough?"

"I don't know. But I can't spend my whole life worrying about what if and not living my life." She patted his chest before he went off again. "I'm not saying I won't be careful. More so now that I don't even feel safe here."

Tate's head fell back before he looked at her again. "I hate that."

"Me too, but I'm going to take Detective Valdez's advice and press charges. Hopefully, I can get a restraining order."

Tate waved that off. "A piece of paper isn't going to stop him."

"I don't think so either, but I want to have everything in place for the next time he comes after me."

"He's not going to stop." Tate's obvious statement held all the inevitability they both felt.

"This isn't what you signed up for."

"Yeah it is. Good times and bad. That's the deal, right? You and me and whatever comes our way."

She went up on tiptoe, wrapped her arms around his

neck, and hugged him tight and didn't let go. "You are the best man I know. Whatever happens, I'm so lucky we've shared this amazing thing between us."

"Don't talk like it's going to end."

"Not if I can help it."

He stepped back and took her by the shoulders. "We're going to have everything we talked about this morning and more."

She gave him a quick kiss. "I hope so." With that, she walked up to the house and went up to the room they shared together. They dreamed of making the cabin home. A space for the two of them to spread out and fill with their things and their memories.

If Clint thought he could jeopardize that or take it away from her, he had another think coming. She was tired of playing defense. Time to take action.

So she showered, changed, grabbed the empty duffel bags so she could pack up more of her things and bring them here, and headed out.

Of course, Tate spotted her coming and met her by her car. "I'll take you into town."

"I'm doing this on my own. Need anything?"

"Just you." The sweet talker, he always knew just what to say.

"I'll be home soon."

He smiled that she called this place home. Truthfully, she'd be at home wherever she was with him.

They shared a goodbye kiss that promised there'd be a lot more of them waiting for her when she returned.

"Don't be too long. I won't have anything fun to do here while you're gone."

She beamed. "I like the fun things we do." She purred

out the words to tempt, tease, and flirt, and also to let him know she had her feet back under her after Clint knocked her for a loop this morning.

She tossed the bags in the back seat, jumped in behind the wheel, waved to Tate, and headed out. A surprise waited at the end of the long driveway and just a few hundred feet down the main road where Clint's car was being pulled out of a ditch where the front end had struck a tree. Not much damage from what she could see, but it could have been a hell of a lot worse. The winding road was dangerous at night with deer and other animals crossing. You had to be alert. Driving it drunk—she shook her head—stupid and careless. He could have killed someone, or been killed if he slammed into a deer.

Well, she wasn't going to be stupid or careless about the situation with Clint.

She had a few ideas of ways to protect herself.

Clint might think she was an easy target. If he came after her again, he'd find out differently and regret it.

Chapter Twenty-Five

Tate spent the last four hours with his gut tied in knots. With Clint in jail, he didn't need to worry about him confronting Liz. He called Detective Valdez to make sure he knew about the arrest. Valdez assured Tate he was working on making a murder charge stick. So far he had no witnesses who had seen Clint with Aubrey out by the lake and bridge.

The trespassing and assault may be the only thing that stuck to Clint.

Tate wanted to hit something.

Liz had woken up happy and excited about their future. Five minutes with Clint and he ruined another day for her.

"She's back," Declan called from the front of the stables where he signed off on a hay delivery.

Tate left the tractor carburetor he'd been cleaning on the workbench, grabbed a rag to wipe off his hands, and headed for the door.

"She looks tired."

Yeah, well, they didn't get much sleep last night and she had a rough morning. But he planned to make sure she had a good night.

Declan slapped him on the shoulder. "I'll finish with the tractor. Go take care of her."

Tate appreciated it, but hated to leave even more work for Declan, who put in more than his fair share of hours. "I'll finish up before I take her to dinner."

Declan gave him a shove toward the house. "Go make her smile."

"My favorite thing to do."

Declan seemed to catch the innuendo and headed in to finish putting the tractor engine back together. The last thing Declan needed right now was more things to solve. If the fix worked, Declan could end his day on a high note.

Ask him, Declan needed *someone* to tinker with instead of the tractor and this ranch.

Liz pulled two stuffed bags out of the back seat of her car and headed up to the house. He followed, hoping to brighten her day. He had a few ideas up his sleeve on just the right way to do that. After all, he knew her better than anyone.

He thought about proposing tonight, but didn't want to tie their engagement to what happened with Clint this morning.

He wanted Liz to look back on the day he proposed and smile and not have a single thing darken the memory.

With Clint haunting her life, Tate wondered how long it would take to find the right moment.

Fuck that. He wasn't going to let another man dictate when he proposed to the woman he loved. But he did have one thing to do before he asked her. Maybe it was old-fashioned, but his mama raised him to do things the right way.

He walked up to the house and found Liz in their room hanging some of her clothes in the closet. It did something weird to his stomach to see her clothes hanging next to his.

She turned and jumped back, pressing her hand to her chest as she gasped with surprise. "You scared me."

"Sorry. I thought you heard me coming up the stairs."

She dropped her hand. "Lost in thought, I guess. How was your day?"

"It sucked. I didn't spend it with you."

A fleeting smile tilted her lips. "I took some time to clean up my place in addition to packing some stuff, which led to sorting out my clothes and bagging some things up that I'll donate. I've got way more than I need."

"Said no woman I've ever known."

Another quick smile. She was warming up and getting out of her head. "Oh yeah? Are you going to build me a huge closet with the addition to the cabin?"

"Anything you want." He tilted his head. "Well, within reason. But I promise your closet will definitely be bigger than mine."

This time the smile lasted a few seconds longer. "What did you do today?"

"Not much. Fixed a busted gate on the bull pen. Checked on the cows in the south pasture. Rescued a cow that got stuck in some mud. Helped the farrier shoe a couple of the horses and trim a couple others' hooves. Tore apart the tractor engine. What else did you do besides sort and pack your clothes?"

"Stopped by and saw my parents. I updated them on the whole Clint situation. They're worried, but happy I'm here with you and your brothers looking out for me."

That made him feel better. "How are your mom and dad?"

"Good."

"Did you mention moving in here with me?"

She stopped pulling clothes from the bag and looked at him. "Not specifically. Like your brothers, they think it's inevitable we'll be together now." She set a pocketknife on the dresser by her phone.

"What's with the knife?"

"I thought I'd carry it with me now. Just in case. My dad gave it to me when I moved in to my own place. It's been in a drawer ever since. But now . . ." She thought she needed it to feel safe.

She'd spent her whole life living like nothing bad would ever happen to her. Not anymore.

Yep. He should have beat the hell out of Clint this morning.

"You know what? Let's go out to dinner." Tate moved past her and went to the closet and pulled out the sexy black dress she'd hung up. He turned and held it out to her. "Put this on." He found a black lace bra stacked with the white and nude everyday ones in the drawer and handed it to her. "And this." He let his gaze roam down to her hip-hugging jeans. "Panties optional." He gave her a wicked smile. "Surprise me."

The smile stayed on her face this time. "How long will that dress stay on me?"

"Most likely through dinner. Once you're back in the truck, I can't make any promises." He tossed the dress onto the bed next to piles of T-shirts and pants, flung one side of the bra around her waist and caught the end with his free hand, and used the bra to pull her in close. "Put on that sexy dress, go to dinner with me, and let's forget about everything but you and me for a little while."

She clasped her hands at the back of his neck. "You are always the best part of my day."

The kiss they shared nearly buckled his knees and had him tumbling her onto the bed. But he held it together and took a step back even though he wanted to strip her bare and get closer.

He released one side of the bra and draped it over her shoulder. "I'm going to shower off the day." He smelled like motor oil and horses. "Get ready."

She had a better idea and hooked her hand in the front of his jeans and tugged him close. "I could use a shower, too. Wanna share?"

"I've been sharing my cookies, French fries, and life with you forever. Why not a shower," he teased.

She reached over his shoulder, grabbed a handful of his sweaty shirt, and dragged it over his head and down his arms as he leaned over. Her eyes landed on his chest and that glint of appreciation in her eyes made him hard and hungry for her.

She tossed the shirt on top of the laundry pile, took his hand, and pulled him toward the door. Once she had him in the bathroom and the door locked, clothes went flying. He appreciated her expediency and thoughtfulness to turn the shower on to heat wearing nothing but pink with white polka-dot panties while she watched him drag off his boots and jeans. He didn't know why, but those dots drove him crazy. Everything about her made him want her these days. And he loved it. And her for being perfect for him.

He kept the condom he pulled out of his jeans in his hand and stepped under the hot spray. He let his gaze follow those dots down her thighs and legs until she kicked the panties away and stood for a second just so he could look at her.

He took a step toward her, hooked his hand at the back of her neck, and coaxed her into the shower. "Come here."

Skin met skin and warmed under the hot water sluicing over them as his tongue slid along hers in a deep kiss he dragged out just so they could enjoy being this close.

Liz hooked her leg over his hip. He slid his hand down her belly and dipped it between her spread thighs and found her wet and slick with desire. Her hips rocked forward and met his wandering fingers. He slid one, then two inside her. She nipped his shoulder and her nails bit into his back. He had her panting and moaning against his neck as she rocked against his hand and shattered with a scream he captured with another deep kiss. She leaned into him and he slid his hand up her body to cup her breast and sweep his thumb over her tight nipple.

She stepped back and took the condom from him. He took advantage of the space and leaned down and took her nipple in his mouth and suckled and licked while he filled his hand with her other breast and made her sigh. He could listen to her do that all day.

He heard the tearing of the condom wrapper and his cock twitched.

She pushed him up so she could get her hands on him. She stroked his length and he let his head fall back under the spray and just enjoyed the feel of her hand working his hard flesh and the water running over his head and down his back.

She rolled the condom on, then turned her back to him, bent over, pressed her hands against the wall, and looked at him over her shoulder. He knew that come-get-me look and gripped her hips and thrust deep, her round rump slamming into his hips as he seated himself deep in her heat. His groan echoed off the walls.

She pulled forward, then pushed back into him. He took her need and moved with her, holding her hips and guiding her back and forth as he lost himself in the rhythm and feel of her. Unable to hold on for much longer with her driving him to the edge with every push of her ass against him, he slid one hand around her hip and down to where they were joined. He slid the pad of his middle finger over that sweet little spot and made her sigh and rock against him.

"Yes, Tate. More," she begged.

He gave it to her, thrusting deep and circling that little nub until her body tightened around his and she shattered. He gripped her hips and thrust deep again setting off another round of aftershocks as her core locked tight around his shaft and he came seconds before his body pinned hers against the wall and he buried his face in her damp hair.

He slipped his hand over her belly and held her against him. "Damn, honey. You okay?"

She snuggled back into him and reached back and

rubbed her hand down his ass and thigh. "I'm really, really good."

He separated from her, touched her hip to make her turn around while he pulled off the condom, opened the shower door, and tossed it in the trash. Liz settled back against the wall so he could lean in, kiss her, and press his forehead to hers. Eyes locked, he traced a finger along the side of her face. "How'd I get so lucky?"

She smiled and his heart jumped. "I'm very patient."

He couldn't help it—he laughed and it filled him with so much love for her he had to kiss her again. "Man, I hit the jackpot."

She slid her hands over his chest and smiled even bigger. "We both did."

He hooked his arm around her waist, picked her up off her feet, spun her around, and set her right under the shower spray. Water drenched her to the point she sputtered and smacked his arm to let her go so she could wipe her face. She smiled and laughed and he just took her in.

"Are you trying to drown me?" Not an ounce of reproach filled those words.

He squirted shampoo into his hand. "I love it when you laugh." He rubbed his hands together, then washed her hair for her, massaging her scalp as she ran the bar of soap over his chest and arms. "I like this."

"We're never going to make it to dinner."

"Sure we will. We'll just have fun getting there."

And they did enjoy the rest of their shower, hands sliding over each other, sweet kisses and love bites that drew them closer and erased all the tension from their day.

By the time they dried off, dressed, and were ready

to leave they were thinking only about each other and what they anticipated doing after dinner.

They held hands on the long drive into town. He couldn't help sliding his hand over her knee and up her thigh to get a tempting peek at what she wore under the dress. Black lace. He'd pull it off with his teeth later. But for now, they flirted and seduced each other with long looks, sweet kisses, and tempting strokes.

Nothing intruded on their intimate night. He took her to her favorite Mexican restaurant. They sat close and talked in low tones, except when he made her laugh. Then she let loose and he just wanted to make her do it again.

He stopped on the way home at the bakery she loved. Minutes from closing, he managed to snag the last piece of her favorite triple chocolate cake. She fed him bites on the long drive and they demolished it well before they made it to the ranch driveway.

The lights were out but the sky sparkled with a trillion stars. They stood in the drive with their heads tilted back looking up at heaven. Then he looked at her and knew he'd found his heaven on earth.

He took her up to their room, undressed her slowly, enjoying all that creamy skin encased in black lace as long as he could endure it, before he laid her on the sheets and made love to her like it was the first, last, everything.

With her head on his chest, he held her close as the night waned and the quiet surrounded them and left him with an overwhelming feeling of contentment.

"I love you," she whispered, but he felt so much more than her simple words, because he felt the wonder of what they'd shared tonight and how it engulfed and connected them in an awe-inspiring way.

"I love you." He gave the words back to her, feeling them as wholly as she did.

He had the woman of his dreams in his arms and a future he couldn't wait to happen.

He thanked God, the universe, and her for giving him this.

No one would ever come between them. No one would ever take her from him. He'd do everything in his power to make her life as happy as they'd been tonight and more. He wanted her to have everything. He wanted everything with her.

And anyone who tried to take that from them better watch out.

Chapter Twenty-Six

TATE WOKE up to a blustery cold Monday morning and a purpose gnawing at his gut. Something he needed to get done today. He and Liz shared a great morning, exchanging flirty smiles as they both reminisced about their amazing weekend together without saying a word. He loved this new thing between them where a shared look said way more than words.

He dropped Liz at work because he also woke up to a text from Detective Valdez that Clint was out on bail. He'd wanted to keep that piece of news to himself until he dropped her off, so they had a little more time to just be together without the outside world intruding. But of course she read the distress on his face and figured it out.

And Clint ruins the day again.

Tate worked at the ranch all day with a ball of anxiety roiling in his gut. Now that he was about to get this done, he worried even more about how this would go.

He stood at Liz's parents' front door and ran his hand over his button-down white shirt and pounding heart. He'd worn black pants and his good boots. He wanted to look like a guy who deserved a woman like Liz.

He took a deep breath and knocked. He shifted his

weight from one foot to the other and back before he caught himself and stood still. Footsteps approached the door. His stomach dropped, but he held it together. He knew the Scotts like he knew his own family. He'd been welcomed into their home too many times to count.

Of course, things got a little awkward during the teenage years when Mr. Scott eyed him every time he came over, probably because he thought like a lot of people that something was going on between him and Liz.

Not so then, but man, flip a switch and he couldn't get enough of her.

Mr. Scott probably didn't want to know about that.

The door opened and Tate tried to hold it together and smile without his nerves showing. He wanted them to see he came with a purpose and that what he wanted mattered. More than he ever thought possible.

"Tate," Mrs. Scott said, looking him up and down. "Are you okay?"

Great. She knew him so well, she saw everything with one look. "I'm fine. Thank you for allowing me to come over and speak with you." He glanced past her to the empty living room. "Is Mr. Scott home?"

"He just arrived. Please, come in." She waved him forward. "We're very curious about your call. While Liz has shared some of what's happening, we know she's holding back details and keeping up a brave front. How is she? Really?"

"She's upset, but doing well." He did everything he could to tip the scales to happy for her every day. He admired her strength and perseverance to push through and not let Clint rule her life.

Tate stood in the living room where he'd played everything from Go Fish to Scrabble with Liz. He'd killed her at War every time. She'd dominated at Battleship. Liz's parents never minded him or any of Liz's other friends dropping by for hours. An only child, Liz never lacked for friends her own age, and for a long time they were like brother and sister, though he never thought of her that way. She was Liz. His friend. The one person who was always there for him besides Trinity and his brothers.

He liked her because she was different from them. She said things differently, and whatever it was about, it just made sense to him.

"Tate?"

He gave himself a mental shake and tried to pay attention. "Yeah?"

Mrs. Scott gave him a knowing smile, understanding this was a different kind of visit from the afternoons he spent here after school. "Can I get you something to drink?"

"No, thank you."

Mr. Scott walked in, hand held out, a curious look in his eyes, too.

Tate shook his hand and tried not to fidget. "Good to see you again, sir."

Mr. Scott's eyebrow went up. "When did Ken turn into sir?"

Tate raked his fingers over his head. "Sorry. It's been a while."

"Time doesn't make us any less friends, I hope." Ken put his arm around Leslie's shoulders and hugged her close. Two indulgent parents staring at him with amused smirks.

He had a feeling they knew why he was here. It didn't make it any easier to do this.

"Let's sit." Leslie held her hand out to one of the club chairs facing the sofa across a coffee table.

He pulled the box from his pocket, held it covered in his hand as he sat on the edge of the seat and put his hands on his knees.

"How are your mom and dad? Where are they this week?" Ken asked, easing them into conversation.

"California. The redwoods, I think."

Leslie sat serene and composed. "How is Drake doing? We heard about his whirlwind engagement and wedding." Her gaze dipped to his hand. A spark of interest lit her eyes at what he held hidden.

"Drake is practically a new man, thanks to Adria." Drake finally got the help he needed with his PTSD. And Tate didn't have to worry about him offing himself or hurting someone anymore.

"Terrible what happened to her sister." Ken shook his head in dismay.

"Adria was devastated, but she's trying to move on with Drake and the store she and Trinity opened."

"It's incredibly popular. We've shopped there a few times. Your sister's casseroles are amazing."

He had to hand it to Trinity and Adria, they'd found their niche in a crowded prepackaged meals market.

"They keep me and Declan well-fed." All this chit-chat made him more nervous.

Leslie leaned forward. "We're so relieved to know

that Liz is taken care of and protected out at the ranch with you boys from that man she was seeing. She told us about him coming to her work while she was talking to that reporter."

Ken's face flushed red with anger. "Idiot showed up at the ranch. I'm not a violent man, but I wish you'd shot him. I don't like where this looks like it's going."

Tate didn't either. And with Clint back out on the streets, it was only a matter of time before he did something else stupid—and dangerous. It made Tate want to rage.

What the hell was Clint thinking? What did he hope to accomplish?

Why wouldn't he back off?

With more women coming forward with claims of harassment, Clint had more than enough on his plate to keep him occupied and away from Liz.

"Tim, the reporter who put the story out, gave us an update earlier. Clint's company fired him. He's facing some potential lawsuits from his other victims." He hated that Liz continued to be Clint's victim. "Clint hired a lawyer but I don't think he'll get away with the trespassing and assault charges."

"He should be behind bars." Anger darkened Ken's eyes.

Tate would settle for jail, but a permanent solution would make Liz's life a hell of a lot better.

"I'm doing everything I can, short of ordering her to stay home from work and at the ranch, to keep her safe. With the amount of pressure on Clint, I wouldn't be surprised if he disappears for a while, if not indefinitely." One could hope.

"Guys like him don't run. They think they can get away with the bad things they do." Leslie squeezed Ken's offered hand.

They'd always seemed to have a solid marriage. He never saw them argue or raise their voices to each other. They had to have their disagreements, but like his parents, they found a way to get through them and past them and find a way to always end up back at happy together.

"Whatever happens, I'll always take care of and protect Liz." There, that was a good opening for what he came here to do. Feeling his confidence return, he dove in. "I love her. I think you've known that for a long time."

They nodded, their indulgent smirks coming back and making him nervous all over again.

"You two have been inseparable since you were practically babies." Leslie's eyes shone with memories and kindness.

"We've always been friends, but it hit me all at once why that is. I don't want to live my life without her."

Both of them leaned in.

"I've always known how much she cared about me. I haven't always been good about telling her how much she means to me. But that's changed, too. I don't want a single day to pass that she doesn't hear me tell her I love her. I want her to know it every second of the day. I want a lifetime to show her how much she's loved." He turned his hand over and showed them the black velvet box.

Leslie gasped and covered her open mouth with her fingertips. Tears glassed over her eyes.

Ken gave an approving nod.

"And with your permission, I'd like to ask your daughter to marry me."

They didn't say anything. They just stared at him.

"Do I have your permission?"

Leslie jolted. "Yes! Of course."

"She's loved you her whole life," Ken said matter-of-factly. "I know this is what she wants more than anything. I've heard it in her voice and seen it in her face every time she talks about you. I know you'll take care of her."

"Yes, sir. Always."

"Enough with the sir, Tate. I appreciate you want to do this right, but relax. We're happy you chose each other. You're a good match. You know how to argue without hurting each other. You two always found a compromise when you needed to."

Leslie added, "Most kids have friends that come and go from their lives as they grow up. Not you two. There was some kind of special that glued the two of you together." Leslie glanced at Ken. "I think it was their sophomore year when oddly enough they were both infatuated and seeing someone else, when we said to each other, 'Those two are destined to be together.'"

Ken leaned on his forearms on his knees. "You two talked to each other more than you did the people you were seeing."

Tate shrugged. "She was always more fun to talk to and be with than anyone else."

"You found something to do with those other girls." Ken winked and waved his hand to stop Tate from trying to defend himself against that embarrassing truth.

"All I'm saying is you two made it through all that, took your time to explore your options, and came to the conclusion that you're better together than with anyone else." Ken glanced at his wife, then spoke for both of them. "We worried you two would settle down together too fast. We wanted Liz to have some life experience outside her relationship with you. You wanted that, too."

"Believe me, it wasn't a conscious thing. I denied my attraction and feelings for her forever." He didn't have a problem telling the truth he'd come to terms with when faced with possibly losing Liz. Even now the thought of losing her stopped his heart.

"Because she mattered that much to you." Leslie's insight erased his fear that he'd have to go through another round of "Are your feelings real?" questions.

"She means everything to me."

They sat back, pleased with his response and at ease with giving him their blessing.

Leslie shot forward with her hand out. "Can I see the ring?"

He handed it over.

She opened the lid and her eyes glassed over again. "Oh Tate, she'll love it. It's perfect."

He glanced at the diamond solitaire with the pretty swirls and filigree setting. "I hope so."

Ken leaned over and checked out the sparkler. "You did good, son. When will you ask her?"

"I'm still working on the how and when, but very soon. So, please, don't give her any hints or anything. I want this to be a total surprise." He checked his watch. "And if I don't hurry, she'll wonder why I'm late picking her up at work."

Leslie stood at the same time he did and handed the ring back. "Are you going to give us some time to plan a proper wedding? Or are you going to be like your brother Drake and hurry her to the I do's?"

He shrugged, knowing he just couldn't wait much longer. "It seems to be in the McGrath blood."

Leslie rolled her eyes. "I guess I better get down to the bookstore and buy every bridal magazine I can get my hands on so we can start planning."

"Good idea. Just give me a little time to ask her." Tate shook Ken's hand. "Thank you."

"Welcome to the family, Tate, though it seems silly to say that since you've been a part of it so long."

"Thanks for always making me feel like I belonged here."

Leslie touched his arm, her eyes warm with emotion. "Don't keep my girl waiting."

Soon, Liz would officially be his girl for the rest of his life.

He had the ring and her parents' permission. Now all he had to do was ask her and get his "Yes!"

Chapter Twenty-Seven

Liz didn't mind taking Detective Valdez's advice to switch her hours from day to day. Making it harder on Clint to stalk her kind of made her feel like she was doing something to protect herself besides hiding. Though she didn't delude herself into thinking he couldn't get to her.

All she wanted to do was get through one day without thinking about him.

She'd prefer to spend most of her day thinking about Tate. Somehow, in all the chaos and drama, they'd created their own little oasis with each other. She'd always known she loved him, but that love had grown and turned into something so unexpected and special now that they were together.

Tate worried about her being at work. She shared his worries, but refused to stop living her life. Besides, they were going to need the money to fix up the cabin and pay for the wedding she hoped came sooner rather than later.

Tate certainly seemed on the verge of asking her something more than once, but then he backed off because of timing or circumstance. Clint had become a dark cloud in their sunny relationship and it had to stop. Because of him, they had to do things they didn't plan, put things off, move things around, and generally organize their life around whatever he did or they thought he might do.

Frustrated and annoyed, she stuffed the receipts she'd been working on into her drawer and went to shut off her computer when an email popped up with an attachment. The subject read Liz Living it Up!

She normally didn't click on attachments from email senders she didn't recognize, but something dreadful stirred in her gut. Somehow she knew what it was going to be, but she didn't want it to be real. Somewhere in the back of her mind she'd thought this could happen, but hoped it wouldn't. Not to her.

Things like this happened to other people.

She clicked the attachment and covered the gasp that actually got stuck in her throat along with the bile she choked back.

Gasps. Moans. Ridiculously fake heavy breathing rang in her ears as she watched a few seconds of the explicit sex scene playing on her screen. She immediately thought, *That's not me!* But it took her a second to push through the shock and realize that her face had somehow been superimposed over someone else's in the video.

It sure did look real.

Too real.

Real enough that other people would believe this if they didn't know she didn't have a butterfly tattoo on her ass and her breasts were real, not that perfectly round. While you couldn't see the man's face, it was obvious a third party recorded the original video. She'd never participate in such a thing.

But Clint sure would make this trash and send it out to humiliate her. After all, he'd done it before. And now he wanted to punish her for her perceived slights.

Heart thrashing in her chest, she shut down the video and grabbed her purse to find Detective Valdez's contact information. Though it sickened her to share this with anyone, she couldn't let Clint get away with this. She was under no illusions that they'd trace this to him. He'd proven to be quite adept at covering his tracks. Computer savvy, he'd managed to send the email anonymously. Making the video look real took skill. Or at least a credit card to get some jerk to make it for him.

She pulled the detective's card out of her bag just as Emmy and a few of the other women who worked at the spa filled her doorway. Trepidation filled Emmy's eyes and Liz knew.

Her heart pounded with anxiety and embarrassment and rage. "You got the video."

Clint must have sent it to everyone at her work. Just like he did to Aubrey.

All the women's eyes darted this way and that, but none of them looked right at her.

"It's not me."

Disbelief covered all their faces.

"The video is a fake." Tears threatened, but she tried to hold it together by focusing on her outrage.

Emmy looked relieved but a few of the others gave her yeah-right looks, even though they were well aware that Clint had been causing her trouble. They'd been so good about watching her back here at work and lending their support.

But still, this was hard for them to dismiss as another of Clint's retaliations.

And in that moment she understood exactly how Aubrey must have felt when Clint did this to her with a real video. How humiliated and helpless she must have felt to take it back and make them unsee it.

The blame and shame should be on Clint for doing something so underhanded and violating, but no, they looked at her like it was her fault. She was the disgraceful one. The degenerate.

Even if it *was* her, having sex wasn't a crime. Everyone did it.

Oh, forget it. No rationalization would make them see her the way they did before they saw the video even if she could prove it a fake. It was in their minds. They'd formed their opinions.

And she was screwed.

Exactly what Clint intended. To hurt and shame her.

Well, she shouldn't feel that way, but she did.

"This is another attempt from Clint to hurt me. He just got fired for harassment. *He* sent the video." She held up the detective's business card. "And I'm going to report him to the police. If you want to believe that's me doing that, nothing I say will change your mind. But it's not me."

"It looks just like you," Janet pointed out.

She didn't know Janet that well, but she appreciated her honesty. "It's a clever doctoring of what I assume is an internet porno movie. I don't know how he did it, but do you really think I'd participate in something like that"—she held her hand out toward the monitor—"with someone filming it? Come on. I'm not that daring. And what reason, other than revenge and spite, would someone have to send it to everyone here? You think I'd want to share that with anyone, especially my co-workers? No way."

The women nodded and shared looks. She hoped she'd made her case, but right now their feelings and judgments about her didn't matter. She needed to get Detective Valdez on this and hope he could tie it to Clint and arrest him for . . . What was the charge? Harassment? It seemed too little for the crime and how this could ruin relationships—or God forbid, get her fired.

If he put it up on the internet, there was no hope of getting it down. Once it was out there, it was out there forever.

Emmy came forward and put her hand on Liz's shoulder. "I'm really sorry this is happening to you."

Liz looked up at her, every emotion roiling inside her, sinking her shoulders and pushing a sigh out. "I just don't understand why he's doing this to me. I didn't do anything to him."

"Bastard," Janet called out.

The other women murmured their agreement. She hoped they remained on her side.

"Thanks for coming to tell me you all got it. I'm not sure if the detective working the case will want to talk to you, but be prepared. Oh, and if you get anything else, please let me know."

Janet waved the others to head out for the night, but turned back and said, "I hope you get him for this."

"Thanks." But she didn't have much faith in the system Clint circumvented at every turn. The trespassing and assault charges might stick, or get pled down to lesser offenses that amounted to nothing more than a fine, but Clint knew how to get away with this kind of thing because he'd done it before without getting caught.

Emmy touched her shoulder again. "Are you going to be okay?"

She shook herself out of her dismal thoughts and tried to focus. "Yeah. I just need to send the email over to the police, then I'm going home."

Emmy glanced out the window through the blinds. "Tate's out front waiting for you. Want me to tell him to come in?"

She shook her head. "This will only take a second, then I'm out of here." Sick to her stomach and drained from this constant onslaught of worry over the next bad thing to come, she wanted to go home and just be with Tate. She'd like to erase this from her mind, but some things you can't forget.

How was she going to tell Tate about this?

The last thing she wanted to do was make him worry about her more.

And she didn't want him getting arrested for going after Clint for this.

Maybe that's exactly what Clint hoped would happen, then he'd get Tate in trouble and out of the way so he could come after her.

Okay, she needed to stop watching *Dateline* and seeing her life in all those stories that seemed so implausible until they actually happened.

She wondered how many of Clint's acquaintances would describe him as the quiet guy next door.

It just goes to show you never really know someone. Or what they are capable of doing.

"I'll see you tomorrow." Liz needed a moment alone to send the email and gather herself before she faced Tate and delivered more bad news.

"Maybe you should take some time off."

"I'll think about it." But she had no intention of doing that because it kind of felt like giving in or giving up. Not her style. But it was getting harder to hold up under the anxiety.

She wouldn't let Clint wear her down.

Emmy left without another word.

The silence in the office swallowed her, but the thoughts in her head kept her amped.

She forwarded the email to Detective Valdez with a short account of how she and everyone in the office received it, that it was undoubtedly a fake, and that she wanted him to investigate and tie it to Clint somehow.

Disgruntled and dejected that nothing would probably come of it, she shut off her computer, grabbed her purse, left her office, locked up the front door behind her, and walked down the path to Tate's truck.

She climbed in and studied Tate, who looked even more upset than she still felt. "What's wrong?" She noticed the button-up shirt and slacks and asked, "Why are you dressed up?" She was used to seeing him after work in jeans and a T, sometimes a flannel.

Tate stared through the windshield not saying anything.

"Tate. What is it?" She reached out and touched his

shoulder. Rock hard, every muscle tense, he fumed on the inside but didn't show it on the outside. "What happened?"

He lifted his phone, tapped the screen, and turned it to her.

UNKNOWN: I had her first

The text set off another round of alarms in her brain and notched her heartbeat up to hummingbird speed.

Tate tapped the video below the text.

Her heart stopped. This time, it wasn't a fake but her with Clint in bed. Not as explicit or graphic as the porno, they were under the covers, but still. Tate didn't need to see her with *him*.

How dare Clint taunt Tate.

No one wanted to see the person they loved in bed with someone else.

Her stomach dropped and she clutched at the door handle as bile rose up her throat. She fell out of the truck onto the sidewalk and threw up in the gutter, retching when her stomach was empty but her body still tried to expel the horror out of her system.

Tate's hands landed on her shoulders and he brushed her hair back into his hand and away from her face.

She swiped the back of her hand across her sour mouth and sobbed so hard her stomach hurt more and her eyes squinted closed but the tears just kept coming.

Tate whispered soothing words at her ear she couldn't comprehend.

Nothing helped ease her mind or heart. She felt violated and exposed. She raged that Clint would do this to her. Film her without her consent or knowledge. Send it to Tate. To anyone. Their private moment, even if she did look back with regret that she'd ever been with him.

Tate somehow turned her around and wrapped her in a hug. "Ssh, you're all right. It's going to be okay."

Neither of those things were true and just set off another round of racking tears that just made Tate hold her tighter.

"I'm sorry. I shouldn't have shown you that."

"H-he s-sent one to e-every. O-one. At work." She gasped for air that wouldn't fill her lungs and buried her face in the collar of Tate's nice shirt.

"What the fuck!" Tate hooked his hand under her knees and picked her up right off the sidewalk and gently set her back on the seat in his truck. He found a couple take-out napkins in the glove box, wiped the tears from her face with one, then handed her the other to blow her nose with. He grabbed the water bottle from the console, uncapped it, and handed it to her. "Rinse and spit, then drink some. Just a little. You don't want to make yourself sick again."

She did as he said, waiting for him to step back so she didn't splash spit on his polished black boots. Feeling marginally better, she took a few sips, then turned to him. "I'm so sorry. I didn't know he . . . You should have never seen . . . How could he . . . I'm sorry. I'm so s-sorry." Tears flooded her eyes again.

Tate reached for her face and made her look at him. "Don't say sorry for him. I'm not mad at you. I'm furious he'd do something so reprehensible. Then again, I should have expected him to make his point to me. He can't stand that we're together."

"It just keeps getting worse."

Tate's thumb swept across her cheek, wiping away more tears. "Not your fault, sweetheart." He touched his forehead to hers, held her for a moment, then stepped back. "Did he send the same thing to everyone at work?"

"No. Worse. I guess. I don't know what's better or worse about those videos." She tried to make her brain and the words coming out of her mouth make sense. "He doctored a porno to make the girl in it look like me. It's an obvious fake if you know I don't have a tattoo and my body looks different than hers." She sucked in a ragged breath and tried to get through another wave of humiliation and rage. "They thought it was real." She still couldn't believe some of the women she'd worked with for so long believed it was her. Even for a moment. "I sent it to Detective Valdez. I'm sure he'll investigate, but . . ." She let that *but* hang because they both knew how hard it was to pin anything on Clint. And in this instance with the videos the laws hadn't quite caught up to technology and what smarmy individuals did with it.

Tate swore. "I don't know what to do here. I want to fucking kill him."

"Anything you do, he'll use against you. More than likely, you'll end up in more trouble than he's in right now."

"I'll let Valdez know I got a video, too. Maybe I won't have to send it to him—I'm hoping Clint only sent the real one to me."

Clint sent him the real one to taunt him, because Tate knew all the intimate details about her and would spot a fake.

Her coworkers got the fake version because the real thing was a lot more boring than the doctored video.

"How much of it did you watch?"

"Enough."

She wiped her hands over her face and stared down at her hands in her lap. "It's not the same with us, Tate."

He placed his hand on her jaw and made her turn to him. "I know that, Liz." He huffed out a frustrated breath. "I've been with other women. You know that. But you don't want to see it. I don't *ever* want you to see it, or have it thrown in your face." He shrugged and pressed his mouth tight. "I wasn't your first. Neither was he. All of that is beside the point. He recorded you. He violated a rule that shouldn't have to be spoken. You sleep with someone, that's between you two. What happens is private unless you *both* consent to something else. And that's not you, Liz. You have to care to sleep with someone."

She pressed her fingers to his lips and shook her head. "You have no idea how much I regret sleeping with him. I was trying to make something out of nothing. After . . . well, I knew there wasn't enough there to be what I wanted it to be, but I was still deluding myself into thinking it could be if only I gave it a chance. Now I know. I mean, I really know that when it's right with someone you don't have to give it a chance or make it happen. It just comes together. Like us."

He kissed her forehead. "Like it's meant to be."

"Exactly." She brushed her hands over his hair. "I wish I could scrub that from your mind."

"Me too, but I'm over it. I'm furious that he has the

video and sent it. I can't hold it against you for sleeping with him. I do question your judgment," he teased even if the smirk didn't quite light his eyes.

"You slept with Marianne." Liz had warned him junior year that Marianne only wanted to use him to get back at her boyfriend for standing her up for a school dance.

"Enough said. We've both made mistakes." Tate paid for that mistake when Marianne made sure Jordan caught them after a football game going at it in his truck. Tate ended up with a bashed-in window, a black eye, and two cracked ribs.

Jordan didn't fare much better. Tate broke his nose, gave him a matching black eye, and roughed him up so bad he peed blood for three days. Jordan ended up forgiving Marianne, but they split when he caught her with a senior and gave her up without a fight.

Marianne hadn't been worth the fight.

She leaned her head back and stared up at the truck top. "Take me home."

"I guess going out to eat isn't such a great idea now."

She rolled her head to look at him. "Is that why you're all dressed up?"

"Kinda." That didn't really answer her question.

Before she asked him to clarify, his phone dinged with a text.

Tate swore, drawing her gaze right back to him. He stared at his phone, then searched the lot with a sweeping look.

"What's wrong?"

Tate turned the phone to her and showed her the

video of her throwing up, crying, and falling into Tate's arms. The scene that played out just moments ago.

She twisted in her seat and looked out the back window expecting to see Clint standing there filming them. Nothing. No one. Not even a shadow moved in the dark parking lot.

"How the hell did he even get my number?"

She thought about it. "We gave our numbers to the officer who arrested Clint at the ranch. Either he memorized it, or more likely his lawyer gave him a copy of the report with all our information."

"Shit."

She checked everywhere, but saw nothing in the parking lot. "Where is he?"

Tate slammed her door and took a few steps toward the end of the truck and yelled, "Come out, you coward." Nothing. Clint had either fled or had sense enough not to face off with Tate. "I didn't think so." Tate walked around to the driver's side, climbed in, turned the key in the ignition, and drove out of the lot. "He thinks he wins by sending me that video, but he won't come right at me."

"Where are we going?"

"To the police station to give Valdez these videos. Something needs to be done about that asshole."

"He's taunting us."

"No, he's taunting me. He wants me to know he 'had you first.' He can get to you whenever he wants, and he's going to make you miserable until we split or you leave me."

"That's never going to happen."

Tate reached over and touched her face. "He wants it to happen. He wants you alone, so he can have you."

Those ominous words sank their claws into her heart and wouldn't let go.

TATE KEPT AN eye on Liz while she wrote out her statement for Valdez. The detective sat on the other side of the desk with Tate's phone watching the video Clint sent him. Liz's cheeks burned red, but she kept her head down and the pen moving across the page.

He didn't know how she held it together so well.

Sure, she'd had a moment. She deserved it. If he didn't feel such an urgent need to hit something, he might cry, too.

It wasn't fair or right.

Valdez slammed the phone down on the desk. "I'm sorry, Liz. But I had to verify it's you and Clint."

Liz glanced at Tate out of the corner of her eye, but didn't say anything.

"The other video . . . well, it's called a deepfake. Viewers will find it hard to tell if it's real or fake. Most won't question it. My guess, Clint used an online service to make it. Most of them are made with celebrity photos over porn stars' faces. Some folks want a woman they think they can never have or who shot them down. There are tools online to make the videos using the slew of pictures people post on social media online."

"Are you saying he used my Facebook and Instagram pictures to make that filth?"

"That and pictures he took of you. Stills from videos he has of you. It's becoming more common. I read about a couple of big cases in LA. One was from Nebraska. A guy had a video made of an ex. He used it to blackmail her."

"And let me guess, he got away with it." The bitterness in Liz's voice stung. Tate wanted to do something to make this right and make it disappear but he couldn't. Which only made him feel useless. He needed an outlet for all this anger. Too bad he couldn't get his hands on Clint.

"Unfortunately, the laws haven't caught up with technology. If he put it up on the internet, it's nearly impossible to take down." Detective Valdez looked as frustrated as Tate felt.

"So this is going to follow me my whole damn life." Liz sat back and stared at the wall of posters of fugitives.

Clint was number one on Tate's Most Wanted list.

"I think it's time for you two to come up with a plan." That got Tate's attention. "What kind of plan?"

"A code word or something to alert the other you're in trouble. Keep more than one phone with you."

Liz pulled two phones from her purse. "Done."

"You're still carrying your old phone?"

"I picked it up at my condo when I packed my clothes. Clint doesn't have my new number." She sighed. "Or maybe he does. If he got yours from the ranch arrest report, he got mine." She shook that off. "Anyway, I thought it best that I know if he's texting or trying to call me."

"Has he?" Tate didn't even consider she'd kept this from him.

"They've stopped now. I think he got the hint I'm not going to respond. There are more rants and pleas for me to come back to him, to understand, then more rants about how I ruined his life and this is all my fault. I've stopped paying attention. It's more of a record than anything at this point."

"Why didn't you say anything?"

"Because I'm tired of him intruding in our lives."

Detective Valdez leaned over the desk. "Can you track each other on your phones?"

"No." At the same time Liz said that, Tate said, "Yes."

She eyed him. "Really?"

"When I bought the phones, the point was to make sure Clint didn't have your new number. But I thought it was a good idea that we could track each other, considering, so I had them add the app."

"Like I said, he probably knows it, but he keeps calling the old one."

Detective Valdez held his hand out. Liz handed over the old phone. Valdez scrolled through the texts and listened to a few of the disturbing and threat-filled voice mails. "Jeez. This guy is off his rocker." He stood and headed for the door. "Let me have one of the guys download a copy of all this from the phone. I'll pass it on to the DA. It proves harassment. There are a couple of veiled threats in those voice mails."

"The video he took of us outside her work tonight was a threat. He's telling us, *I can get to her anytime I want*."

"Proving that's what he intended is harder than it should be." Valdez walked out and left him with Liz.

He reached out and held her hand. "How are you holding up?"

"Great. I love having strangers watch me have sex." She glanced over her shoulder as Detective Valdez handed a guy her cell and Tate's. "You know they're all going to watch that video and say it's evidence."

"You have nothing to be ashamed of."

Her lips scrunched into an incredulous frown. "That doesn't make it any less humiliating."

"I know. I'm just trying to find any way to make this better for you."

That took the wind right out of her. "You make it better just by being here."

"He's been close enough to scratch you and take a video of the two of us. I want him locked up."

"Six feet under would do me just fine."

The vehemence in her voice surprised him, but he got it. "Include me in that," Tate confirmed. "I'm sure a lot of other women feel the same way. Valdez is right. We need to talk about a plan for what we're going to do when he comes back."

"For you? Or me?"

"Both."

And so Tate and Liz talked out every scenario they could think of for Clint trying to take her, hurt him, and vice versa. Valdez gave them some help and pointers on how best to protect themselves, but the general consensus remained: Clint was coming and nothing would stop him next time. It was just a matter of time, and how and when he did it.

Chapter Twenty-Eight

Clint had wanted to ignore the summons from Detective Valdez to come down to the police station to answer questions. The cop had it out for him. He wanted to link Clint to Aubrey's death. Not going to happen. He'd pulled off the perfect crime.

And he'd done it again last night.

Tate had to be reeling from seeing the video of Clint fucking Liz. No doubt Tate saw on her face how much she wanted and enjoyed it.

Tate would never get that out of his head. Tate would know Liz liked it better with him.

And why wouldn't she. He'd been the perfect lover and boyfriend. She'd see that and regret leaving him for a guy who only wanted her now because Tate didn't want anyone else to have her.

Everything had been fine until Tate and Aubrey confused Liz. She'd chosen wrong, and now she'd get what she deserved.

Detective Valdez walked in with a folder tucked under his arm and a paper coffee cup. He barely spared Clint a glance and settled his gaze on Clint's attorney. This time he wouldn't answer any questions without being lawyered up.

"Thanks for coming in." Detective Valdez sat in the chair across from him and his attorney, leaned back, took a sip of his coffee, and tossed out the first question. "Where were you tonight between the hours of six and seven p.m.?"

"At home having dinner and watching *America's Got Talent*. I love that guy who throws knives at his wife." He nearly laughed when the detective's eyes widened with shock that he'd say such a thing.

"Was that on?"

"DVR." Clint wasn't stupid. He didn't have a verifiable alibi. But the cop couldn't say he wasn't at home—alone—watching a recording, eating fried chicken from the grocery store deli.

"Did you record an intimate night between you and Liz Scott?"

"Don't answer that."

Clint ignored his lawyer. "Liz and I shared many intimate nights together. We were dating."

"That's not what I asked."

"Don't answer," his lawyer advised again.

Clint dismissed the warning. "Liz and I liked to watch ourselves." No crime in that.

"Did you text the video to Tate McGrath?"

"Don't answer that." His lawyer repeated himself.

Clint made a show of patting his pockets. "You know, I lost my phone. I had it in my car when I ran into the store to pick up dinner, then"—he held up his hands—"I don't know what happened to it."

Detective Valdez glared at him. Clint used the same story Tate had told—about a missing phone and the texts sent to Liz breaking up with her.

"So you didn't send the video to Tate?"

"Did the video and texts come from my client's phone number?" Finally his lawyer said something helpful.

Detective Valdez's glare intensified. "No."

"Then why are you questioning my client?"

"Because he made the video."

"Liz made it with me. Maybe she sent it to Tate to make him jealous." Clint shrugged and gave the frustrated cop a smile that only made him glare harder.

"Did you also make a deepfake video superimposing Liz's face over another woman in a porn video?"

He laughed. "What? A deepfake? I don't even know what that is."

Photoshop had nothing on what computer-savvy nerds could do to a video. The one he'd had made was so good, even he believed it was Liz getting fucked. It made him hard just thinking about it.

The cop didn't believe him. "How did your lawyer get ahold of you tonight if you lost your phone?"

"The same way you did. He called the house. I know it's old-fashioned, but I still have a landline." And several prepaid cells.

"You're facing serious charges and allegations from the women you work with. Aubrey wasn't the only one you made a sex video with and sent to her coworkers."

"I never did that."

"It just miraculously appeared in every employee's inbox?"

"She craved attention of any kind. Even her threats to kill herself were ways that she tried to get attention. She had a twisted mind and a destructive streak. She loved the drama and getting people's sympathy. She tried to blame me for everything and get everyone on her side, fawning over her, when all I ever did was try to help her."

"Yet Aubrey's story is similar to the four women's stories who came forward at your work. It's similar to what's happening to Liz right now. It's a pattern that repeats for the women who have the misfortune of knowing you."

"What can I say, I have a type. They all leave happy, but when I move on, the jealousy comes out."

"Is that why Aubrey warned Liz away from you? That's why she had a restraining order? That's why Liz now has one against you?" The detective handed over the form.

His lawyer read it alongside him.

"She did this because she wants Tate to believe she's in danger when that is the furthest thing from the truth. But I bet she's got Tate's full attention."

"They're closer than ever." The detective's eye glinted with pride that he'd delivered that gem.

"But will it last with all this Liz drama? I don't know why women feel the need to create chaos to keep a man's attention."

"I don't know why you think anything you do will break them up. Taunting Liz. Sending the videos. Showing up at the McGrath ranch and assaulting her. Do you really think she'd want you over Tate, who cares about her enough to protect her from you?"

"He only wanted her after I had her."

"Yeah, and you wanted him to know you had her first."

Clint couldn't help the smile. "She picked me over him the first time Tate and I met in the bar. I bet he's pissed about that and still wondering if she doesn't really prefer me."

"She doesn't. She's living with him and never wants to see you again." Detective Valdez tapped the restraining order. "Whatever you think you're getting out of this, you're wrong. She loves Tate. He loves her. All you're doing is proving to her that Tate's the better man."

He stood so fast he toppled the chair, and slammed his hands on the table.

Detective Valdez stared up at him, looking bored, but Clint had his attention.

His lawyer clamped his hand around his arm. "Don't say a word." To the detective he said, "This interview is over. Unless you have proof my client actually committed a crime, we're leaving."

Detective Valdez leaned back like he had all the time in the world. "Everyone knows what you did and what you're still doing. It's all over the local news. You've lost your job and are facing charges. Quit while you're ahead before you end up in jail or worse."

"Is that a threat?" Clint didn't really take it seriously. So far, the cop had nothing.

"Liz is smart. Strong. Determined. She's not going to just keep taking it. Tate will do just about anything for her. He'll protect her with his last breath if it comes to that. Careful who you piss off."

Clint gave the cop a fuck-you glare and walked out.

Tate, a restraining order, nothing would keep him from Liz.

Chapter Twenty-Nine

TATE HELD Liz's hand and walked her toward the cabin. He wanted to get her out of her head and focused on their future, not the past, or what they were facing with Clint on the loose and causing trouble.

Liz stared up at the cabin. "What are we doing here?"

"Planning."

"But Drake and Adria haven't officially moved out." Depending on the work going on at their house, they moved back and forth between the two places.

"Only for a few more weeks. Then this place is ours." He walked up the porch steps, pulling her along with him.

"We shouldn't be here when they're still living here."

"Drake and Adria are at work. They won't be home for at least another hour. And I asked them if it was okay if we came over and sketched out a plan for expanding this place." He unlocked the door—because of Clint, they locked everything now—and held it open so she could go in ahead of him.

She stopped short in the entry, spun around, covered her mouth, then dropped her hand and said, "What is this?"

"Dinner." The table was set for two. White dishes, silver place settings on green napkins, half a dozen thick round candles, their flames dancing, Liz's favorite pink peonies with white snapdragons filling a crystal bowl, and a bottle of wine chilling in an ice bucket. "Roast chicken and potatoes, crispy just like you like them, broccoli and cauliflower with cheddar sauce, and cheesecake with fresh strawberries for dessert."

"Tate, this is amazing."

He pulled her close. "It's been kind of crazy lately. I wanted to do something special and unexpected." He wanted them to have a worry-free meal. Here. So they could get a feel for the place and dream about the future they both wanted.

So he got together with Trinity and Adria and set this up. The smile on Liz's face told him he'd pulled off the surprise.

She went up on tiptoe and kissed him softly. So much promise lingered in that simple kiss. "I love it. Thank you. And it smells great."

They'd both lost their appetite last night after handing over the videos to Detective Valdez. They drove home, the radio down low, Liz's anger simmering as she stared out the window and studied the stars. They snuggled on the couch, neither of them wanting to talk, and watched a movie neither of them remembered much of when they headed up to bed and a restless night.

Liz hung out at the ranch today, not really doing anything, but thinking about how she couldn't face everyone at work and being pissed that the owner asked her to take a few days while they evaluated what happened.

It wasn't fair. Neither was Clint getting away with it and murder.

Tate wished all of this was over already. He didn't want to think about it and worry about Liz anymore.

"Let's eat." He nudged her toward the table and held the chair out for her to sit.

She glanced up at him, smiling all the way to her eyes, and squeezed his hand. "Thank you, Tate. This is really lovely."

"Truthfully, I've never done anything like this, so I asked my sisters for help."

She squeezed his hand again. "I appreciate the thoughtfulness and effort."

He leaned down and held her gaze. "You mean so much to me, Liz. I want you to know that and never doubt it." He didn't know why it seemed so important for her to believe it, but he needed her to with everything inside him. He wanted her to know nothing Clint did would change it.

"I know you love me, Tate."

"More than I can possibly say."

"Nothing is going to happen to me. I'm not going anywhere." Somehow she knew his deepest fear.

He hated the things Clint did, but it was more than that. Tate knew, deep down, Clint wanted to take Liz from him. He wanted her to pay for his imagined slights.

He wanted to torment and ultimately kill her.

Tate would do everything in his power to keep her safe.

But what if it wasn't enough?

I need her so much.

Liz leaned forward and pressed her forehead to his

and stared into his eyes. The green depths in hers turned solemn. "He can't touch *us*. He thinks he can, because he destroys beautiful things. Relationships. Aubrey. Sex."

Making love to Liz was a kaleidoscope of sensations and passion. Beautiful didn't even come close to describing it.

"He took those things and twisted them up and wrecked them. I don't know why, but he can't have nice things. When they shine in his life, he smashes them.

"You hold on, Tate. You find a way to make things better. You make me smile and laugh and feel like I matter. You know how to use your strength to be gentle and kind and still protect and fight for what you love."

"You matter. You're the only woman I've ever loved. You're the only woman I'll ever love." He didn't plan this, but went with it and dropped to one knee.

She gasped.

"You are and will always be my best friend. I want you to be my partner for life. I want you to be my wife."

He patted his pockets. "I've been carrying around your ring for what seems like forever and now I don't have it with me."

Her eyes went wide. "You bought me a ring?"

He nodded. "I didn't want to wait. I had to get it for you. It's at the house. Doesn't matter. I'll put it on you later. I've already asked your parents."

Her eyes softened with appreciation and glassed over. "You did?"

"They gave us their blessing. Now all I need, sweet Lizard"—she laughed under her breath that he used that childhood nickname—"is for you to make me the happiest man in the world and say, yes. Will you marry me?"

She leaned in and kissed him with tears streaming down her beautiful face. One long, sexy kiss, then a dozen all over his face and with every peck she said, "Yes. Yes. Yes." Until she was giggling and he was scooping her up into his arms and twirling her around.

"Yes!" he repeated. He let her body slide down his until he could kiss her one more time. Long. Slow. He sealed her promise with a kiss neither of them would ever forget.

He wanted to make love to her, but remembered how much she deserved the candlelit dinner, time for them to just be together, and enjoy each other's company here where they'd make their home. So he set her on her feet, cupped her face, and stared into her bright love-filled green eyes. "I can't wait to call you Mrs. McGrath."

"I have old-school notebooks filled with doodles and me practicing that name."

Of course she did. "It'll be yours soon, but I was yours a long time ago."

The buzzer on the oven went off.

"Dinner's ready." He nudged her to sit and poured her a glass of wine.

She scrunched her lips. "Wine's not really my favorite."

"Try the Riesling. It's not dry like a red or Chardonnay. It's sweeter. You'll like it."

She took a sip, both of them ignoring the incessant oven buzzer, and smiled. "That's nice."

He smiled, happy she liked it. "Points for Trinity. I told her we'd just drink beer. She said you'd like this and it goes with the chicken." He shrugged and headed for the stupid, annoying buzzer, shut it off, pulled the oven door open, releasing the amazing smells—chicken, garlic, melted cheese—and pulled out the pans and set them on the stovetop.

"Want some help?"

"Nope. I want to do this for you."

"Then I guess we're off to a good start. You cooking and me enjoying a glass of wine. Being married to you won't be half bad." The lightness and teasing in her voice did his heart good. They needed more fun and less drama in their lives.

So he teased right back. "I don't mind making Trinity and Adria cook for us every night."

She laughed at that.

He finished plating up the food and headed for the table. "Trust me, if you leave the cooking to me, it'll be pancakes, eggs, steak, and potatoes all the time because that's about all I can cook that turns out edible." He set her plate in front of her.

"I guess we'll have to take turns."

He sat and picked up his fork. "Works for me." They both dug into the food and settled into the wonder of their engagement.

"What kind of wedding do you want?"

Her question kind of surprised him, because he hadn't really thought about the details, except that she'd be his wife. That's all he really wanted. Except for one other thing. "Fast."

She laughed again. "It took me forever to get you, now you're in a hurry."

"I know what I want. You and me here, making more memories."

She placed her hand over his on the table. "You're

sweet." She glanced around the open kitchen and living room. "I like this setup, but we should expand the living room. We'll need the space for the kids."

He raised an eyebrow. "Something you want to tell me?" They'd been careful, but things happen.

She chuckled. "Not yet. But I'd like to try sooner rather than later. I'm not getting any younger."

"Whenever you're ready."

"Really?" Her eyebrows shot up. "You want to be a dad?"

He chewed a roasted potato bite and nodded. "I'm a little terrified, but also excited. Drake and Adria are expecting. I think it'd be cool to have our kids grow up together."

Her eyes went soft and dreamy. "Me too. But I think we should have some time for the two of us. Six months. A year."

"I'd like that." They'd shared this whirlwind romance, though it had been a long time in the making. Still, he'd like them to enjoy it for a while. As husband and wife. He wanted that commitment.

She wiped a drip of cheese sauce from her mouth, set her napkin down, and asked, "I'm sure you've thought about the addition. What's the plan?"

He told her what he had in mind, taking her suggestions and wishes, adding them to the plan in his head. "I found an architect to draw up the official plans. He'll need a couple weeks to get it done."

"I'll pay half the cost."

"I've got the money for it."

"Tate. We're partners. We'll figure out the financials together."

"I want to take care of you and give you everything you want."

"I want to do the same thing for you. So how about we do it together?"

He sat back and stared at her a little frustrated but also glad she wanted to work with him and not spend money they didn't have. "Is this how we're going to fight in the future?"

"Ready to make up with me?" Her sexy smile faded when a series of texts came through on her phone. She pulled it out of her back pocket and read them. Her face paled. "Oh God."

"What?" He leaned forward and put his hand on her shoulder, ready to hear about whatever terrible thing Clint had done this time. Because it had to be him.

"It's Ava. My neighbor." Her eyes glassed over and filled with a devastated look he wanted gone. "My place is on fire."

"Jeez." Tate never expected that. "Just your place, or the whole building?"

Liz texted Ava. "It started in my place. The fire department is there trying to get it under control before it spreads." She stood and glanced around for her purse. "We need to stop at the house for my bag and get over there."

"Leave it. Let's just go."

"No. I need my ID and insurance information."

They both knew Clint probably had something to do with the suspicious fire. He'd figured out a way to ruin another day for him and Liz.

If Tate got his hands on Clint, it would be the last time.

Poor Liz. If her place had completely burned, she had nothing but the clothes she'd brought here. That was something, but Tate hated that Clint took everything else she owned.

Fucking asshole. When will we be rid of him?

They had all they needed here, but still. She'd worked hard to create a home that reflected who she was and what she liked. She'd filled it with *her* things. Her memories.

Possessions didn't matter in the grand scheme of things. Still, the loss sucked for her.

But as long as they had each other, they had a hell of a lot more than most.

And maybe this time, Clint would get exactly what he deserved.

Chapter Thirty

Liz stood beside Tate, hands clasped tight, staring up at her blackened balcony. Then the roof caved in, smoke and flames still licking at what was left of her place. Stunned, numb, and unable to really process it, she didn't cry or think. She simply watched the fireman on the fire engine ladder holding the hose, the intense stream sending up more plumes of smoke where it flooded out the flames.

Neighbors gathered on the sidewalks watching the show. Her downstairs neighbors huddled together. If the fire hadn't destroyed their places, the water sure did.

Ava stood beside her and Tate. "What do you think started the fire?"

"Not what. Who." Tate bit out those bitter words.

Ava sighed. "I thought maybe that guy would do something. But this?"

Liz didn't want to believe it either, but . . . She simply couldn't dismiss the notion that this had Clint written all over it.

He could have hurt or killed someone.

He didn't care. All he wanted to do was destroy Liz's life.

She shook off thoughts of Clint and focused on Ava.

"I'm glad you called. Thanks for getting the fire department here so quickly."

"I wish I'd gotten home a few minutes earlier. Maybe I'd have seen something to nail that guy."

With the flames out and the fire department personnel losing their urgent intensity, people started walking away, going back to their places, grateful it wasn't them. She didn't blame them for feeling that way. She simply wished all this bad stuff would stop happening to her.

Detective Valdez joined them. "I spoke with the fire captain, told him to treat this as a suspicious fire. They've got their arson specialist ready to go in once it's safe."

"Any hope the fire didn't destroy any and all evidence he did this?"

"They'll probably be able to determine it was intentionally set. Linking it to Clint, well . . ."

She understood the detective's frustration all too well.

She couldn't help but think of what she'd lost. What he took from her. The locket her grandmother left to her. The dishes her parents got her when she moved in. All the photos she had from high school. All the silly notes Tate had written over the years. All things that she'd wanted to show their kids one day.

Tate's phone dinged with a text. He pulled it out and frowned at the message.

"What's wrong?"

"Maybe nothing. Drake's at the shop with Adria, but neither of them have seen Trinity since she went out to toss the trash in the dumpster." Tate read the incoming texts. "Her car is still there." Tate raked his fingers through his hair. "Shit. They found her phone in the bushes."

"You don't think . . ." Clearly they were all thinking it. Clint took Trinity. "Why would he take *her*?"

Angry lines marred Tate's forehead. "To piss me off. Lure me away from you." Tate shrugged, his face a mask of concern and rage.

Detective Valdez got on his phone and ordered officers to *Almost Homemade* to check things out. "I'll head over there now. Call me if anything else happens here."

She hugged Tate. "Maybe she dropped her phone without realizing it. Maybe she saw someone outside, an old friend shopping downtown, and she went over to talk to them."

"Why not go into the shop to talk?"

Liz grasped at straws and tried to rationalize Trinity disappearing without telling anyone. They'd all been on alert since Clint started his campaign to ruin Liz's life.

"Miss Scott, can I ask you a few questions?"

"Sure." She stepped away from Tate to speak to the firefighter. "Thank you for putting it out so fast and saving my neighbors' homes."

"Unfortunately, yours is a total loss."

A car alarm sounded close by. Tate touched her shoulder. "That's my truck." Suspicion filled his eyes. "I'm going to check it out."

Before she could stop him, he rushed off and the firefighter asked her, "Any pets in the home we weren't able to save?"

Thank God she didn't have a cat or dog. She didn't know if her heart could take a loss like that. "No."

Tires squealed as a car engine revved.

She turned toward the sound just as a silver sedan barreled toward Tate walking down the middle of the parking lot street. "Tate!" She screamed too late to warn him. The car hit him just as he turned and instinctively jumped. He landed on the hood, sliding up and into the windshield with a crack of his head, and rolled right over the top of it, down the back window and trunk, hit the pavement and toppled again as the car sped away.

She ran before she really thought about it but found herself sprinting ahead of the firefighter and landing on her knees next to Tate. He rolled to his back and put his hand beneath his head. He pulled his red-soaked fingers away and stared at them. "Fuck."

Her heart pounded so hard in her chest she thought it might crack her ribs and pop right out. "Stop moving." She ran her hands over him, trying to make him stay still.

He looked up at her, his eyes filled with shock and pain. "I'm okay, sweetheart."

"N-no y-you're not." Tears slid down her cheeks. She grabbed his wrist and showed him his bloody hand, even as he squinted his eyes in pain.

Three firefighters squatted around him. One gently laid Tate's head back on the pavement. "Lie still. You took a hard hit to the head. Let us check you out."

One of the guys had Paramedic emblazoned on his back. He took the lead, pulling stuff out of a big bag he carried, and pressing a thick gauze pad to Tate's head. It quickly turned red.

"You're bleeding so much." She didn't want to believe what her eyes saw. She wanted to go back two minutes and tell Tate not to worry about the truck alarm and stay with her.

She wanted Tate to be okay.

"Head wounds always bleed a lot. He'll need stitches. Probably has a concussion." The paramedic glanced at one of the other firefighters. "Anyone get the license and call it in yet?"

"Already done," a fourth guy walked up to them. "That guy didn't even slow down."

"It's probably the same guy who set my place on fire," she volunteered, rage ringing in her voice. "I'm going to fucking kill him." She meant it all the way to her soul.

Everyone stood there staring at her.

"Please. Help him!"

She held Tate's hand, but he kept pressing his elbow to his side.

The paramedic noticed. "Ribs? Bruised or broken?"

"Fuck if I know. They hurt like hell." Pain etched every line on Tate's pale face.

The paramedic started poking and prodding, prompting Tate to expel a whole slew of colorful swear words.

They got the backboard ready to roll Tate onto it.

"Step back, miss. Let us get him ready for transport to the hospital."

She didn't want to let him go. She kissed the back of his hand, sorry to have pulled on his arm and making him wince with pain at the movement.

"I'll be okay, sweetheart." He didn't look it. His face had gone deathly pale. Every breath seemed to cause him more agony.

She knew he'd eventually heal, but still, it took everything she had to release his hand and step back.

Every wince and moan made her stomach turn and her heart break. She hated seeing Tate in this much pain, knowing she was the reason for it.

Clint would pay for this. One way or another, she'd make him sorry he ever met her.

Her old phone dinged with a text. She pulled it out of her purse and stared at the picture, her mind not registering what she saw until clarity returned and horror filled her heart and mind.

"No."

Trinity, face pale and eyes wide with fear, lay in a heap in the trunk of a car that was the same color as the car that just hit Tate.

She covered an agonizing cry with her fingers to her mouth, but it lodged in her throat when the next message popped up.

UNKNOWN: If you want her to live walk out to the main street by the sign and get in the car

She stared down at Tate who'd closed his eyes as another wave of pain washed over him when the paramedic checked out his leg where the front end hit him. She didn't want to leave him, but she couldn't risk Trinity's life and not do what Clint wanted.

The police would find her. They had a plan. It didn't include Trinity's kidnapping, but ultimately, she knew what Clint wanted and what he'd do.

She backed away, hoping no one noticed while they worked on Tate.

They'd take care of him.

He'd want her to do whatever she had to do to save his sister.

Tate would never forgive her for bringing this destruction into their lives if something happened to Trinity.

She needed to take out Clint once and for all.

Hidden behind one of the big fire engines, she sent Drake a text to help Tate, found her new cell in her purse, tucked it into her sock at her ankle, pulled her jeans over it, and sprinted out of the parking lot and toward the main road. The sign was only twenty feet away from the entrance to her building. A *red*, not silver, car idled by the curb at the bus stop.

She walked right up to it, opened the door, stared inside, shocked to see the person behind the wheel.

"You? Why would *you* help him?"

"Toss your phone."

Liz pulled it out of her purse, held it up, and threw it back onto the grass in front of the wall surrounding her complex.

"If you want to get that Trinity lady back before Clint hurts one more woman, get in."

She hesitated for a second, the need to go back to Tate so strong she could barely make herself leave him, but in the end, for Trinity, she slipped into the front seat and gave herself over to the inevitable. But not without thinking through her options and the impending possibilities.

Clint thought she'd come, complacent and ready to surrender to her fate.

Never.

Chapter Thirty-One

TATE CURBED the urge to punch the guy who kept squeezing and prodding his throbbing leg. The world kept spinning, lights flashing in his eyes in time to the thumping of his heart echoing in his skull, along with the throbbing pain at the back of his head. Squinting set off another round, so he closed his eyes and hoped they'd pump him full of drugs soon because the intense pain in his ribs throbbed with every excruciating breath.

"What the hell happened?" Drake's voice shocked him into opening his eyes.

"Hit and run," the paramedic announced. "We'll transport him to the hospital shortly."

"Is he going to be okay?" Deep concern filled Drake's voice.

"The head injury is a concern, but he's alert and talking, so . . ." The paramedic left that hanging.

The longer Tate lay there, the worse he felt as the adrenaline rush wore off and the pain and reality set in.

Tate stared up at his shocked brother. "What are you doing here?"

"Liz texted me '911 come to my place.'"

Tate glanced around, surprised she wasn't by his side. "Where is she?"

Drake scanned the area, having a better view standing than Tate did lying in the road with firefighters all around him. "I don't see her."

Tate tried to sit up, but the paramedic held him down, and the pain nearly had him puking up his guts. "Man, you've got a major head injury. Stay down."

Tate waved him off, but the bile rising in his throat made him lie back. "Did she text anything else?"

"It didn't make sense, but she wrote 'Trinity storm.'"

Tate rolled to his side, clamped his jaw as a shock of pain raced through him, dug his phone out of his back pocket, and read a copy of the text on his cracked screen. He swore, tried to breathe through the wave of fear, and hit the app that tracked her phones. "One of her phones is close by." He pointed toward the wall and the main street. "The other is moving toward the lake. He's got her."

Drake's face paled. "Give me your phone. I'll go get her."

Tate shook his head, rolled up, stood, and rocked side to side, completely out of it for a second. He thanked God for the adrenaline rush that shot through him, sweeping away the pain that came with every little movement. Determination didn't stop the wave of dizziness or him wobbling on his feet, but Drake steadied him with both hands on Tate's shoulders.

"Go to the hospital. I'll take care of her," Drake promised.

Tate shook off Drake's hold and stumbled toward his truck. "No. I'm going."

"Sir," the paramedic called. "You need a doctor and your head examined."

Tate wondered if he meant not only for the injury but also for leaving in his condition. It was crazy. He felt like shit, but if Liz needed him, he was going after her.

And God help Clint when Tate got his hands on him.

Chapter Thirty-Two

Liz couldn't believe this was how Clint planned his showdown. But she shouldn't have been surprised. She'd actually predicted he'd repeat the same behavior, just like he'd done with all the other women. Especially Aubrey.

Clint did what worked for him, but she wasn't going to be his next victim.

"Where is Trinity? Is she hurt? Is he holding her somewhere?" Liz couldn't bring herself to ask if Clint had already killed her. Just the thought broke her heart.

"We'll find out when we get there." Clint's pawn slammed her hand on the steering wheel. "You know, I'm a victim here, too." Her eyes narrowed with fury. "He gets away with everything. He thinks I'll do anything for him. And why not? He makes you want to please him so he'll be kind and make you feel like you're special. When he's mean, you try harder to get back to the way you know it can be again. But then you realize you can't get back the way he was in the early days when he cast his spell on you, because he can't carry off nice and kind for long. Right?"

"Uh . . . yeah. You've been his assistant for a while,

haven't you?" Liz had seen her twice, three times maybe, at Clint's office when she met him there for lunch, or after work to get drinks or dinner.

"He convinced me he loved me. He was so warm and attentive in the beginning. It was fun to carry on our affair without anyone in the office knowing about it. Of course, he was seeing one of the other girls, too. He got bored of me and moved on to others, always stringing me along, saying just enough to make me believe we'd be together again. He knew just what to say and do to get me to keep coming back." She slammed her hand on the steering wheel again. "I'm so stupid. I fell for it every damn time."

"He's ruined the lives of every woman he's ever charmed."

"Charmed? He lied. He hurt. He made promises. He didn't mean anything that came out of his mouth."

Clint talked a good game in the beginning, but it all fell apart when his desires and demands weren't met, because he never considered what would make the woman in his life happy. He thought *she* wanted to please *him*. He wanted her to be his everything. But that was a two-way road.

"I'm sorry he hurt you."

"That's the least of my worries. He knows things about me. He's got videos."

Liz understood all too well the shame and embarrassment Clint inflicted by using those videos to keep his victims compliant. Or in her case, to humiliate her. "He's done it to me and others."

"Yep. I'm just one of many." The hurt in those words made Liz's heart ache.

"You're just the latest obsession. He makes you feel like you're the one. But you're not." Pain filled her eyes.

Liz had a feeling she spoke more to herself than Liz. "What's your name?" Liz wanted to connect with her and find a way to get her on Liz's side.

"It doesn't matter." The resignation in her voice scared Liz.

If she really didn't think she mattered, what would she do?

She pulled into the parking area by the path that led up to the Lover's Leap bridge, parked the car, turned off the engine, and sat for a moment. "Some things, you just can't fight. But everything comes to an end."

That ominous statement settled like a lead ball in Liz's gut.

What does she mean?

Is she with me?

Or against me?

She turned to Liz. "Let's not keep him waiting."

TATE SAT BEHIND Adria in the back seat of the truck. Drake drove like a maniac, but Tate didn't care so long as they got to Liz in time.

Adria turned in her seat, phone to her ear. "They found Trinity." The relief in Adria's voice didn't even come close to how happy Tate was to hear that.

"Clint drove her a couple miles from the shop, took the picture to send to Liz, then pulled her out of his car, and pistol-whipped her, but she's okay. He wore a mask, so she can't positively ID him, but she knows like everyone else that it was him. He dumped her on the side of the road. She flagged down a passing car.

She's with Detective Valdez. They're on their way to meet up with us at the lake." Adria narrowed her eyes. "She refused to go to the hospital, too."

Tate and Drake shared a look in the rearview mirror. McGrath stubbornness won out.

Tate had trouble breathing through the pain, but his need to get to Liz overrode good sense. He needed to see a doctor about his head and ribs—and soon—but he wouldn't until he found Liz.

He hoped his injuries wouldn't prevent him from helping the woman he cared about more than his own life.

Adria rolled her eyes. "He's sent backup to the lake. He says to let the cops handle it, but he knows you're not going to do that."

"Fucking right." Tate pressed the heel of his hand to his throbbing head. "I'm getting her back and making sure Clint gets what's coming to him if it's the last thing I do." It might be.

"You look a little . . . gray." The worry in Adria's eyes touched him.

It also reiterated what a colossally bad idea this was, but he had to do it. He couldn't leave Liz to face off with a maniac on her own no matter how bad his injuries.

They'd talked about this, planned for the inevitability of it, but he never once thought she'd have to face Clint alone.

"Wait. Was Liz in the car when Clint let Trinity go?"

Adria asked Valdez and shook her head. "Trinity said no one else was in the car."

"Was Trinity in the car when he hit me?"

Adria did the whole relay thing, asking Detective Valdez, then filling him in on the answer. "Yes. But she didn't know what was happening. She's really upset to hear you got hurt."

He blew that off. "So she was in the car with him when he hit me, but Liz wasn't in the car when he let Trinity go." Clint must have rented the silver car after he drove drunk and hit a tree on the road before confronting Liz in the stables at the ranch.

"If Liz didn't leave in her car, and she wasn't in his car, then who took her?"

"He's got help," Drake filled in the blank.

It hurt to think, but Tate tried to piece things together. "Who the fuck would help him?"

"We'll find out. We're here." Drake pulled the truck in behind the red and silver cars, blocking them in and making sure no one made a run for it in one of the vehicles if this all went south.

So long as he got Liz back in one piece . . . that's all that really mattered.

Drake turned and leaned into Adria. "Lock the doors. Do not get out of this truck."

"I'm coming with you."

Drake shook his head. "You are the most important thing to me. You're pregnant. I can't help Tate if I'm worried about you."

Adria scrunched her mouth into an angry but resigned pout. "Fine."

"I love you." Drake kissed Adria, took the rifle Tate handed him from the rack hanging in the back window, and got out.

Tate followed him with the pistol he took from the

lockbox under the seat. Unsteady on his feet, lights flashing in his eyes, and the pain becoming more than he could handle, Tate wondered how long he had before his body shut down on him. He felt his energy waning, but he rushed down the path toward the falls and bridge, letting the adrenaline do its thing and feed his determination to get to the woman he loved before he lost her forever.

That thought bolstered his energy as did the sound of Liz's voice up ahead.

Chapter Thirty-Three

LIZ WALKED ahead of Clint's assistant, not knowing if she'd help or hurt Liz, and headed for an even bigger threat. She spotted him the second they rounded the bend in the path that dipped down a slight incline to the bridge that spanned the rushing falls, which cascaded over huge boulders, and ran down into the lake.

The waning sunlight highlighting the rushing water turned the spray to bursts of yellow, orange, and pink. Once the sun dipped below the hills and trees, this part of the lake would turn dark quickly.

The raging creek and lake were a beautiful sight to behold at sunset, but it didn't hold her attention. She kept her gaze locked on Clint standing with his back to the railing, the lake behind him, and a smile on his face that looked both charming and menacing because she knew the man behind it.

"Where is Trinity?" She glanced over the bridge and the long fall down to the rocks and water, thinking of poor Aubrey.

"I got rid of her."

Liz put a hand on her roiling stomach and gasped, tears gathering in her eyes.

Clint's anger drew lines in his forehead. "She's not

part of this. If you'd just listened to me, seen that I was the man you were supposed to be with, none of this would have happened. *You. You* were the one."

Clint's assistant stepped up beside her. "And what about me? What was *I* to you?"

Clint cleverly gave the assistant an adoring smile. "Our time came and went, but you are invaluable to me. You know that."

Liz knew the truth. She spoke to the assistant, but kept her gaze on Clint. "You're here because he needs you to take the blame. He thinks you're so devoted and beholden to him because of what he's holding over you and how much he thinks you love him that you'll do anything for him. Like bringing me here. But after he kills me, he'll throw you over that rail just like he did Aubrey and say you were jealous of me, because I made a mistake leaving him for Tate and I wanted *him* back. You didn't want me to have him, but he didn't want you, so you killed yourself."

"That's ridiculous." The surprise in Clint's eyes said she'd hit the mark. He stared at his assistant adoringly. "I've come to realize who is important, who I can count on, and how much you mean to me, Kelly." He spewed those lies, then turned to Liz. "You're trying to ruin my life, talking to that reporter, making those women come forward, blaming Aubrey's tragic death on me."

"You've got the whole wounded party thing down. But I'm not buying your bullshit. No one does. Aubrey warned me away from you. You saw her with me. You forced her up here and you killed her."

"You can't prove it. The cops can't. No one can."

"I can."

Kelly's bold words made Liz and Clint both turn to her.

Kelly pulled a gun from her back and pointed it right at Clint's chest.

His eyes went wide, but then he dismissed Kelly as a threat with a shake of his head and a sad smile. "Oh, Kelly."

Her eyes narrowed with fury. "You think I don't see how you use me, but I do. The day Aubrey died, you came back to the office all sweaty and acting weird. I'd know. We'd been together long enough for me to recognize when something was off. You changed your shirt and *threw* it at me, *ordering* me to get it dry-cleaned. I work for you, but I'm not responsible for your fucking laundry. That's not my job. Neither are the blow jobs you insisted on in your office or making reservations for you to take out some other woman!" Kelly relaxed her rigid frame and gathered herself, then gave Clint an insincere smile. "I didn't get your shirt cleaned. I kept it, because I noticed the stain on the front. Remember? You said you spilled ketchup on it. Now, I'm no forensic specialist, but the stain looked suspiciously like spit and blood. I'll just bet Aubrey fought back and you smacked her across the face." She put her hand on her own cheek, like she knew just how Clint liked to assert his dominance and punish. "I've had to clean blood out of my own clothes thanks to you."

Clint took a menacing step forward. "Where is it?"

"Safe."

"You know what happens when you don't do what you're told," Clint warned, still dismissing the threat of the gun and Kelly's resolve.

"You throw me off a bridge," Kelly suggested, understanding that Liz's prediction was probably the right one.

"I would never do that to you," he swore, sounding convincing, but she and Kelly saw past the tricks and manipulations, the cooed words meant to soothe so he got his way.

"You did it to Aubrey. Why?" Kelly asked, genuinely hurt and sympathetic to Clint's other victim. "Because she didn't do as she was told and stay out of your business?"

"That's exactly it. Isn't it?" Liz asked, stepping next to Kelly, both of them standing against Clint.

Clint leaned in, fury in his eyes. "She got what she deserved for interfering."

Liz tilted her head. "That sounds like an admission of guilt to me. Coupled with the shirt, I'm sure that's enough proof to put you behind bars for the rest of your life, you cold-blooded murderer."

Clint shook his head. "Nothing is going to happen to me."

"You're going to jail, you bastard." Tate's voice rang out from behind her.

Liz turned just as Tate stepped out of the brush and onto the trail right at the bridge. She wanted to run to him, but Clint grabbed her from behind in a choke hold and dragged her back against the railing.

Kelly backed away from Tate as he stepped onto the shadowed bridge, the gun still trained on Clint. And now on her, too. She hoped Clint didn't get *her* shot.

Liz pulled at Clint's arm around her throat with one hand at the same time she pulled the pocketknife from her pocket with the other. Lack of air, or the quickly fading light, dimmed her vision. She didn't have much time before she passed out, and hit the release to make the blade snap open, then turned the knife in her hand and drove it into Clint's thigh.

Surprise was on her side. He released her to grab his leg.

She fell to her knees coughing and choking, trying to get air.

Tate rushed forward, gun drawn, but Clint pulled the knife free, and grabbed Kelly by the shoulders. He pulled her in front of him just as a shot rang out.

Tate froze, gun in the air.

Liz didn't know who fired, but Tate didn't have a wound, so she turned to Clint and Kelly, who had her back to Tate as Clint held her facing him. His eyes went wide as he stared down at Kelly.

Clint's hands fell away from her shoulders to his sides. He dropped on his ass, then fell back, blood spreading across his abdomen, turning his white button-down bright red. He clutched at his stomach and gasped for breath.

Kelly stood over him with her gun pointed at his chest. "You ruined my life!" She fired the gun over and over until it made only a clicking sound.

Along with Liz, Tate stood there watching shocked and frozen as the bullets slammed into Clint's body one after the other, more blood spreading over his entire torso.

Kelly kept pulling the trigger though the gun was out of bullets, her eyes wide and desolate.

Liz stood and reached for the gun, taking it from Kelly's hand, though Kelly didn't stop staring down at Clint.

"He ruined my life."

Before Liz registered what she intended, Kelly stepped over Clint, planted her foot on the lower slat of the railing, and pitched herself over it.

Liz dropped the gun and tried to grab her. At the last second, Liz wrapped her fingers around Kelly's hand, sending Kelly's legs toppling over her head until Kelly swung facing the lake.

Tate grabbed Liz's waist before Kelly's weight pulled her over the railing.

"Let me go!" The desperation and anguish in Kelly's reckless words broke Liz's heart.

"Don't let him win," she begged. "Hold on. I'll pull you up." She tried to reach down with her other hand but Kelly kicked her legs and fought to get free.

Drake suddenly appeared beside her and made a grab for Kelly, but Kelly reached up and pried Liz's fingers away and fell.

Drake missed Kelly by half a second.

Liz, hands held out to Kelly, stared as Kelly dropped and hit the rocks and dark rushing water. "No!"

Without Kelly's weight holding her over the railing, Tate's weight and grip pulled her back and she fell on top of him on the bridge.

He let out a bellowing moan filled with pain and went limp beneath her. She rolled off him, saw the blood pooling under his head as his eyes rolled back and closed, and her heart stopped.

"Tate!" She held his gray face. "Tate!"

But he didn't move. Didn't blink. And she feared she'd lost him forever.

Drake sank down on one knee beside her and put

his hand on her back. "Cops and paramedics are here. Move back so they can help him."

She didn't want to let him go. She wanted to hold on to him for the rest of her life.

Kelly slipped away from her. She wouldn't let Tate do the same.

She leaned down to his ear. "Don't you leave me, Tate McGrath. You're supposed to marry me. You promised. And I'm holding you to it."

Tate pressed his cheek to hers before he went limp again, giving her hope that he'd heard her.

Drake helped her move back and out of the way of the paramedics who quickly replaced the gauze pad at the back of Tate's head. They rolled him onto a backboard and strapped him in, not wasting any time carrying him to the ambulance waiting in the parking area.

Liz barely got a chance to kiss him goodbye before they took him away.

Drake held Adria against his side. Liz sat at his feet, back against the railing and the rushing water that swallowed Kelly and took her away.

Detective Valdez squatted beside her. "You okay?"

Numb. Wishing the image of Kelly falling out of her hands didn't replay in a loop in her mind. She didn't know how to answer, so stayed silent on that subject and said, "I want to go to the hospital with Tate."

"Soon. I need your statement."

"It's like I predicted and you probably have on video." She glanced over at the camera that she knew about and Clint didn't attached to a nearby tree. When she and Tate planned for what might happen while they were at the police station reporting the sex videos, she told the detective that she thought Clint would stick to habit and what worked and eventually he'd come back here.

She hated being right.

"He wanted to tie up loose ends. I have a feeling he was planning on leaving before the shit really hit the fan."

"Officers are at his home. They confirm he had his bags packed and a plane ticket to Mexico."

"Where his money would go further and he'd be out of your reach."

Detective Valdez nodded. "Probably."

She raked her fingers through her hair and held it away from her face. Elbows on knees, head down, she ran through the events with the detective who'd been just a few seconds too late to see the ending Liz hadn't seen coming.

"Kelly worked for Clint. She was his assistant. It seems she knew everything going on in his life. She was one of his victims. Used. Abused. Manipulated. She'd endured a lot. He ordered her to take me."

"Videos," the detective guessed, scribbling notes on his notepad.

She nodded. "I didn't know she had a gun. I went with her because I wanted to get Trinity back."

"She rode in the ambulance with Tate to get the cut on her head checked out where Clint pistol-whipped her. She needs stitches and probably has a mild concussion. Nothing as severe as Tate's."

Her stomach pitched as the replay of Tate tumbling over Clint's rental car replayed.

Silver lining. Trinity was all right. For a little while there, Liz thought Clint had killed her when he said he "got rid of her."

"At first, I thought Kelly was helping Clint, but when she spoke about getting Trinity back, I wondered if she really wanted to help me." Liz got it now.

Kelly watched Clint fall for one woman after the next, using Kelly, but never treating her the way she deserved. When all those women came forward, Aubrey died, and Clint wanted Kelly to clean up after him by dry-cleaning the shirt, then bring Liz out here to end her, too, Kelly snapped. Deep down, she had to know Clint was just using her again, and this time Kelly would pay for what Clint had done.

"He thought he could get away with everything. Rent a car. No one ties it to him for the hit-and-run attempted murder. Sweet-talk and use Kelly to take me. She kidnapped me, he didn't. I die just like Aubrey, he blames that on Kelly, too. He kills Kelly by throwing her off the bridge. Suicide. The jealous lover kills the woman who took away the man she loved and herself."

"But Kelly didn't play his game."

"He'd pushed her too far. Used her for the last time." Liz wanted to thank her for stopping Clint from hurting her or anyone ever again. She didn't want to understand why Kelly took her own life, but she'd seen the pain and misery in her eyes and couldn't deny that Kelly simply couldn't face the consequences of what Clint put her through. *I'm so stupid. I fell for it every damn time*. Kelly didn't want to feel that way or be Clint's victim anymore.

Liz would have to live with the fact she couldn't save her. She'd tried. And right now, it felt like the biggest, worst failure of her life.

"Kelly kept the bloodstained shirt Clint wore when he killed Aubrey. It's probably at her house."

"I'll send someone to check her place and their office." Detective Valdez waved an officer over and whispered the orders before he gave Liz his attention again.

Exhausted, talked out, and too worried about Tate to care about any of this, she kept it short. "You can see the rest on the video." She looked up at the dark sky. "If he'd waited a little longer, it'd be too dark out here for the video to capture anything." She waved that away and tried to focus. "Kelly shot him to protect herself. And me. Then something snapped inside her. It's like she couldn't kill him enough."

Liz raised her head and let it fall back against the railing post.

Drake put his hand on her head and rubbed his fingers through her hair. "You couldn't have held on any longer. She nearly dragged you over with her."

She appreciated the comfort Drake offered even if she couldn't feel it right now.

"Tate saved me." Broken ribs, a massive concussion, excruciating pain, none of that stopped him from holding on to her and pulling her back to safety. Back into his arms.

"Kelly fought her way to be free." Liz couldn't think of it any other way. Because you had to be desperate to escape to do what Kelly did.

Liz stared at the scrapes on her hand where Kelly pried herself free.

Adria bent beside her and wiped a tissue across Liz's cheeks. "You tried to save her, Liz. You did everything you could to hold on to her. Like everything else, her death is Clint's fault."

Detective Valdez stepped closer. "Take her to the hospital. Get her checked out and back with Tate." He crouched and put his hand on her arm. "Without you, Aubrey's parents might not have ever known the absolute truth about her death. This will bring them closure. You knew Clint was coming. You anticipated him. You helped stop him. Without you, he'd have kept hurting people and destroying lives." He squeezed her arm, then stood. "I'll be in touch."

Drake hooked his hand under her arm and helped her up. Adria took her hand as they followed an officer with a flashlight back down the trail to where Drake left his truck parked behind Kelly's car and Clint's rental.

"He really thought he'd get away with everything."

Adria hugged her to her side. "He didn't. And everything is going to be okay now."

"Only if Tate is okay."

Drake held the truck door open. "Declan just texted me. They're monitoring Tate, but he's restless even with the drugs they gave him."

She took the back seat and pulled her cell out of her sock.

"So that's how Tate tracked you." Drake nodded his approval.

Liz confirmed with a nod. "Dropped the phone Clint knew about and kept the one Tate got me with a different number." While Clint probably told Kelly to make her get rid of the phone so she couldn't be tracked, Liz wondered if Kelly followed through so she could carry out her execution without being stopped by the cops.

Kelly went out to Lover's Leap with her own plan, knowing she was walking to her death and determined to take Clint out first.

"Tate didn't want to lose track of you."

"I don't want to lose him." She hit the speed dial for Declan.

Drake closed the door and walked around the truck and climbed in behind the wheel next to Adria up front. He started the engine and maneuvered around all the cop cars to get them out of there.

Declan finally answered on the third ring. "Hey, how are you doing?"

"Are you with Tate?"

"Yeah. He hasn't woken up. He lost a lot of blood and there's some swelling in his brain."

Liz appreciated the update and honesty. "You told Drake he's restless."

"Yeah. I keep talking to him, letting him know I'm here, but it doesn't seem to help for long."

"Put the phone to his ear. Let me talk to him."

"Good idea. Go ahead."

"Tate, honey, it's me Liz. You are going to be okay. I'll be there soon. I love you so much. You rest. I'm on my way. I love you."

Declan came back on the line. "He seems to have relaxed. You're just what he needed."

"If he gets restless again, remind him I'm on the way. We should be there in a half hour, maybe less."

Drake sped up for her. She'd pay the speeding ticket. The only thing she cared about right now was getting to Tate.

Chapter Thirty-Four

LIZ STARED at Tate lying so still in the bed. Nurses came and went hour after hour. The doctor assured her he'd be all right. He wasn't in a coma, just a pharmaceutically induced deep sleep. He needed rest and time.

Well, he'd had thirty-nine hours of nonstop sleep and if he didn't open his eyes soon, she might scream.

The worry gnawing at her gut made it impossible to eat. Every thought in her head turned into a prayer for him to wake up.

She'd barely slept at all. Maybe three hours, if that. But she hadn't left his side. She'd parked her butt in the chair, taken his hand, and refused to let go. Not until he regained consciousness.

Not until he came back to her.

The doctor backed off the sedative hours ago. At this point, she'd take one little sign that he knew she was there with him.

Then again, the last time Tate stirred, he'd set off the alarms on his heart monitor. His blood pressure spiked. The nurses rushed in and told her it was probably just a bad dream.

Tate had mumbled unintelligibly for a moment. She'd squirmed her way between the doctor and nurses tending him, pressed her forehead to his, and whispered, "I love you," over and over again.

And just like that, he'd settled into a deep quiet sleep again.

And so she'd sat sentry at his bedside praying, *Please don't leave me.* The words on repeat in her head and in her heart.

They'd finally discovered the depth of their feelings for each other. Yes, she'd always loved him. But what she felt now eclipsed that limited notion of what she'd felt growing up and being his friend. Her heart simply couldn't take living a life without him now.

A hand settled on her shoulder. She hadn't heard anyone come in and jumped.

"Liz, honey, you need to take a break. You haven't left or eaten since you got here." Her mother wanted to take care of her, but all she wanted, all she needed, was to be with Tate.

"I'm fine."

"You're not. After what you went through . . ." Emotion choked off the words.

Liz reached up and put her hand over her mother's. "I can't leave him."

She brushed her fingers along his wrist. His hand lay limp on top of hers. She wanted him to feel her, to know she was there. He wasn't alone.

"He'd want you to take care of yourself."

"If I was in that bed, I'd want him here with me." Tears stung her eyes. "He saved me. Without him . . ." She shook her head, unable to explain how she felt about what happened on that bridge. How even in his condition, he'd risked his life for hers.

He was hurt because of her.

A ball of regret and guilt settled in the pit of her stomach along with her unyielding worry for Tate.

Mom brushed her hand over Liz's hair. "It's not your fault. He doesn't blame you for anything that happened."

"Clint tried to kill Tate because he wanted to punish me."

"Oh, Liz, don't own Clint's terrible actions."

"Ever since Tate and I got together, it's been one horrible thing after the next. Why the hell would he want to marry me?"

"Cuz, I. Love. You."

Liz gasped, stood, and stared down into Tate's barely open blue eyes, so grateful and overjoyed to see him finally awake.

Tate's eyes scanned the room. "How long have I been here?"

"You've made me wait on you for going on two days." Tears spilled from her eyes. "I thought I lost you." Relief swamped her whole body.

"You swore you'd marry me in kindergarten. You can't get rid of me now that we're about to do it." His mouth tilted into that cocky grin she loved.

She pressed her hand to his beard-stubbled cheek. "Are you okay?"

"Couldn't get any better. You're here."

She held his face and pressed her cheek to his forehead. "You almost died."

"Good thing I didn't, because I live to be with you." Tate adjusted his position and winced when he turned his head.

She leaned up and held his head still. "Stop moving. You've got sixteen stitches in the back of your head."

He reached up, dragging the IV line with his hand, and touched the swollen lump hidden beneath a thick bandage. He stared up at her. "Are you okay? Did you get hurt?"

"I'm fine. I promise," she added when he looked her up and down.

His brow furrowed. "That woman killed Clint, right?"

"Yes. He's dead."

The tension went out of Tate. "Good."

"They found the evidence that he killed Aubrey, along with all the videos he'd made."

His eyes narrowed. "More of you?"

She glanced at her mom, not really wanting to discuss it in front of her.

Mom got the hint. "You know what, I think I'll go tell your family you're awake." Her mom dashed out.

Tate held her gaze. "Tell me."

She gave him the truth. "He was obsessed with me. He'd sit in his leather chair, staring at the sixty-five inch TV on the wall playing a slideshow of pictures of me. Some I knew he took. Others were candid. He recorded me without my knowledge on our dates. I thought he was checking emails or something and never really paid much attention that he kept his phone in his hand all the time."

"So he'd just sit in the chair and watch you and . . ."

"Get off on looking at me." The uncomfortable conversation about all this with Detective Valdez yesterday still unsettled her.

A nurse came in to check on Tate, cutting off any questions he had about the other disturbing things they'd found at Clint's place. It wasn't worth talking about anyway. She wanted to put the whole thing out of her mind for good.

"How are you feeling, Mr. McGrath?"

He closed and opened his eyes. "A little slow, but okay."

The nurse checked his blood pressure and entered it into her tablet. "Probably the pain meds, but I'll let Dr. McIntyre know. He'll be in soon. Can I get you anything?"

Tate held Liz's hand. "I've got everything I need right here."

The nurse smiled at both of them, then headed out.

Liz propped her hip next to his on the bed and stared at their joined hands, so grateful he was awake and alive.

"It's over, Liz. He's dead. He got exactly what he deserved."

"I know. It's terrible, but I'm glad he's gone." She didn't want to think about Clint or the horrid things he'd done anymore.

Tate squeezed her hand to get her out of her head. "What about that woman?"

"Kelly. His assistant at work."

Clint used and harassed so many women, but he'd really hurt Kelly in a way that changed her. Just like he did to Aubrey. They wanted him to love them. They just didn't see Clint wasn't capable of love. He didn't care about anyone but himself. They got caught up in his charm and how he'd say all the right things and dismissed the way he acted. They couldn't reconcile the two opposing things, so they craved more of his attention and dismissed the way he hurt them.

"Did she make it?"

Her chest went tight. "I couldn't hold on to her. She broke free and fell into the rushing water." She brushed her fingers over the scratches on her hand.

Tate shifted his hand in hers to cover them. "I thought you were going to go over, too. My heart stopped when I saw you tip over the railing. I wasn't sure I'd grab you in time."

She lifted her shirt. "You held on."

"Jeez, Liz. I'm sorry." He brushed his fingers over the four purple bruises on her side left by his fingers digging into her body as he kept her from going over the bridge with Kelly.

She pulled up the other side of her shirt. "I have a matching set."

"Do they hurt?"

She shrugged. "Doesn't matter." She took his hand again and held it tightly. "You saved my life."

"I would have shot Clint myself, but Kelly got in the way. I didn't want to hurt her. I only wanted to save you. I could feel myself fading and my head hurt like hell, but I wasn't going to stop until I knew you were safe and we could be together without him haunting our lives anymore."

Liz agreed. Clint took up too much of what should have been a happy time for her and Tate. He tainted everything and everyone around him.

Still, she hadn't quite gotten over the whole ordeal. "I just can't stop seeing Kelly falling. Drake tried to help."

"I was too late." Drake walked in behind her, along with Declan and Trinity. "I missed her by a few inches." Drake's dark expression matched exactly how Liz felt inside.

Just a few more seconds and they might have saved her.

Tate studied the cut on Trinity's temple and her black eye. The swelling had gone down, but she couldn't open her eye all the way yet. "Are you okay?"

Trinity rushed to his side and wrapped Tate in a hug that made him wince, but he still held on to her. "I am now that you're awake." Trinity stood up and brushed her hand over Tate's hair, making sure not to mess up the bandage around his head. "You scared us."

Tate searched Trinity's oddly blank face. They'd all noticed something off about her. Understandable after what Clint put her through and Tate being unconscious for so long. Maybe now that Tate was awake and doing well considering his injuries, the wall she'd put up to hide her emotions would come down.

They all needed a little time to let this settle and allow the shock and nightmares to fade.

Tate noticed Trinity's brave face, too, and held her arm to try to comfort her. "I thought the worst when Drake said you went missing."

"I thought the worst when he shoved me into the trunk." Trinity visibly shook, but tried to pull herself together by wrapping her arms around her middle. "I'm fine. How are you?"

"Kinda tired."

"You need to rest." Liz rubbed her hand over his chest. "You'll probably be here a couple days so they can monitor the concussion."

"My brain feels like it's stuck in first gear."

Declan put his hand on Tate's leg. "Sounds like you're back to your old self."

Tate smiled at the teasing. "I have a head injury. What's your excuse?"

Declan gave Tate a mock glare. "Looks like I need to hire someone fast. You're going to be no good to me with those cracked ribs."

Tate put his hand over them and winced when he tried to take a deeper breath. "We all know you've been dragging your heels on that because you can't stand to give up control."

"Na-uh." Declan refused to admit what everyone could see.

"Uh, yeah," Drake agreed with Tate. "It's not complicated. Hire a couple guys with experience and put them to work."

"It's not that simple. I need to train them to do things the way I want. Besides, I haven't had time to find anyone because I'm always putting out a fire at the ranch." More excuses.

And the mention of the word fire, Declan frowned at her. "Sorry about your place."

"I'm insured." She'd use the money to buy whatever furniture they'd need at the cabin once they renovated it. Everything else she lost . . . well, she couldn't get it back. And nothing was more important than the fact she and Tate were still alive. And together.

Tate caught Declan's eye again. "Hire some people. I'm getting married and taking Liz on a honeymoon. Somewhere with a beach." Tate looked at her. "I told your mom I'd give you a few months to plan the wedding of your dreams. Can you whittle that down to . . . I don't know, next week."

That shocked her. "Tate, we can take our time. There's no rush."

"You've had from kindergarten to now to figure out what kind of wedding you want."

"You're serious."

He eyed her, dead serious. "As a heart attack."

"Well, if you're going to have one, this is the place to do it," Drake teased.

Liz brushed her hand over his shoulder. "We'll talk about the wedding when you're home."

Tate held her gaze. "We'll stop at the courthouse and get the paperwork on the way home."

Liz shook her head. "You're relentless."

"Like you said, you've been waiting on me a long time. I'm ready." He pulled her hand so she'd lean over him. "We don't know what's going to happen, or how long we have. Anything can happen. I want to marry you. Now. So we can live every day we have together as husband and wife." Tate pointed at Drake. "Look how happy that grump is."

Drake smiled at Adria walking in the door carrying a duffel bag.

"They're ridiculously happy together." Tate held Liz's gaze. "Let's be that happily married."

Tate wanted to put all this Clint stuff behind them and move on with their lives.

And what better way to start than by embracing the love they'd found and getting married with their family and friends surrounding them. That's all they really needed.

Liz couldn't contain her smile. "I'd marry you anytime, anywhere." She'd break it to her mother gently. The two of them, with Trinity and Adria's help, could put together a beautiful wedding and reception in no time. She didn't need anything extravagant.

She just needed Tate.

"And if you want to actually be standing at the altar, you need to get some rest so you can go home."

"So *we* can go home." Tate settled into the bed as his eyes drooped. "Don't go." He held her hand so she couldn't get up.

"I'm not going anywhere."

"The rest of us are headed home to check on things while you get better," Declan said.

"If you hired some help, you could take some time off, too." Tate didn't open his eyes while he delivered that statement, which meant he missed Declan flipping him off. The smirk on Tate's face said he knew his brother had done it anyway.

"I need to check in at the shop." Trinity leaned over and kissed Tate on the head. "I'll be back."

Adria dropped the duffel bag next to the table beside Tate's bed and patted Liz on the leg. "I brought you a change of clothes and some basic toiletries. I thought you might want to clean up in the shower here."

Tate opened his eyes again. "You must be tired, Liz. If you want to go home . . ."

She shook her head. "I'm staying." She touched Adria's arm. "Thanks for thinking of me."

"Of course. We're family."

They all made her feel that way.

Everyone said their goodbyes to her and Tate and left together. Her mom and dad poked their heads in for just a second to say goodbye, and then finally she was alone with Tate again.

She stood and stared down at him. "I don't know what I would have done if I lost you."

Eyes closed, he surprised her by mumbling, "Never going to happen."

She leaned over and kissed him softly, loving the feel of his warm lips pressed to hers. "Sleep. I'm going to take a shower, but I'll be right back."

He found her arm and tugged. "Climb up here with me."

She missed being close to him, too. She couldn't wait to hold him again. But . . . "I'd love to, but you take up every inch of that bed and I don't want to hurt your cracked ribs."

Tate's mouth scrunched into a disgruntled pout. "When we get home, I'm never going to sleep without you again."

She kissed him, though he might have fallen asleep right in the middle of it. She smiled down at him and brushed her hand over his forehead. She'd wanted him since they were kids. Now she had him. And nothing was ever going to come between them again.

Chapter Thirty-Five

Two DAYS after getting out of the hospital over the weekend, Tate opened the door and frowned at the man standing on the porch. "Detective Valdez."

"Tate. May I come in?"

"Don't take this the wrong way, but I hoped I wouldn't see you again." He held his arm out to welcome Valdez in anyway.

"I get that a lot." He glanced around the living room and into the dining room. "Is Liz around?"

"Upstairs."

Valdez tilted his head and stared at Tate. "I heard she quit her job."

Tate rolled his eyes. "You mean the owner suggested she might want to take some time to get her life together."

As happy as Liz was to have him home, she'd had a hard time letting go of what happened. After suffering so many traumas, she had recurring nightmares.

But they were trying to look to the future by focusing on the wedding plans.

This Saturday she'd be his wife. Officially. Because he already thought of her that way.

True to his word, they stopped at the courthouse on

the way home from the hospital. He had the marriage license. Now all he needed was his bride's I do.

Liz descended the stairs. "How are you, Detective?"

Valdez shook Liz's hand. "Tired as always. It's good to see you."

Tate put his arm around Liz's back and held her close. "Would you like to sit down?"

Valdez shook his head. "I just came by to check on both of you and to deliver this." Valdez handed Liz an envelope. "Clint's father came to town to claim his body. We had a long talk about what happened. And how it happened. Mr. Mayhew blames himself for not doing what he could to get Clint the help he needed after Mr. Mayhew moved out of their family home. He hinted that he'd become someone he didn't want to be anymore taking care of his mentally ill wife and out-of-control son."

Liz exchanged a look with Tate, then turned back to Valdez. "What do you mean?"

"Mr. Mayhew didn't go into detail, but inferred there were other incidents in high school and college. Clint's behavior became too much, so Mr. Mayhew cut him off and sent him to work here in Montana, hoping the smaller town and simpler life would change him."

Liz opened the envelope and showed Tate the check made out to both of them. "Two hundred thousand dollars." Awe and anger filled Liz's voice. "Why?"

"He can't change what happened, but with that money, he's hoping you can change your life. Aubrey's and Kelly's parents, along with the women at Clint's work who he harassed got some, too. He knows an apology won't give you back the home you lost or the peace of mind Clint stole from you. But it will pay Tate's medical costs and get you started on your new life.

"If Clint lived, he'd have gone to prison for murdering Aubrey and attempted murder for Tate, arson, all kinds of other charges. Clint can't pay for what he did, but Mr. Mayhew wanted to do something because he knew an apology wasn't of any value to you after what Clint did."

Tate wasn't sure how he felt about the money. He wanted Clint to pay for what he'd done. Death seemed too good for him.

Did a big payday make up for what Clint had done to him and Liz? No. But it did make it easier for them to live the life they wanted.

"We could use the money for the cabin renovation and put some away for a rainy day." Liz stared at the check and saw possibility, because she wanted so desperately to put the past behind them.

He liked that about her. Yes, she struggled to move on, but she had the determination and will to keep moving forward and get a little better every day.

"Please tell Mr. Mayhew that we're sorry for his loss." Tate could be the bigger man and understand that the guy had lost his son. That probably meant something to Mr. Mayhew even if Tate and Liz were happy to be rid of Clint from their lives.

"He said if you were amenable, that he'd like you to know how sorry he is. He hoped you'd understand that the hardest thing he had to come to terms with was that he couldn't help someone who didn't think anything was wrong with him."

Liz touched Valdez's arm. "Tell him we understand. And that actually helped." Liz turned to Tate. "I see it now. He really thought he could make someone love him."

Tate kissed her on the head. "Who wouldn't want to be loved by you? I know what it feels like, and I wouldn't give it up for anything."

Valdez shifted from one foot to the other. "I'll be on my way. If anything else comes up, I'll let you know, but the cases are closed. I wish you both well."

"Thank you, Detective." Liz waved goodbye with the check in her hand.

Tate closed the door and turned to Liz. "This feels like it's finally over."

Liz nodded. "I think so, too." She looked at the check. "We can afford the wood beams in the living room and a stone fireplace in the master bedroom."

Tate grinned and shook his head. They'd had grand plans for the cabin, but had to lower their expectations because of what they could actually afford. "Okay, but only if we buy a really soft rug to put in front of it so I can make love to you in the firelight."

She hooked her hand around his neck, careful to miss the stitches still in his head, and pulled him close. Her chest bumped his and he held back a wince when his ribs protested, just like he did last night when he finally made love to her again after getting out of the hospital. His body ached something fierce from that car hitting him, but damn if he didn't need her desperately.

Just like now.

He pressed his forehead to hers and stared into her

bright green eyes. "You look happy." For the first time since everything happened, he saw genuine joy in her eyes.

"I came down to tell you I got a call from Shady Trails Retreat."

"That high-end hotel and spa that opened last year on the outskirts of town?"

"Yes. I submitted my application before they opened, but they hired someone else, who apparently didn't work out."

"They offered you a job?"

"Yes!" Pure joy lit her eyes.

"Did they know you lost yours?"

"No. It just worked out." She deserved something to go her way. "They want me to start next week, but I told them I'm getting married. I thought they might go with someone else, but they said they'd wait for me to start."

Tate kissed her again. "That's great, sweetheart."

"No, the great part is that the pay is about forty percent higher than my old job."

Even better. "You deserve it. You work hard and you're great at your job."

"I also get two free spa treatments a month."

"Fancy," he teased. "I'm really happy for you."

"Be happy for *us.* This means we can stop worrying about money and just live our lives, happy right here."

He hugged her closer. "I only want to be with you."

"Isn't that a song?"

Tate smiled. "If it is, we'll dance to it at our wedding."

Chapter Thirty-Six

TATE STOOD under the massive cedar trees near the orchard on the property. He brought Liz out here a couple days ago to show her one of his favorite spots on the property. The cabin they now had architectural plans for was made from cedar cut right here on the property. She loved the spot. All their friends and family were gathered and filled the chairs they'd put out on both sides of the flower petal–strewn path that led right to him.

Liz wanted an elegant country wedding. At first, he didn't know what that meant. But between her mom, Adria, and Trinity, they put it together in record time. They'd have the simple ceremony here among the trees, then walk back to the house where he, Declan, and Drake had built a temporary dance floor in the pasture surrounded by long tables decorated with green linen cloths and topped with white dishes, crystal glasses, and vases filled with Liz's favorite pink peonies, white snapdragons, and greenery, silver place settings, and dark blue napkins to match Trinity and Adria's bridesmaids' dresses.

Adria added something to the tables that took him back to their early school days. Bowls of grapes sat beside cake plates with stacks of chocolate chip cookies. The very items they'd traded at lunch more than once, but especially on the day Liz boldly told him she was going to marry him.

He should have listened. He shouldn't have fought it so hard.

He should have known she was right.

He made her wait on him a long time.

And here he stood, everyone looking at him in his tux standing next to the justice of the peace waiting on his bride.

Drake and Declan stood at the back near the road where the black SUV pulled up. Adria got out first and took Drake's arm. Trinity followed and took Declan's. They walked toward the aisle as the music started. "Songbird" by Fleetwood Mac accompanied them down the aisle and the lyrics about love struck him right in the heart because he felt his love for Liz grow each and every day.

Trinity and Adria were beautiful in their dark blue dresses. His brothers were cleaned up and admittedly handsome in their black tuxes. The elegance to this country affair.

Drake released Adria to stand opposite Tate, gave him a smile and a smack on the back when he took his position as best man next to Tate.

Declan separated from Trinity and walked up to him, put one hand on Tate's shoulder, the other on his face, and gave him a huge smile, then stood beside Drake.

And that's when the wedding march began and he looked down the aisle and there she was, beautiful in her white strapless dress. His elegant bride. Rhinestones and pearls encrusted the entire top of the dress at her breasts, then nothing but white satin draped in a perfect line down her torso, hips, and legs where it flared out at the bottom. He'd never seen her look more . . . amazing.

With her deep red hair bundled at the back of her head in waves that created a loose bun encircled by rhinestones, swept back from her gorgeous face and bright green eyes and the smile she gave him . . . pure happiness.

Her parents, Ken and Leslie, stood on either side of her.

Liz carried a pretty bouquet of white roses in one hand and hooked her arm through her father's.

They walked down the aisle toward him and he couldn't take his eyes off her.

It took all his self-control to wait while Liz turned to her mother for a kiss on the cheek, then one from her father before Ken took Liz's hand and held it out to him.

Tate clasped hands with Liz.

Ken placed his over their joined ones. "Take care of each other."

"We will," Tate promised.

Ken and Leslie took their seats across from Tate's mom and dad, who'd left their RV at a campsite in the California redwoods and flew in for the ceremony.

Liz faced him and squeezed his hand. "I'm going to marry you," she whispered, making him smile and taking him back to kindergarten and her bold declaration.

"Na-uh." This time he teased, instead of denying what seemed fated.

They shared a laugh that eased their nerves and excitement.

The justice of the peace put his hand over theirs. "Some things are inevitable, like the sun rising every morning. Like the love Tate and Liz share that led them here today. And so we gather to celebrate their very special relationship.

"It's not often you meet someone in childhood and they remain your best friend for life. Even rarer, that the friendship that kept them close all these years turned into a love of a lifetime.

"Marriage is a union. And though Tate and Liz have shared that bond for most of their lives, they've invited their closest friends and family, the people most important to them, to watch them take this next step in their joined lives.

"They have written their own vows. Tate," the justice of the peace prompted.

Tate took a deep breath and met Liz's brilliant, welcoming green eyes. "I love you. I've loved you practically my whole life. I picked you for Red Rover, dodge ball, to be my teammate and my best friend." He squeezed her hand. "I picked *you* to be my wife. We've shared a million memories. I can't wait to make a million more with you as my partner for life and the mother of our children. I promise, no matter what comes our way, I will always be by your side. I will protect you, hold you, provide for you, and be everything and anything you need me to be. I will always love you."

Liz squeezed his hand and blinked back tears. "I

always knew I loved you. That love never wavered. It never will. You are a part of me. I will always be the one who comforts you when you're down, the one who loves you through the ups and downs, the one who makes you laugh, and rubs your back when you've worked too hard. I will be your council and best friend who supports you in everything you do. I will try every day to be the wife and partner you deserve because you are the man I want, I love, I need. I will always love you," she echoed his final vow back to him.

The justice of the peace took over again. "Liz and Tate will now exchange rings as a symbol of their commitment."

Drake handed Tate the two rings Tate had picked out for Liz. He'd offered to give her the engagement ring as soon as he got out of the hospital, but Liz asked him to surprise her on their wedding day. Something to look forward to after all that happened.

He loved that their relationship was about them, not a ring or what he could give her other than the love they shared.

Trinity handed a ring he didn't even get a glimpse of to Liz. She handed her bouquet off to Trinity and turned back to him with that same beautiful smile he got to wake up to every morning now.

"Tate, take Liz's hand and repeat after me. I give you this ring as a symbol of our love."

Tate held Liz's hand and repeated those words and the rest . . .

"For today and tomorrow, and all the days to come. Wear it and remember that my love is always present even when I'm not." He slipped the diamond solitaire on her finger, enjoyed the hell out of her surprised smile, then slipped the diamond eternity band on right next to it.

"Tate, they're beautiful." She held up her hand to admire the rings.

His chest swelled with pride seeing his rings on her finger and knowing she'd wear them the rest of her life as his wife.

"Liz, take Tate's hand and repeat after me. I give you this ring as a symbol of our love."

Liz repeated the vows that held a promise he not only believed but knew she'd never break. She held up a black carbide band, perfect for a guy like him who worked with his hands and didn't need anything fancy. She held the ring up and tilted it so he could see the inside inscription.

LM loves TM

Liz McGrath loves Tate McGrath. He wondered how many times she'd written that in her notebooks over the years.

"I almost had it inscribed with Lizard's Love."

He couldn't contain the belly laugh. Everyone in the crowd, including his brothers and Trinity and Adria, busted up laughing.

Liz slid the ring on his finger. He squeezed his hand and opened it, unused to wearing anything on his hands. But he'd get used to it because he had no intention of taking it off.

"Tate and Liz, you've professed your love by exchanging vows and symbolized your commitment by exchanging rings. Before you kiss your bride, Tate, there's just one question I need you both to answer.

"Liz, do you take Tate to be your husband and promise to love, comfort, honor, and keep him, in sickness and health, good times and bad, forsaking all others, and be faithful to him as long as you both shall live?"

"I do." God, her smile. It lit Tate up inside.

"Tate, do you take Liz to be your wife and promise to love, comfort, honor, and keep her, in sickness and health, good times and bad, forsaking all others, and be faithful to her as long as you both shall live?"

"I do." He could barely contain his own smile.

"I now pronounce you husband and wife. Tate, you may kiss"—Tate hooked his hand at the back of Liz's neck and drew her lips to his before the guy could finish with—"your bride."

Tate held the kiss, his heart pounding with joy, and his future brighter than it had ever been.

He ended the kiss by pressing his forehead to hers. "I love you."

"I love you, too." The love in her eyes dazzled him.

"It's my great honor and privilege to be the first to introduce Mr. and Mrs. McGrath."

Tate took Liz's hand and turned to their cheering guests. He kissed the back of her hand right next to the sparkling rings he'd slipped on her finger moments ago.

Drake and Declan both slapped him on the back, making his cracked ribs throb, but he was too damn happy to care.

Liz took her flowers from Trinity and accepted a kiss on the cheek from his sister and Adria.

Their friends and family stood as he led Liz back

down the aisle and the photographer he'd completely forgotten was even there snapped photos of them.

His brothers, Trinity, and Adria hung back with him and Liz to take pictures as the guests made their way back to the stables and the party waiting to happen.

They posed for what seemed like a thousand photos, but his and Liz's smiles never wavered because this was their day to shine and bask in the love that held them together all these years. They knew it would see them through the years to come.

Everyone headed back to the ranch, leaving him alone for a moment with Liz. Finally.

"I can't wait for everything that's to come."

She wrapped her arms around his neck and kissed him softly. "No matter what, it's you and me, cowboy."

Keep reading for a sneak peek at

LOVE OF A COWBOY

the next book in the McGraths series
by Jennifer Ryan

Coming March 2021
from Avon Books

Chapter One

SKYE KENNEDY snuck toward the master bedroom, drawn by Gabriel's harsh voice and the ominous feeling she couldn't ignore. She peeked through the ajar door and stared, horrified by the anger blazing in his eyes. Gabriel held Lucy trembling in front of him, his hands fisted in her linen shift dress, his body bent toward her as she leaned away, his face an inch from hers.

Skye didn't recognize who Gabriel had become.

The boy she grew up with had turned into a very dangerous man.

Poor Lucy. She couldn't get away. Not that she tried. Fear held her wide-eyed and docile.

Lucy's fear echoed through Skye.

"What will my bride think if you bring that bastard into this world?" Rage and disgust filled Gabriel's unbelievable words.

They stopped Skye's heart.

If she wasn't mistaken, in this case, "bride" referred to her.

Skye didn't like being told what to do, which is why she'd never agree to be his wife.

But several of the other Sunrise young ladies couldn't wait to marry the men Gabriel—in an unprecedented dictate—handpicked for them. They thought it an honor to marry into his inner circle of tried-and-true, trusted friends.

Believers in his new vision for Sunrise.

She didn't believe in Gabriel's new direction. It led them down a dangerous road. And if the rest of the Sunrise Fellowship community outside Gabriel's circle of friends knew what he was doing behind their backs, they'd cast him out once and for all. But for the sake of the community and all they believed in, Skye worked in the shadows to find a way to take down Gabriel without him turning the tables on her for going against him.

Right now, she feared she'd taken too long to oust him, and Gabriel was about to do something else to prove how far he'd strayed from their ideals.

Tears streamed down Lucy's pale face. "I didn't mean for it to happen."

Skye had no idea, nor did she care, that Gabriel had been sleeping with Lucy.

Gabriel pulled Lucy even closer, their noses nearly touching. "Who did you tell?"

Lucy patted Gabriel's chest with one shaking hand, trying to soothe him, but nothing, not even the child she carried, seemed to calm Gabriel's ire. "No one. Just you. Please, Gabriel, he's your son."

"Skye will give me strong sons. *She's* the only one worthy to be my wife."

He'd always had a thing for *her.* She avoided him when possible. When that didn't work, she tried to be kind like she'd been taught, but careful about how much attention or interest she showed Gabriel.

She didn't want to give him the wrong idea.

Not that he cared what she wanted either way.

"*She* will stand beside me. Not *you*."

Never. Not going to happen.

A desperate plea filled Lucy's eyes. "But you said I was chosen."

Gabriel sneered at her. "You were. To serve me. And you've served your purpose."

So cruel.

He was one of those people who thought everyone loved him and you were lucky to be *his* friend even when he was unkind.

He held himself in high regard, thinking himself better than everyone else.

Tonight he proved to be far lower than the worst of them.

"You will not have this baby."

"I won't give him up," Lucy wailed.

Gabriel shook her. "You'll do as you're told!"

Lucy's gaze dropped and she shook her head. "You can't make me." Her defiance set Gabriel off.

He shook her again, making her head snap back and forth like a rag doll's. "You will!"

"No!" she shouted right in his face.

He shoved Lucy to the floor and kicked her right in the stomach, sending her body sliding across the hardwood toward the dresser. "Why are you trying to ruin everything?"

Skye pressed her hand over her mouth to cover her shocked gasp.

Lucy screeched, then let loose an agonizing wail.

In a blind rage, Gabriel kicked her again, then

stomped his big booted foot right into her thigh as she tucked her legs to her chest to protect herself from further harm.

Too late.

Lucy's piercing scream echoed in Skye's ears.

Bright red blood spread and saturated Lucy's white dress.

Gabriel stood over her, his breath heaving in and out with the fury still tightening his muscles and etched in his face.

Lucy stared up at him, her teary eyes wide and wild. "Why?"

Gabriel gave no answer for his horrendous behavior. If he felt any remorse for his child and what he'd done, it didn't show.

Lucy clawed at the material, dragging it up her thighs, and stared as blood spread and pooled on the floor between her legs. She clutched her belly. "No!" Pain etched lines on her distraught face.

Skye wanted to rage. She wanted to help Lucy, but fear locked her in place, witness to the horrifying tragedy. Stuck in this terrible nightmare, her mind couldn't make her body move.

Lucy stared up at Gabriel, her eyes huge and filled with grief and blame and unimaginable sadness. "Y-you k-killed him."

Gabriel stared down at Lucy. "He was never meant to be." Those flat words left Skye cold.

He squatted next to Lucy. Skye hoped he'd finally help her. But no, he gripped her jaw tightly in his fingers and glared at her. "My son will be born to my *wife*, not some whore."

How had so much malice corrupted his heart?

Shame washed over Lucy's face, but she retaliated. "Skye w-won't have you. When she f-finds out . . . you plan to m-make her . . . m-marry y-you . . . tomorrow, she . . . she'll . . . re-refuse you."

That truth narrowed Gabriel's eyes and filled them with renewed fury. He released Lucy's face and backhanded her, splitting her lip and sending her sprawling on her back. Her head cracked against the floor and her tear-drenched eyes fluttered.

Gabriel pointed his finger in Lucy's face. "No one refuses me. I am the supreme leader of Sunrise."

No, he's not!

There was no such thing here. They worked in co-operation with one another.

But Gabriel wanted to be treated like some patriarch. He demanded people's respect, but hadn't earned it through his words or actions.

Tonight, he'd proved he'd lost all reason.

Lucy's head rolled to the side and her eyes locked with Skye's through the crack in the door. "Love is free." Lucy's breath slowed. "Love is kind." Lucy sucked in a shaky breath as the blood pool between her legs grew wider and she looked up at Gabriel. "You will never have love, because y-you're cruel." Air whistled as she inhaled. Then Lucy exhaled, "Ruunnn," though barely a sound left her lips.

Lucy bled out and didn't breathe again.

Skye watched the soul disappear from Lucy's beautiful hazel eyes. Her heart broke and her mind reeled. She should have done something. Anything to stop this.

But her brain found some reason and whispered the disturbing truth: *Get out of here before you're Gabriel's next victim.*

He couldn't be reasoned with or deterred from his deadly path.

Ever since his dad died two years ago, he'd changed. Grief gave way to acceptance of his leadership role at Sunrise Fellowship and morphed his childish selfishness and tendency to push the limits into destructive subterfuge.

He lashed out at those who didn't go along.

Anyone who questioned or defied him suffered his punishing disapproval, fury-fueled tantrums, and petty retribution.

What had once been a peaceful community of people living a quiet, simple, self-sustaining life had become corrupted by power and greed. In one short year, Gabriel had tainted their community-first home, built on cooperation and the farm everyone worked to sustain them.

She took Lucy's last request to heart, found that her frozen limbs loosened with her resolve to do what she'd been planning for the last few weeks. She backed away on silent feet, and though she didn't run, she left the man who stared down at the young lady he'd used like she was nothing. The man who in cold blood killed his child and an eighteen-year-old girl and talked as if he ruled the good people who lived their lives in peace at Sunrise.

She tiptoed down the hallway to the home office she'd worked in since she was fourteen, when Gabriel's father noticed her aptitude for math. He taught her accounting and gave her a purpose greater than the farm chores she'd performed her whole life.

She didn't bother to go to the phone and call the police. Gabriel's corruption had spread to them as well and it disheartened her to know she couldn't turn to the authorities for help. Which left her only one option: run. There had to be someone outside their community and town who could help her stop Gabriel and what was coming.

The threat of discovery made her heart thrash, but she tried to stay focused, fought the fear, and did what needed to be done so she could get what she needed. Otherwise she'd never be able to take Gabriel down.

She went to the rug in front of the sofa, folded it back, and pushed it away. She pressed her shaking hand on one of the boards and the secret panel popped loose, revealing the safe embedded in concrete. She spun the dial, her trembling fingers barely working. She didn't know how much time she had before Gabriel left Lucy and called for his trusted "guards" to help him cover up his crime. Every beat of her heart amped her anxiety as she twisted the dial to each number, gripped the handle, turned it, and lifted the door open. She didn't sort through folders and envelopes, just pulled everything out.

For a split second she stared at the stacks of cash, disgusted by how Gabriel earned them. She thought about the other women he was hurting and the people who'd get hurt if he carried out the plans she'd spent weeks uncovering.

She hadn't stopped him from killing Lucy, but she would find a way to stop him from hurting anyone else.

She wasn't a thief. She believed they were all better

off when they worked together and shared the rewards with everyone.

But if she was going to get away, she needed help.

She snatched one of the thick packets of cash and stashed it in her cargo pants pocket.

As she'd uncovered Gabriel's illicit activities and the threat of being caught meddling in his affairs drew ever closer, she'd feared she'd have to run, but she never thought it would happen like this.

There was no time to cover her tracks. She stuffed the files and papers into the messenger bag hanging on the back of Gabriel's desk chair, pulled the strap over her head and across her body, stared at the picture on the desk, and wished the man she'd admired had been a better father. If he'd disciplined instead of spoiled and coddled, maybe Gabriel would have turned out to be a better man.

With little to no consequences ever imposed on him, Gabriel had become entitled. Now he wanted to be some "Supreme Leader."

She rolled her eyes at the absurdity of it.

Ironic when Sunrise taught cooperation and equality for all.

No one person, not even Gabriel, dictated their lives. His ego had grown to astronomical proportions. Lucy paid the price for his belief that he could say and do whatever he wanted without repercussions.

Skye planned to teach him a lesson he should have learned long ago.

But to do that, she needed to get out of here before Gabriel discovered what she knew, what she'd done, and came after her.

Even with the police on his side, Gabriel would not get away with Lucy's murder. She'd find a way. And she knew someone who could hopefully help her. And the others.

Infused with fear and desperation, she ran from the office for the front door and snuck out with barely a click when the door closed behind her. She leaped down the porch stairs and hit the gravel path leading back to the great hall and other cabins. She wanted to follow Lucy's command, but she kept her head and walked like she had not a care in the world when she had a million thoughts and fears circling her mind.

She didn't want to alert any of the guards who patrolled the property. No one but her questioned why they needed them. Did everyone think someone was out to steal their bumper crop of apples?

No. Gabriel hid something much more valuable and dangerous on the property.

If he discovered what she'd done with it, she'd suffer the same fate as Lucy.

If Gabriel succeeded with his campaign to brainwash everyone into thinking his way would bring them unimaginable prosperity, she feared for everyone's safety.

What she saw for Sunrise's future frightened her.

What used to be home, a simple life on this thriving farm, now felt like corruption of everything she'd been taught to believe in and trust.

Gabriel had always pushed the boundaries. His father had tried to reel him in with reason and appealing to his better nature.

Too bad Gabriel didn't have one.

Now, no one even tried to steer Gabriel away from the dangerous path his compass pointed him down.

No one dared.

So she'd have to be the one to put up the roadblocks and stop him before he reached the point of no return and more innocent people got hurt.

She arrived at the cabin where Gabriel had ordered the young women who were to be married off tomorrow to gather for their last night as bachelorettes. She had been told to join them and enjoy the treats Gabriel had arranged for the ladies before their morning weddings and the reception brunch.

She wondered how Gabriel planned to get her to walk down the aisle.

Didn't matter now. She wouldn't be there.

Neither would the other women. She hoped. They deserved to make up their own minds about whether or not they really wanted to marry Gabriel's men—his guard, as she thought of them.

She rushed into the cabin and stopped short when she spotted the ladies sitting in a group, enjoying tea and cake. Such a sweet scene compared to the gruesome one she'd left at Gabriel's place.

The young ladies stared up at her, shocked by her sudden entrance, worry and resignation in some of their eyes.

Sue stood and took a step toward her. "Skye, what's wrong? Has something happened?"

She didn't have time to explain. If Gabriel caught her with the files she took . . . if he knew she'd seen what he'd done . . . she didn't want to think about what he'd do.

Maybe some of these young ladies wanted to get married. She'd bet, given a chance to really think things through and make their own decisions without Gabriel's influence, they'd choose differently.

"Skye, are you okay?" Sue took another step toward her, wanting to help.

They all did. They were all so eager to help, so eager to please.

And that would be their downfall if they continued to just go along without questioning Gabriel and his motives.

"Would you like to leave?" The broad question raised some eyebrows.

Alice surveyed the spread before them, then looked up at her. "But what about our party? We don't want to upset Gabriel by leaving without finishing after he did this for us."

No. No one wanted to upset Gabriel.

"Gabriel suggested we see a movie." It was a treat they weren't likely to pass up. Once she got them away from the farm and Gabriel's influence, she'd explain what had happened and let them decide if they wanted to return and get married—or not. She hated to lie to them, but telling them about Lucy's murder would only delay them longer. They'd panic. "If you want to go, we have to go now." She waved them to come along.

Finally, they abandoned their cups and half-eaten plates of food and headed for the door, happy to get away for another special treat.

Alice stopped next to her and smiled. "Gabriel has been so kind. He's given us so much. I worried about marrying Michael. He's so much older than me."

Yeah, the twelve-year age gap should make Alice wonder what they really had in common and if they could make it long-term.

"I barely know him," Alice went on. "But Gabriel has done so much to make this a wonderful experience. I know it's meant to be, just like he said." Alice uttered the words, but a lot of fear and reluctance filled her eyes.

Skye wondered if she'd been that naïve and stupid at seventeen. Had she ever blindly followed without question?

No. Which is how she got herself into this predicament.

"Alice, Gabriel can't force you to marry Michael."

"My parents want the match, too."

That was a lot of pressure for a young lady.

She didn't understand how Gabriel managed to dupe everyone into believing his grand plans.

Yes, Gabriel had spent weeks pushing his agenda and convincing the Fellowship that the matches created stronger family bonds and guaranteed future generations of Sunrise stewards.

The other members didn't know Gabriel was just covering his ass.

"As his wife, I'll help him to become his best self and give him children, a family, and stability so he can fulfill his purpose."

Gabriel liked to spout big ideas like that, but his words held no substance. They sounded good, especially to the young, impressionable women who wanted a fairy-tale life.

If she asked the other four women why they'd agreed

to get married without a lengthy courtship, she'd probably get the same exact answer.

None of them were prepared for reality.

Back when Gabriel's father headed the Sunrise council, she might have agreed to a similar match if he'd suggested it, but she'd have wanted time to get to know the man first, to be sure. A man and woman should be tied together by their shared beliefs. They should be best friends as well as lovers.

She figured that out when she was sixteen and fell madly in love with Joseph. She tossed reason to the wayside and went to great lengths to see him as much as possible. She even snuck out for their romantic rendezvous. But like all young love, it was fleeting—especially when she caught Joseph kissing Renee.

And looking back now, she realized she'd never had another serious boyfriend because Gabriel had always been lurking in her life, trying to keep her all to himself. And it worked, because the other boys accepted there was something between them. Like Gabriel, they believed she was meant for him.

She'd simply put guys on the back burner and focused on her job and making Sunrise the best it could be.

"Alice, you're only seventeen. Do you really want to be a wife and mother so young?"

"Babies are so sweet. I would love him or her so much."

Of course she only thought about a cute baby, not what it would be like to take care of an infant day in and day out. Yes, a baby brought a lot of joy into your life, but taking care of them was a lot of hard work. And a husband . . . Alice had no idea what it meant to take care of and be a partner to a man. To have her life and decisions tied to that person.

She hooked her hand around Alice's arm and tugged her out the door. When she got the girls out of here, she'd have a talk with Alice and the others about the reality of marriage and family, so they made informed decisions about the rest of their lives without pressure from Gabriel or their families.

The others had already piled into the van down the road.

Skye wanted to find her parents and sister, but feared she'd already taken too long to get away before Gabriel discovered her. She needed to get out of here before he found her and killed her to keep her quiet.

This was so much bigger than Lucy's murder.

Her family didn't know anything. She hoped they'd be safe. Gabriel couldn't get rid of them without explaining or raising suspicions. Not now.

Ten feet from the van, Joseph stepped out in front of them, rifle hanging down his back by the strap over his shoulder. Guns at the compound were new, too. "Hey, Skye. Where are you going?"

Skye tamped down her rising panic, pushed Alice to keep walking to the van, and tried to talk her way out of this. "Gabriel suggested I treat the girls to a movie tonight." The false brightness in her voice didn't seem to alert him that anything was wrong.

Since their relationship had ended in disaster, all their encounters were fraught with tension. She hoped he took her anxiety as remnants of her resentment toward him.

Joseph stared past her down the road to the girls. "Are they excited about their weddings tomorrow?"

Hesitation filled his voice and skepticism filled his eyes.

"Why wouldn't they be?" She wanted to know if Joseph was still blindly going along with Gabriel or if he'd finally started thinking for himself again and saw the reality of what Gabriel was doing to Sunrise. To all of them.

"I wonder if they really know what they're getting into." His cynical expression answered that and made her think he didn't wholly go along with the impending marriages.

She took a chance on the slim hope that he finally had doubts about Gabriel's new plans for Sunrise. "I'm going to make sure they know they have a choice."

Joseph gave her a firm nod.

And she took another shot at getting through to him in case it would help stop Gabriel. "Go to Gabriel's place. You'll see who he really is."

With that, she rushed off to join the girls at the van with hope in her heart that exposing Gabriel to Joseph would have a domino effect and he and the other men would finally stand against him.

She climbed behind the wheel knowing that was a long shot. She shifted the bag of evidence onto her lap. It and the other things she'd hidden were probably her only hope of putting Gabriel in a cell where he belonged if she got them to the right authorities.

Alice leaned over. "I'll hold on to that if you'd like."

"I've got it. But thanks." Skye put her shaking hand on the bag, turned the key in the ignition, and hit the gas to get them out of there. Everyone fell back in their seats, then let loose a holler.

They thought they were out to have fun.

She knew better.

No telling what they'd say or do when they realized where she was really taking them.

As she drove through the gates, she took a moment to think about what she was leaving behind, but it only made her heart ache more, so she shut off her brain and drove.

Lucy deserved justice and she planned to get it for her. One way or another.

Alice leaned forward, staring out the windshield. "The movie theater is the other way."

"I'm going to make a stop. I think you'd all benefit from talking to someone about your upcoming marriages." She hoped she was doing the right thing.

"Like a counselor?" Bess asked.

"Very much like that." A legal counselor, who could advise the fourteen-year-old, who of all the young brides needed the most help because she already had a baby on the way.

"I'm nervous," Julie confessed. "But the flowers are going to be so pretty." She covered her complicated feelings by talking about pleasant things.

"My bouquet is filled with pink peonies." Alice beamed.

"I made this really pretty floral crown with baby white roses and orchids," one of the other girls chimed in.

It seemed easier for them to follow Julie's lead and stick to the simple things.

They grew all kinds of fruits, vegetables, and flowers on the farm and in the greenhouses and sold them at farmers markets along with the other goods produced at Sunrise. It's how they sustained the compound.

"Mine has pink roses and blue hydrangeas." Beth's voice didn't sound as exuberant as the other young women caught up in the weddings. At nineteen, maybe Beth was one of the ones unsure of sprinting down the aisle.

The others responded to her restrained tone and fell silent, as if Beth's quiet resistance amplified their unspoken fears.

They should be afraid.

Skye had gathered pieces of the odd things happening at Sunrise. Taken one at a time, they didn't seem to be anything more than a ramp up to increase production for much-needed repairs, renovations, and expansion. But put together with the slow changes to the culture and philosophy they'd lived by for decades, alterations that Gabriel forced with his persistent ways, it painted a picture that went against everything she'd believed in her whole life.

Lucy's death proved someone had to stop Gabriel before it was too late.